PEACHY

THE FIRST BITE

CAMRI KOHLER

This is a work of fiction. Any resemblance to actual persons, living or dead or actual events is purely coincidental. Although real-life locations or public figures may appear throughout the story, these situations, incidents, and dialogue concerning them are fictional and are not intended to depict actual events nor change the fictional nature of the work.

First published in the United States of America 2023 by Lake Country Press & Reviews

Cataloging-in-Publication Data is on file with the Library of Congress.

ISBN: paperback 979-8-9860748-6-3

ebook 979-8-9860748-7-0

Author website: https://www.camrikohler.com/

Publisher website: https://www.lakecountrypress.com

Editor: Samantha Costanilla

Cover: Zoe Norvell

Formatting: Dawn Lucous of Yours Truly Book Services

For my mom and dad.
Don't worry, you guys did great.

And for Dylon.
Say something nice.

CONTENT/ TRIGGER WARNINGS

The Peachy Trilogy features dark and potentially triggering content. I hope to be as thorough as possible, please contact me on my website if you feel a CW/TW has not been included in this list.

In alphabetical order:

- Alcohol Use
- Animal Death
- Blood
- Death
- Depictions of Bullying
- Drug Use
- References to Abuse
- References to Suicide
- Self-Injurious Behavior
- Tobacco Use
- Violence

PEACHY PLAYLIST

PEACHY PLAYLIST

1

THE CABINET WAS UGLY, the color of a lost cigarette or a neglected toilet. When I was a kid, it was white. Obscenely so. The box had glared, almost hummed, in the sun like an alien spaceship. Now it was rotting, fading to a hideous yellow as I aged. The matching twin bed frame had done the same. The furniture so bland and ubiquitous that I could hardly even call it "girl." Just storage enough for any breathing human being, or maybe a spoiled dog. The walls still held the band and zodiac posters from my teen years. My mattress still boasted the unnatural orange stain near the center. But the cabinet didn't look the same at all.

My alarm blared, vibrating my phone against the yellowing nightstand. I turned it off within seconds but continued to lie there like a frayed sweater. Simply existing in my bed for long stretches of time had become routine to me. I didn't like my grandmother knowing I was awake.

After I did nothing for as long as I could excuse, I sat up and whispered a curse into the surrounding silence. This old mattress would kill me one of these nights. I opened and closed my mouth, smacking my dry tongue against the foul morning residue. Frowning at the rotten cabinet, I swung my feet off the side of the bed and crossed the hall to the only bathroom in the house. I locked the door behind me. It smelled like bleach.

I couldn't remember the exact day I had last washed my hair,

1

but knew I was due. Having no time for a wash today, I settled for raking my fingers through the curls of my amber blonde hair a bit more violently than was comfortable. Loose spiraling strands fell into the basin of the sink, fell lighter than feathers across my toes. They itched.

I washed the hairs down the drain of the sink while I brushed my teeth. I spat blue froth mixed with stringy pink blood, which bubbled over the newly formed hairball. I swallowed some mouthwash—fresh breath would even out my greasy hair—and I sat on the edge of the tub, enjoying the cool porcelain.

After putting on my grungy white polo shirt and a pair of jeans, I shuffled out my doorway as if lost. The exit was down the hall, past the other bedroom and the big open space that amounted to a kitchen and living room. In one of these rooms waited that looming, sickly vulture of a woman. I was full of trepidation and simmering resentment. So early in the morning.

The door to her bedroom was closed. She only closed the door when she wasn't in it, ruling that I was not welcome inside without a chaperone. Past the blockade, the kitchen was shabby and sparse, but notoriously spotless. To the north of the kitchen were the archaic blue couch and bulbous-backed television set, the only furniture that made up the living room.

And there she perched: a tall, angular, ash-gray brunette. This woman and I looked nothing alike. My being small, curved, and pink compared to her boney towering frame. My grandmother's name was Pamela. Her friends called her Pams.

Pamela was ramrod straight on the blue fabric couch, the bottom of which sagged lower than her ruined, wrinkly chest. The TV was too loud. My mom used to start each day of her adult life with the news fed to her from her favorite local news-caster, Timothy Peters. That a grown man would be called "Tim-othy" was incredibly repugnant to me. Pamela unabashedly played the station every morning.

Timothy looked striking in a navy suit and a "fun" tie, which was tipped in threaded orange and yellow flames. "It is hot, hot,

hot out there, folks!" What a charming spin on the terrible drought that had plagued Utah annually.

I didn't want to look at her. But.

Her eyes met mine as I turned my head. She held her trusty flyswatter tightly in her spindle fingers, swinging crazily at the flies who seemed to constantly hover around her person, regardless of the season or her pristine surroundings.

"Good morning, Francesca," she said irritably, alluding to my late awakening. I had always been "Francesca" to my grandmother. Being called that had bothered me to no end throughout my life, and I knew this was the exact reason Pamela had never conformed to Frankie like everyone else.

"Morning, Pamela." She hated my use of her name just as much as I hated Francesca. Her mouth turned down in a gargoyle grimace and she took another swat at her ever-present pests. I could hear them buzzing from across the room. Even at night, I heard them.

There was no time left to be berated and my lateness had never stopped her from throwing a good bitchfit. When Mom was here, we used to tolerate one another, with strenuous effort, but the effort was there. After she died, and I had planned on selling anything that would catch a good price, Pamela moved into her house with me. Pamela announced to anyone within shouting distance that she was worried about my ability to cope, but we both knew she was worried about all the old shit that cluttered this house. After her arrival, there was nothing to sell. All the valuables vanished during my work hours.

I hated her here. We were two prickly weeds who had lost their spring flower, just growing useless and petulant around nothing worthwhile. I stood behind the couch and stared at Tim's fun tie for a respectable amount of time before turning to the door.

"Are you leaving? You haven't eaten anything." Pamela adjusted her avian weight but didn't move to get off the couch.

She glared at me until I met her eyes. Her disdain was worthless if I didn't acknowledge it.

"I'm not hungry." In truth, I had only eaten half a bag of Cheezy Poofs the night before and I was starving. But if I ate, she'd criticize whatever I made or would insist on making me something herself. She would stalk around the kitchen complaining about her wrists and ankles. She would only make enough for me and would prattle about some hap dash snack she would settle for later—crackers, an apple. Pamela, the Martyr. I despised when my grandmother prepared food for me, especially when I was forced to stand in the kitchen and watch her do it. I'd rather go hungry, and often did.

"Remember what we talked about last night, eat something healthy. For once, you will eat something healthy. If you're just going to rot in your room every day, then you need fewer calories. I don't want to find any slimy chip bags under your bed again," Pamela snapped, waiting, begging me to argue.

Over the last few months, I lost the drive to fight her. I merely considered her face and gave a tight smile. She raised her flyswatter above her sharp shoulder and followed the bugs fiendishly.

I stepped again towards the front door, giving my grandmother a sparing glance. Pointy, too skinny, as if she were a bag of tent poles. Her white collared blouse surrounded her limbs like a blanket. She loved how she looked; I regularly caught her admiring her bones in anything reflective. I wondered how long we'd have to haunt this house together.

ASPEN RIDGE WAS an unfortunate little town. Walking fully across it to Jim's Family Grocery took twenty-five minutes from our isolated two-bedroom rambler. The fastest route was an unin-

4

spiring and lonely road that divided two fields of tall, yellow grass. Utah was always dry, but our recent summers were dangerously so, filled with heatwaves, wildfires, and bad air. I could already feel sweat pooling under my chest and between my thighs, though my lips were as dry and cracked as salt flats. My clothes clung to my body, uncomfortably tight. Since my move back home, though I refused to use Pamela's repeatedly offered scale, I guessed I had gained somewhere between ten and fifteen pounds. That didn't bother me. It bothered Pamela and *she* bothered me.

After every minute of walking, I habitually pulled up my jeans and pulled down my shirt, attempting to cover the creeping pale flesh in between. The sock of my right foot had fallen inside my shoe, exposing my heel to the worn rubber backing of my sneaker and causing a loud *squeak!* with each step. I walked between the fields like a clown entertaining an empty big top. The constant *squeak!* jeans up, shirt down, made me overpoweringly self-conscious. I surveyed my surroundings with every embarrassing cycle.

"Oh god!" I choked, slapping a hand to my nose. The sudden smell had me doubled over. Potent and sour, like the black grime beneath a dumpster. It clung inside my nostrils like curdled honey. I dry-heaved before I pulled up my shirt to cover my nose and mouth. I had to expose my soft stomach for too long a time as I walked the stinky distance. The coughing started up again at a decomposing pile on the side of the road. My shirt was wet at my mouth. "Oh."

A dead dog lay on its side, sizzling in the oppressive heat. I approached it carefully, afraid I might lose last night's pitiful dinner. I expected a cesspool of maggots and beetles to fill an animal producing such a stink, but there were no bugs on this dog. Its hide was stretched over its ribs tightly. The fur on its face had pulled away from its snout, exposing its jaws in a vicious snarl. The teeth remained whole and sharp. It looked like it had been here for weeks—dehydrated like jerky, dry and shrunken—

though I was sure the dog wasn't here when I walked home from work yesterday.

I imagined the carcass rotating its leathery head toward me, grinning over its pointed canines. I inched closer, reaching my hand to test the savage fangs—

The grass beside me rustled suddenly. I jumped, pathetically pulling my shirt down. The rustling sound continued closer, low to the ground—a snake. I backed away from the animals into the center of the road. Snakes in this area weren't venomous, usually, but they were always unnatural and terrifying. I had almost forgotten the dog when the smell assaulted me once more. I shoved the damp cotton back to my face and jogged north.

After I stepped through the automatic doors at Jim's, I slowed my walk down to a crawl and crossed into the backroom to find my apron. All the employees shared only two coat hooks for their aprons in the storeroom, and I was digging through the dozens of egg-crusted green fabric when I heard someone approach over my shoulder. Heavy feet.

"Morning, Miss Hughes." Scott. The boss. Scott looked like your average middle-aged father: plump, balding, and a little sad. Scott resembled soft serve. He wore a crisp green apron over his button-up shirt and tie. Scott's tie was not fun at all.

He looked around to ensure no other employees were in the vicinity. "I've been meaning to catch you. You should really take your uniform home and wash it. I've noticed some ... gunk on it for a few days now and it's, uh ... unprofessional. Could you take it home with you tonight and clean it up some? Yes?"

At least Pamela could spit it out. I inwardly rolled my eyes and thought of all the crusty residue and dried milk I just waded through to get to my own—cleaner—apron. Usually, I was apathetic toward Scott. It was only during moments like these that I hoped his children bullied him or his wife fucked the neighbor.

I answered slowly, "Sure, Scott. It'll be clean tomorrow." He

6

gave me the straightest smile I had ever seen and turned toward his office.

After a few steps, Scott held up his pointer finger, "Oh, and one more thing, Francesca," *Ugh*. This guy too. "You were a few minutes late today. Don't let it happen again, please." Rather than risk speaking openly, I replied with my own straight smile and turned away, hiding the disgusted lift of my lip.

I worked the usual seven degrading hours I was accustomed to. I dealt with a blazer-clad asshole, who ripped up an expired coupon and threw it in my face; a powdery old bat who dropped not one, but two full gallons of milk onto the hard floor; and an endless parade of co-workers talking of hikes and movies and children. I hid in the storeroom for the last hour of my shift, pretending to stock when I heard any noise, but primarily sat on the floor in my favorite dark corner.

I left early, having not seen anyone in a while, and took a six-pack of Gold Star home with me. It tasted like sweat-soaked bread, and as cheap as it was, I didn't feel too bad about taking it. It was a lower ABV beer, and I could finish all six before I got home. I would throw the empties in the neighbors' garbage bins. Pamela would never find out. I left the store through the loading dock.

To avoid the stinking dog roast, and to ensure I'd finish my pack, I would take the long way home. The road I normally took formed a straight line between starting point and destination. I would instead turn left, right, and then right again, my day's journey forming a perfect and unnecessary square. The square connected many of the remaining homes and plots of land in town. Due to the globs of random townies I would certainly come across, I would have to be discreet.

I squatted between two cars in the back of the parking lot and pulled the pack out from under my rolled-up "unprofessional" apron. I chugged until my ankles couldn't hold my weight anymore and then collapsed back onto my tailbone. I stretched out my legs and proceeded to finish the can lounging on the asphalt. I drained my drink, burped with my mouth closed, letting it filter out my nose, and relieved my palms of the many tiny pebbles wedged into my pink skin.

The streets were bare. After I drank my second can behind a lone trailer, and my third beside a dying, crispy shrub, I felt free enough to walk through the tall grass on the side of the road. I hopped onto the pavement when I heard any slithering and crouched down when I passed homes with large windows. I crept by a couple of trucks that were sitting on the road's shoulder, waddling around them like a hunched-back penguin. One truck I recognized as Mr. McCormac's. I risked a glance through my hair at the driver. His head was tipped back and his mouth drooped open, spittle at the corners. He was taking a nap behind the steering wheel.

Mr. McCormac was always nice to me and my mom. He brought us a bag of apricots every year from his trees. He was a busy guy, probably hiding from his wife, who, from what I'd seen, thought a quiet moment was a moment wasted. She must have four lungs. Too bad they weren't tits. "Ha! Could you imagine?" I mumbled, snorted, and scooted forward on my hands and toes. "Rest easy, old man."

I was beginning to feel cheerful at the prospect of home and tried to remember where I'd stashed my Cheezy Poofs. I lifted my fifth beer to my lips and looked across the field beside me. I neared the spot exactly across the square from that dead, dead dog. I could still smell it from here. Impossible.

I coughed a wet cough, and from the side of my eye, saw a patch of white, like a glare of sunlight, rise from the pavement. It waved hazily beyond the grass in the blazing heat but was otherwise unmoving. "What the ..." bubbled from between my parchment lips.

I weaved to the wire fence surrounding the field of grass, dry shoots going up my pant legs and crunching underfoot. I was about to duck under the cords, the white something was larger now, when I vomited a full eight ounces of fluid at my feet.

The smell of acid and yeast lifted from the wasted foam as it puddled above the hard earth. Spit hung from my mouth in stringy loops. "Too fast," I heard myself. Burping again, I shook the grass shards from my jeans. I dropped my last Gold Star in the grass sadly and looked back across the field. The white shape was gone.

The caustic rotten stench creeped back around me as I neared my driveway. I breathed through my mouth, and though it made me queasy, like eating decay, it almost helped.

The house was still spotless, but the reek filled the empty spaces like a gas. I jogged into the bathroom with my eyes on the carpet. Pamela didn't comment and relief flooded my gut as I locked the door.

I jerked around toward the washer before I'd forget, grumbling about Scott and ripping my apron over my head viciously. As I opened the door again, I glimpsed my reflection in the mirror and did a double-take. My eyes were a deep, dark red. Knots of hair had escaped my hair tie and hung in dirty ropes down my face. Yellow spit from my regurgitated Gold Star was strung out of the corner of my mouth and stuck to my cheek. I dunked my head in the sink and drank from the faucet, smearing cold water over my flushed face. It was exquisite. I found one of my mom's hair clips in the vanity drawer and pulled my hair up into a messy ball. Wadding up some wet toilet paper, I scrubbed at the puke spatters on my polo and flapped the cotton in the air to dry.

Going for casual, I swung the door into the wall with a bang and strolled down the hall. Her bedroom door remained shut, so I ambled back to the living room and arranged my expression, hoping I appeared worn out and sober—which was basically true—and experienced a strong sense of déjà vu.

It was the exact scene I had left this morning. Pamela sat on the edge of that blue fabric couch in front of the television. Her eyes were vacant, as if she had seen it before. The flyswatter was at home, clutched in her vengeful fist across her lap, as flies hopped from surface to surface of her.

"Hey, Pamela!" Too loud. "Why are you still watching this? You hate the evening anchors." I was still wet and nervously chatty. Pamela didn't respond or even acknowledge me. I didn't feel the peace that I'd always dreamt would accompany her silence. "Grandma? You hear me?" She ignored my uncomfortable endearment and continued to stare forward. "Yeah, um, I look pretty awful, right? Have you been outside? There's this smell out there. Thought I would try and clean up a little. Guess a shower would have done the trick, huh?" I huffed a laugh. Nothing.

"Pamela?" I approached her timidly, expecting her to start hissing like a teapot. Even now, I tasted the pungent dead scent on my tongue. Pamela's eyes were wide, but they looked through the television. Her lips were parted and as crinkly as brown leaves. I leaned in close to the mouth, closer than I'd been to her in years, and searched for words within it. My eyes were hardly an inch away and I felt no air hit my face. I reached out my fingers and pressed those lips. The skin was cool to the touch and stiff. I moved to cup the cavernous cheeks with my still-wet palms.

A lone fly landed at the corner of one green eye, buzzing. I waved the bug away with disgust. Undaunted, it returned, again and again, lingering over the juicy red crevices of the gooey orbs. I pushed the eyelids down, the thing buzzed against the back of my hand, relentless. The eyelids felt as if they were fighting my fingers, inviting the bug inside. I pushed against Pamela's skin. Pushed until I was scared.

"Oh," I breathed.

My grandmother was dead.

2

THE BODY HAD BEEN TAKEN away hours ago, but the stain of it stuck to my fingertips. Though I was now the cleanest I'd been in days, my wet hair making me shiver in cotton sweatpants, I could still feel my grandmother's dead lips in my hands. I wondered if this was shock.

My eyes remained dry as I had called the police earlier, and when the voice on the other end of the line asked, "Is this an emergency?" I sorted through what constituted an emergency before speaking. "No, it's not."

Pamela was old, obviously, but she wasn't *that* old. In her late sixties, I thought. I didn't know too much about the woman, but my mother never told of any health conditions or scares. Maybe throughout every one of those long, long decades, Pamela had been slowly starving herself. Speculation, of course. The police or medical examiner or whoever handled these things would call when they had a cause of death.

This was as sudden—more so if I were honest—as my mother's death, but the police assured me it was most likely due to some mundane risk that came from living past fifty. I couldn't stop myself from morbidly wondering how long it was after I left her on that couch that she had stopped breathing. I remembered how I'd found her ... it was exactly as I had left her.

There was a soft, rhythmic knock on the front door. I didn't lift myself off the bed and so expected further knocking. Instead, the front door eased open and closed in my ears. The footsteps that followed were measured and slow. I wasn't surprised he was here, but I would still ask how he knew. My bedroom door fell open in the dark before Ben stuck his head inside.

"Hey, Frank," he smiled easily, as if this were just another day. Which I supposed it was. His mouth lifted so naturally, as if at rest when turned upward.

He paused, asking for permission, then slid his lean body through the door and onto the foot of my twin bed. Ben was tall, 6'2", with thick toasted skin from a life in the sun. He was outside every chance he got. What little hair he had was dark and shaved close to his scalp. He never grew it out; I wasn't sure if it was closer to black or brown. He had a few holes in his face where he had pierced some feature and had then grown tired of the jewelry, and those holes now blended in with the freckles that dotted his nose and dark eyes. His long arms were spackled in black lines and symbols, tattoos that my mother had found *interesting*, and Pamela always abhorred. They were one of the reasons she hated and probably feared Ben.

Today he wore a busy tank top covered in animated dinosaurs and loose green carpenter pants over rubber flip-flops. I normally would smile in return to his greeting, but that seemed something like impolite. He silently crossed his ankles, an uncharacteristic gesture.

"How did you find out?" I asked. I wondered if his presence would make me want to cry.

"Scanner," he replied with a shrug. Of course, it would have been reported on the police scanner Ben kept in his living room. He bought it years ago, when his loud, underage parties were regularly being called in by his neighbors, even though they lived a quarter-mile from his house.

He didn't throw many parties these days but claimed that having it still came in handy from time to time. If you could call something like this handy.

"You found her?" he asked. My eyebrows squished together

and I turned my hand over limply in my lap. Pink fingers. "You okay?"

"Probably better than I should be." I didn't feel the sadness or the guilt, the anger, the relief that I was waiting for. A teardrop, some chest pain. Something. His quiet made me want to continue. "She seemed fine this morning."

A tawny finger crept into my field of vision. It was etched in ink triangles and x's, painting over several deep grooves in his skin. I'd always wondered if he experimented with scarification before the tattoos, though I'd never asked. He stretched his pointer and middle finger out to mine, brushing them so gently I couldn't be certain of it. I hated being touched. Ben knew and accepted that. His fingers stroking mine was the equivalent of a bone-crushing hug. I pressed back softly, the pink of my skin lightened delicately before I crossed my arms against my chest. That was enough.

"You smell nice," Ben noted, unbothered by my with-drawal. "That's new." I smiled for the first time genuinely that day, surprised at the tug of my left cheek. He stuck his roaming finger in my ear and shook it around. "Squeaky clean."

I jerked my head and snorted. "You're too sweet."

"You should stay at my house tonight. And not just because you smell lemon-fresh for the first time in your life. Watching baking competitions just doesn't spark the same fervor without you there." He moved my wet hair over my shoulder, touchy today, and began digging through my now-yellow cabinet. He found one of my old duffels and threw it on my lap. "Outside clothes too, not just jammies."

"Jammies can be outside clothes," I grumbled as I flipped the duffle upside down and shook it over my blankets, watching strands of hair and dust fall out of its corners. "Since when do I need a bag for your place?"

"It's an open-ended invitation. I only have so many shirts, and your nasty digits always leave stubborn mystery stains." He held a few items to his nose before throwing them all back to the carpet.

I ought to feel embarrassed, but I didn't feel much of anything. Two generations wiped out in a year. My grandmother was gone. My mother was gone …

When I hadn't moved to pack, Ben lowered his eyebrows and raised his voice, "Did you want me to get your shit together *for* you?" He kicked a dust-covered piece of black something onto the bed. I grabbed whatever it was and tossed it in the bag before rummaging around on my bed where I tended to dump my clean laundry.

I had packed a few trusty t-shirts and something denim when I felt another clump of hair lift. Ben slowly twirled my hair around his finger, and I watched like an anxious animal as it fell in a spiral. "You sure you got it?" His finger stilled, suspended before my face. "Princess?"

"Think I won't bite that off?" Ducking to avoid his hand, I dragged myself to my dresser and started stuffing fabric in the bag. There wasn't much in there, since most of my clothes lay soiled on the bedroom floor. Once I had enough to keep myself somewhat dressed for a week, I scoffed from behind my hair. "Princess?"

"Please don't start." He lifted one matted gray sock from the carpet and hastily tossed it in my tiny trash can.

I crossed the hallway to the bathroom, shouting behind me, "I'm assuming you want me to stay on this soap kick I'm on?"

"Might be a nice change!"

I took a plastic grocery bag out from under the sink, filled it with bottles, and threw it on top of my duffle in the hallway. I found one of my two pairs of shoes by the tub and slid my bare feet into them. Unsure of how long I would be away, I packed my boots too. I looked up to find Ben watching me with an exasperated expression. "Should probably chuck most of this back in the wash. Better safe than sorry." He lifted my duffle to his shoulder, it was hardly bigger than a purse. "Can we please go now? I haven't eaten and I know you haven't either."

Ben beat me to the door and left it open. As I crossed the room, it pulled my eyes like a beacon—that blue fabric couch. It had transformed from a boring symbol of our mediocrity into an eerie, almost malevolent thing, like a Victorian locket or a blood-stained diary. I thought I could see the stain of her stuck in the fibers. I should have cleaned it, or hurled it out on the lawn. If I touched the cushions, would my hand come away covered in it? In the stain?

I slammed the door behind me and locked it.

Ben's car was a loud, ugly piece of trash, but it ran, which was more than I could brag about—I traded my unremarkable car in for not enough money after I returned to this town and had resorted to walking everywhere since. His vehicle was a plastic-looking red Volkswagen sedan with rust around tires that were too big for the body. Ben wasn't a car person and had never minded my constant berating of it. He would just smile, placating, and rev the rattling engine.

The door protested as I pried it open. The leather seats were cracked and almost always painfully hot to the touch. Whenever I sat in this car I was overwhelmed with the scent of cigarettes, though Ben hadn't smoked in the last year, and a woodsy-dirt smell, though Ben never hiked. Those things combined with the underlying chemical aroma of paint that followed Ben everywhere.

My forehead beaded with sweat as we reversed away from the house, my once cozy clothes now swamped and heavy. I popped my knuckles, relaxing with each audible release. I knew Ben hated the sound, but he let me go about it in silence.

On the edge of town, near the freeway, Ben inhabited a very well-kept one-bedroom bungalow that sat alone far from the road. He told me his uncle had inherited the house decades ago, but the man preferred his place in New Mexico, allowing Ben to move in at seventeen. I thought his uncle must have been completely batshit to allow a teen like Ben to live alone in a house during his senior year of high school, but I couldn't deny the success of the place. Ben took pride in his home, keeping it clean, touching up the white finish, and maintaining the yard. He even kept a flourishing herb garden around back which he nurtured and utilized in his cooking. Ben had taken to adulthood in a way that made me jealous, but not enough to dig my own garden.

BEN SPRINKLED salt over the orange pan, some sort of pasta with oil and fresh basil. He had allowed my small assistance of dicing tomatoes, but stood close behind me, gnashing his teeth with every uneven slice. Finally, one of his chomps was so dramatic I held the knife over his scarred hand resting on the counter. He waited in the other room for me to complete one vegetable—or fruit?—and banished me to the table.

I traced the patterns in the artificial wood finish until he brought out two mismatched bowls and a couple of beers under his arm. "Thank you, Chef. I could have done more but a neurotic harpy took my knife," I growled.

"You're so welcome, Princess. I would have brought you a suitable wine pairing … but I don't like wine." He shrugged, ignoring my irritation. He spun a bite around his fork and tucked it into his mouth neatly before taking a gulp of his beer. I took a swig; it was no Gold Star. "I have a little gift for you," he continued, focused on his dinner.

I paused, a forkful of untidy noodles inches from my chin. "Why?" I wasn't interested in some sorry-your-grandma-died something or other to remember today.

Ben held his hands up in defense, guessing the path of my thoughts. "First off, you're so welcome, asshole," he snapped with an eyebrow raised. "Second, this was handmade a while ago. I just haven't seen you in a few days." His jaw clenched in defiance as he stared me down.

"Handmade?" I took a few quick crotchety bites without tasting much. I slowed down, at risk of choking, and slid a mound of pasta to my tongue. Delicious. Of course it was. "Is there a reason for this present?"

He returned his attention to his food. "Must you always be so irascible?"

"Doesn't this dinner count as a homemade gift?" I asked, dipping my pinkie into the saucy remnants of my meal and licking it clean. Ben was oddly engrossed in my piggishness and smiled. When he did, I pitied every person of whom he'd ever asked anything, including myself. His teeth were perfect behind his curved lips, but it was the stuff behind the smile that always got to me, somehow both teasing and genuine. My lips tilted up in reluctance. "Fine, God, I concede! Hand it over then."

He finished his beer with a dignified quiet, "It's in the bedroom." After taking our empty dishes to the sink, he sauntered toward the back of the house. "Would you care to join me?" He winked over his shoulder.

I flinched in distaste. His light flirting was rare, scary, and always caught me off guard, like someone who carried a gun you nearly forgot about until they held it to your temple. He flirted with everyone, generally, but often held back when we were alone to keep me at ease. No doubt he knew how it disarmed me and had used it to his advantage now, as revenge for my rudeness.

The thud of my bag on the linoleum interrupted my panic. "If you want to change into something a little less rank," he chuckled, disappearing into his room.

My stupid face had the balls to blush.

I flopped onto his squishy queen mattress, almost as familiar as my own bed, and far more comfortable. The room was simply furnished: a steel-framed queen bed, a hand-me-down desk that held his painting supplies, and a dresser to match. His walls were what held the real interest of this place. They were radically covered in his sketches and paintings in various mediums and sizes, some black and gray, some exploding in color. Some were framed on canvas and others were printer paper held up with Scotch tape. Charcoal and pastel, acrylic and watercolor. I thought I saw my own hazel eyes staring back at me from a few pieces, but fearing I was being egotistical, had never asked.

Ben dug around in his closet, rifling through some very loud shirts. He opened some built-in drawers, closing them immediately, before he finally retrieved my gift. He inspected it closely in his palms, as if it were a loan document.

He turned around and dangled a woven bracelet in the air above me. It was unprecedented in its peculiar beauty. Nothing about it stood out or held any particular charm, but it was captivating all the same. It wasn't made with anything from a jewelry store, more like found objects. The brown fray of rope interspersed with mismatched pebbles from the mountains drilled through and threaded precisely. It was all strung together with a lock of thick black thread, it shone in the dull overhead light of Ben's bedroom. "Wow," I whispered. It was more strange than pretty and I liked it. I tried to grab it, but Ben took my wrist and tied the bracelet around my bones himself.

"Perfect fit," he said. His intense eyes found mine, which I instinctually avoided.

I got to my feet and began to peruse the room I'd been in a thousand times. My fingers trailed along his eclectic collection of knick-knacks: a copper lighter, a plastic Zen garden filled with blue Pixie-Stick dust, a common pink flower that had died and dried years ago. My bracelet shared something like kinship with this assortment of junk. I touched them all. The dead flower was surprisingly soft, silk petals, the color brighter than I thought as I stroked its face.

"TV?" Ben's voice was steady, calm, but I jerked as if sleeping. "It's pastry week," he added with impatience.

I TOSSED, intermittently conscious despite how cozy I was on Ben's caramel-colored leather sofa. We made it through three episodes of baking drama—Ben sketching, my toes pressed against his thigh in an almost normal way—when my lids began to droop. I watched his chalk spin into a curl, a curl just like mine, when I finally gave up the fight. He jostled me when he shoved a pillow beneath my head. The fresh scent of detergent filled my nose.

Ben left in a hurry, clearly wanting to give me privacy to be upset. He had made up the couch for me after an argument—he'd wanted me to take his bed for my extended stay. He only relented after I took his pillow and comforter; he would take the guest bedding from the closet. Grief deserved a higher thread count, he said. The wood and smoke scent clung to his duvet, just like his car, and I liked that a little.

I hoped in this alone time, in the somber darkness, I would finally cry. My eyes remained cold, clear, and dry. I ran myself over with memories of Pamela, trying to force a reaction, but I, frankly, didn't have much in the memory bank. Most of the reel involved Pamela chiding me for my laziness, my eating, my weakness. She rarely smiled, and when she did, she was derisive.

I had never once liked her. But I thought I might miss her with enough time. In the way that people tied by blood are supposed to miss one another. I remembered my earlier comparison for Pamela and me, the two weeds. I used to find comfort in the idea, that at least the two of us were missing something so much better than we were. And *her*, I did miss.

Whether it was the loss finally kicking in, a homesickness, or the certainty that I had never felt so lonely, a single hot tear swelled between my lashes. It was trapped there, pooling onto my eye. The blurriness was a warm one and I thought that sleep might be within reach. I turned my head to the side and began to fade. The last thing I saw was Ben's trusty scanner, the plug stretched out haphazardly on the floor …

My eyes opened at the sound of feet in the hallway. The edges of the room melted into each other until I couldn't find the edges at all. I rubbed my legs together but there was no heat. I stilled, feigning sleep—it might have even been real—then Ben leaned over me.

"You're gonna miss it, Frank!" He ripped me off the couch and I was lighter than air, "Come on! We need to hurry!" The click of a door being opened and closed. Outside. The two of us. I couldn't remember finding my shoes, but they hugged my feet as Ben led me through the crispy grass, held my hand.

My shoe squeaked against my ankle with each step, it almost grounded me. The world was a fuzzy animal. I was looking at it through water, the pool of my eyes. "Ben, I can't see. Everything is … smeared." He towed me along faster. His hand was attached to mine. I could discern trees ahead.

We entered the line of aspens, and I felt a new fear of the woods. I had grown up with these trees, played in them as a child. But never in the dark, never in this swirling, surreal reflection of reality. I didn't trust my eyes. I could only hear Ben leaping and gliding far in front of me. Our arms stretched between us like warm taffy. He would vanish completely, along with my hand, if I didn't keep up.

I saw a subtle worn pathway angling down into a shallow valley. I followed Ben, moving infinite angry branches away from my face, the ground shifting like mounds of restless snakes.

Without warning, without a hint, I was suddenly surrounded by music, singing, as if the voice was right beside me. It was the most angelic sound I had ever heard, stinging my eyes in its magic. There was no such thing as music before this, there was no such thing as sound. It was irresistible, hypnotic. It was agony to know it. "Benny?" I heard my own plea.

Dropping my hand, he yelled, "Come on!" once again and

walked under a low-hanging blue branch. It stabbed into the stark night like a knife. My hand was cold. I ducked to follow him.

In the small clearing of trees was a roaring bonfire, much taller than me, though I never saw or smelled smoke surrounding this place. Naked bodies writhed around the flames, devastating, inhuman in their freedom and loveliness. I didn't know which body was singing, I couldn't perceive faces. The skin was endless, cosmic, but the sound was clear. It shattered me, broke me entirely. I collapsed to my knees. The bodies moved around me as if I weren't alive.

Ben's back was to me, very near the flames. He stripped off his shirt, exposing his bare torso, shiny black and orange in the fiery glow. His tattoos continued down his ribs on both sides like the shadowed arms of a stranger. They seemed to flicker and flex in the firelight like the dancers around him. The tears I had childishly thought I deserved before now finally dribbled down my cheeks. I had never witnessed a sight so glorious.

For so long I watched, haunted, I hardly noticed the kneeling figure. He was fully clothed, sweat dewing down his neck and glimmering like diamonds in his skin. He was still, so still I would have guessed him unconscious, but he held his eyes open, shockingly wide. His mouth lifted peacefully, as if in a dream.

I noticed Ben approach the dreamer, though my eyes repeatedly bounced back to the spinning dancers. The naked bodies writhed as the song swelled around them. Ben reached toward one of them, a girl with shining dark skin, and came away with a bowl overflowing with green.

He turned back to the happy kneeling man, and Ben's smile radiated in my chest. He caressed the foreign face. I had only a moment to envy that stranger before Ben extended a graceful finger into his face and popped the left eye from its socket.

3

I JOLTED OUT OF SLEEP, my cheek adhered to the inside of my elbow and caked with drool. I was afraid, afraid of the woods and the fire. The man, there was the … hypnotized man … his eye. I sat up more gradually, expecting to be surrounded by the tall horde of trees I was kneeling in just moments before, but instead was twisted in a deep gray comforter. The smell of the woods still hung over me in its fibers.

"Morning, Princess!" Ben shouted from the loveseat, making me duck my head in nervous surprise. "Ten in the goddamn morning and she's finally up," he muttered insolently to himself as he walked out of the room. My face felt purple with heat, though inside the house was a cool seventy degrees.

I looked through the archway leading to the kitchen. Ben, in his tattered grandpa robe, took mugs down from the cupboard. He methodically chewed a cinnamon stick poking through his lips. It rolled left and right between his teeth while he poured coffee. The smell was so rich, the fear I had been submerged in began to ebb, but the drool picked back up.

"Isn't sleeping late warranted in this situation?" My throat felt full of gravel and gum. I sounded like a toad. "Grieving granddaughter and all?" I rolled my shoulders with a crack.

Ben ignored me. "I'm not bringing this to you in bed. Come sit outside with me." He didn't look back as he opened the side screen door.

I shambled like a zombie into his bathroom first. I started when I saw my reflection. I was a stranger.

My eyes were bright and alive, no traces of sleep in them. My cheeks were flooded with color, a healthy color—rose—and for the first time in what felt like years, my lips weren't peeling away. They looked soft and plump. My hair even seemed lighter, the blonde tones more prominent.

The bright eyes fell as I remembered the figures in my dream, Ben included. I could not help envying their otherworldly beauty. Even with the sudden health boost that came with half a day's sleep, even at my best, I was nothing but a rueful voyeur to them. My newly tenderized lip lifted as I rolled my eyes with my reflection.

I had accepted my appearance when I was young, not loving it or hating it. The sole exception being my hair. I loathed my hair. I spun one strawberry curl around my finger like a noose. It was mashed and frizzy from sleep—looking like a dead ginger cat in the gutter—but even after strenuous effort, it was horrifyingly doll-like. I already appeared younger than my twenty-three years, barely looking eighteen if I wore makeup and fifteen without it. My hair added to my childlike appearance. It pushed strangers and acquaintances to be sweet with me when nothing made me more uncomfortable. Fortunately, it didn't take them long to notice my proclivity for unpleasantness.

My skin was my favorite feature. I never experienced break-outs, even as an angst-filled teen. It was a very non-fussy attribute, unlike my hair. But, if anything, that just gave me an excuse to shower less. I hadn't owned face wash since eighth grade, preferring only hot water on my skin, which I now splashed over my cheeks and down my neck. I used my over-sized shirt to dry my face and took the opportunity to judge my smallish tits and round thighs. Nothing to cry about. But how ridiculous would they look next to the bodies by the fire? Shaking off the frightening dream, I used the toilet and followed Ben out back.

Completely in character, he only had two reclining patio chairs and a small table outside. Though he had been well-known for big parties a few years earlier, he never had much furniture for guests. I was still grateful for the end of that phase, having never been a partier. Not that I didn't love drinking. I did. I just preferred it away from roaring, obnoxious crowds.

The chairs faced a backyard of shorn grass yellowing in the sun. I knew he didn't appreciate having to let his plants, including his grass, wither and die, but he also wasn't one for waste. A true dilemma for him. His herb garden was visible to the left, thriving with life. He had sacrificed the grass for those green beauties. Beyond his yard was a patchwork quilt of landscape: grass fields, aspen trees, and mountain face. My eyes froze on those trees, imagining the figure on his knees.

Ben pushed the free chair noisily across the cement then slid my cup of coffee closer to the edge of the table. The smell was the best bait he could use on me. He pulled the spitty cinnamon stick from between his teeth, used it to stir his drink, clinked it on the rim, and returned it to his mouth.

"How'd you sleep, Frank?" he asked before sucking the coffee off the stick.

I leaned back in the chair, the sun's heat beating against the top of my head. I gave myself lots of time, drinking most of my coffee at once. Cream and cinnamon.

"Ugh! Did you stick that disgusting thing in my cup?"

"You wish, babe." He winked, his stick stuck on its side between his teeth. "You sleep okay? I thought I heard you moving around a lot." He looked back to the surrounding scenery, his smile in place despite the cinnamon.

I felt a twinge of paranoia. Even if the fire and the eye-gouging were a dream, what if he did leave the house?

"I slept okay. Weird dreams." My pinkie trailed the handle of my mug. "How did you sleep?"

"Slept like a baby that sleeps better than a baby." The cinnamon stick made another appearance before flipping back

24

over his tongue. "What do you want to do today? I don't work until Monday." He worked painting houses locally and as far as the Salt Lake Valley. Ben didn't care what he was painting, he seemed to love it all the same.

I hadn't told Ben that I was scheduled to work in a few hours. Surely with what happened, I could get the day off.

"I should probably call Scott and explain … and I should talk to the medical examiner or something, right?" I took a quick, anxious sip. "There needs to be a funeral—am I the one that plans that funeral?" Of course it had to be me. I probably had family somewhere, but my grandfather was dead, and I had never known my own father. I was an only child. This wasn't going to be something I could ride out with a bag of chips and a DVD set.

My mother had been cremated. Pamela and I scattered the ashes in a mountain spring that she loved. At least, that's all I would say to the nosey people who would ask. But my grand-mother never let me touch the urn or scatter anything up on that mountain. She never even warned me before she dumped them to the ground like old food down a garbage disposal.

Not that I resented my horrible dead grandma. Not at all.

"Yeah, all of that." Ben grew concerned with my zoned-out silence. "But what do you *want* to do? None of that sounds like something we're going to enjoy."

I scowled. Ben was always taking care of me. I fought him every step of the way, but it was like yelling at the sun. It was just his nature.

"Well, a movie might be okay. But I always ruin the show for you when I can hear people talking."

"Or breathing."

"Or," I continued, "food would be fine, but we could just eat here and save money. Same situation with a bar."

"Plus, it's ten in the morning."

"We could go buy some DVDs." I thought of the pathetic movie collection I had at home. The discs existed on the same shelf as the half dozen books I owned. Each had been given to me as a gift and I'd been meaning to pick out a book for myself. I liked reading well enough. I liked the quiet of it. "Or, um, I haven't been to the library in a while." I had never been to the library. My lack of interests and hobbies would be disappointing at a time like this, but hobbies tended to take up a lot of time.

His reaction was instantaneous. "Cool. But let's go to the bookstore instead. The librarians around here are assholes."

෴

BEN SUGGESTED he be the one to call Scott at Jim's Grocery. I shunned his mothering but not as much as making phone calls. In truth, I did not want to talk to Scott, didn't want to defend myself to him, which would be inevitable. Because whenever I had to defend myself, chances were good I was getting fired.

I left him in the kitchen to take a shower and brush my teeth. I brought my grocery bag of toiletries in the bathroom with me, but used his toothpaste when I saw the brand was better than mine. Curious about his soap, I gave it a whiff. It smelled more like the ocean than the woods. My brows pulled together as I took my own lemon-scented body wash into the shower.

After I toweled off, my hair hanging in soaking, knotty spirals down my back, I dug through my bag in search of a suitable outfit. I held up a pair of shorts, nonplussed. I wouldn't have brought these if I'd been paying attention. Or if I ever did laundry. I generally wore jeans as a rule and had always felt uneasy showing much of my skin. It made me tug at my clothes consciously or otherwise. But I couldn't deny this heatwave, and I was too proud to tell Ben he was right about the laundry. I slid them over my thighs and stuck my head in a boxy white t-shirt.

I walked back to the kitchen, scrunching my hair dry in a towel. Ben sat on the counter next to the sink, still on the phone

26

but obviously talking to someone else; he couldn't have talked to Scott for more than a few minutes. He was listening intently to whoever it was when his eyes followed me through the archway. His eyes flicked down to my bare legs and then up to my face, his expression unfathomable. It made me nervous. Had he ever seen my bare legs?

"Later," he barked before ending the call and hopping off the counter. Ben changed while I'd been in the shower. He was wearing what had once been a basic crew neck with a realistic picture of a wolf howling at a lightening strewn sky—before he cut off the sleeves, opening them up past his ribs—plus cut-off denim shorts and Sperry's. Similar symbols to those that decorated his arms and back were tattooed on his shins and calves, though they weren't as noticeable under the leg hair. Stubble sprouted along his jaw; I stole his chance at the bathroom.

"Scott hopes you are doing alright, and he says to, quote: take as much time as you need, I guess," Ben voiced in a decent impression of my boss. "Wanna go to Salt Lake? Best used bookstore in the state on Main Street."

"That's a forty-minute drive," I said, muddled.

"Sick of me already, Frank?" he grinned at me with obvious skepticism. He knew he was the only person with whom I liked spending any time. "We can stop for gas on the way. I swear we'll make it back by sundown." He held his right hand up in a Boy Scout salute before transitioning to finger guns. He emptied both magazines before throwing my wallet at me, grabbing hold of my sleeve, and whisking me out the door.

"JELLY?" Ben asked in the Dunkin' Donuts drive thru.

I nodded. "And a giant iced coffee." I offered him a handful of quarters that had been bulging the side of my wallet. He looked revolted, so I poured them into his center console. I had a bad habit of taking the sporadic quarters dropped in the Take-a-penny/Leave-a-penny tray at the grocery store.

He got six donuts for the road and an iced coffee for himself as well. The greasy box of fried dough and melting chocolate smelled heavenly. Ben took a maple, slid the box into my lap, and put on his oversized sunglasses. He got them at the gas station, and he loved how he looked in them.

"I still think you should have bought the red ones," I speculated, pulling a jelly donut out for myself. "Black is timeless, but boring."

"Boring!" He coughed up glaze onto his lip in offense.

"Just a bit."

"It's called being understated, not all of us are avant-garde risk-takers like you, Frank." He rubbed the white fabric of my t-shirt between his sugar-free thumb and forefinger. "Quite the fashionista."

I slapped his knuckles with a grunt, and he immediately ripped a piece from the jelly in my hand and tossed it into his mouth.

My nose scrunched with displeasure. "You know there's another jelly in the box that I wasn't eating?"

"You go ahead, I'm not a jelly fan."

I lifted my lip in agitation and took a sip of my coffee—it was shockingly sweet but refreshing in the sun. Ben's AC worked in scattered icy storms, surprising us every few minutes with a blast of cool air before noisily sputtering back into the void.

"So, what's so special about this place?" I asked. I hated driving when I didn't have to, even riding passenger. For the most part Ben knew that, and as guilty as I often felt about it, he kept our hangouts around Aspen Ridge.

"It's huge for a thrift. Two stories, genre rooms, floor-to-ceiling shelves. I thought you would prefer the variety of options compared to the single book aisle at the grocery store." He shoved his straw in his mouth for a big slurp. "Or I would, anyway. Plus, everything is nice and cheap. Just like you,

Frank." He grabbed my chin affectionately, shaking my head. I slapped his hand away and he grinned before continuing, "We could get some food or something afterward, you know, lots more to do in the city than at home."

He flicked his eyes over to me behind his glasses, always checking, despite his light tone. He sensed my reluctance for road trips but wasn't going to voice it. Communication was not my specialty, so I reached over and touched his hand on the steering wheel, awkwardly pressing the tips of my fingers to his skin. His arm stiffened under my hand, but he gave me some privacy, eyes on the road while I touched him.

"Thanks. For this," I mumbled in a small voice. It wasn't eloquent, but it was words. I put my hand back in my lap and took a long pull of coffee and sugar.

WE ENTERED the store through a heavy glass door with an old bell attached. No need to pay for street parking on the weekend so Ben encouraged me to take my time. The smell of the books was overwhelming. It wasn't a smell to which I was accustomed, but one I instantly understood: brittle paper—like lumber—and smoky dust. I stood just inside the doorway to take it all in. Shelves lined the walls eight feet high. The second floor was visible above them, stationed over half of the ground floor like the most surprising balcony. The book storage was eclectic and diverse, steel bookcases and round wooden tables, TV stands and shoe racks, all overflowing with books. There was even a space that looked like a closet filled from floor to ceiling with VHS tapes and DVDs.

I wandered the first floor, trailing my hands along the worn spines. They were paperback and hardcover, old and new, popular and obscure. I enjoyed reading the backs of them, the stories people could come up with.

I lost track of time in the quiet building, picking up half a dozen novels before even reaching the fiction. I had to repeatedly exchange books as I came across titles I had never heard of, and then again for others I had repeatedly heard of. I smiled to myself at the thought of putting a few on my small shelf at home. I didn't have many possessions that I liked.

My arms shook under my pile of books, plus three VHS tapes in damaged paper covers— Pamela had brought her old VCR over when she moved. I would probably need to put a few items back, but each comparison between them seemed impossible and unfair. I had already cut them down to the most out-there or the most exciting. I began searching for Ben. He would help me decide, or at least take half the load from me.

Weaving between the shelves with my load was a challenge. I moved cautiously throughout the store and found a back room floored in white laminate with metal ladders along the walls. I searched each corner without any luck, but found the staircase leading to the upper balcony.

My foot caught on the lip of a couple of stairs, but the books held. I took a moment at the top to appreciate the view. There weren't many people in the store and that both comforted and depressed me. I hoped the owners were getting enough business. It was much smaller on the second floor—only one shelf lined the back wall behind four tiny tables, all unoccupied.

I looked over the railing to the floor below, searching for Ben's shaved head. I saw his inked arm holding the handle of the front door from outside. He stood inside the entryway. I must have taken longer than I thought. Gradually, I eased the books out of my arms and onto one of the empty tables. Praying that no one would loot my stockpile, I rushed downstairs.

I hustled around the mismatched furniture of the room easily with my arms free, making my way to the door. I was only feet away when I sensed a troubling bout of intuition—I didn't want Ben to know I was watching him. I moved to a low hexagonal table beside the display window and picked up a paperback. The cover alluded strongly to romance. The content didn't matter, I flipped to the middle conspicuously and pretended to read. I caught a few "slick slits" and "quivering cocks" that stood out on the page before I thought I could risk a glance.

Ben wasn't alone. He faced the store but was not looking at me. His attention was held by a woman, whose back was directly in front of the window.

Her skin was an opulent dark umber, almost charcoal, and even through streaked glass, it looked soft. Her hair was heavy and black, like smoke shrouding her, falling in waves to the middle of her back. She wore a dress I would have never dared to—floral, light, and short. Ben reached out and squeezed her hand tenderly, and she let him, before pulling the handle of the entrance door wide. She spun gracefully on her heel, walking in the other direction, her face in profile. I inhaled in awe.

She had a velvet, heart-shaped face, but a strong nose that was flawlessly straight. Her lips were the fullest I had ever seen, the top almost too full, but the oddity only made her lovelier. Her cheekbones were smooth and round, they glistened in the sun. Her eyebrows were sharp, angled over honey brown eyes. She was radiant. Inhuman.

It was the dancing woman from my dream.

4

THOUGHTS RACED through my brain like starving rats in a maze as I hid behind the shelter of books. I grappled with the reality of the magnificent woman. It wasn't that I created a correlation between her face and the dancer of my dream, but that my memory had slammed the complimenting puzzle piece into place with a confident force. It was her.

Had Ben mutilated a human being? Had he dragged me along to watch? Why couldn't I see or hear well the entire night? Was I drugged?

Denial at such ideas punched me in the cortex. I switched gears, going with another possibility—or more likely the *probability*—that my imagination was running wild and I didn't watch Ben pluck an eye out of a face. If I chose to believe this, Ben had still planned to meet this unknown woman out here. That's why he wanted to make the drive, and probably who he spoke with on the phone. I didn't have as much reason to feel hurt by this option, but hurt seeped through me just as well.

My thighs burned and I began to bob on my ankles. One thing was certain. Ben had kept things from me. My heart stung because of it.

I scanned the store furtively but didn't see his shaved head above the shelves. Without consciously deciding to do so, I began to mash the eye-gouging dream into a repression box. It couldn't have happened. I wouldn't consider it. Not right now.

This—the beautiful face and the touch of her hand—that had played out right in front of my very awake and very red face.

I moved slowly and with many unnecessary stops. When I reached the staircase, I felt slightly more in control.

"There she is," Ben announced to the room as he walked through its doorway. He scrutinized my naked arms. "You didn't find anything?" His face fell in disappointment. I nearly told him I hated the store, that I wanted to leave and never come back, just to sustain that expression. But after two seconds of seeing that alien downward curve to his mouth, I knew I could never go through with it. I was so weak.

"Ben!" I squealed, perky and loud. His eyebrows shot to his forehead. "I found some books, and some movies. They're upstairs. I just didn't want to carry them everywhere while I, you know, browsed." I about-faced to the stairs and Ben followed behind me.

"Lordy! We should have brought a wagon for you, Matilda." He grinned at my leaning pile of books on the table. He picked up a few for examination and his smile grew. I detested how much pleasure he got from this.

"Children's books?" He simpered, holding up one of the two I had collected. Then he reached for my orange VHS.

"I don't need to get all of them," I countered defensively. "I was just picking up stuff as I went." I kept my eyes on the books, toying with them so I didn't have to look at him.

"Well, you were lucky enough to pick up gold. Good ol' Lemony." He gave a book a pat and waited for me to respond. When I didn't, his hands started stacking, organizing books by size. "You take half and I'll take half, then we might make it to the register in one trip," he said and scooped up the larger tower. He turned for the stairs, and, in spite of myself, I hurried to take my own stack into my arms.

I set the books on the counter just as gingerly as I had upstairs. I liked them organized by size.

"Is that all?" the cashier's rickety voice chaffed. He was easily the oldest human being I had seen upright. His face caved in on itself like an ancient and poorly baked soufflé. I was concerned the muscles and bones of his quaking hands would snap under the weight of some titles, and I considered holding them up for him to scan. His eyes narrowed, as if he knew what I thought of him, and I averted my ogling while he worked. *Dusty old goat.*

Ben reached into his back pocket for his wallet. Already shaking my head, I fussed, "Don't. This is my stuff and I'm not planning on sharing it," I pushed my unruly hair back from my sweaty forehead. "I can buy my own things."

"I was the one who didn't want to go to the goddamn library, otherwise everything would be free for you anyway," he growled, wallet still out.

Ben's short temper only shortened my own. "You already gave me the bracelet. I'm not a charity case." I wondered if he had bought the dancing woman any books. Or donuts. Blood filled my face.

"$77.55." The cashier croaked, obviously bored with our exchange. The numbers might have been the last thing that decrepit voice box would ever say before collapsing into dust.

I slammed my credit card on the counter like a lunatic. The cashier didn't react in the slightest, he simply slid the card expertly through the machine. Ben was silent beside me, and I felt his vexation beat against my skin like the sun outside. After I signed the receipt, he rubbed his head in agitation and grabbed the paper bags from the dying book master man.

"Let's get some food," he sighed. "Your cranky ass needs a beer."

∼

WE WENT to a local place with a tiny outdoor patio, equipped mercifully with misters overhead. I refused to look at Ben, even though my temper had drained at the prospect of lunch.

"What can I get the two of you to drink?" The server appeared at my elbow. I didn't recognize any of the microbrews on the menu, they had intense names like The Devil's Dance and Skeleton Key.

"A pint of anything," I ordered lazily.

"Make that two steins of whatever you recommend," Ben corrected. His arrogance and showy politeness were so infuriating. He grinned at me like he knew exactly what I was thinking.

"You know you are, unequivocally, the most annoying person on the planet when you pull shit like that."

"And you know that you would have ended up with a second pint anyway," he retorted. "And a third … and a fourth."

I didn't want to be eased by him. I wanted an explanation but was too afraid of how insane I'd sound, to his ears and mine. Folding my arms, I watched the people around us enjoy their food and silly conversations. I found things to hate about them all, like the offensive color of a hat or the way they moved their feet under a table.

Our drinks arrived and I drank before ordering, creating an uncomfortable silence for the server. The brew was pleasantly sour, pineapple-y. I hoped it would clear my mind enough to form a plan, or muddy things up enough to make me unafraid. In a hurry to get it over with either way, I drank half of it before I put the glass down.

"Thirsty?" Ben asked, amused, as the server left to get our order to the kitchen.

I nodded an affirmative, avoiding his eyes. I watched my legs through the honeycomb pattern of the table's metal frame. They almost appeared tan, my skin insatiable for sunlight.

"Is there a reason you haven't looked at me since we left the bookstore?" Ben asked.

I took another big swallow before I surrendered and made eye contact. There was that stupid face of his: warm and cocky and inviting. "Yes, there is."

He laughed when he realized that's all I had to say. I held his eyes for an eternity, surprised at my ability to do so. His mouth twitched as I lifted my glass. "So, Cleo upset you?"

I froze, taken aback, the stein touching my lip. I let beer soak my tongue but set it back down without swallowing. So, he knew I had seen them and was blatantly unbothered by that fact. Humiliation tackled me and I wasn't feeling especially brave yet.

"Cleo?" I asked innocently.

"Cleo. The woman you saw me with outside the store today," he volunteered. "She wanted to come in and meet you, but I told her I'd like to speak with you first. About her. And me. And you."

My eyes popped and my mouth pulled down in the corners like a troll's. "What the hell is the matter with you?" His eyebrows rocketed upwards. I checked the other tables and lowered my voice. "You aren't seriously discussing some sex thing with me? This couldn't wait a couple days? And she had to come here to—"

"Slow down there, Frank!" He held up his finger as he took a drink, then hid his mouth with his hand. He had the nerve to giggle at me. "This isn't as serious as my asking you for 'some sex thing.' I realize the timing could be … better." His eyes widened with the fact. "But certain things have been set in motion, so this really can't wait, Princess." He took a swig. "As much as I might like it to." He eyed my nearly empty glass. "We should get two more. Drinking will help if we're actually doing this."

I threw up my hands. "My mind just went right back to sex."

The server's timing was impeccable. I forced a pained smile as he set my tacos on the table. Ben thanked the man for his burger and asked for another round. Once he was out of earshot, Ben played with his huge sunglasses and looked at me with something like pity.

"You might as well take a few bites, it'll get cold once I get into it."

I did as he suggested, eating wildly. I hadn't had restaurant food, outside of fast food, for months. Not to mention that cold tacos were subpar, and I knew I would be asking a lot of questions. He was acting so obscure and strange. Our server set another full stein in front of me.

Ben leaned back and folded his hands over his stomach. He tilted back on the hind legs of his chair several times, stirring small doses of anxiety beneath my sternum. I drank deeply while I waited for him to spit it out.

"The hardest part is always the beginning," he mused, rubbing his shorn hair, lost in thought for a while before eyeing me seriously. "Do you have anything you want to talk to me about?"

I sat across the table in stubborn silence, causing Ben to huff with impatience. "We have to get all this fear of lunacy out the way," he groaned, raking a palm across his mouth.

My eyes shriveled, held open too long. I pictured his skin in the firelight, rippling, golden. I took another drink.

"I know you have had something on your mind today," he spoke slowly, as if I were mentally deficient. "I want you to be brave, Frank. I want you to tell me about it."

I followed the freckles surrounding his face, he had earned several dots in the sun. The boyish speckles floated beneath his eyes like dust mites in an attic. I shook my head. The beer was hitting me, a gentle shove. If he wanted brave, then he could have it.

"I had a dream last night," I started, my words unwavering.

"Did you?" He wasn't asking for a confirmation or asking to be polite.

"I'm … I'm not sure."

He considered my dizzy eyes with a hawk's focus. After I looked away, he leaned forward in his chair and began stacking the empty plates, pushing them to the side of the table. He held his glass in both hands. "Go on."

I took a sip, already half gone, hardly detecting its sour on my tongue. "You left the house and I followed you. You went into the woods ... and I followed you."

I set my chin on the table, my nose pressed against the stein. Through the glass, I saw a hazy Ben nodding in encouragement, and that made me wish I were alone. He didn't act like I was telling him a dream, he acted like I was rehashing one he already knew.

"And ..." I breathed. He waited expectantly, fingers pressed white on his glass. My hands began to shake. I threw back my drink, pouring some up my nose, as the confirmation struck home. I coughed. *Oh no.* "Oh ... no."

Ben's hands shot up in defense. "Frank, Frankie, listen, everything is okay, everyone is okay. I promise. I promise, alright?" he desperately assured, moving his hands over my own stiff fingers, clenched in dense balls.

The server approached to take our plates and, sensing I was having some sort of episode, excused himself quickly.

Ben waited until he was back through the patio door. "This is going to take a while, it's much more complex than what you saw." His eyes were packed with panic. "You're a part of this now, and I need you to keep an open mind. Can you do that for me, Frank?"

"Are you saying I'm culpable? Like a witness?" He couldn't possibly be threatening me like that. Not Ben. Ben, my best friend. Ben, who last night stole an eyeball.

"Everyone is okay," I heard him again.

Wanting to stop the questions, I felt myself nodding. Lying was simple. We were lying.

He exhaled in relief. His hand returned to his head, and he bit down hard on his lip. His finger scratched at his skull. The same one that touched my hands. The same one.

"Do you believe in ghosts?" he asked. "Spirits? Monsters? Witches?"

My head wrenched backward on my neck as I sputtered. "What?"

"Witches," he enunciated. "Do you believe in things like that? Has anything strange, anything inexplicable, happened to you? Around you? Can you think of anything like that?"

"I think I'm ready to go home."

"Damn it, Frank!" he whispered aggressively, his fist hitting the table. Immediately, his hand loosened and his eyes lost focus, as if his battery died.

After an inexplicable moment, his stare flashed back to my face. "A different route then," he stated nonsensically before he reached across our table and grabbed my knife from its napkin. Without hesitation, Ben cut a deep groove into the stiff tissue of his palm.

"Ben! What are you doing!" I flailed my hands around in no helpful way before thrusting my napkin over the bloody skin. I held it to him tightly. "What does this have to do with anything? Bleeding everywhere tells me nothing! It's on your glass—"

"Shhh. Frank, try and calm down." His blood was like a paint stroke on the reflective stein surface. He gripped my hand over his own, creating a fleshy totem pole on his side of the table. I didn't pull my hand away. I thought I could feel his blood rushing to the new wound.

He traced the veins on my wrist tenderly and, after some flinching, my heart rate subsided. I felt his pulse slow with it. His fingers were long, his hands so much bigger than mine. My palm began to sweat, but Ben didn't seem to mind. He held onto me for a very long time. I sucked in some much-needed oxygen and my shoulders lightened.

"There," he soothed. "Better?" I nodded again, afraid my voice would betray the truth. "Keep breathing, okay? I can explain everything." My head bobbled in response as he pulled our hands apart. Mine flopped heavily on the table, tugging the napkin that I'd used as a bandage along with it.

Ben inspected his palm, a knowing smile pulling his freckles closer to his eyes. He held his hand out to me as if asking for a high five. I squinted at it, disconcerted. "We don't do that."

Annoyed, he reached farther out to me, his palm inches from my nose.

I yanked the hand towards me, searching, then snatched up the napkin, unfolding it to its full size. Crimson spotted it in dark cherry blossoms. I must have been dreaming. Again.

The slice in Ben's palm was gone.

⟋⟋⟋

"YOU HAVE to come out eventually, Frank!" Ben yelled from outside the bathroom door. I leaned on the slippery vanity, going over what I had just witnessed. I visualized the fire in the woods, the blood-soaked hand. I had seen them both, and yet they didn't exist. After I realized Ben's hand was fine, his skin stretched between my fingers like a bewildering map, I threw my wallet on the table and fled. I had been in this damp public toilet ever since.

I took a deep breath. A lot of people were magicians, illusionists. Maybe Ben had simply picked up another eccentric hobby. "So, you're into parlor tricks now? What does that have to do with Cleo? Or the woods?" I asked through the door.

"Come out and I'll explain. I'm not going to scream in front of all these innocent people." Then he shouted, "Just one second, sir! Her granny just died."

I heaved the door open and found him leaning against the wall. He appeared a bit miffed, but also a bit unsettled. He so rarely seemed less than comfortable.

"Hello again. Are you ready to talk?" He paused for one heartbeat, "Or you can hide under the table like a baby?"

"Babies don't hide under tables. Not intentionally." His chiding was irksome, and my eyes narrowed naturally. I stepped out of the bathroom.

"Wonderful. Let's go sit in the car. There's blood all over the cutlery." He gave a flippant wave and led me back outside.

It was still scorching hot; the sun wouldn't set for hours. I was dreading the burn of his scalding leather seats. Ben squinted through his buggy glasses toward the raging sun as we walked to his Volkswagen, and in an unexpected move, he held open the back door for me.

There was a browning fabric seat cover draped over the bench, keeping my thighs from both burning and sweating more than they had to. I slid over for Ben, and he slammed the door behind him, rust flakes tainting the air. He was so close. The smell of his sweat lingered in the cigarettes and dirt. I scooted away from him.

"That wasn't a parlor trick." He wasted no time. "People like you and me and Cleo can do certain things—"

"I didn't do anything! You were the one! You cut yourself and that man, you did something to his eye!" I jabbed a finger in his face.

"I know, I know! Would you listen?" he shouted. "Please?" I forced my lips together in a painful slash. "Now, whether you're ready or not, things are about to change for you. People like us, we're born like this. But we become stronger when we're together." He tossed his hands around as he ranted. "It's much easier to let yourself slide into—I don't know—our abilities when we're together."

Ben was being brutally vague. "Abilities? Then what are you? And we've been together for years. What does that have to do with anything?" I sucked my lip into a bite. "Did you do that? That thing with your hand?"

He laughed nervously. "I'll try and take those one at a time. What are we? Many things." His eyes met mine before darting away. "Witches, monsters, superheroes," his voice trailed off and he cleared his throat. "Power is in the eye of the beholder and all that." He grinned without humor before he grabbed both of my sweaty hands in his and kissed them. I was almost diverted, and I tried to tug them back before he continued, "I've never wanted to rush this. When your mom died, I was going to tell you. It was a bad time, emotionally, but it was time."

"My mom?"

"But then Pamela came and she just … she drained you of everything. You barely left the house, or your bed even. You were pulling away." Ben spoke so rapidly I struggled to catch the words. "I waited too long. I just wanted to see you. The rest didn't seem as important." He set the back of his hand on his knee, running his finger along an angry patch of skin on his palm.

I unconsciously reached out toward the peculiar spot. The skin looked bizarre, like it had extended across an old wound and pulled the opposing skin back across the divide. It bunched like bad stitching on a t-shirt. I wanted to touch it. He had just knifed himself in this spot twenty minutes ago. In that very spot. The blood proved it. But it had healed itself. Almost instantly.

"Did you do this?" I asked again. The sun burned red through the tinted windows.

Ben shook his head. "You did."

His nonsense had become beyond annoying. "I can assure you, I did not do that. You are losing it, Benjamin! Are you hallucinating? Or fucking with me?" But the scar was real, I thought, mystified. I reached for his palm, running a finger across the bumps of new skin, unable to resist any longer.

"When you touched my hand. The napkin was there, but your skin was on mine." He illustrated gently, squeezing my fingers. "It felt warm."

"I felt warm too. That's how the sun works."

He shook his head. "It always feels warm." He brought my fingers to his cheek, pressing the tips against his rough stubble. And I felt it. The warmth didn't come from outside—it came from within him.

"Those of us who are … gifted, are given certain affinities," he uttered, his jaw moving beneath my hand. "It's something special about us that we do without thinking, a certain faculty that happens on its own. But, with practice, and with time, those faculties can be strengthened." He took another deep breath. "It's what we are. And what you are, specifically, is a healer. Restoration—" Ben's words stalled at whatever expression crossed my face.

"Magic," he whispered.

I had never heard him speak with such care, even after Mom, and despite the logic sitting mulish in my brain, curiosity overpowered reason for a moment. "What do you do?"

He beamed at my sudden interest, at the possibility to explain. "I'm a seer. I can see things that might happen." He seemed proud. "There are limitations, obviously. But it comes in handy. Sometimes."

"Always the handyman," I said before asking sardonically, "You're a fortune teller? Tarot cards and palms?" I snorted and wished I brought a beer out here with me. "Does your friend go by 'Miss Cleo'?"

His frown was peeved but brief. "The cards are just a tool, they aren't necessary. Palms too, but only because direct contact strengthens the sight." He scooted closer to me, filling the space I'd created.

"The visions are hard for me to control. But I only get better with age," he leered. He sounded like the Ben I knew, and it was wonderful. "It used to be, I could only see flashes through my own eyes, my perspective of future happenings. After some time and practice, I could see through the eyes of others." And the wonderful was gone.

"Right." I gave a patronizing pause. "So, you think I'm a 'healer'"? I pictured myself in scrubs with glowing hands.

"I know you are. Or at least, I know your affinity is restoration, and that blankets a lot of possibilities. This is the first time I've seen what you can do in real-time, and I gotta say Frank, it needs work." He poked at his scar like a fungus. "Normally, I'm not wounded when you touch me. Which we both know is rare. But whenever you do it's like … I just spent a weekend at a wellness spa. Rejuvenating." His expression grew peaceful.

"Oh my god." I buried my face in my arms.

"I'd hoped you find out on your own, that I didn't have to tell you like this."

When I didn't respond, Ben babbled in a rush. "We can all do more than our affinity—spells," he clarified. "But they don't come naturally. Every outside spell has a price. The more difficult the spell, the higher the cost. There are different ways to go about it, but pain is a great offering." He held out both his arms to me, an illustrative display. I didn't follow at first, then understanding clicked into place. I ran my hands through the air above his arms.

He gave himself every one of these stark tattoos. They filled his skin totally, at least what he could easily reach. They piled on top of each other several times on the inside of his left forearm. He had filled every gouge and slice with ink, hundreds of them. Some were straight lines like tally marks, others were shapes and doodles—a smiley face, a lightning bolt. A few were frighteningly deep, their scars rising high above the rest like tree roots breaking up a sidewalk.

"It's better to look like the spooky tattooed guy than, well …" he said simply. "Plus, the ink is rather becoming, don't you think?"

I couldn't help but flinch at his implication. I shook my head and tried to follow along. "Why did you think I can do this if you've never seen it before?"

Ben became bashful. "I saw you. Us. Together. A long time ago, before I had gained any semblance of control over this thing. And we are all so alone when it starts. So, I found you." He hit me with another acute stare. "I would have found you eventually, without trying, or I would have never seen it. I just, sort of, hurried things along."

I didn't know what to say. Our entire friendship was based on a bunch of magic tricks? Pamela's death had conveniently forced his hand? But the part where he came to find me … I liked that. But— "Is that why you moved here? What about your parents? And your uncle just happened to have a house in my hometown?" My questions dripped suspicion.

His face hung. "I really did emancipate myself when I was sixteen." He covered his eyes with one hand and rubbed his head with the other. "But the house I live in is mine." He looked up to me in earnest. "I bought it when I was twenty."

No. This was too much information at once. I wanted it to stop. Still the words dropped from my mouth like stones. "But I met you in high school. We were seniors," I asserted. "We were together. Before you were twenty."

Ben pinched his nose, then brought his hands into his lap, fidgeting. "Yes, we were." I skimmed through every memory I had of him in school. He was there with me, he had a red back-pack that matched his car. Our schedules never lined up because of his interest in art and my lack of interest in anything. "I had to meet you. I knew we were going to be close. But you hardly ever left your house. Even then, you were so goddamn reclusive. I needed you to know me."

I added up the years. "Six years … I met you six years ago. You're twenty-six? And you've been, what? Stalking me? Since I was seventeen." My mouth couldn't close, I tasted the salt of our sweat in the air.

Ben lowered his eyes and moved back toward the door. He looked crushed.

"I'm twenty-seven," was all he said.

"Twenty-seven. Right." We had just celebrated his birthday last month.

At his confirmation, I popped the burning metal handle. At first I walked, then I ran. I didn't want him to see me unravel.

He didn't come after me anyway.

5

I DON'T KNOW how long I lasted. Probably not very; I had the stamina of a chubby toddler. But I sprinted until my sides screamed, then I jogged until my nose ran, until I thought I had put at least a mile between us. As angry and as estranged and as disturbed as I felt, I imagined him sitting in the backseat of his car, smashed up small under his hands. "Good."

His age was immaterial. His two ages were not so dissimilar, less so than seventeen and twenty-one, I concluded, realizing that's how old we *actually* were when we'd first met. Ben had snuck into my life, he had come to my school, had known where I lived. He knew my mom and Pamela, gotten to know them. He manipulated me into trusting him. He hardly touched me. He teased me and argued with me. Sat quietly with me sketching while I drifted internally. He never pushed me, knowing I needed space.

Ben had been a focal point in my life for six, nearly seven, years. I was irreparably altered. He had bent my universe completely out of whatever the hell shape it was supposed to be before he walked into it!

I remembered when I first met him. It was at his house. All the kids I worked with at the local sandwich shop were talking about a back-to-school party the new guy was throwing. It only took the disclaimer, "There will be alcohol, parental figures notoriously absent," to persuade the entire student body to show. Now I knew how he'd managed to obtain all that alcohol.

Of course, I just wanted to go home after work, but my coworker would not shut her gooey glossed mouth when my mom came in to pick up dinner. My mom even drove me to the party, knowing there would be drinking, but desperately wanting me to socialize with living people. To prove that I was one myself.

Throughout the night I was unfriendly, curt, and judgmental. I went as far as to drink an entire beer alone in the new guy's bathroom, much to the chagrin of one very sick sophomore. After I had a decent buzz going, I walked around outside his home in the raucous dark. A handful of kids were scattered about the yard, smoking their parents' weed and blowing each other in the grass. The smell of it all was faint in the crisp fall breeze. Once I had made it around back, hoping no one would notice me, I slid down the siding of his house. My butt planted on the cool cement, and I finally softened. As I'd tilt my head for a drink, I watched the stars peek over his roof, and I'd wished every party could be just like this.

Even so, someone did notice me sitting there. Thinking back on it, if everything he said was true, he must have been searching for me. Or maybe waiting until I'd had enough to drink that I wouldn't growl at his approach. I heard his sliding glass door hit the frame and froze. Dreading that someone would see me and ask why I was sitting outside, alone in the dark. And I would have to lie and say I wasn't feeling so great, that I just needed some air. It would probably work, but would be exertion nonetheless.

He strolled out onto his patio, very tall from where I was sitting, and stood by his lonesome. This was the first I'd seen him, and as he was the only unfamiliar face in this town, I knew who he was by deduction. I thought he must be so odd to throw a party only to wander by himself. He hadn't been at the beer pong table or at the counter mixing drinks.

He pulled a pack of cigarettes out of his pocket and stuck a stick between his lips. He didn't smoke like the other kids I knew. This was something he did alone. He inhaled deeply, closed his eyes—he found something in this.

He wore a pair of exercise pants with snaps down the sides and a lively Hawaiian shirt that was hardly buttoned. Dressed like that, he would have drawn attention in a town as small as Aspen Ridge, even if he weren't from out of town, or as heavily tattooed. He took another deep drag and I saw his shoulders loosen. I felt like I was intruding on a tranquil and intimate moment for this man. Then again, that's exactly what he was doing to me.

He looked out across the lawn and noted his visitors and their various suckings with obvious disinterest before spotting me on the ground. I waited, bored now, for him to say the lines that were expected of him. But he only watched me, taking another smoke every now and then. His arm swung down from his mouth, smoke clouding his face, with such an easy grace. When he registered that I wasn't going to speak, he ambled over and sat down on the ground within arm's reach of me.

I wasn't sure if I preferred this or the predictable script I had imagined. I admit that I preferred *him*, an unknown, to the people I knew. He seemed to be relatively noiseless, but his closeness was unsettling. He continued to smoke and I continued to drink, and neither of us said a word. I would look at him sometimes from the corner of my eye. He had a strong jaw, almost boxy, and I caught the shine of a lip ring in the moonlight. Even still, I tried very hard to ignore him, to go back to my stars.

After he finished his first cigarette, he pulled out a second, offering me the pack in the same moment. I curled my lip in distaste. I enjoyed watching people smoke, it would seem, but I didn't care for the gravel and tar taste. I held out my beer to him in a matching offer. He lifted his eyebrows, and with avidity, reached out to take it. I pulled it away before he got his hand around it and finished the can. I did not share. He snorted next to me.

I wanted another beer, but I was reluctant to leave this quirky little rendezvous. He didn't seem to feel the same, finally rising to his feet and walking back in the house. I pulled out my phone to call my mom—I had been here much longer than an accept-able amount of teen social time anyway—when he sidled back out through his door, a can of beer in each hand. He slid back down the wall, stretching the drinks out in front of him. Once he was settled, he opened the first and held it out to me with his maculated hand. How chivalrous. I suppressed my smile; I didn't want him to know I was pleased, but took it happily. He beamed at my acceptance. We both sipped at our drinks and watched the sky as party guests gradually filtered away someplace.

Once the night became hushed, and I was the only one left, I stood up, my knees popping. He followed suit, towering over me, but didn't move to enter the house. Instead, he reached out a hand from a distance. "Ben," he said to me.

Nearly satiated by both his silence and his aversion to my classmates, I timidly extended my own and embraced his hand in a weak shake. He squeezed my palm vigorously until I gave the same pressure.

"Frankie," I finally conceded.

∾∾∾

HE HAD SEEMED to understand me immediately. I'd never felt anything like it. My stomach surged at the knowledge that Ben had, perhaps, known me before I had ever met him—on the incredibly off-chance that anything he said was real. I should have been more suspicious when it had all started. He had been so … excited! Always bursting with happiness to see me, to blow off any other plans to stray around town in apathy with me. He was never offended by my grumpiness and constant rebuffs against his touch, he simply stopped asking if I wanted him there and instead began showing up at my side, at school during the day and at my house at night. Without the opportunity to say no, I became more than accustomed to his incessant presence, I craved it.

～

I STUMBLED into a big park with a well-worn mulch path around the corners. There weren't many people out enjoying the place with this heat, just a few homeless individuals napping in the grass under a thicket of trees. I meandered through the turf, ignoring the path, until I found my own shade. I fell to the ground in swampy exhaustion. There were some yellow-type flowers around the base of the tree, a few of them stomped and broken, which, so unexpectedly, made me think of my mother.

She wasn't like Pamela in the slightest, and after her own teenage rebellion, she had struggled to understand my desire to just stay home. She loved to dance. She would move to any music playing whether it be at the grocery store, or the hospital, or my graduation ceremony. If there was no music, she would sing her own songs and grab the nearest bystander by the arm, forcing them into an unwilling waltz. She had fiery hair that fell to her waist in silky ringlets and striking jade eyes. I was a diluted secondhand version of her, like the color had been sucked out.

Men adored my mother. I'd regularly come home from school to find a new admirer sitting at the table while she cooked up something colorful, spicy, and delicious. Her energy and our frequent visitors did not make us popular with the town, and that never seemed to bother her. She loved the cow fields and the nearby mountains. She found the expanding rumors about our family entertaining; they endeared her to them further.

I felt guilty now, for wanting the things that I did. I wanted to leave. I hated the town, I hated the people. But mostly I wanted to get far away from her frenzied energy and her endless parade of scumbag suitors who weren't looking for a new frizzy-haired stepkid.

I resented that I was my mother's inverse.

My mom said very little about my biological father when I was young. Eventually, I stopped asking about him. She always told me, as delicately as she was able, that he hadn't asked for me as a daughter and she had never pressured him to commit. Just like the myriad of boyfriends with whom she kept company in my teens. Just like me. She never pressured me to finish my homework, never pressured me to apply for scholarships, or to find my dream job, or to even keep a steady, uninspiring job. She just let me follow my fancies.

And I hated her for it.

I wanted pressure, I wanted her to yell at me. To push me to try. A part of me even yearned for her to rant about Ben's constant presence. Wouldn't a normal mother do that?

And that's why, at nineteen, I left her to move to a different, uglier piece of Salt Lake City than where I sat in the grass now. I had saved up enough from the sandwich shop to get my own crappy apartment before I got a barista job at a coffee house nearby. Ben would still hang around my place whenever he worked in the area. He would cook us dinner and listen to me go on about my shitty job and my piling bills and my non-prospects of any kind. But he was just a reminder of what I left behind, and I canceled our plans more often than not. My mother called every day.

After her accident, I traveled back home to go through our junk. I'd find myself looking at her things until dark and I'd reason it was too late to drive. I'd sleep in, nestled in my old bed, until my manager got sick of my absence and fired me. I was elated until Pamela walked through the door without knocking. That was months ago. Six months ago.

I rolled over in the grass to get closer to the flower. The petals looked pudding soft, I couldn't help reaching out to skim my fingertips across each. I wasn't disappointed, I rolled them between my fingers. My hand traveled along the stem to the stomped brown bits in the center, and I missed her.

As I held the dead flower, the stem plumped. The silky wilted petals opened and stretched. The colors of the blossom brightened while the plant straightened itself proudly and faced the sun. Alive.

I breathed in the scent of the now healthy bloom and savored this season for the first time all year. I pinched myself hard inside my elbow.

"Ow! Shit." I glared at the beautiful flower. "Are you fucking kidding me?"

My hand still held the fresh flower by the petals. They were warm.

I shook in denial, but without thinking, reached out for another wilted plant beside the first. Before I could connect, my spine tingled like static. I scoured over my shoulder. The nappers still lay at rest, eyes closed. My head craned left and right. Nothing looked amiss, but the tingle remained. Someone was watching me. I turned back to the flowers, peeking through my hair sporadically for my voyeur. They were getting closer.

"It's disorienting, I know. But, wow, you have an enchanting gift." I whipped my head around in the opposite direction than I'd been expecting. The speaker was within touching distance and stood over my shoulder, her shadow disappeared in the shade of the tree. I looked up at Cleo, unprepared for the additional heartache her beauty caused. She appeared a little older than me, clearly a woman—there wasn't an ounce of childhood naivety or androgyny about her. Her expression was so warm, I nearly closed my eyes to escape it. This face could take anything from me.

I searched the park once more for whatever had given me that funny feeling and saw nothing. Anxiety stirred in my chest when I considered what they may have seen me do, but like a magnet, my eyes returned to Cleo and my anxiety was erased. Feeling the irrational urge to reach out to her and touch, I smashed my hands into the dirt and roughly forced myself off my knees. I brushed the clumps and rocks off my skin, refusing to meet her concerned eyes. Looking at her made me feel like someone else.

"I'm Cleo," she introduced, "but I'm sure you already knew that. We were worried … So, Frankie? Right? You don't like Francesca. I'm sorry this was sprung on you. I'm sure I'm not the person you want to see. But are you okay?"

I hated that this dream woman pitied me. I hated that her words made me want to cry. "How did you find me?" I asked, feeling completely pathetic.

She was embarrassed by my question. "Well, Ben knew where you ended up once you did. He thought you might not want to see him …" She shrugged her perfect shoulders. Her skin smoldered in the sun. I shook myself internally and forced myself to listen to her. "Hence, the leaving him in his car."

"So, he sent you?" *Coward.*

Again, she looked sheepish. "Not exactly. I've wanted to meet you for so long now. I know how you're feeling and I'm being incredibly selfish, but I couldn't help myself. Are you absolutely hating me right now?"

Yes. But when I saw her miserable expression, my instincts screamed to soothe her. "Uh, no. No. Nice to meet you, Cleo. I'm just a little—" She smiled, and I had to close my eyes again. "—caught off guard. By all of this. And, uh, you know. You." I risked a glance and caught her nodding. She knew the effect she had on people. "I'm Frankie," I said redundantly. "So … it's true? And you, you're like Ben?"

"That's right, and like you. It's so unbelievable. It takes time, a lot of time. And support from people like us." Her face suddenly hardened and I took a step back. "I hope you aren't terribly upset with Ben. He looked so hurt when I left him."

She grabbed my shoulders and I was both horrified and exhilarated. She rubbed them up and down like she was keeping me warm. I loathed unfamiliar touch, but I practically fell to my knees and thanked her for the contact.

"Everything will make sense soon, I promise," she vowed. I did not want to go back to the car, but my head was bouncing up and down on my neck, desperate to keep this woman happy. Her smile put the stars to shame. "Wonderful!" She let go of my shoulders but took one of my hands before turning away. I saw a glimpse of self-satisfaction on her face and I did not trust this woman.

Walking with Cleo was like taking a tour of Salt Lake City. With the hand that wasn't holding mine, she pointed out structures and streets, telling me whether they were worth a cover fee or if the service was bad. Her hand soaked in my sweat, but she never let go.

"Did you like the food at Stella's? It's not the best spot in town, but they have a great patio. Don't you think so?" Cleo asked.

"Stella's?"

She giggled. The sound was wind chimes, and I bit my cheek to keep my head. "Where you went to lunch! Did you like it?"

I thought back to lunch and I could hardly remember what I ordered, let alone how it tasted. "I think so." She put her hand to her chest and looked at me like I was a puppy that couldn't climb a stair on its own. Such a face was insulting, but my mouth stretched into a silly grin for her.

We were crossing the street to the Stella's parking lot now and I saw Ben leaning against his car, head down. I waited for Cleo to drop my hand, which she didn't. She was virtually skipping as we reached him. He lifted his head when he heard us on the pavement, and his expression transitioned from worry to fierce relief. The relief was so visible and profound I very nearly felt remorse for leaving him. "Bastard," I murmured.

Cleo steered me to the backseat of Ben's sedan. Once I was

belted inside, she finally released me and shut the door. Without her skin on mine I felt more like myself: incensed. She circled back around the trunk of the car before she opened the driver-side door. I stared at her in the rearview mirror, baffled, before Ben slid into the seat next to me. His eyes were entreating and anguished. He didn't say anything, but his face was positively begging me to let him sit at my side. Figuring my only option was to run back into the street and drown in my own sweat, I groaned and mashed my face into the back of the driver's seat.

Ben did not put his seatbelt on, but turned his body to face me. He put his feet over mine, the back of his calf resting against my shin, and encircled my fingers in his own. I cringed, but then he held my hand to his forehead, his eyes closed reverently, and gave my knuckles a swift kiss, just a brush of his lips, before placing them back in my lap. His immense gratitude was unexpected—he probably knew I was on my way back before I did.

Cleo pulled out of the parking lot and got on I-15. She rolled down all four windows, not even attempting the AC. She'd driven this car before, and she shifted expertly. I felt stupid for not realizing she had been in Ben's life all this time.

No one talked for the bulk of the drive, which seemed against Cleo's nature, but she was happy. The radio squeaked, and she hummed sweetly along to each static song. Every few moments Ben would stroke the back of my hand with his thumb or bump his leg against mine. Each touch less unnerving than the last. From time to time, I would shift positions, throwing an elbow into his ribs or stomp on the toe of his Sperry, pleased with each grunt spewed from his mouth.

We were ten minutes outside of town when my cell phone rang. Without having to ask, Cleo rolled up the windows and turned the radio down.

"Hello?"

"Hello, am I speaking with Francesca Hughes?" a woman recited.

"Yes," I answered hesitantly.

"My name is Amanda Wells, I'm with the medical examiner's office. I'm calling in regard to your grandmother, Pamela Hughes."

There was an expectant silence. "Okay."

"We have reached the cause of death in her case. She experienced cardiac arrest, which isn't uncommon for a woman her age."

My eyebrows pinched. "She had a heart attack?"

"No, Miss Hughes, a heart attack is a blockage in the blood. Cardiac arrest is the sudden failure of the heart, by which I mean the heart stopped beating. I'm very sorry for your loss." Her voice was wooden, but I couldn't begrudge her that. "Should I arrange for the deceased to be picked up by the funeral director? Perez Family Funeral Home will handle everything from here."

I didn't know what else to do with the deceased. "Okay. Thanks," because, what else was there to say. I hung up the phone and let it fall to the side.

"Pamela's heart stopped," I informed the car. "That's what did it."

Ben and Cleo exchanged weighted expressions in the rearview mirror. My suspicion piqued, my hackles raised. My mind was connecting dots, slowly and painstakingly, but I was definitely realizing something. I played back what Ben had said to me earlier: I couldn't join him in whatever this was with my grandmother still around, with her grip on my life so suffocating. Something about my pulling away, but it was time …

I shivered despite the heat and resisted the urge to leap from the moving car. "Did you?" I whimpered, wide-eyed.

Ben snorted in disgust. "I know I haven't been honest with you but I'm not sure I deserve that." He faltered when he saw our entwined limbs. His jaw clenched. "Maybe I do." He cupped my chin, and my twitch was insubstantial after all the exposure. "But *I* didn't kill your nana, Frank."

The emphasis was perfectly clear. Ben didn't kill Pamela.

But somebody did.

6

I WAS calm in comparison to discovering the truth about Ben. It could be because when I found her, I was already inundated with the knowledge that there was something abnormal, something overpoweringly wrong about Pamela on that couch. It was the utter absence of the unfamiliar—nothing was knocked over, she hadn't tried to stand up, the shades weren't drawn. It was the normalcy of the entire scene that made it so obvious that there was something very not normal about it.

"Who, Ben?" I demanded, feeling vengeful. I even cast a furtive glance at Cleo behind her back.

He put his big sunglasses on and stared up at the burning sky. "I don't know. Like I started to tell you in the car, when I see something, it's not like there's a camera set up that I'm watching through, I see through someone's perspective. The more time I spend with a person, the more often I see through them. I hadn't seen anything important concerning Pamela since she decided to move in with you."

I curled my lip. "You could have warned me."

His features all pulled together as if there was a bathtub drain in his nose. "I was in her head when it happened." He kicked the loose pebbles of his driveway. "A vampire got to her, looked like."

Cleo gasped at this ridiculous revelation. Ben's foot swung harder, rocks pummeling the side of his car.

"Hands were on her. The palms were on both sides of her head." He held his hands to his cheeks in illustration. "They just rested there. They weren't Pamela's hands. And her sight just drifted away to nothing."

I imagined Nosferatu sneaking in to kill my grandmother with his claw-like hands. "Vampires? Vampires and witches and … wendigoes," I finished lamely, "Oh, my." I stomped back to the car and leaned my head on the hot roof until it hurt. "You have got to be fucking kidding me." I bounced my head against the steel.

"Vampires are witches, Dorothy. It's just a classification. Their affinity." He yanked my shirt, pulled me away from the car. I wrenched the cotton from his hands. "They're like life-drinkers. I've never met one before. Creepy things." Cleo nodded vigorously beside him. "Groups of us, covens or ilks, some have life-drinkers and they are powerful commodities. Rare. Each slightly different than the last. But they are not an easy people to control, for murder-y reasons."

The sun sank below the crest of the mountain, and I feared my mind was sinking with it. Either that or it was about to explode and leak out my ears. I couldn't think of a response that didn't involve the words *insane* or *crazy*. I couldn't think of anything. I just turned to the front door and waited for Ben to open it.

We all entered the house and simultaneously sighed at the cool air. I fell onto the couch like a bag of sand. I couldn't remember living a longer day. I didn't even bring my books in from the car. Cleo was unaffected by any of the news I received today. She hustled into the kitchen and began taking various bottles out of Ben's cabinets and refrigerator—she knew her way around—and made herself a cocktail.

Taking his glasses off, Ben lowered himself down between my knees, propping his chin on my thigh. If it weren't today, I would have locked myself in the bathroom to escape the intimacy. He turned his face, resting his cheek against me, and watched me watch him. His eyes were afraid, but less than before. I was coming around to his charms.

"Frankie. I'm sorry," he whispered.

I was a smirk away from saying everything was alright. I wanted to make him happy infinitely more than I wanted to care about his stalking and his secrecy and his lies. I detested that I had nearly forgiven him already, that after I'd returned to the car, it didn't feel so revolting a thing. It didn't seem fair at all. I grazed his cheekbone. He had pretty cheeks. And then I cocked back my arm and punched that dainty bone with everything I had.

Ben yelped and clutched his face, falling backward to the floor. "JESUS, FRANK! My fucking eye!"

"You should have seen it coming twice!" I yelled back. In truth, I hadn't aimed for his eye, I just wanted a good cheek shot. But the angle was bad, and I had never done that before. My knuckles were screaming.

Cleo sniggered from the kitchen. "I am so happy I was here for this," she sighed happily and dropped a few ice cubes into her drink.

I clenched and released my fist when Ben wasn't looking. There wasn't any blood on his face, I realized with disappointment. He held his eye and scowled at me. "Cleo how about you give me some of *my* ice out of *my* freezer for *my* face instead of *your* drink?"

That got her laughing again as she put a few cubes in a dish rag and brought it over to Ben, who had stretched out on the floor. He ripped the bundle out of her hand and said, "Thank you," venomously.

"I hope you feel better," he sniped at me, "my eye is swelling up like hemorrhoids on a roller coaster." He gingerly pressed the pack to his face and clicked his jaw left and right as if I hit that too.

"Such a baby," I muttered.

"If that isn't the baby calling the baby, baby."

"That doesn't even make sense!"

He guffawed, the laugh swollen with contempt, and water began running down his neck. Sure enough, when he pulled the ice away, his eye had puffed up and was closing in fast. My mouth twisted up. I did feel much better.

I was tempted to ask Cleo for a second batch of ice for myself, but Ben would never let me live it down. I settled for easing my hand along top of the couch cushions as I laid back. That punch took my last reserve of energy. My eyes fluttered closed. I heard Cleo mumble something about a "spare eye" to Ben, but was too far gone to listen.

WHEN I OPENED my eyes again, it was dark, other than the flickering light of the TV. Someone had covered me with a blanket. A wave of nausea hit at the thought of sleeping out here while Cleo and Ben were secluded in his bedroom. Until I heard a snoozing body on the loveseat across from me. Ben was tangled in a thin sheet, his head flat on the seat of the couch. Cleo must have taken the bed.

I'd been asleep for hours. "Are you still there?" flashed on the screen. I found the remote on the table and turned off the TV.

From what I could see of Ben's face, his eye was purpling nicely. I searched my heart for any stray guilt over that punch and found nothing but satisfaction. I cracked my neck and my back using the armrest of the couch and got to my feet. The clock on the stove blinked 12:53. My clothes were wrinkled and stiff from the day's sweat-fest. I padded to the back door and snuck out for some fresh air.

It felt wonderful outside, a cool breeze tickling my skin. I lifted my right hand to the moonlight for inspection. The knuckles weren't swollen or red—a victory.

I stretched loudly now that I was alone and sat in one of

Ben's reclining chairs. My ass had barely made contact when a resounding crack echoed through the swaying fields. My pulse quickened. I reasoned that there was plenty of wildlife around here—deer, rabbits. Still, I watched the fields for far too long to think I convinced myself of anything. The familiar and unwelcome sensation that someone was watching me needled my back, tickled my spine.

"Hello?" I called, knowing there were ears to listen. The wind paused, curious at my exclamation. Silence. "Come out!" I shouted in an attempt at bravado.

They were close. It was as if they beckoned me using my own nerves and muscles. I wanted to walk into the field, farther even, to the foreboding woods. I needed it, to scratch at the intense itch. I was past questioning, I was acting.

The dry grass hurt my feet—someone had removed my shoes as I slept. It was uncomfortable, but that didn't matter. My certainty crashed with waves of excitement. Something magnificent was just beyond the edge of those trees and it was waiting for me. I felt its urgency echo my own.

My foot caught on a rock and I fell forward to my hands. There were more rocks waiting, my palms and knees struck down hard.

"Frank?"

Ben? I pushed myself back to get a better vantage point and glared over my shoulder. I only saw his dark silhouette in the yellow glow of the porch light. I hadn't noticed the bulb flick on behind me.

"Frank, where are you going?" he asked. His voice was relaxed, not at all alarmed by my streaking to the woods after midnight.

I rubbed my skinned palms on my shirt and inspected my foot. I had a slash near my toes, it was bleeding. Nothing to write home about. I stood and looked back towards the woods, but the inexplicable impulse to chase had gone as rapidly as it came.

I had acted like a sleepwalker, and I was terrified by the loss of control. I had lost my agency to a sound in the woods. Shame bloomed in my guts. There was nothing out there.

"I was just going for a walk," I yelled back to Ben as I carefully made my way to his porch. The stiff grass was much more painful this time around; pebbles and dirt stuck in the blood of my foot. "I needed to clear my head is all." I wanted to hide the wound from him.

Even with one eye, he noticed my limp. He walked out into the grass a few feet and helped me onto the cement. I only resisted a little. "Were you under the impression that you had shoes on?" he asked politely, settling me into one of his chairs. He held my foot up to the light, tipping my chair back. He drew one of my hands down to the wound and pressed my fingers over the blood like a Tupperware lid. "Now, what was this whole adventure about?"

"Who knows," I didn't want to lie to him, though he deserved it. "I feel like I'm going off the deep end here." I smiled weakly, but Ben addressed my facetiousness with a grave expression. He sat down in the opposite chair. "Your eye looks hideous," I chided, changing the subject.

He reached up and prodded it, the purple swelling would be all the more hideous tomorrow. "Impossible," he said, looking wistfully into the fields. "You got quite the swing in though." He tossed my hand from my foot and studied the wound. The bleeding had slowed, maybe even stopped under all the dry crusty stuff. But if the skin was supposed to have healed into an ugly scar like it had on Ben's hand, we were both disappointed.

His mouth rainbowed. This wasn't what he expected, but I wasn't particularly surprised. "Why didn't it work?"

"Just put your hand back. And keep it there, okay? Might take time." I nodded but wasn't optimistic. Bristling under his worried gaze, I changed the subject again. "What does Cleo do?" She was already so intimidating. I wasn't entirely sure I wanted to know.

"She's a siren," he answered off-handedly.

Siren? Did he honestly mean, "A mermaid?" I slapped my hands to the arms of my chair without thinking and Ben pointed strictly at my foot. I covered it again with my hands.

His smile was small. "She's walking around in the desert, isn't she? These are all just classifications, Frank. People have misconstrued our talents since ... always. They only got the gist of it and romanticized us in poems and stories. You know how Greek sirens would lure sailors to their doom? That's a poetic tragedy. Contorting witches, those of us with affinities, into non-human monsters while conveniently warning the townsfolk of what we can actually do." His eyes darted between my foot and my face. "Her beauty and her voice are a scary dangerous combination. It's a miracle I knew what she was before I met her." He shuddered.

At the mention of her voice, a memory stirred that had somehow, impossibly, fallen to the wayside in the upheaval that was this day. Her naked body swaying in a mob of dancers with Ben at the forefront.

"What happened last night?" I asked. "If everyone is okay, then what did I see?"

He clenched his teeth in a goofy expression, like the whole ordeal was nothing but a very awkward situation. "Well, that was Cleo's idea. She's got quite the brain in that body of hers." He shook his head, impressed by the woman, yet again. "We needed to do a ritual. Needed to find out about the new witch in town, the one who paid your granny a visit. And we needed you to be there ..." Struggling to explain everything he put his hands on his head. "Cleo came up with the plan years ago, but I saw that the timing wasn't right. The timing was never right to ... to introduce you. Until now. She thought this way would, sort of, get you into the thick of things without you going into shock. An introduction to magic under the guise of a dream."

The headache returned behind my eyes. I would never reach the end of all the explanations, all the questions. "Real then … That was real." I checked in on my foot as a brief distraction. There was no scar yet, if it had closed at all. "Who were all of those people with you? Just random nude townies?"

He scoffed at my absurdity. Yeah, *I* was the one being absurd. "That was all Cleo. She's been working with her affinity for a long time. She can throw certain illusions to help … persuade those who need … persuading."

He was choosing his words carefully, but my fear of Cleo increased with every facet I learned about her. "And who was the guy?" I considered ending my question there, out of the guise of politeness, but what was the point. "The guy whose eye you fish-hooked."

"He was a consenting adult," Ben insisted immediately, extending a finger to emphasize his point. "That man was happy to help."

"Did Cleo make him 'happy to help'?"

"What goes on between Cleo and her partners is none of my business. But he's fine, I treated him with healing herbs—cone-flower, ginseng, and the like—before the sun even came up, though all things considered, he could have used your help more than mine." His eyebrow lifted as his eyes drifted. "But he looks very jaunty in an eye patch."

I had never considered my own righteousness much before. I wasn't an overly empathetic person, but if Cleo was involved, then there was no choice for the man. The situation irked me, but I wasn't sure if it irked me enough.

"What happened to me? I don't remember anything after that." Not that I had tried too hard to remember.

"Oh, you fainted. But the enchantment was finished once the ritual ended. You were there for the good part." He grinned and I anxiously popped my knuckles. The good part must have been the naked dance and the mutilation. "I carried you home afterward."

I pulled my hair forward to cover my flushed face. "So, what did the eye do? Did you see the person that killed Pamela? The vampire or whatever."

He exhaled in a gust. "Not yet. We needed the eye for a—" he searched for the word, "project. One you need to be awake for, and you need to participate."

Participation required. The thought made my stomach heave and my mouth sweat. At least the eye had been procured without my fingers, the hard part was over. Small silver lining. With any luck, Cleo wouldn't sing again.

I considered Cleo's personality, at least what she had exposed me to. She seemed charming and affectionate, a real people person. It made some sort of sense, what she was. "Why am I a healer? Shouldn't I have a doctor-like vocation? Shouldn't I be nurturing or warm or anything like that?" I was haunted by fresh yellow flowers.

His eyes flickered to the wound on my foot before he answered. "Real gifts are never asked for, Frank. You only get to choose what you do with it. You could tell every sick human being to fuck off while you grow the healthiest orange grove in the west if you wanted." He raised an eyebrow as if daring me to do just that. "I saw the flower in the park." He chuckled at my surprise. "Well, not 'saw', but, you know, saw." He tapped his head.

"And what about the rest?" I asked, ignoring the instinct to deny his precognition. "You said we could do other stuff too."

"We can start the other stuff tomorrow." He stood and stretched. "And unless you want to sit on the ground for three or four hours and drink with me, we should hit the couch."

He put his hands on the armrests of my chair and leaned down toward my face. I heard my sharp intake of air. He had been so close to me today, it was overwhelming. He smelled like salty sweat and garden soil.

He nearly pressed the skin of his cheek against the skin of my own. His mouth almost brushed my ear. I felt his soft breaths against me. He inhaled deeply. I wondered if he was smelling me too and my face warmed. He lifted his other hand to my hair and dug his fingers in, pulling at the roots. I swallowed audibly and shivered.

He moved his face to kiss my temple. His lips were dry. And then he drew back completely. He righted himself, gave me a cheeky smile, and strolled inside. "That's for the punch!" he called out to me from the dark.

7

I STEWED in that moment all night—until the dark turned gray and my eyeballs burned—and through my vigorous shower the next morning. As Ben sure as hell knew.

I stepped out of the steam, determined to act unbothered and laid-back. I would not let his—what? Breathing on my ear?—fluster me more than it already had. I brushed my teeth and combed out the tangles in my curls with my fingers. It had really frizzed out over the last few days. My upsurge in cleanliness was drying out my hair, and the skin of my face was flaking.

I examined my bare feet. The scar from the fall last night looked older than the eight hours it was. Days old, maybe. I was no doctor, but it had closed. The scabbing was almost ready to peel. Ben implied it should have happened in seconds; he wasn't prepared for these results.

I crouched down and toyed with the hard scab. "Wow." Even if he wasn't impressed, I certainly was. I so rarely left my room growing up, so rarely had gotten injured.

I was already out of bottoms to wear. I should have paid more attention to what I put in my duffle. I stood in the bathroom in my flamingo patterned underwear—the elastic pulling away from the cotton—and a well-worn muscle tee that read "World's Best Dad." It used to be Ben's, but I claimed it years ago.

I could ask Cleo to borrow something, but I'd honestly rather wear something of Ben's. She was staying in his room anyway, so I opened the door and peeked out, looking left and right, though a woman in her underwear is not the most salacious thing Ben's ever seen. I swiftly crossed the hallway on my toes, and burst through his door, shutting it behind me.

So, naturally, Ben was sprawled languidly across his bed. I took in his long body as he zeroed in on my panties. An eternity passed before his eyes crept up to my face, and a sly smile stretched his cheeks. I was torn between leaving the state—Washington had always seemed very nice—or playing it cool. I bit my lip once, good and hard, and I remembered my vow: unbothered and laid-back.

"Hey." I folded my arms across my chest and leaned back against the door I'd just slammed. His expression was unmoving, unless his simper had grown impossibly smugger. "So, it turns out, I only had one pair of shorts and they're, um, gross after yesterday. I can get some more clothes today." I evaluated my cuticles stupidly and made a click sound with my mouth. "But could I wear something of yours over to my house?"

He let his eyes wander over to his dresser after taking in my full form once more. His dickishness tested my restraint, but I refused to be the one to fold simply because I was mortified. Nothing new to me.

He rolled off the bed and moved across the room like a sleepy cat in a sunbeam. He was clearly enjoying himself, and I knew the second I said anything, he'd win. He rummaged through his drawers, sporadically leering back at me. At long last, he found a pair of small, swishy running shorts and threw them into my arms. I didn't waste any time and yanked them up to my belly button. Ben's mouth was crushed to one side as if resisting the impulse to laugh at me. I pretended not to see.

"Can you drive me to my house? There's a lot I need to do."

He nodded, his mouth held closed. Thank god for small mercies.

Cleo was relaxing in Ben's backyard as we left, reading a

book under a humongous and fashionable sun hat. I tried very hard not to imagine what they would get up to while I was gone. It was like picking at the scab on my foot.

I told Ben I would need to look through Pamela's things and decide what to keep before getting one of those giant city dumpsters out to the house. It was still unknown whether she wanted to be buried or cremated or turned into a tree. The next stop after this was the funeral home.

Ben kept his thoughts to himself throughout the drive. I didn't know if that was better or worse than knowing what was happening in his fat head. I could feel him looking at my legs behind his shades. My outfit was a little at odds. The squeaky heel of my sneaker had finally broken through, so I wore my black moto boots with his swishy shorts and muscle shirt.

Ben didn't exactly appear inconspicuous either. Before we left, I saw that the purple bruised eye had become nearly black, with soft sheens of green and blue that would only expand outwards in time. His glasses covered most of his face, but it was probably uncomfortable. I had gotten the punch in, no need to punish him further.

"Let me fix your face," I offered, reaching across him to his cheek.

He dodged my hand as if I were wielding a knife. "You are not touching my face." He shoved his palm to my nose, swerving the car. "You see the scar? Amateur hour. You need practice before I let you 'fix' anything else."

I lifted my lip and crossed my arms tightly. If he didn't want me to touch him, that sounded like a win/win in my book.

He idled in front of my house, that stupid smile back in place. My resolve to appear unbothered was wilting—he was too bothersome for such a thing. I jumped out of the car and didn't look back as I walked up the drive. "Thanks for the ride," I yelled, my eyes on the house.

"Dick," I added under my breath.

"No problem." I heard the crunch of dirt beneath tires as he backed out. I had my key in hand. "Frank?" he shouted behind me. I paused, facing the door. "I love flamingos."

I flipped him the bird over my shoulder. He laughed like a braying jackass before speeding down the road.

My resolve was al dente.

There were two sorry-for-your-loss gifts on the front porch—a floppy house plant that reminded me of a Basset Hound, and a bouquet of dead grocery-store daisies. Both had suffered in the heat and neither had a note attached. I cursed as I unlocked the deadbolt and crossed the threshold. I half expected Pamela's ghost to rattle the furniture, but I sensed nothing other than the stale warm air of an empty house. Pamela had moved in so quickly after my mom died, I'd hardly experienced the silence.

I dropped the houseplant in the corner and the daisies on the carpet. I avoided the couch unequivocally—that would be the first thing in the dump. Death rolled off it in waves. My arms prickled with goosebumps as I went through the pantry and the fridge. I thought I should let Ben get a look at my current food supply; he'd get more use out of these *ingredients* than I would. I stood in the middle of the kitchen for a long time, fighting a desperate urge to go to my room and skip all of this. I would work fast.

Before I searched through Pamela's things, I grabbed a plastic razor from the bathroom and stuffed it in my back pocket to take back to Ben's. I should shave my legs. Not for Ben … for the summer heat.

If I had ever felt like a bigger ass than I did right now …

Then I pushed open my grandmother's habitually closed door. The darkness was startling, her blinds were closed and the curtains closed over them. Her bed was made, the handstitched forest green quilt pulled up past the pillows. It looked exactly as I would imagine the room of a dead person—twice over, actually. Clean, flat, depressing. I opened the wood-paneled doors to her closet, though I already knew I didn't want to keep her clothes. I could donate them all to Goodwill to appease any guilt I might feel one day.

The dresses were all long and lacy and frilly. She had a few shapeless pastel skirts and a single pair of creased salmon dress pants. She always dressed like she'd been on her way to church, though she didn't practice in any way I knew about. I grabbed the first dress on the rack: black, floral, good as anything to be buried in.

Doing my best to take my time and not rush to my room, I went through her nightstand, secretly terrified I'd find a vibrator in its drawers. But of course, I didn't. She would have been more pleasant otherwise. She had a neat pouch of cough drops, a silk sleeping cap for her hair, a few pieces of jewelry, and a small moleskin journal. I would take the jewelry; I never wore the stuff, but I could give it to someone else one day, if I ever had someone to give it to. The journal was the real interest piece. I took one of Pamela's pillowcases from her bed, leaving the pillow, it smelled too much like my grandmother—flowers, bleach, and heavy hair spray. I put the jewelry inside the makeshift sack and dropped the pillowcase to the hallway floor before I fled toward my bedroom, out of patience with this whole performance. I opened the book to the first page. It was an entry from three years ago.

With the journal in one hand, I turned the knob to my room with the other, wondering if there were any Cheezy Poofs left. My eyes were on my grandmother's elegant script, so I didn't notice the figure standing at my window. As I stepped into the room, I felt the same intoxicating sensation that I had the night before. Before I could look up, a new voice spoke.

"Hello, Francesca."

IT WAS A WOMAN, slight but powerfully built. She was another person who had clearly spent a great deal of time outdoors. Her skin was burnt brown sugar, and her long, tangled hair was bleached white from the sun. Her eyes were almost as light, so pale they were like glass shards between her eyelids. They had a slight downward angle to them. A scar sliced down from her hairline through her left eyebrow, barely discernible in the pale hair. She had a button nose and wide lips. It was a staggering appearance, and one that was out of place in her casual outfit made up of loose canvas pants and a tank top; even more so next to my homely furniture and taped-up magazine cutouts.

"Hello," she said again before I could speak. I was both entranced and afraid, as if I were trapped in my bedroom with a mountain lion who could speak English. She hadn't moved, but her eyes were sharp and so intensely focused on me.

"Why are you here?" I stuttered, taking a step back toward the hallway. She tracked the movement but remained motionless. That hadn't been the question I intended to ask. I should have asked who the hell she was, but it was as if I already knew her. I had never seen this woman, her remarkable features, but her presence felt familiar to me.

"Because you're here," she said. Her voice was faint and raspy like a smoker's. Her mouth fell open and her head tilted to one side as she watched me. "I don't want to hurt you, Francesca. I wanted to see you."

My heart raced around my chest. "How do you know my name?"

She didn't appear at all abashed. One side of her mouth lifted. "I've been nosey. I discovered more about you while you've been away." She took a measured step in my direction. "My name is Jessamae."

This woman acted as if breaking into my house and going through my things was a normal, not criminal, thing to do, but I felt hunted by her.

"And why did you want to see me?"

Her thick brows lowered over those sea-glass eyes. "Don't you feel it?" she asked, taking another step forward. I took another step back. Her grin continued to lift as if she were charmed by my ignorance, or my fear. Another step. We were only a few feet apart now.

And then I did feel it. The magnetic force pulling me was strong now, almost painful. The pressure I sensed last night from the woods, it was here in this room. It was pulling me to *her*.

"You were in the woods."

Jessamae continued towards me. I didn't back away.

"I was in those woods. You left me waiting for some time." She didn't appear annoyed by the fact—she appeared nothing short of elated. "But I am patient. I waited for you still today, and I will wait for you again."

"Why are you here?" I repeated. She was muddling my head.

Her smile extended fully for the first time. It was chilling. She was captivating in a way entirely other than Cleo. When Cleo smiled, I wanted to run to her, when this face smiled, I wanted to flee. A bear trap hiding in a wildfire. It was haunting, and I was ensnared.

"Look at you," she purred. She was close enough to touch me. And she did. Her hand lifted and curved around my chin, her thumb finding the dimple there. I trembled into her skin. She traced the outline of my lips before she pressed them softly with one finger, as if she were hushing me. "Such a peach."

My trembling grew to shaking. I wanted to run but I was cemented in place. I wanted so much, I was more of a wish than a person. Her dark hands followed the lines of my face, tickling under my jaw. She inhaled.

Her body molded into mine. Tilting my head up, she inhaled again, deeply. Her lips danced against mine in not quite a kiss. She lifted her face as if lost in thought before she looked back into my eyes. I could see my hazel reflected in hers like mirrors. "I'll see you soon," she promised. And was gone.

~∾

"FRANKIE! FRANKIE!" Ben shouted from the front of the house. I hadn't moved from the same spot in my doorway, but Jessamae was nowhere in sight. Had she gone out the window?

I couldn't feel my legs, and I didn't trust them to hold me up if I moved. Then Ben was behind me. He crossed his arms around my ribs and held me to his stomach. I hardly sensed the heat of him. He spun me around so fast my spine cracked. He gripped my shoulders, panic in his eyes.

"Where did she go?" He searched the room, cranking his head from side to side. His hands frantically ran over my entire body, down to my ankles and up my back. "Did she hurt you? Do you feel tired?"

"I'm okay," I breathed. He smashed my face between his hands and started what looked like a breathing exercise, bunching my hair up under his palms. Deep inhale, hard exhale. I had no trouble giving him this time. I'd forgotten how to walk.

"I didn't see her nearly until you did, until I was home." He crushed me to him again, his arms around the back of my head. "Jesus Christ."

"Why are you breathing like that? She didn't want to hurt me." Or so she said.

Ben's hands dropped to my shoulders and pressed down. "Frankie! That was the vampire! What else would she be doing in your house?" He shook me like a ragdoll.

I jerked back from him, slipping and landing on my butt. Ben took my hands, extending them above me like a marionette's. I batted his hands away and pulled my arms to my lap.

I hadn't even considered it. Pamela had never crossed my mind. Now, after the fact, it was humiliatingly obvious.

She killed my grandmother, and then had been waiting for me.

I didn't like Pamela. But I might have loved her, or something like it. Familial obligation to give a damn one way or the other. Jessamae had taken family from me. She had taken the only blood relative I had left. She could have killed me just as easily.

The fact that she could kill me did not change my fear of her. Her ability to end my life was no different than anyone else's, really, and I'd seen her as a predator from the start. But wiping out the last of the Hughes line was clearly not her plan. She was tracking me, learning about me. She didn't want me dead, at least not right now. I feared the connection between us just as much as I feared her.

Ben rubbed his eyes, already exhausted though it wasn't even noon. "Let's get the hell out of here, please? There's something else I'm adding to our agenda today. But we really should attend to Pamela first."

THE FUNERAL HOME was only a few blocks from Jim's Grocery, in what you could call the metropolitan area of Aspen Ridge. It was a nondescript building with beige stucco and few windows. The grass around the building was well maintained, with the light and dark crisscross pattern from being very recently mowed. "Perez Family Funeral Home" was displayed in steel letters above the door. One of the more tasteful businesses in town.

Ben held the door for me like he was Gene Kelly singing in the rain, his big sunglasses in place to obscure his eye. His spirits always lifted so abruptly, it was hard to dwell. I propped my new pair of gas station shades onto the crown of my head. Ben surprised me with them when we got back to his car. They were the red ones I liked, but much smaller than his own. My tantrum over another gift was a small one. Ben owed me.

The building smelled like a cramped flower shop, like Pamela. The arrangements in the lobby were dated, the colors evoking 90's prom pictures. There were no coffins on this side of the building. I could see some caskets on display through a pair of double doors and was anxious about the cost more than anything else.

"Good morning, Miss Hughes," a suit greeted me pleasantly. He looked to be in his fifties or sixties. The suit wasn't tailored to fit him and hung a bit loose over his rounded gut. He had a head full of thick dark hair and his drooping neck was pristinely shaved. His expression was kind, and I was curious as to if he really enjoyed his work.

"My name is Gabriel. I am so sorry for your loss." He actually sounded sincere. "I'm here to help your family in this time. Whatever arrangements you need, I'm happy to fulfill them."

He shook my hand and then Ben's, who introduced himself as a friend of the family. Gabriel guided the two of us to a pale and stiff sofa between two enormous wreaths on sticks. The floral smell was sickening.

"I understand your grandmother, Pamela, passed away two days ago of natural causes," he read the details from an iPad he produced. I wiggled uncomfortably, thinking of Jessamae. "Have you already posted an obituary or announcement?" he asked.

"Oh, shit," I blurted before I could stop myself, "I'm sorry. I just, uh … no I haven't." Before she moved in with me, she had lived in another city, Lehi or Alpine or somewhere around there. Her friends across the mountain had no idea she was dead.

"That's alright." His face crinkled up in a smile. "I can take care of that if you like. Something in *The Salt Lake Tribune*, perhaps? I can submit some general information, or something more personal if you want to do that."

He was very good at this. He was not offended by my curse or my lack of preparation. He deserved that pretty grass outside.

"General information would be okay, thanks." Ben reached over and patted my knee before giving a light squeeze. His touching had increased so dramatically over the last few days, I didn't even twitch. He was exposure therapy-ing me.

Gabriel smiled at the two of us before pulling a pamphlet off an end table near him. "There are several options for your grandmother. Let me begin by asking, would you like to host a funeral or a wake?"

I wasn't certain how wakes worked, but I knew guests were necessary, and I hadn't been to a funeral since my grandpa's when I was five or six. I didn't have the funds or the interest in spending more money on something symbolic. I rolled the pamphlet into a tight tube in my hands.

I tried to formulate an answer that didn't illustrate just how far my naivety, or apathy, extended. "I think the smallest reception possible. Please. We don't have much family." We didn't have any family.

"I understand." He typed something into the iPad on his lap. "Any religious practice that you would like us to honor?"

There was so much more to being dead than I knew. And the truth was, I didn't know my grandmother. "I don't think so." I was fairly certain most gods asked their followers to not be raging hags. Rest in peace.

"It's sounding like the right fit for you may be an intimate burial or cremation. If I may be so bold, I would recommend a casket. That way those who care about her could visit her resting place," he offered.

That would be a decent compromise, but I was still waiting for the big ugly price tag. "Is a casket very expensive?"

He considered me with compassion. I tried to see myself through his eyes: a young woman barely out of childhood with no money or family being towed along by a heavily modified man. Ben put an arm around me as if to demonstrate my helplessness, and Gabriel's expression became a little unhappy.

"Please don't fret over that, Miss Hughes. We will find something superlative and, I promise, we will stay within whatever budget you propose."

I thought if I pushed out a tear, I could get this thing for free. However, Gabriel was one of the few people from whom I would feel uncomfortable stealing. Even if I couldn't afford it, I would pay him.

He showed us through the eerie room of display caskets, and we found a biodegradable model—I had no idea whether Pamela wanted to be buried or burned, but I brought the dress as a just-in-case, and this seemed like a safe middle-ground—for five hundred dollars. I had an inkling that it cost much more, but

Gabriel would hear nothing of my protests. At least I could cover that with the bulk of my checking account.

"Our next steps include choosing a plot, headstone, and burial service," Gabriel said, propping up his iPad.

I pounded my face against the edge of his stately oak desk. I went back in for a second bang but was thwarted by Ben's fleshy hand. He put his arm around my shoulders and whispered in my ear, "Go wait outside, okay? I'm going to talk to him for a second."

Ben was known to make quick decisions. I stood clumsily, rubbing my forehead, and left the room. The cost of this whole thing felt insurmountable. I hoped Ben wouldn't play the sad little girl card too hard with this man. He shouldn't lose money. I wished I could just bury Pamela in the backyard like a dog, but with how things were going, ghosts were real, and she would float around the house for the rest of my life, bitching about what I'd done.

That house was mine now, and it was filled with the possessions of two dead women. And now there was a murderous succubus camping around the place, maybe even sleeping there. The notion was only faintly violating, and I didn't like that at all.

Ben walked out of the office alone, letting the door swing shut behind him. He pressed his hand to the small of my back and escorted me out into the sun. The hot air felt gritty, like desert sand in my mouth. I should sell the house and move to Alaska.

"What happened? What's the final number?" I asked him, dreading the answer.

"Five hundred dollars," he replied without looking at me. He drove us from the parking lot, turning onto the main road in the direction of his place. "We have to grab Cleo, then we're taking a little drive. Sorry about all the trips, Princess. But with that Casper lady hanging around your house, plus how slow your foot healed after last night, we need more info. There's a guy I know. He can help us out."

What he said swirled around in my mind like toilet water until something stuck. "Why do I only owe five hundred dollars, Benjamin?" My eyes narrowed. "Are they going to throw her in the box and then push her out to sea?"

He gnashed his teeth in irritation. "Please be reasonable, Frank." He gave me a moment to be reasonable. "You will pay me five hundred dollars, and I will pay the funeral home. Granny will have a beautiful view from the least expensive lot in the cemetery, with a straightforward headstone, in the coffin you picked out for her." He spoke to me as if I were red in the face, pounding on the dash in opposition. I didn't want to be predictable. But ...

"What is your problem? I could have gotten a loan!" I shouted, ashamed of my inability to afford a dead grandmother. Ben owed me, true, but not a burial service. The dryness in my chest meant tears might come soon if I didn't get a grip on myself. "You need to stop doing this! I am an adult, and I can do things for myself!" My current behavior aside.

"You! Are! Welcome!" he yelled back at me, practically shaking the windows. He appeared to regret his outburst imme-diately, he circled his middle finger and thumb over his temples. "Listen. I realize I don't drive a Ferrari or a spaceship or some shit, but I do have money!" Yelling again, he attempted to steady himself. "I'm a stellar investor, have been since I was eighteen." He knocked his knuckles on the top of his head. "You can pay back every cent if you want, you'd probably enjoy it more knowing how much I didn't want it."

I chewed on the inside of my cheek, opening the slimy skin. "I should just sell my stupid house," I whispered. "At least I'd come out of this debt-free."

Ben pinched the cheek I'd been chewing and pulled it away from my gnawing teeth. "I'm not a loan shark, Frank." He pulled one of my curls out long and then watched it spring back into place. "I'm the love of your life." He unleashed the power of his taunting smile on me and grabbed the wheel with both hands.

His tone was light-hearted, but a nervous shudder tickled my ribs. The plastic pink razor in my pocket seemed to grow, suddenly uncomfortable under my butt cheek. I was such an ass.

~

WE IDLED at Ben's to pick up Cleo and to drop off the new round of clothing I packed. I'd need to do a load of laundry before I put any of it on, so I sat, a bit fidgety, in the front seat of the Volkswagen in Ben's running shorts. My legs appeared tanner, and they were smooth—I ran the razor over them sloppily while I used the bathroom—nothing like the limbs I'd known. I looked at my face in the visor mirror and I had never appeared healthier. I looked like I drank eight glasses of water every day and always ate my vegetables. What a liar my face was.

Cleo approached the car in high-waisted shorts and a crop top. Her legs were gut-wrenchingly flawless. I peeked again at the legs I had just been admiring. "Nope," I uttered to their mediocre expanse.

She slid into the back seat, disgruntled when Ben wouldn't hand over the keys. She put her headphones in and discreetly ignored us for nearly an hour, though Ben and I didn't talk much. The air in the car felt strange after our argument.

We pulled off the freeway when Cleo yanked the earbuds out of her ears. "Where exactly are we going, Ben? We can't be going to Chelsea's, she went east months ago."

"We aren't going to Chelsea's." Ben evaded her question, something that did not escape Cleo's attention. She stared at Ben in the rearview mirror, but he refused to meet her eyes.

"Why did we need to leave anyway?" I grumbled, sick of the car.

Cleo rested her head on the shoulder of my seat. Heat came off her skin. "You need some practice. I saw you work with a flower, and Ben saw you in that restaurant, but you couldn't heal yourself last night." She was incredibly informed. "So, though Ben is being secretive and cryptic with us, it's safe to assume he's taking you to someone with either talent or knowledge." Cleo finished with a small smile for me and a glare for Ben.

"How long have you had your powers?" I turned to her, suppressing the urge to ogle. I wasn't sure if "powers" was the right term, but it seemed as appropriate as anything.

Her small smile shrank, like she was trying to be amicable but didn't want to speak of it. "It's something we're all born with, but my abilities presented themselves when I was very little. As long as I can remember."

"How does that work? What exactly makes the powers 'present themselves'?" I didn't want to push her, but I was struggling to grasp these concepts. "Why are mine only showing up now?"

"Several circumstances can inhibit things. For example, you don't like to be touched, but your ability requires touch." She turned her head against my seat so she could study my face. "At least for now. And the only relationships you had for most of your life were with non-magical women. Both of whom caused you to isolate yourself even more." I shot a glare at Ben. He'd told Cleo way too much. "Don't feel bad. You had family. That's not something to resent. I was in the foster system until I was fifteen. By then, I'd already had a firm handle on what I was." Though her voice was melodic, her tone was terse.

I normally would never pry into someone else's business. I hated the sensation when it happened to me, but I was very ambivalent about this "affinity" of mine. Like I had been thrown into the ocean, the depths too dark to decipher, surrounded by giggling mermaids. Especially Cleo. I pressed on.

"You were never adopted?" Looking and sounding like she did, there had to have been a line across the country to raise a little girl like her.

"I was fostered many times." Her eyes grew severe and

distant. "It didn't work out." Her mouth twisted in hatred, disfiguring her angelic face into something frightening. I turned back to face the windshield, shying away from the siren.

After another thirty minutes of driving, Ben turned off the highway abruptly and headed up a steep mountain trail. His car did not appreciate the rocks and craters along the path. We bumped up and down, banging our heads against the roof more than once. After crossing through a shallow creek, the path became dark, shrouded in the shadows of towering spruce trees. The road was eventually obliterated by boulders and stones. We had to leave the car and walk another hundred yards before we even saw the house.

It was a sprawling, modern glass box secluded on the side of a foliage-covered cliff. Its architecture was both futuristic and minimalistic, reminiscent of the American 1960s. The walls were glass-paneled in their entirety, stretching up three stories. Each panel was lined in a dark and expensive-looking wood. There was an attached garage off to the right of the front door that would fit at least eight cars in its caverns. This was a person I would have allowed to pay for a headstone.

I wanted to stay at the back of the group as we exited the car, intimated by the façade. Sensing my hesitation, Ben, once again, put his hand on the small of my back and led me up the stone path to the house.

He knocked three times on the door, which was simple and wooden, but colossal. After some clanging noise on the other side of the door, it swung open.

"Hey there!" the homeowner boomed. This zealous man was tall, taller even than Ben. He had a blonde circle beard he kept short around his mouth, which was beaming at us all like we were lifelong friends. He had light skin with pink undertones and light eyes, a very fair fellow. He looked strong underneath his informal clothing. A big hand circled around a glass of clear liquid. He had a jacket on, and a baseball cap pulled low on his head.

"Are you serious, Ben? Him?" Cleo growled.

The man mashed his lips together to tame his huge grin. "Hello, Cleo, it's nice to see you again. You look ravishing, as always," he greeted her with a mischievous gleam in his eye. She made a disgusting noise in the back of her throat, like clearing phlegm, but otherwise ignored him. "Oh, and another lovely lady friend." He winked at me. Holding his other hand to his chest like we were a miracle on his doorstep, his eyes passed between us giddily. "Good lord. My, oh, my."

"May we come in now?" Ben asked with impatience.

"Don't think I forgot about you, Benjamin. You look better than either of them, baby." He reached out with his non-drinking hand and slapped Ben's shoulder vigorously. "Come on in, you beautiful creatures. Can I get you a drink? Tequila?"

He led the way through what was probably called a foyer, it smelled like a department store. We followed him to an expansive and blinding white kitchen with a full bar open on the shiny island, which I thought might be as big as my bedroom at home. Everything came in extra-large—the cabinets, the windows, even the shiny espresso machine. It was all steel or granite as far as I could see. It was painfully bright and did not inspire comfort. Our host got some glasses from a fancy alcohol cart and began pouring tequila in all of them.

"Frankie, this is Patrick." Ben gestured to our bartender with an annoyed fondness, who then looked up at his name cheerfully. "He's been around for a very long time and has an almost creepy—" Patrick only smiled wider at the term, "—knowledge of all things supernatural."

"I'd be happy to help, not that you asked," Patrick said close beside us. He handed one glass to me and another to Ben before going back and getting a third glass for Cleo. When he offered it to her, she turned her back to him and walked across the entire floor—which was extensive, to say the least—to stare out the windowed walls of his home. Unperturbed, he kept both glasses to himself and rejoined the two of us.

"How old are you?" I prodded rudely, not that this person seemed easy to offend. "You don't seem much older than us."

"Awe, you're sweet." He stirred his drink with his finger and sucked the liquor off. "Well … in a way you're right, and in a way, you're wrong."

When I waited expectantly, confused, Ben explained, "He's a shifter. They tend to have incredibly long lifespans."

An image of the Wonder Twins filled my mind. Surely this man would be dazzling in one of those purple jumpsuits. "A shifter?" I repeated.

Patrick interrupted before Ben could respond by exuberantly clinking his drinks against the rims of ours.

"A werewolf, baby girl!" he shouted before draining both of his glasses.

9

"NOT IN THE classic horror sense. I wish. Not even a wolf at all. Just a big hairy beast that somehow manages to be even stronger than I am right now," Patrick narrated as he poured himself another glass. He smelled the alcohol with glee. I tried to do the same and gagged. "Most shapeshifters become something with a heightened ability, something sort of avian to fly, or something small to hide. I get raw strength." He shot the liquor back. "And sex appeal."

"Think of all the poor woodland creatures that have loved and lost him," Ben said with a straight face. Patrick nodded at the tragedy.

"You don't need a full moon?" I asked intrigued, thinking he might laugh at the question.

"I don't need it. But all of us are more in tune with our abilities when the moon is full. I can change at will, and I also change when I do not will it." His eyes were grim. I poured myself another shot of tequila and Patrick dipped his chin in approval. "Should we go to the library then? All of us?" he asked loudly and pointedly at Cleo.

She scowled, torn between her evident hatred of Patrick and her desire to be involved. "Fine. But get within three feet of me, and I'll have you begging for death by morning."

"Three feet?" Patrick glanced down at his pants. "You flatter

86

me." He pushed himself off the granite countertop and left the kitchen.

We traveled through several scantily furnished, shimmering rooms before entering what looked like the inside of a computer motherboard. The walls were lined with drives and blinking lights in varying colors. A few large screens were dispersed between the bits of technology with a bunch of nonsense text scrolled over a black terminal, updating every few seconds.

"Quite a book collection you have here," I mumbled before draining my tequila. My jaw tightened at the burn.

"Thank you, it is very nice. And I'm not being at all sarcastic." He circled his hand in front of me with distaste. "I've had all the books and papers scanned, so they really are somewhere in here. But I don't trust you with any of this." He gestured with both arms around the room.

Patrick approached one of the drive storage racks, and after tapping several keys arbitrarily, he pushed a random square inward, like a VHS into a VCR. A panel along the wall behind me slid to the right, inside of the next row of drives. It was dark inside the doorway. I was surprised he hadn't hung torches along the walls.

He had opened a secret passageway. I appraised Patrick with my eyebrows at my hairline.

"I know," he was elated. He guided us inside.

It wasn't a passageway at all, but a small, brown, low-ceilinged room. It was filled to the brim with encyclopedic volumes and assorted leather-bound books. There were a few overstuffed armchairs and one quaint loveseat under the glow of standing lamps. It was very cozy.

Patrick was clearly impressed by his own collection. "It took years to sort through all the fantasy and the wishful thinking to find tomes written by people like us. Or at least someone involved with witches. The real stuff."

He turned on a lamp and sat in one of the squishy chairs, looking like a pompous professor in a zip-up. He stretched his long arms out in a welcoming gesture. "Feel free to read every-thing in here, but most of it won't pertain to you, baby girl." He turned to face me with an air of superiority. "We all run a little different. You'll need the books on restoration. You are on the restoration train, am I right? I am." He tilted his glass towards me like he was guessing my astrological sign.

"That's what I've been told." I squinted at Ben who wasn't paying attention. He was scanning the titles printed along the leather-bound spines that surrounded us. "How'd you know? Are you like Ben?"

Patrick flapped air through his lips. "No, thank the good lord." His eyes bounced to Ben before returning to me. "He's talked about you for a few years, that you were coming." The side of his mouth lifted at his phrasing. "But if I may be serious for a second, every one of these books will say the same thing at some point: You can't do anything, outside of what your amateur hands can do naturally, until you rid yourself of your brain blockage."

"Brain blockage?"

His face *did* harden, serious for the first time. "You have to stop thinking that all of this is bullshit, that it's not real. This is what's real for you now. Once you figure that out, you can step up to the plate." He pressed the tips of his fingers together like a villain. "You can't do much if you don't believe. Didn't you ever watch Barney?"

I turned to the books to avoid his knowing stare. I was a logical person. Logical people knew that the supernatural was for malnourished, live-in-their-mother's-basement weirdos. People who wanted so desperately to be special that they became formulaic in their fantastical justifications. As much as I may have wanted it once, I accepted I was nothing special years ago. Even after seeing Ben's palm heal, and the flower rise in my hand, in the back of my head I had called myself, and everyone else, crazy.

But Ben wasn't delusional, as strange as he could be. Cleo

was startlingly easy to believe—she had seemed more than human from the start. This boisterous man, Patrick, didn't seem malnourished or psychotic. He exuded credibility in his stuffy armchair, hidden away in this very posh home. I was resting on possible—I could at least trip into probable.

I didn't have time to dawdle, not with Jessamae in town. I pulled the pink razor from my back pocket and popped the plastic cover.

"Are you shaving right now?" I heard Patrick ask, bemused, as I held it to the thin skin inside my inner elbow. I slid it sideways along the blade and bit my lip at the fear of cutting too deep. Cleo rushed forward and took the razor away from me, looking scandalized. Patrick coughed tequila down his chin. Ben remained calm, but his eyes were bright and alert as he watched.

Blood oozed from the wound. I wrapped my fingers tightly around it. Closing my eyes and thinking healing thoughts—imagining my skin coming together obediently—I tried to force myself to stop bleeding. It had been so easy with Ben, with that yellow plant in the park. It would be easy now.

I lifted my fingers, and they were sticky with bright red blood. I looked to Ben, feeling betrayed. "It isn't working!"

He came to me and placed my hand back on the seeping cut. With some uncertainty, he turned to Patrick and asked, "She couldn't heal herself yesterday either. What do you think?"

Patrick tugged at his short beard in thought. "Are you sure she's got any magic in her?" He wiped drops of liquor from his jacket. "Maybe the hair had you fooled. You know, women used to be burned as witches back in the day because of their hair? But you don't have to worry about that around me." He bit his lower lip. "I love strawberries. Lots of antioxidants."

I unconsciously reached for my hair before I dropped my hand, blushing. "I healed Ben! And I brought a dead flower back to life."

Patrick's face lifted. "I didn't know you were a gardener."

Ben snorted from behind Patrick's chair. I glared at his back.

"How about you take your glasses off, Ben? Something wrong with your eyes?"

"You should eat more strawberries," Patrick smirked. Then the realization hit, and he understood Ben's sunglasses might not be a fashion statement. "Wait, what's wrong with your eyes? How dare you hide behind such ugly sunglasses in my house?"

Ben threw me a vengeful look before answering, "Don't worry your giant head about it. She'll make it up to me later." He walked along the longest wall of the room and pulled a volume down.

Patrick's laugh boomed around the small space. "Oh, I can't wait to see that," he leered. "But as I was saying, before I was so wonderfully interrupted," he winked at me again, "she probably can't heal herself."

Ben's mouth tightened as he studied me. "She is healing, her foot went from open to scabbed overnight. It's more rapid than mortal, but much slower than expected."

"Well, sure. She'd still have the restoration magic in her. I'd bet she heals rapidly without trying. How did she heal you, Mr. Magoo?"

Ben mimed laughing, "Aren't you a card." His glasses remained in place. "She touched me. It took a couple of minutes at most."

"Okay. So, touching herself," Patrick smiled again, "it wouldn't be the same. Contact with her skin worked for you. But she's sort of covered in her own skin already, you see." He needlessly gestured to me, waving his arm up and down.

"Your wisdom truly knows no bounds," Cleo rolled her eyes so hard I'm surprised they didn't get stuck back there.

I frowned while I considered what Patrick said. That didn't seem like a bad deal. Even if things worked slowly, I was given a safety net. I wasn't as vulnerable as I always believed myself to be.

Patrick placed his empty glass on the low table in the middle of the room. "Well, it looks like we have work to do. We're going to need an energy-boosting elixir. I'll just roll the bar cart in here," he announced before dashing from the room.

∽

I SLAMMED DOWN YET another empty glass. Everyone had told me that drinking might better allow me to accept my new normal and rile my confidence. I was currently working on levitating a lime wedge off the floor. Ben decided I should stretch my magic muscles before I gave healing him another try, and neither Cleo nor Patrick volunteered for test-dummy duty.

The lime had shaken a few efforts ago, and nothing else had happened since. My shins were covered in shallow cuts. Each had closed so quickly, that as the blood dried up, I'd make another nick. With each new mark, I dipped my thumb into the bead of blood and pressed it to the fruit. Patrick cringed at the bloody mess.

"It's the easiest way!" Ben insisted again. "The fresher the wound, the stronger the magic. And killing a goat would be tough in this little room."

"Nothing in my house is little," Patrick said.

The corner of my mouth quirked but then immediately fell as the lime remained stubbornly affected by gravity. "Is there some sort of incantation, some Latin I could say to make it float?" I snarled.

"It doesn't work like that," Ben explained. "Speaking certain words that people made up themselves, no matter what century they did it in, is just ego," he said, swirling his half-empty glass in the air. "Belieeeeeve, Frank."

"I'm trying!"

"I know Latin," interrupted Patrick, who was three sheets to the wind and dancing alone to some reggae fusion he was playing through the house's Bluetooth. "Coitus. Cum laude." He held up a finger for each one. "Homo erectus."

Though Cleo refused to hurt herself, she had been putting in a lot of effort for my cause. She sat behind a large stack of musty books; to her left were volumes she deemed useless to me, and to her right was a much smaller stack that I would need to read. She found time to shoot irritated glares at Patrick with each turn of the page.

"How long will I need to cut myself?" I asked, poking at my candy cane of a leg.

Ben curled onto the floor beside me, crossing his legs. "For spells outside of our affinity, they take much more ... *oomph*. You know our reputation for utilizing newt's eyes and dead men's toes and other bits of things in potions. Right? Things like that that can help you. Symbolic things. Blood and pain are powerful and always on hand." His scarred skin seemed to glimmer in the light, emphasizing his point. "Magic comes with a price."

He bounced his foot to the beat of the music, and I bobbed my head on my neck. The music wasn't so terrible after fourteen or fifteen songs.

"Why do I need to float stuff anyway?" I asked, making another small slice with a kitchen knife along my calf. I didn't want to destroy my only razor. "Shouldn't I be making force fields or something?"

"You can't even levitate a lime, Princess," he reminded me with annoying sympathy. "You aren't ready to force any fields." He took our glasses to the cart and poured another splash of clear liquid into each. "How about this. If you can lift the lime one foot off the ground," he held up a finger to show me how much one was, "then I'll let you fix my eye." He whipped off his glasses dramatically.

"Ho!" Patrick yelled, pointing at Ben's head and splashing his drink around the room. "Look what she did to your beautiful face! My respect for her has grown, almost as much as your disgusting eye."

I laughed with him but was tempted by Ben's offer. I got on my knees and leaned over the lime, posing my hands in front of me. Working to ignore my self-consciousness at how stupid I looked, I thought less of floating the lime than of believing that I could. A lime in the air was just as real as the lime on the ground. It was as possible as holding it in my hand, tossing it in the air. It was real like I was real, this room, these people. I wasn't dreaming.

The tiny green wedge began to ascend. One inch, two inches—

I was so surprised that it plummeted back down around three. My small audience applauded. "That's right! I'll drink to that!" Patrick cheered, sloshing tequila on his chin.

"Beautiful, Frank! That was beautiful. Room for improvement, but something." Ben lifted his glass to me, his mocking grin infectious.

I clapped for myself. "I'll show you improvement," and turned to Patrick. "Do you have human snacks in this place, or are there cats and squirrels in your fridge?"

"You've got a lot of sass for someone that can't lift a lemon past her knees."

"She lifted a lime, you hairy buffoon," Cleo corrected.

"But I actually do have human snacks. Go look in the kitchen and bring them back for us. Thank you," he said, his eyes closed as he swayed to the music.

I pushed myself up thoughtlessly and weaved around the furniture as I exited.

It was a long trek to the kitchen. I may have gotten lost on the way, but eventually, I found myself under the bright overhead lights reflecting off the ubiquitous white stone. It took too long to find Patrick's fridge, which resembled a shiny closet door. I opened it and was disappointed. He had rows and rows of elaborate water and juice, but nothing to eat. I leaned into the cool air, feeling increasingly hot and stumbly.

"I probably should have gotten you some dinner before we left," I heard Ben stammer.

I turned around and sat against the shelves of the fridge.

"No, no. You—" my words sounded swirled, I swallowed. "You mother me too much, Benny." I pulled open the nearest drawers. "Werewolves have to eat. Help me find food."

He began opening cupboards and appliances. His black eye faced me, the shades blooming like a watercolor, but much uglier than anything Ben created. As I watched, it pulsed under the bright kitchen lights in a tease.

I strolled across the room, grabbing handles as I walked. I inspected the spaces he had already checked as I approached. When I was within reach, I sprang! My arm barely moved before he gripped my wrist, restricting me.

"Really? You thought you could use the element of surprise against *me*?" he scorned.

"I have before!" I flung my left hand up—and got devilishly close to his black and blue skin—before he snatched that wrist too.

"Why won't you … just let me … help you?" I grunted as we struggled.

"You haven't lifted the goddamn fruit enough yet!"

We knocked against open drawers and countertops. I fought him wildly. After getting one hand free, I craned my neck and bit his prevailing hand, white-knuckled on my wrist. He pushed me back against a counter with his body and bent down to bite my trapped arm in retaliation. "OW!" I squealed, squirming in his arms. "Isn't this what you want! For me to be a healer? For my willingness in all of this!"

He folded his arms across his chest, his face impenetrable.

I poked him in the shoulder, the rib. Two quick, hard taps.

Ben didn't move. "Knock it off, Frank."

"What are you so afraid of?" I jabbed him in the chest. "With your incessant touching. Pulling on my hands, twirling my hair!" I hit his cheek and forehead. I clutched his jaw in my vise-like hand. "Isn't this what you want?"

He got a hold of my limbs and smashed them both against his chest. "You are so annoying!"

Before I could bite him again, he leaned down angrily and he kissed me.

My eyes gaped open, and my head snapped back. "What the hell are you doing?" But Ben pushed into me hungrily, his mouth moving again on mine. And I was kissing him back.

For once, I was not self-conscious, I was not afraid of his searching fingers. I felt him, all of him. The warmth I'd sensed from him before, blazed into wildfire. There was a burning need in his aggression. His hands found my hair and drew me to him, *wrenched* me to him. His craving matched my own. The skin of his arms, hot under my hands, wasn't enough. I held them to me, working impossibly closer. His tongue slithered between my lips. I tasted the tart lime and the burn of the liquor. I was wrecked, lost in him, in the sensation. His rough cheek scratching mine, his hot breath on my skin, his soft lip between my teeth. My hips undulated against him, and he moaned in response. He lifted me onto the countertop and pushed himself roughly between my legs.

My hands were under the back of his shirt, my fingers digging into his shifting muscles. I felt the ridges of his tattoos under my palms. It made me shiver with pleasure to know them. He released my hair and slid his fingers down my body to cinch around my ribs. I was dizzy, panting, breathless, as his teeth nipped my bottom lip, followed by the slick trace of his tongue. He pushed harder against me, and I heard my head smack a cupboard, feeling no pain. His hands traveled down to my hips, and his thumbs wrapped around the tops of the bones there. Not low enough. I wanted to consume him, and to be eaten alive.

Ben pulled back, his eyes wide in horror. His pause lasted only a moment before he hurled me toward the fridge, his body folding around me like a cage. I had left the fridge open; it chilled my scorching skin. Then the house shattered around us.

The room collapsed with a high and deafening shriek as glass shards flew through the kitchen and covered its innards with fine powder, like a crystal bomb. A scream built in my lungs but all I managed was a feeble whimper. My hands clung to the skin under Ben's clothes, my body tense with shock. I must have been hurting him.

It wasn't until the crashing and the tinkling fell silent that Ben stepped away from me. I was stiff and ungainly, jammed into the shelves of the fridge. Plastic bottles and smashed juice cartons littered the tile around me. I stood up on weak legs and closed the refrigerator with care before walking deeper into the room. I was wearing my boots, but every step cracked underfoot; it was an uneasy experience. I followed Ben to the source of the explosion.

One of the glass panels that encapsulated Patrick's home had been destroyed. Pieces as thick as my thumb littered the floor like chunky diamonds. They coated the table, and there were fragments inside the drawers and cabinets that we had left open. Warm air crawled in through the new opening and coated me, thick as a wool blanket.

"I didn't do that … you couldn't have done that …" Ben stated quietly. "So … who—"

Cleo sprinted into the kitchen and slipped on the clear bits of house, catching herself against the kitchen island. She looked from Ben to me to the ten-foot hole in the wall. She appeared discomposed for the first time since I'd met her. Patrick trailed in after her, his face impassive as he took in the shattered window, the glass dust, all his open cabinetry. His gaze shifted between the two of us—Ben stood at my right hand—and the empty space that once was his window.

"Which one of you blew up my house?" he asked. His demeanor filled the kitchen with blistering tension that made me want to inexplicably scream. Once Ben stood in front of me—his hand reaching back with index finger extended, asking me to remain quiet—I understood.

Patrick was changing.

10

PATRICK BLINKED RAPIDLY, as if ticking. His eyes looked strange, too big, and too dark. "Who broke my fucking window?" His breathing was deep but forced, like a woman in labor.

Ben held up his hands in a peaceful gesture and stepped forward, slow and steady. Patrick's eyes followed his movements with quick precision. "It's alright. Just some broken glass. Right, buddy? Nothing to get worked up about. It's alright. Just keep breathing."

Patrick's breaths appeared to ease, his fists flexed open. He closed his eyes. "It wasn't us," Ben assured. And with that assurance, Patrick's eyes popped in understanding—this was the act of an outsider—and his precarious control shattered as completely as his window.

He clawed at his face in a desperate attempt to stop the inevitable, grunting with the effort of it. His lips bulged outward from his face like an ape. He ground his white teeth, straining his jaw and disfiguring his mouth further. His fingernails extended into bone-colored hooks that scored his skin. The skin paled. It looked unnatural, too tight for the muscles within it. Patrick lifted his enormous head and met my incredulous stare. His pupils had blown up to fill his entire eye, flooding the whites, as though his irises were a ruptured dam.

I was rooted in place, beyond stunned. The charming and jovial man who I'd gotten to know in the last few hours was a monster. But my psychological response was much more unsettling. I was invigorated. I wanted him to change. I had found something I could not explain away. Magic. In front of my eyes. Patrick had shown me he was more than human. My survival instinct held me back, but I yearned for this, was enthralled to witness, to experience, what would happen if he could not regain control.

Ben was forcing me backward, blocking me and my view of the beast entirely. "Patrick? Patty boy? Just breathe, remember to breathe. You can come back from this." His words only pushed Patrick further over the edge. White fur burst from his knuckles and cheeks. His zip-up was bulging and protesting as it stretched.

Cleo rushed around the kitchen island to stand at my side, her hands mirrored Ben's, held up in front of her chest. "Calm down, Patrick."

The beast let a bellow explode from its jaws, its fangs longer than my fingers. The dishes shook inside the pretty cabinets, and I forgot to breathe. With a final build, the jacket shredded, and what was once Patrick straightened to its full height. It resembled a gorilla, but leaner, and very tall, nearing seven feet. White fur sprouted from its appendages, head, and back. What skin remained had taken on a reptilian quality—scaled but very thick.

"Run, Frank!" Ben shouted, but I'd been affixed to the kitchen floor.

Cleo yanked me off my feet as Patrick lifted a glossy modern barstool and tossed it our way as if it weighed no more than a glass of liquor. The stool smashed into the wall behind me. It decimated the drywall and reverberated off the tiled floor. Another roar shook the room, and I finally gained the sense to get the hell out of the way.

I scuttled backward on my hands and feet, desperate to find purchase and stand. The coal-black eyes targeted me—they were primal, unrecognizable. The monster stalked forward on longer, thicker legs, the balls of its hairy feet easily supporting its gargantuan weight. It crossed the room in three bounds before it seemed to smack into an invisible wall.

Its confusion didn't last long. The beast clawed at the barrier. A furious shriek pounded against my ear drums. "Go, Frank!" Ben ordered through his teeth, his arms contracting with an unseen effort. I took advantage of the miraculous obstacle and got to my feet.

A strange smoke abruptly filled the room. It was a dark, midnight blue. I couldn't sense the source, but the haze was palpable as it surrounded us. I could breathe through it easily and it didn't have a scent, but my vision was completely eradicated. Ben's sweaty fingers found mine through the blue fog. He hauled me out of the kitchen, sprinting all-out and cracking my arm in its socket. Enraged snarling echoed through the house. It thrummed in my ears and panic dewed my hands. The monster could be anywhere.

The smoke didn't extend far, and when my eyesight cleared of it, I saw we had fled into an elaborate dining room. A teardrop crystal chandelier hung above a table that sat twelve. The chairs were rigid, white, and spindly, contrasting exceptionally with the dining table. The tabletop was made of dark gray cement, and was thicker than my forearm. I could only appreciate the mass of it when the heavy thing flipped onto its side with a shaking, resounding *boom!* I lost my balance, fumbling against Ben's chest. Ben pushed me down roughly on our side of the boundless stone plate.

"Stay down!" he demanded over the sounds of the irate animal now stomping from room to room, searching for us through the dissipating smoke.

"You stay down!" I retorted through my teeth.

The pounding footsteps got louder as it roamed back in our direction. Ben forced his hand over my mouth and held a finger up to his lips. His face was only inches from mine, and, foolishly, as the predator sought us out, I was struck by his appearance. His cheeks and lips were flushed. His skin glowed with health, and I thought his shorn hair might have grown slightly. It looked closer to a deep brown than black, I realized.

The eye I punched and bruised just last night was positively perfect.

The beast rounded the corner, its hefty feet smacking against the floor. I heard its shallow breathing, smelled its sour sweat.

Trembling, I pulled Ben's hand from my mouth and climbed messily to my knees, still drunk. His eyes flashed in warning, but I shook my head in return. My fingers curled around the edge of cement, and I dared to peek around the corner of the tabletop.

The beast was right outside the dining room entryway. Its snout lifted to the air, and my heart plummeted to my heels. I ducked back behind the table knowing we were doomed; its disorientation wouldn't last long and it would soon smell us just as I smelled it. The horrible silence stretched on. I covered my own mouth to smother my breaths.

Ben touched my shoulder to soothe my choked breathing, and stupidly, instinctually, I slapped it away. The sound of the rejection sliced through the room and a roar of victory followed it.

Ben and I jumped to our feet and circled around the huge table, always keeping it between us and the beast. "Patrick, it's us!" Ben screamed as we paced.

Snarling in frustration, the thing moved to jump the stone block, its claws curling over the edge and scraping against its surface. Before it could hurdle the furniture, Cleo appeared in front of me. Then a second Cleo materialized behind the beast, then a third was at the table. Three Cleos danced around the monster, tempting its drooling jaws.

Its jowls snapped closed over a finger, a wrist, but each time contact was made with a Cleo, her body would vanish and reappear elsewhere. The animal wailed in agitation, swiping fiercely with its claws in all directions as sirens flashed in and out of time and space.

"Plug your ears! Now, Frank!" Ben hollered before sticking his own fingers in his ears. I paused for a moment in silly defiance before I did so. With his head, he gestured back toward Cleo's act of defense.

I could hear the muffled echo of the beast, then I heard something more. Garbled but lovely. Cleo's mouth gaped open for long stretches as she held the beast's crazed gaze. Was she screaming? She was hauntingly calm, her lips moving but nothing else. She wasn't screaming—she was singing.

The beast shook its thick neck and scratched at its own scaled ears in effort to escape the music. Its snout curled back from black gums and it charged at the nearest Cleo apparition. But the beast had clearly retained some human intellect. Because before he could reach the woman, he switched targets and slashed the opposing Cleo in a massive arc of its arm. Her shoulder opened like cellophane, and she collapsed to the floor.

"No!" Ben yelled. But the monster wasn't finished. It approached Cleo prudently, checking its rear and sides for copies of her. "Touch me!" Ben ordered, turning to me from behind our weak shelter of two dining chairs. For once, I listened without a fuss.

I held his hand as Ben approached the duo. At the touch of him, warmth enveloped me. Sweat beaded down my forehead and neck, and my hair felt heavy and wet around me. I struggled to breathe, but I didn't release his palm.

The beast paid us little notice. Ben's free arm lifted, his wrist bent as if resting on glass. And as the beast bent down to ravage Cleo's exquisite features, it swung its claw and struck another wall. Familiar with the blockage, it pounded at the shield with angry fists. The invisible force pushed violently back at the monster, flinging it into the dining table and bending its spine backward, over the table's edge at an unnatural angle.

The animal bleated in pain, its gargantuan form crumpling in a pile. Its breathing was jagged and fast. Ben stepped cautiously toward it, but the beast exposed his teeth in aggression, halting Ben in place. Its enormous head turned around, the scales of its cheeks rippling strangely in the light. The beast strenuously dragged itself up to all fours, favoring its right side. With a painful roar that shook the beautiful crystal of the chandelier, the monster skirted from the room on broken bones.

The tinkling of glass across tile emanated from the kitchen. Sparing a look for Cleo and me, Ben hurtled to follow Patrick.

I dropped to my knees and mashed my hand into the bloody well of Cleo's shoulder. It fountained between my fingers.

"I can fix this! I can fix this!" I willed desperately. I didn't know if Cleo was warming beneath my touch, or if her blood was warming me.

With both hands, I pushed against her shoulder as if giving compressions, and I finally felt the ripped skin and muscle beneath the blood. Adrenaline pounded through my bloodstream as I kneaded her shoulder like seeping, soupy dough. Cleo's wild eyes found mine, pleading, as I was. She was shuddering, almost bucking against my weight.

"I can fix this!" I screamed at her as I forced her back to the floor, straddling her hips. I tried to balance my weight between my legs and my hands. I touched the bone exposed underneath the slippery meat of her.

Ben rushed back into the room, sliding on the red flooded tile. He took in the horror of us. "Fucking help me! Please!" I yelled. Cleo's shaking had yet to slow, and I gritted my teeth against her strength. Turning away from Ben, I focused all my energy on her.

"He's gone. Patrick jumped out the broken window. He'll be in the woods for a while." Ben said. Then, moving with heartbreaking patience, Ben squelched through the blood with careful steps before crouching down at Cleo's head. He brushed sticky hair from her face, and Cleo's eyes found his. "It will work," Ben whispered to her.

I tasted salt in my mouth, and I cried out angrily, hating my useless tears. I smacked my tongue to erase the taste when I realized with a pause that I wasn't crying, I had swallowed some of Cleo's blood.

It didn't taste sweet—it didn't taste like anything other than what it was. But it stuck to my tongue and lined my throat like honey. I searched for more on my lips.

"It will work," Ben spoke to me now. "It will work. Believe it, Frank."

"It will work," I repeated. My tongue swept each of my teeth.

Ben turned back to Cleo with a gentle expression, her shock appearing to subside. As the blood clotted in her body and the river of it seemed to dry up at last, I felt the skin under my fingers twitch like trapped butterflies. Her tear was closing.

"See?" Ben said.

~

"YOU MAKE FORCE FIELDS?" I belted, squatting down and holding out the dustpan. "Are you fucking kidding me, Benjamin?"

Ben's smile was answer enough, but still he responded, "I had my first vision when I was seven years old, things have … progressed since then. The psychic fields didn't start until recently. Turned out my affinity wasn't so much precognition as mentalism. I mean, I already told you I see through the eyes of others in my visions. I can also see through the eyes of others in the present. That developed in my early twenties."

He swept the obstinate glass crumbs into the dustpan. We had searched the entire kitchen, but eventually found the maintenance tools in the garage. They still had the tags on them. After we mopped up all the blood—thank god for the ubiquitous tile in here—we righted what furniture we could and began to clean up the remaining damage.

"Cleo developed her ability to cast illusions. And her body itself, like her hair—probably her teeth and fingernails too—can be used in enchantments," Ben continued, his eyes on his work. "Patrick, even as a human, is much stronger than a human, and faster. His body is hard to break but heals easy." He looked wistfully to the hole in the house. "He's no window, that is for certain." He swept up the last glass particles. "And he's a lone shifter, but a natural alpha. People instinctually follow him. He climbed the corporate ladder in no time ... back around the turn of the century."

I jerked up in surprise and nearly spilled all our hard work. I clapped my newly freed hands over my eyes. "I am never going to get used to this." Then, dropping my arms, I tilted my chin. "What was it? Your first vision."

Ben dumped the glass into the trash and set the broom beside the fridge. He wiped his hands on his shorts before he answered. "I saw my nanny take cash from my father's wallet."

"Did you tell?"

His smile grew to shit-eating proportions. "Our dog got ahold of that wallet somehow. My mother's too." He stared at the ceiling, fondly reminiscing. "But the vet didn't find any paper or plastic in his stomach. He must have passed it all. Quite the garbage disposal, that pup."

"Well," Cleo started, waltzing into the kitchen and dabbing at her shoulder with a white hand towel, "the scarring could be straighter." She pulled her hair over her shoulder and examined the faint line. "But it looks much better than Ben's. For that, I thank you, Frankie."

I nodded with my eyes down, still ashamed and afraid at my reaction to her blood. I hadn't told Ben; he had been too preoccupied tending to Cleo and supporting my efforts. It took over twenty minutes to close the wound completely, which wasn't surprising considering that Patrick nearly amputated the woman. And once it was finished, Ben had thrown Cleo's arm over his shoulder, leading her to a guest bath to get cleaned up. I hadn't felt jealous. I was busy licking the red stain from my hands.

My lizard brain took over; I hadn't given it a second thought.

Or even a first thought. By the time I had any control over myself, the blood was gone.

"I love the scar, myself," Ben complimented, gathering the books from Patrick's library into a cardboard box he found folded in the garage. "Normally, your skin is so boring."

"What a refreshing change that is to hear," Cleo said with a grin of her own.

~~~

CLEO OFFERED to drive us back to Aspen Ridge. She said she felt fine and wouldn't hear of any of our concerns. I thought she might want to focus on something else for a while, but I would never say that aloud. She didn't want to discuss Patrick's attack.

"I never saw a car following behind us," Cleo professed to our otherwise silent car as we neared the base of the mountain. I'd also been considering the identity of tonight's perpetrator, and I was sure we all had a good hunch. "They weren't targeting Patrick," she furrowed her brow in concentration. "You were both in the kitchen?" Her tone was marginally too innocent. She appraised Ben's freshly healed eye a little too closely.

"I didn't see anything outside," Ben replied honestly from the passenger seat. I blushed, remembering his mouth on mine. Yes, we were both in the kitchen. No, we didn't see anything outside.

Cleo tapped her fingers on the steering wheel, ruminating. "The vampire?"

"Are we on any other hit lists?" Ben asked, rubbing his hair, unhappy with its growth.

"But did she know about Patrick? Why shatter a window? To scare you?" She spoke more to herself than the two of us. Which didn't matter one bit—we didn't have the answers. I had been confused about Jessamae's intentions as well. If they weren't to kill me, then why follow? The mystery intrigued me. And as unsettling as the concept was ... *she* intrigued me. The shame was there somewhere, but I couldn't dig deep enough to sink in it. Not yet.

"Stop the car," Ben demanded.

Cleo hit the brakes, kicking us all forward. Ben hopped from his seat, and I heard splashing under his feet. We were parked on top of the small creek we had crossed to get to Patrick's mountainside estate. I couldn't see Ben clearly by the dim lights inside the car, but he bent towards the water before swinging back through his door. He held a small, smooth rock that he'd taken from the river. "Thank you, m'lady," he told Cleo before she began driving again.

"We have more to do tonight. Stop at a grocery store on the way back. Jim's will be closed, so find something on the way," Ben instructed.

We soon pulled into the parking lot of a Target near the freeway. He turned around in his seat, his face appearing between the headrests. "Frankie, would you please buy a six-pack of that nasty shit you like to drink? Red Star?"

"Gold Star," I corrected with an indignant scowl. "But we're finally doing something I want to do. So I will." I popped the handle, stomped my blood-soaked boots on the asphalt, and banged the rusty door shut. I ignored Ben's, "Do you need any cash?" and marched inside.

$5.89 for a sixer. I wished I could steal them as easily as I had from Jim's, but thought it would tip my moral scale even further on the side of evil after my behavior this evening.

Then I did myself one better. My feet were wet with sweat inside my boots. All my socks had been dirty, and my naked feet were hot and stinking. On a sudden whim, I stopped in the women's intimates section and picked up six pairs of black ankle socks before hurrying to the self-checkout.

I glimpsed at myself in the security camera and was once again startled. My hair had grown. A lot. Maybe six inches. It appeared blonder than ever, golden with pink hues. The sheen of my curls was noticeable, even in the low-resolution security feed. I remembered Ben's healthy radiance at Patrick's, the hair growth. Had our kissing triggered this? And even the sporadic touching, to a lesser extent, before that?

"Damn me," I mumbled, my steps unsteady. We should have never kissed. I had lost myself completely in the feel of Ben, in the heat. I remembered wanting to eat him. And after my psychotic episode with Cleo's blood, I reevaluated that urge with self-hatred.

What if Ben felt the same about me? He had described my smallest touches as equitable to a wellness spa yesterday. Were his feelings—I groaned inwardly at the word—*romantic*? Or was he getting off on my touch in more ways than one?

11

BEN OPENED his door and was out of the car before we had properly stopped. I heard him knocking around in the kitchen from the front yard. Inside, as I rounded the arch, he fished a steak knife and a serving spoon out of a drawer, and a large blue salad bowl from beside the stove. He plopped his odd river rock in the bowl and rushed out back, leaving the screen door open for Cleo and me.

He placed the giant bowl on the ground near his herb garden with the rock inside it. He walked carefully through his herbs, trailing his fingers along their aromatic leaves. Cleo and I watched him, perplexed. At least, *I* was perplexed. Reading Cleo was like reading Latin—outside of *coitus*, that is.

Ben eventually paused with a sad droop to his shoulders. He crouched down and tugged at the base of a pokey-looking shrub, coming away with a long stem of needles dangling soil from its hair-like roots. He wove through the proud rows of vegetation and pulled up a second root, a fat-leafed plant with little yellow bulbs. I smelled the rich soil from here.

He slipped back inside, nearly at a sprint, leaving us standing useless in the dark, but was back in a flash. Cradled in his arms were several fat candles, and in his hand was a small white box, the kind you would keep a necklace in. He placed the candles around the yard, and I felt a pang of apprehension at the idea of fire on such dry grass.

Ben placed the biggest candles at four evenly spaced points around the bowl, a diamond formation. "Cleo, would you please bring out an item of clothing?"

Cleo shifted from foot to foot at his request. "Couldn't I bring out a hairbrush instead?"

"Only if you love it."

Cleo groaned at his bizarre instruction and dragged herself through the screen door.

"And Frank. Honey. Baby!" he crooned. "You have the hardest job of all." He held his hands together in prayer, the herbs nestled between them.

"Of course, I do. Should I sit down for this?"

"No, you really shouldn't. We need you to run, Princess. Enough to work up a sweat."

I was at a loss for words, sputtering like a goldfish. "Now I know you're joking."

"I'm actually not." He squished his face in an apologetic expression. "It's just until you work up a sweat, enough to collect in this." He wedged a mashed paper cup from his pocket, what dentists hand you before you spit. The wax of the rim was peeling away, and the body was contorted with creases. It had clearly been used.

"Have you done this before?"

"Once or twice. Waste not." He kneeled behind one cream-colored candle and extracted the copper lighter I'd always seen on his nightstand. "Better get moving, Frank. We'll get everything else prepped."

"Uuuuuuuggghhhhhh!" I wailed as I began to jog.

"Do you want to cry instead!" Ben offered from the diamond of candles.

I ran in a circle around the property, passing his grass, his herbs, his car, his porch, until I saw him again. "I might cry anyway!"

But in truth, my breathing wasn't as labored as I'd come to expect. My knees didn't even pop with the impact of my feet. "I could run all night." I huffed to myself over my bouncing stride. "Or at least all hour."

That wasn't necessary in this heat, however. After four laps, I felt a trail of sweat dangle perilously from my chin. I held the cup to my jaw and kept running. As I passed our preparation center, I saw that every candle was now lit, with the bowl, my beer, Cleo, and Ben at their center. As I ran to their side, I heard them snigger together at the cup-chin-run chore into which I'd been forced. "Laugh it up!" I shouted. "I'll remember this next time Patrick takes a piece out of you!"

I finished my lap and hustled to the circle, taking the cup from my face. It looked to be half an inch of my juice.

I lifted my lip as I approached the peanut gallery. "Having fun over here?"

"Nothing but," Ben drawled with a simper. "Ready? Stand over here." He guided me to his left, Cleo's right. "Here we go."

He knelt and indicated we should do the same. "A stone from beneath running water," he gestured to the river stone at the bottom of the bowl. He then twisted his torso and reached behind him. "Rosemary and bay." He placed the long green growths into the bowl, bending them, and wincing while doing so, to fit within the dish.

Ben sat back on his butt, pulling his feet out in front of him. He retrieved his steak knife from its resting place in the grass beside him. He took off the rubber flip-flops he'd worn that day, and with a nasty zeal, cut a deep lesion into the sole of his foot. I gulped at the sight. It was less unexpected than it used to be, but still more than I wanted. The knife left a gnarled fringe to his skin.

He perched his dripping foot over the edge of the bowl, his blood flowed black in the fickle light.

"Okay, Frankie, will you please empty one of your beers into the bowl?" he asked. "You can have the other five."

I didn't smile. He wasn't being funny, but I did as I was asked. The crack of the tab under my fingers was loud. I poured. The foam fizzed enthusiastically. Its yeasty funk hit my nose and I felt the powerful urge to puke. The last time I drank the stuff was still such a recent and pungent memory. My mouth filled with saliva, and I swallowed it back.

"Now drink one," Ben urged.

"What?" I blurted, fearing he had read my mind.

"Drink one of the beers."

I, again, did as I was asked, appeased that I could get the swell of spit out of my mouth. Ben smiled at my compliance. I had chugged back nearly half the can, forgetting the vomit sensation and enjoying the taste.

"Now spit," Ben directed.

"What?"

"It has to be a personal sacrifice. I know how much you love that shit."

I grumbled waspishly but did as he said, hocking a big beer-soaked loogie into the bowl.

"Give me the rest." He held his hand out.

"Why? I did what you said."

"I also know how much you hate to share."

I threw the almost-empty at him but he caught it easily. "So annoying," I muttered, suspecting he had seen my throw before-hand. Ben swirled the Gold Star around his mouth before spit-ting it in the bowl and tossing the empty aside.

"Terrible," he croaked through the foam.

I burped with my mouth closed and earned a disgruntled look from Ben. "My mouth was closed!"

"Dump your sweat into the bowl, please."

I splashed my sweat into the bowl, giving the little cup a good shake, and hurled the garbage across the yard. "You're welcome."

Ben ignored me. "Cleo, would you please take this," he handed her the knife, "and this," he gave her a bright yellow stretch of fabric, "and cut it to pieces?"

She didn't hesitate, and with her nimble fingers, she had the blouse in scraps atop the frothy mixture in less than a minute. "Thank you, Cleo," Ben said with a sad smile. "Now cry."

My incredulous eyes shifted from Ben to Cleo, but Cleo would not be perturbed. She had such control of her body, it seemed she could use it in any way and on command. Her eyes immediately flooded with anguished tears, and it took all my restraint not to cross the small space and hold her to my chest. She positioned her fingers under her lashes, soaking them in saltwater, and then dipped her hands into the bowl at our feet. She remained taciturn, and I sensed her resentment. Cleo was not a crier.

I began to wonder if her vivacious introduction to me was anything more than bait, if it were also a tool for her use, like her body. Despite the bubbly and warm masquerade she put on— was it only yesterday?—when we'd met, she now struck me as pensive, austere, and sharp. With a pinch of sarcasm. I felt a smile pull my mouth.

Cleo lifted her hands from the mixture in the bowl and cleaned the residue off her skin with her tongue. My smile was dashed, and I curled my lip in revulsion. I couldn't knock the blood-licking after my performance tonight … but my spit had been viscous.

When I tore my eyes away from that freak show, Ben held the small white box in his lap, his foot still suspended over the concoction. I felt a bullet train sort of dread as he lifted the box's lid. "Let's all thank Daniel for this baby blue," Ben said as he tipped the gift delicately, rolling the succulent organ out of the cotton bedding and onto his palm. It looked soft, like a poached egg, and if it really was blue, I couldn't discern it. I only saw pink.

Ben slid the eyeball and its reaching bubblegum veins into the bowl. The orb bobbed for a moment before it sank below the foul brown froth. "The third eye," he said.

"Now, everyone, put your feet in the bowl." Learning to act without hesitation, I wrenched the sweltering boots off my rank feet.

"Our sacrifice had to be personal in order to use the third eye.

We each sacrificed a small happiness as well as our sweat," he nodded to me, "our blood," he paused, "and our tears," he bent his head solemnly toward Cleo. "What we're hoping to find is the white-haired witch. My sight is limited, and by using the third eye, we will see the world as she did in the days before she killed Pamela Hughes." His mouth mangled in hatred. It was unreal to see that expression on Ben's face, which had always rested in a smile.

Cleo removed her sandals from her manicured toes as I wiggled my newly freed piggies in the warm air. I timidly dunked them into the brew, terror-stricken at the possibility of squishing the looming eye underneath. Ben, always the gentleman, tucked his feet under mine and pressed the eyeball to the bottom of the bowl. Cleo then stacked her toes on top. The bubbles flattened out, and our stacked feet became visible through the russet red haze of the mixture.

Ben fell backward and hit the grass with a soft thud. Cleo fell in succession before I caught up and did the same. The stars were dazzling.

We waited. I wouldn't permit myself to think this would fail. I had seen real magic tonight. This would work.

And it did. The stars faded and moved as though they were fireflies, blinking in and out of existence. Then I was blinded. I wanted to sit up at the sudden nothingness before my eyes, but held my pose. Before I could suck in a breath, a swirl of images blended together in my mind like a dream. The colors were too bright, as if the contrast was turned up on a television set.

I WAS SURROUNDED by aspen trees, their sharp smell tingled pleasantly in my nose. I raised my strong, tanned hands to stroke the trunks adoringly. An ugly weed climbed the roots of one of my trees. It only took the lightest of touches to shrivel it back down to the earth.

It was night, the moon hung loyal and heavy in the blue sky, but I could see the details of the pale-barked trees as if it were high-noon.

I was on a path, headed for something unknown. After I'd arrived in the West, Las Vegas, months ago, I had unconsciously drifted in this direction, seeking it out. As I got closer, within the state lines, the lure became strong and undeniable. It felt wrong when I strayed too far from it. And though I did not know the thing I was hunting for yet, here I was.

I broke through the veil of trees and came upon a house. It was a small brick dwelling with peeling shutters and cloudy windows at the edge of this scattered township. The lawn was dead under the moon's rays. I stretched joyfully beneath them. My prize was inside these walls, I could sense it. The magnetic pull shook inside me.

I approached windows that were obscured with curtains. Window after window, blocked. I circled the building until I felt it. It was a woman, fresh, a blindingly bright life. She was on the other side of the wall. She had magic in her, it was mirrored in myself. Such vibrancy she had tucked into her skin! And her shell was fracturing, like magma destined to burst from its crust.

I then sensed a second life in the home. Older, withering. Mortal. I resisted approaching the girl now, while there was a second life to consider.

I stayed near her overnight and listened to her breathing change as she awoke. She remained still as the sun rose for quite some time. She was forcing her vitality back, trapping it within her like a tiger in a cage.

The old mortal padded across the house to her room several times. I tracked her steps to the only unobscured window in the house, a television room. I watched her sit and shake her head, disappointed.

The woman, almost a girl, eventually got up from her bed.

Her feet dragged beneath her. She didn't want to leave her room. The old one mumbled to herself after she left, using words like "lazy" and "ungrateful."

I hurried to follow the trapped woman with rose-colored hair along the streets of her town. She seemed a nervous little spring blossom, looking around herself with unease regularly. I stayed within the Creeping Foxtail growing along the road, bending low and willing my steps to be silent. She hardly acknowledged the life growing around her.

She shuffled unhappily into a grocery store, Jim's Grocery, whose name matched the logo on her unflattering shirt. I waited a long time for her to leave again, and grew anxious when she didn't. Surely, she wouldn't spend all day in this place that she hated. After several hours, I walked in to check on her. It didn't take me long to track her down, even as wilted her energy.

She moved like the dead, less than a specter—she lacked the passion specters embodied. She swept the floors around her, numb to her own existence. She performed numerous asinine tasks—stocking cans, scanning juice cartons—as if she were nothing more than her hands. I feared for her. Watching her suffer, deprived of life, was like watching myself suffer. I ached for such waste, and I would not stand helpless while something so precious was thrown away.

I walked her home that evening from far back in the grass. She carried brightly colored snacks in her arms. I fretted over her. I fretted over her aloneness.

A stray dog crawled out from beneath a car as the sun set, finally finding relief from the heat. The animal was hungry, nearly starved. It stalked behind the woman in desperation. I could not allow her to be harmed, not when I was so close. The dog followed the pavement, legs bent low, avoiding me and my scent. I crept in on its heels. Once I was close enough from my cover under the Foxtail, I leapt. It didn't have time to cry out. I drained it efficiently and silently. I drained it of everything, watched as it shriveled, heard the crackle of it crumbling in on itself, its innards desiccating. This would avoid attracting more animals to her daily route.

She waited a long time to enter her home after she reached it. The relative inside made her uncomfortable in her own skin, such a disgrace it was. I had never felt such vitality in a witch or such a powerful link to one. Her magic pushed against her delicate shields like the bud of a rose, the buds of a thousand roses, in spring. Like fruit. She needed me as much as I needed her.

The girl hurried past her roommate, striving to avoid contact or conversation. "Hello to you too, young lady," the woman croaked like a raven. "I see what's in your hands, don't hide it from me. You're always hiding from me." Anger flared in my blood as I watched from the window. "You need more vegetables. Why don't you ever bring vegetables home from the store?" She swung a fraying flyswatter at a flurry of black bugs.

"I'll bring something else home tomorrow, okay?"

"Something healthy. You don't exercise enough to eat that junk. Why don't you ever exercise? Your mother was always so slim, and she made all her meals herself. Organic. How come you never buy anything organic?" She resented the young woman's curves, was probably jealous of them. The woman was crackly, pointy, like a praying mantis. But the woman clearly felt insecure at the woman's words, tugging at her clothes.

The girl turned and headed to the back of the house. "I won't bring junk home tomorrow. I'm tired … grandma." The word sounded unnatural from her lips. "I'm going to lay down."

So, it was the grandmother. I couldn't fathom the disdain with which she spoke to the daughter of her child. She frightened the young woman, forced her to hide alone in her room, in her shell. Her magic would never fully develop under this guardian, keeping her imprisoned.

It wasn't a choice—I would help her. I didn't want her to be in the house when I took the old woman. She didn't need to see that just yet. She was still green. I would come back after she had a moment alone, she seemed to enjoy those. Then I would explain to her what she was, what I was. I would teach her how to be. She would never have her light diminished with me.

Morning came both too soon and too late. The girl's breathing shallowed as she woke. She went through the same motions she had the day before: toilet, sink, dress, door.

"Good morning, Francesca," the grandmother snapped. Francesca, a fitting name for this spark.

"Morning, Pamela," she returned weakly. I could see her fading through the grimy window, fire stirred in me like a cobra.

"Are you leaving? You haven't eaten anything." She swung her flyswatter around like a sword.

"I'm not hungry." Both Francesca and I were dreading another speech on her chosen eating habits. But I hadn't heard her eat anything but a few chips the night before. She was skipping meals.

"Remember what we talked about last night, eat something healthy. If you're just going to rot in your room every day, then you need fewer calories." My breathing spiked. I'd only endured this woman for two days. Insufferable.

The grandmother only spoke to Francesca when she was leaving or entering. Though she harassed and complained, she was pushing her to stay hidden away behind her door.

Francesca showed a strained smile to her grandmother and fled, only allowing herself a single scowl of dislike before leaving. It wasn't the reaction I knew she was eager to release. There was a rage in her that I desired to see, so much about her was volcanic.

I stayed under cover until I couldn't see Francesca shrinking on the horizon any longer. Then I stretched towards her bedroom window. I struggled with it, but it eventually released with a sigh.

I moved with an unnatural swiftness, and only moments later I was in her dark bedroom. It was covered in dust, hidden under soiled clothes.

I moved noiselessly as I entered the hallway. Though I

despised this woman, Francesca's family didn't need to feel superfluous pain or fear. The grandmother stared at the TV, a permanent sneer etched on her sunken face as she swung absent-mindedly at the insects.

She took no notice of me. Instead she stared, empty, at a news report flashing on the screen. I went to her. I leaned over the back of the couch, placing my hands on either side of her face. There wasn't much left in this one anyway, and I didn't feel sorry. I felt her drain under my fingers as if she were running away. Her eyes remained open, but they saw nothing more.

12

MY SIGHT CAME BACK GRADUALLY, a cloud in the wind. The candles had burned down into weakly shimmering puddles; we had obviously been watching Jessamae for hours. I splayed my hands in front of me, reacquainting myself with my light skin and clumsy fingers. I let memories and sensations from my own past wash over me, getting comfortable in my body again.

Feeling Jessamae's emotions and experiencing her thoughts was surreal. I'd expected to watch her as a bystander, but of course, there were no hidden cameras, as Ben said, and we hadn't crafted a time-travel elixir. Still, her private thoughts were an invasive, violating, fascinating surprise.

My power, of course, she recognized days ago, months even. But she *saw me*, who I was, and she—somehow—cared for me. Pamela's murder proved that, in an unnatural way.

But my grandmother wasn't a danger to me, her disdain for me aside, and Jessamae knew it. She killed Pamela for me, and therefore ultimately, for her. She had thrown me into this new world with gentle killer's hands.

Anger filled me, teeth to toes. I had already forgiven Ben for his lies, but that didn't change the fact that he had choreographed our entire friendship, altering my life for that vision of his. Now Jessamae felt she had some magical stake on me, seeing me as her protégé that she could mold. How many people would decide they were entitled to my future?

I looked at the other anchors of the triangle. Cleo had her head in her hands, bent forward over her knees. She didn't seem saddened, but that she was concentrating very, very hard. Ben, however, was positively fuming. His mouth twitched as if he wanted to yell at something somewhere. His eyebrows pushed tightly together over his incandescent glare. "A lot of good that did us!" he shouted, unable to restrain himself. "She killed Gran, but why did she follow you? We didn't learn a goddamn thing!" He pitched the caustic bowl into the side of the house, splattering the stew onto his windows and patio furniture.

"Jesus, Benny! She did it to—I don't know—unleash my magic! You don't need to throw that shit everywhere." The liquid was strangely clear on the walls but smelled vile.

"How do you know that?" Cleo's question was quiet.

I squinted at her in the dark. Her honey eyes were serious.

She didn't know. In front of me, Ben appeared the same, except enraged. Both of them didn't know. What had I done? How could I have been buried so deeply within her, just me? This wouldn't go over well, not at all.

"It's just, you know, what she saw. Pamela was ... unpleasant. I wouldn't leave my room when she was around. Jessamae,"—their heads twitched like hunting dogs' at the name —"the witch, the vampire," I sputtered. "She didn't seem to like it. I mean, did you like it?"

The connection between Jessamae and I, it felt like a bad thing. I was ashamed of it.

Ben continued to glower, unconvinced, but Cleo tipped her head in consideration. "She did leave you alive. It's possible she crossed your path, sensing another witch, and took a shine to you, I suppose." Her full mouth puckered in concentration. "Although, it still feels a bit outlandish to purely be coincidence. We can agree she isn't looking to hurt you. I think. For now, at least."

"We can't agree on that," Ben barked. "She killed an innocent woman on a whim. Pamela was a horror show, but she didn't deserve to die for it. We can't determine the witch's intentions because killing is second nature for her!" His features deflated like an air mattress as he looked at me. "It's not enough. She could change her mind and drain you on impulse."

Regardless of what I gleaned from Jessamae's recent thoughts, I couldn't argue with him. But Ben must have seen how she touched me in my room—at the memory I fidgeted uncomfortably—and Jessamae had been excited to see me. She actually seemed less inclined to hurt me than most acquaintances.

Ben was absorbed, watching the fleet of expressions cross my face. He waited it out with weary eyes. "Are you alright, Frank? I know that you and Pams weren't exactly besties but that couldn't have been easy to watch."

"I'm fine," I said offhandedly. In truth, seeing Pamela through Jessamae's perspective had only expanded the distance I felt toward her and her death. A flare of shame swelled knowing they'd all heard exactly what Pamela thought of me. My habits, my choices, even my weight, she had used them to make me feel so much lesser. I wished the others hadn't seen that.

I turned to Cleo to avert Ben's scrutiny, but she was gone, leaving nothing but a round imprint in the dry grass. I couldn't blame her. I had dragged her through another day that felt two weeks long.

I stood without looking at Ben. There was too much embarrassment reddening my skin.

First, I practically suck his tongue out of his face. Then he sees how weak I was around my harpy of a grandmother. Finish off with his witness to Jessamae's intense fixation, which he couldn't have ignored even without her inner monologue.

I plodded, exhausted, to the couch that had become my personal bedroom. I wasn't sure if I would ever sleep in my twin bed again. Was I expected to sleep in Pamela's starched sheets? The thought made me sick.

I fluffed my pillow and huddled into Ben's gray comforter. It was late, essentially morning. I thought I might feel a little less humiliated once we slept off all this excitement.

SOMETHING WOKE ME SUDDENLY. My heart went wild, I flipped my head around frantically to find the disturbance. It was impossibly dark in the house. I saw tall menacing shapes throughout the shadowed corners of the room. I stared without blinking until my strained eyes adjusted to the darkness and the shapes fled. Ben was swaddled in his sheet, snoring softly. I was accustomed to that sound; he hadn't woken me.

I didn't want to leave the safety of my couch, but I couldn't see anything amiss in the living room. I searched the kitchen from my bed for something out of place. I saw the muted green glow emanating from the digital clock on the stove. It gleamed against the fridge and the porcelain of the sink. Nothing. I looked down the hall for any sign of Cleo. The dark sat in total stillness. I told myself I'd been having a bad dream, but the hairs on the back of my neck prickled against my flesh and my heart refused to slow. I folded myself up onto my knees silently and craned my neck around the obstructed corners of the room. Leaning my body far off the sofa, I peeked out Ben's screen door and nearly jumped out of my skin.

Eyes. Those phantom eyes were right outside the door, watching me, gaping at me. They glowed in the night like water under the moon. Her hands pressed against the door on either side of her, hard. Her fingertips flattened out from the pressure. Our stares locked and she lifted her lips in that bone-chilling smile. I was staring into the mouth of a wolf. She leaned forward, her breath fogging up the glass in big steamy circles. She looked deranged. I had feared her during the day, in my bedroom. She had been alien and predatory. But in the dark, under the faint light of the crescent moon, she was the most formidable and sinister thing I'd ever seen.

My breathing hitched. I was terrified she would break the door under her hands, would walk into this room, those eyes never leaving my face. But the door wasn't what stopped her; she could come in. Eventually, she would come in.

A lock of my hair lifted gently into the air. It seemed to hover and spin around my head. I looked back at Jessamae. Her hand had left the glass and was twirling around whimsically near her face.

She was playing with my hair. Through the space between us, she was playing with my hair.

She touched her fingertips back to the glass, and I felt them on my cheek. They were warm and rough against me, unmistakably there. Jessamae closed her hand delicately into a fist and stepped away from the door. She stared at my terrified expression for just another moment before she ran off, back to the forest.

THE SUNLIGHT SHINING red on my eyelids was both magnificent and cruel. It meant that I had finally drifted into a dreamless sleep after seeing my visitor, and there was a sense of safety under the sun. As illusionary as it was. Last night's tequila, however, made the sunshine quite painful.

I smelled the comforting aroma of coffee and opened my eyes. The mug was inches from me on the corner of Ben's coffee table. I sat up without a sound, disappointed in the lack of popping in my joints, and reached for the cup gratefully. It had cooled, but was almost warm in my throat. There was a folded slip of lined notebook paper under the mug.

I had to go to work. Please stay with Cleo until I get back. Dinner @ 6:00

I took another gulp of coffee—even cooled it was excellent, made exactly as I liked it.

In all the hullaballoo, I had forgotten Ben had to make a living. That *I* had to make a living. I hadn't talked to Scott all weekend. The burial for Pamela was tomorrow morning, I would call him after, or the next day. I needed to grow up, go home, and clean out just about everything. But I didn't want to leave my friends just yet. They were the only reason Jessamae was hesitating.

The image of her at the door last night was so bedeviling that it should have been a nightmare. But I remembered her rough skin on my cheek as though she were still here. I remembered the cold sweat on my face and the thump of my heart. I remembered enduring the painful need to pee all night because I was too afraid to leave my blankets. I jumped off the couch now and ran to the bathroom.

Once my hair was detangled—mostly, its length had become unmanageable—and my teeth were brushed—I skipped the shower today, my skin was tight and dry from being so clean—I sat at the dining room table with a second cup of coffee and the books we had taken from Patrick's the night before. I know I had been tipsy, more than tipsy, but how I didn't notice there were only three books to examine was unfathomable. We had two on restoration, and one on eradication—Jessamae's specialty. I added my grandmother's journal to the pile, prepared to have a study session, hoping that one day I could open the secondhand books I'd bought at the store.

Before I could flip to the first page, Cleo stepped elegantly into the room in a silk robe with her luscious hair on top of her head. She waved at me half-heartedly before pouring herself some coffee. She sat at the table with me, seeming crabbier than I usually was in the morning. She slid one of the restoration books towards herself and began flipping pages without a word. I enjoyed her company.

The other restoration manuscript was a memoir, written by someone like me between 1902 and 1911. His name was Samuel C. Foster, and he was in his forties when he discovered what he was. His wife had died in a hurricane along the Texas coast, and soon afterward, he cut off two of his toes in a woodworking accident. Before he even made it to a doctor, he found that the wounds had closed. Within another two hours, two stubs began growing out of his foot. By nightfall, he had two new squirmy toes.

He performed various self-mutilations before he deemed it his own prowess and not a miracle, at one point pulling out eight of his teeth and watching as they each grew back through his gums. He opened a private church focused on healing the ill and the disabled, in which he was referred to simply as "The Doctor." He placed his hands on his patients and within twenty-four hours, their ailments were entirely cured. "I've never known that to lose my love, my wife Teresa, that I would gain such purpose! I am almost moved to thank her for passing on from this life. She gave me mine," he wrote in 1906.

His delight didn't last. He was hosting nightly sermons, and by 1908, he began to change. He felt exhausted after each "treatment." He began to show signs of rapid aging: wrinkles, soft bones, aches and pains. His hair fell out the year after that, then his teeth. They never grew back.

"All along, I was giving my life to my patients. They each will live on, long after me, with pieces of myself within them. They suckled at me, mewling kittens, until I was empty. Nevertheless, as I lay in my home and breathe my last breaths, I regret nothing." 1911.

What a disturbing image on which to end. I was told everyone's affinity worked a little differently, but that didn't mean that I couldn't also be giving my vitality away in my magic. Samuel had uncovered what he was in his forties and died after another decade. I could be dead by my mid-thirties. If I ever started feeling drowsy after a spell, then no more playing doctor.

Cleo held her steaming mug in both hands, only a few pages left of her manuscript. As she reached the end, she finally spoke. "Okay, so this is written as a study performed by the head of a coven who had a healer in her group." Cleo put her coffee down and flipped back to the front of the book. She held a single page up for inspection. "There's no date, but it was written with a typewriter, so it was within the 19th or 20th century." We had a history buff over here.

"The leader was a dragon, meaning she could naturally produce and control fire, fascinating witches, dragons, and she observed the behavior of her group members and their magical progression. The healer—though she always refers to him as such—doesn't sound like a healer at all. She found that when he touched the wounded or the ill, he became more powerful. While many aged around him—," she paused and looked up to me, "a witch's lifespan is often longer than a mortal's, so who knows for how long," she turned back to the book, "—he remained suspended in time as a young man. He was feeding off the pain and the sickness of others. So rather than healing, he was taking their pain into himself. It's unusual, but his body seemed to thrive on it.

"Her final hypothesis was more of a hunch, but she believed that the pain was affecting his mind. Her coven was having severe accidents too often, their skin hanging open after reporting small falls. The man would, of course, steal their wounds, and inevitably get stronger. He was expelled from the family, and she never tracked him down. It sounds like she feared him and with good reason."

She shut the book with theatrical timing that was fitting for such a tale. I gave her a brief synopsis of Samuel's stint as The Doctor. Both examples of what I could become weren't all that attractive to me. Die young or become a third-party pain junkie.

Cleo noticed my conflicted expression. "It's too soon to tell in either case, but I don't think you'll end up like either of these men, okay? We need to learn more about what is happening to your body when you heal, then we can come up with a game plan." She assessed the other two books across the table. "Why don't we take a break? I could use some sun, and you could use some practice."

I pictured Jessamae's eyes shining in the darkness and shivered. "I can multitask," I insisted, and I brought the books outside with me.

Cleo stretched out like a flower in the sun, a smile playing softly on her face. I sat in the grass with my coffee to one side of me and the books to the other. My leg was striped in small, dried scabs from the cuts I made last night. I wrapped my hands around them and tried very hard to concentrate. I closed my eyes and pushed on the meat of my calf, but time and time again, the scabs stubbornly remained. I threw my head back in exasperation.

"It's healing. You may think it's slow, but you're healing much more rapidly than anyone else would be," Cleo said, her face skyward.

"It's my confidence. You guys keep telling me about my untapped potential."

"Maybe, but as much as I loathe to say it," she groaned emphatically. "I think Patrick is right about healing yourself. But even if he is wrong, your hand clearly isn't helping." She noted my vexed expression. "No offense."

I shit-talked under my breath about know-it-all pirate killers.

The stories about sirens seemed fairly spot on after getting to know Cleo. She embodied enchantment. Even knowing what she was, I doubted I could fight her seductive spell.

I replayed the healer horror stories from Patrick's books. I couldn't think of a legend to fit the healer accounts, nothing like the legends of sirens, or dragons. Or even oracles, like Ben. Probably because the storytellers in a healer's scenario, the humans crafting the legend had nothing to fear from people like me. If they knew what I could do, I'd grow to fear *them*. Greedy things, people.

I squinted at the sky. It would be hot later, but cooler than it was yesterday. The idea lifted my spirits. I thought of Ben working, wherever he was. At least he wouldn't have to be as sweaty in those stiff painter's pants of his today.

What we did last night was the best kiss I'd had and the worst mistake I could make. Thinking of him between my legs made my stomach clench. Now I would always know what he could be doing to me if I let him. Did he think my lips were too dry? Too rough? Did I have bad breath or sticky spit? I put my arm to my mouth to test the texture of my lips. Soft.

Sensing prying eyes, I turned to catch Cleo watching me with a smirk.

I swiped a book from the pile beside me to appear busy. As I flipped random pages, I picked out my mother's name near the center. This was Pamela's journal. I turned back to the beginning to start the first journal entry with general disinterest.

For several months, each passage held similar motifs. Beth ignored Pamela at Costco—she was cut from the Christmas card list. Tracy had gotten a scandalous divorce; the whorish woman was gunning for her husband's money … her husband of thirty-five years. Really playing the long game, Tracy. Pamela feared she might have a mouse in the house. This is the focal point of her life for a long string of days. Blah, blah, blah. Yadda, yadda, yadda.

I stopped and restarted a passage written on April 3rd two years ago. She wrote of me.

That man was in Aspen Ridge. Andrew, or Alan. It's practically a sin to speak of him in this family. Ridiculous! I don't see what all the fuss is about. I hope he'll be able to find that girl in the city. If I had her address, I would give it to him myself. He wants to see Francesca, and he absolutely should. Look what's become of that girl without the proper influence of a father.

13

MY MOTHER LIED TO ME. My entire life she had been lying to me. The whole secrecy and betrayal brigade that had been beating me to death over the last few days was getting old.

My father was interested in knowing me, he'd come to visit, soon after my twenty-first birthday. He knew that much about me, it seemed. And she'd sent him away, told him I'd run off, probably, and that either she didn't want him to find me, or she didn't know where I'd gone. If so, that hadn't been true—she'd helped me move.

And Pamela had been told never to speak of him, she had never uttered a word about him to me, this Andrew or Alan. As much as she thought I needed the influence of a father, she must have felt some satisfaction at withholding the information. Otherwise, why not say something after my mom's accident? It wasn't loyalty holding her back. The concept didn't align with Pamela.

Cleo asked, "Find something riveting in that diary? A garden party, perhaps?"

I didn't want to share this with anyone yet. My future seemed to belong to so many people, my past should stay mine for a little while longer. "A lot of excitement over a possible rodent situation. I hope the edge of your seat is comfortable."

She gave a subdued little chuckle. This was the most fun I'd seen her have since I met her.

That my father existed somewhere did not change my current predicament. I needed practice. I needed to be strong. Then once everything got settled, though I wasn't sure how that would happen just yet, maybe I could research Andrew. Or Alan. I shut the book.

Cleo sat up in her chair. "Move over."

"Huh?" I grunted.

"Move over." She stood above me, her face entirely in shadow.

I had changed into an oversized t-shirt and some boxer shorts that morning, my knees and shins had reddened in the sun. I rolled over onto my side, too confused to argue.

Where my calves and heels had rested in the yellowed grass was now flooded with green. Unlike the surrounding lawn, these odd spots of grass were soft and long and lush.

"How am I doing this?" I shouted. "Why do I have to focus sometimes and others it happens without even trying?"

Cleo folded herself beside me with dignity. "First, I would suggest that some tasks are more difficult than others so they naturally would require more work." She side-eyed me like I should have known that already. "Second, let's consider what we know you've done. Ben's hand, the park flower, Ben's eye." She, again, gave me the side-eye. "My shoulder, and the grass. Okay. What were you feeling or thinking while healing Ben's hand?"

I scrunched my face in thought and stared stupidly into the sun. "Uh, I was sort of panicking. Then Ben held my hand over his hand." I held my fists up to illustrate. "And he helped me breathe."

"You were focused on Ben?"

"Mostly."

"And what about the flower?"

I ran my hand through the stiff grass beside me. "I was thinking about my mom." As I said it, the memories rushed back in a waterfall. I felt the grass soften under my skin.

Cleo noticed the change and watched my hand sway over the ground. "Ben's eye?" She kept her stare on my hand, but her eyebrows peaked. "Focus on Ben?"

I nodded, afraid to speak. "And Ben helped me through the

work on your shoulder. He was encouraging me most of the time." I didn't mention the surge I'd gotten from Cleo's blood on my tongue, but it had been electrifying. A large patch of grass had grown entirely green now, as I reminisced about it all.

"Mmhmm …" She eyed the lawn's evolution. "Well at the very least, it seems like Ben helps you concentrate, or he relaxes you if you're upset. He makes you happy," she paused, "something like that. Try holding him, or your mom, in your mind while you work."

I tickled the brown patches lightly, watching them green.

"How about we try working with the elements?" Cleo suggested. "The whole lawn will take a lifetime and it won't last the week anyway."

She stood tall on her long umber legs and took off into the house. As Ben did last night, she returned with a candle. She set it on the patio table while she surveyed the porch and the surrounding plants. She paced along Ben's herb garden, her eyes sharp and low.

"Lose an earring?" I called.

Cleo straightened. "That's very funny, Francesca." I'd never seen less humor in a face. "I'm looking for a bug. An earwig or a spider."

"For?"

Her eyes popped and she bent swiftly at the waist. She strolled back to me with her hands cupped and held out from her body. "Here we go. You can pay for the magic with this," she beamed at me. "Come over to the table."

I moved nervously to her side. I did not care for live bugs, and I did not care for dead bugs.

She opened her hands like the claw in a prize dispenser. A chunky black beetle fell to his back, trapped on its shell on the table.

"Smash it, then we'll get to work."

"Of course," I sighed. My hand hovered timidly over the struggling insect.

Cleo urged, "Just do it."

"I am!"

I hesitated a second longer, then brought my fist down on the thing. It crunched like a pair of glasses underfoot.

"About time," Cleo growled. "Now, in a way, the elements are cognizant beings, and each has specific qualities to them. You give them an offering, as you just did, and attempt to channel them. The first step is to feel them around you, acknowledge them."

I suppressed an eye roll, knowing neither Cleo nor the elements would appreciate my sass. I closed my eyes and sent my feelers out.

I sensed the earth beneath me, the breeze across my face. There was some presence of water in the sky, I knew, though the feel of it was negligible. The elements surrounded me, cool and patient. But, unlike the first three, fire was difficult to hold. A lightning strike, evading me entirely.

I reached for the earth. The soil under me was solid, almost sinewy, veined with roots. Sensing its abundant growth beneath me was like taking a big breath or drinking a glass of water in the middle of the night. Its relief was subtle, twirling as it reached, blooming in my muscles. The air on my face was playful and amorphous, circling my head and lightening my weight on the soil.

"Now, light the candle," Cleo's voice interrupted me.

I opened my eyes and brought my attention to the wick, willing it to burn. Fire was hard to grasp, I couldn't sense its comfort like I could the earth and the air. I inhaled and attempted to find the fire, to feel its qualities. Hot. That was obvious. And it wasn't hard to channel heat out in the sun's rays. Hot, unpredictable, dangerous. Wildfires, bonfires, campfires, fireworks. Celebratory and deadly.

The fire reached out to pet my skin, and it excited me. Blood heated my cheeks and my breathing sped. Rather than try to hold it, I let it use me. Like a conduit, I invited the fire in, to burn through my incendiary nerve endings. It traveled through me, hot and fast. It was thrilling. The scald moved too quickly to hurt. The light sting was electric. I was struck.

The candle ignited.

I fell backward, bonking my head in the grass, luckily missing the cement. My skin tingled as I took in gulps of warm, dry air. All of this to light a single candle?

"It's an intimate experience," Cleo chirped happily. "The earth is my favorite. Fire can be very intense. It will be a lot harder for you in the house, just try to work with whatever is offered to you." She slapped one of my bare feet in camaraderie. I didn't move, still regulating my heartbeat. Cleo laughed at my exhausted bliss. "Maybe we should have started with water."

～

I PRACTICED with Cleo throughout the afternoon. I did like water quite a bit. It was tireless and strong. It tasted clean on my tongue and boosted my focus, like I had dosed myself with Adderall. I managed to fill a small plastic cup with water, indoors no less. Admittedly, I did struggle, as I often do. And there was a morbid pile of crushed insects on the counter to prove it.

"This is great," Cleo tittered, holding up the cup for display. "If Jessamae comes for you here, you can conjure a puddle under her feet. She'll slip and fall to her death."

My brows flattened, unamused. "I think I've made a lot of progress after a single weekend of trying."

"I'm just saying, I don't know why Ben is pushing so hard for you to build up your skills when they won't help against a witch like Jessamae, anyway," Cleo said, dumping the water down the sink. She was a blunt person, Cleo.

"Because you should never underestimate simplicity," Ben interjected, closing the front door and dropping his car keys on

133

the coffee table. I smelled the oily, chemical aroma of paint from the kitchen. "Look how successful Kraft Mac and Cheese became. Against all odds." He walked through the kitchen archway and kissed me on the back of my head. I blushed at the action. Then Ben took Cleo's hand in his and kissed her lightly on the knuckles. *Shit.*

"What have you two been up to today?" he asked as he walked back into the living room. "I didn't see any trouble."

Cleo updated him as she leaned against the archway. "Frankie made considerable progress harnessing the elements. Neither hide nor hair of Jessamae. But that doesn't mean she wasn't keeping an eye on us."

I doubted she had been anywhere near us today. Our link hadn't been thrumming as it had before when she was close. But, I rebutted, if she broke the window at Patrick's, I hadn't felt her then. Though I had been a little distracted at the time.

I didn't want Ben or Cleo to know how great an impact she had on me. I kept my mouth shut.

"Marvelous. Just let me shower and change, then we can go to dinner," he said. He rubbed the scruff growing on his chin before taking off his shirt and leaving the room.

His note said nothing about leaving the house. "Are we not eating here?" I asked his retreating form.

"Cleo might be eating here. I haven't asked about her plans," he called back.

"My plans are to order a pizza. I might even take a bath in Ben's very neglected bathtub. Thank god I can make my own bubbles." Cleo shook her head in resignation. "But we are in desperate need of a second car if we are going to be staying here much longer."

She was eating here by herself while Ben and I went elsewhere. I considered asking Cleo in that moment, while we were still alone, if anything had ever happened between her and Ben. If anything was still happening between them. I was scared she would laugh, or worse, she'd pity me—or worse again, she would candidly affirm my fears. How could I ever compare to Cleo, who was somehow intelligent, powerful, and the most beautiful being on this planet? I did not want her knowing I was just a little too curious about Ben's love life. She would certainly tell Ben if I asked.

I distracted myself, wondering how I would channel the earth. Grow a tree? I imagined Ben nurturing his garden with nothing but his nimble hands, cooperating with the soil. It wouldn't work very well without payment. He must have used a watering can. There was so little moisture in the air to channel, even I could sense that.

"Is that what you're wearing?" Cleo asked insultingly as I stared out the kitchen window.

I surveyed my ensemble. "Does it look like what I'm wearing?"

She held a hand to her temple. "Is that what you are wearing out of the house tonight?"

I considered my limited wardrobe. I didn't manage to get any laundry done today. That meant I would choose between dirty shorts or dirty jeans. Neither option was pleasant.

Cleo watched my predicament play out with impatience. "You'll borrow something of mine. We're going to have to take a shopping trip to the city shortly. I'll bet you don't have anything black for tomorrow either."

She was right about that. At least, I didn't have anything suitable for the burial, black or not. Shopping for clothes with a siren sounded like a truly bizarre experience. I wasn't certain I could endure it. I saw the bold and pretty things she wore. It was nothing I would ever pick out for myself.

Rolling her eyes at my apprehension, she filed behind me and turned me toward the hallway. She frog-marched me to Ben's bedroom.

"I HAVE my cell if anything fishy happens!" Ben yelled from the car. "But I might not have service, so, probably don't call."

Cleo lounged against the doorway. She was back in her silk robe with an attractive cocktail in one hand. She waved her fingers against it and disappeared inside.

I was buckled into the passenger seat, very unhappy in a short summer dress. It was a deep pine green and sleeveless. Gold buttons trailed down my chest from the sweetheart neckline. I felt shockingly exposed, but I liked the color.

I had tried on several pairs of too-tight denim jeans, fruitlessly tugging them up my thighs, before we both realized a dress was the best option. "Or a skirt and a crop top," Cleo suggested, to which I about kicked her. The only thing that stopped me was my own desperation for something clean and presentable to wear, for once, this week.

Cleo's feet were two sizes bigger than mine, so I was stuck wearing my black moto boots. At least I had socks this time.

Ben drove in the direction of the freeway; I didn't know where we were going. Somewhere without service, I deducted. There wasn't much food in Aspen Ridge worth sitting down for, and it appeared that Ben wanted some sit-down level nourishment. He was as dressed up as Ben ever was, wearing a short-sleeved button-up shirt that was actually buttoned.

"What's the special occasion?" I asked as I reached over to rub his shirt between my fingers.

"I could ask you the same thing," he said, eyeing Cleo's dress. "How does it feel in there?"

I curled my lip at the length of the thing. "It's okay, only slightly freakish." I scratched my thighs to illustrate my point. My tan had persisted. Not "tan" by anyone else's standard, but my skin was turning champagne in color and was faintly less milky by the day. When I saw myself in the mirror in this dress, I couldn't deny that my hair had a nice shine, and it was much fuller. It stood out against the dress. I remembered Samuel's book, as well as the book of the dragon, and the sudden health boost frightened me.

Ben pulled off the road sooner than expected. The gravel trail led to a rough version of a natural cul-de-sac. It was a place I knew. Boasting some of the best tree cover in town, kids in high school would drive out here together and bounce their cars around. I glanced nervously at Ben, panic-stricken but also embarrassingly excited. This seemed outside of Ben's character, but maybe this was where he brought his girls once he knew they were interested … No, I didn't believe that. That's not why we were here. I tried to ease my mind and breathe.

He parked his little red car in the expansive shadow of the trees, it was still light out and we were alone. We both stepped out into the warm evening. Ben took a large backpack out of his trunk and strapped it on his back.

"Ready, Princess?" He grinned under his oversized shades and took off toward the edge of the wood. We were hiking? *Lovely.* I lowered my new shades from my crown with a grimace. At least I had my boots on, and the bodice of my dress was tight, but it flared out naturally at my hips—it would be bearable.

"Don't worry, it's not far. It's just a place I like to go to clear my head. It's nice." He looked back at me with his stellar smile.

"Is there a five-star French restaurant out here?" I asked, trying to disguise my increased wheezing as we climbed.

"You in the mood for snails, Frank?"

"I don't think I've seen a French restaurant within fifty miles of here. No wonder, with it hidden away like this." I grabbed a branch to pull myself up a steep rise. "Pretty though."

Ben chuckled as he led me deeper into the forest. We walked for another twenty minutes, and the sun began to droop. It looked too big and too bloated, reddening behind the trees. Ben lifted himself up a large boulder and turned back to offer me a hand. I took it in my right with the other on my skirt, worried about my butt peeking out of the dress. At the top, there was a small clearing above the rock. The ground was almost entirely flat, the stone exposed through the pine needles. It was a good-sized circle to play a game of chess. Or to have a picnic.

Ben unzipped his bag and retrieved a thick flannel blanket. He spread it out over the stone and dirt before folding himself on top of it cross-legged. He patted the rock, inviting me to sit. I curled my legs beneath me, again, painfully aware of my butt.

Continuing to unpack from the ground, Ben pulled out a green bottle of moscato and two plastic water cups, unused I hoped. He popped the cork of the bottle effortlessly before he poured a fizzy dollop into a cup and pushed it my way. I drank deeply, parched. It was fruity and crisp.

"How is this so cold?" I asked, relishing the cool cup between my hands.

"The bag is insulated," he explained, pouring a healthy amount of wine into his own cup. He held the rim of his drink out to me, "Cheers."

I tapped my cup to his, though it was nearly empty now, and he smiled for me.

"What are we cheers-ing to?"

"To your health," Ben quipped. He refilled our cups, making them feel like expensive crystal flutes. "A lot has happened in the last few days. I thought you might want to …" he shrugged his shoulders, his shirt had somehow unbuttoned since we sat down, "talk about it." He leaned back on his elbows.

I flashed through the events of the last few days. I worried that supernatural brain of his somehow knew about my connection to Jessamae, or that my father had come around and wanted to know me. Or about my very un-casual interest in Ben, my fear of his past with Cleo.

He had left things open, and I didn't want to say anything incriminating. I would start off safely: General Q & A. "Where does the magic come from? Is it genetic?"

Ben took a sip before answering. "It is. But the gene is recessive. It could lay dormant for multiple generations, or for multiple years in a person. A lot of witches live out their lives, or at least the bulk of their lives, with nothing more than a few unexplainable occurrences, never knowing what they're capable of. Because our consciousness is tied to human normalcy, some of us must lose that attachment to normalcy before the real magic triggers. Families, friends. Or," another sip, "so I've read. We create covens, we band together and make our own families a lot of the time. Blood-bound magical families are rare."

"How come?" This was better than the History Channel.

"We aren't as fertile as regular people. A magical coupling has a pretty tiny chance of conception. Chances are better if you reproduce with ... regular people, non-witches. Which also doesn't happen often. We're attracted to the power in one another." He held my eyes fiercely. "It's like we all flunked human biology. We are probably the only creatures that are not driven by reproduction." He gave me a slow once-over as if I forgot my pants again. His timing sucked—this might have been the least sexy sex discussion I'd ever had. "Maybe it's the universe keeping things in check. You know, if everyone is magic—"

"Then no one is," I finished for him. He pointed at me in affirmation.

I swallowed my second cup of sparkly booze, and I felt a familiar boost of bravery. "That's what you and Cleo are? A coven of misfit toys?"

Ben laughed and finished his own cup. "And you, Frank. I know it's new for you, but it isn't for me, and not even really for Cleo. I saw us together a very long time ago. Family." His smile had lost any semblance of tease. He was utterly genuine, and he was ecstatic.

I smiled, thinking I needed much more practice to fit into such a tight-knit group of weirdos. I needed practice all around. "Do you see anyone else joining the club?" I regretted asking immediately.

Ben's glee faltered. He reached into his pack and took out square plastic containers. I had an inkling that he knew exactly who I was thinking of, as terrifying a devil as she was. "No," he said. He checked the insides of the containers surreptitiously. "That doesn't mean it won't happen, obviously. But I don't see anyone coming any time soon."

He offered me one of the boxes, which I took while he refilled our cups. I opened it to find a very handsome sandwich: prosciutto, arugula, and some sort of goopy cheese. He then handed me a smaller container with fresh pear slices inside. He had made all of this himself, and my heart hurt with the sweetness of it all. I was incredibly unworthy.

"Ben ..." was all I'd managed to say as I touched the bread crust.

"Have you and Cleo ever been together?" I blurted as loud as a car backfiring. I couldn't bear not knowing any longer.

Ben's face erupted in astonishment. I wasn't sure how his visions worked, but regardless, I was surprised he didn't see that one coming. He shook his head like a wet dog, ridding himself of the thought.

"No! No. Really no. No! Cleo doesn't date. She doesn't do any of that. Least of all with me! Well, maybe not least of all— not that I'm saying there's a chance." He was practically incoherent in his assertion. "Cleo and I have never even *considered* each other romantically."

I raised an eyebrow in doubt.

He raked his hands down his cheeks. "I know what she looks like, yes! I've seen her, believe it or not. I knew what she was before I ever met her. I knew how I'd feel about her before she knew I existed." He paused, smashing his features and dropping his hands to his lap. "She's had a rough go of it. Cleo. She's strong, almost diamond-hard because of it. She would have never trusted me if I ever saw her as anything other than a very important friend. That's all."

I took a moment to process that by taking a bite of my sandwich and throwing a few pears in my mouth. The flavors were magnificent.

I assumed with a face like Cleo's, people would, at all costs, protect a child like her. It made me sad to imagine the reality, to conceive of what she must have suffered, being so devastatingly lovely. I had never considered the lengths people would go to, the levels they would sink to own such a face, to claim it. Beauty was not always something to envy. Maybe.

He'd made his relationship with Cleo clear to me, but I still had no idea where *I* stood with Ben. I needed to know more.

"So, you saw both Cleo and me before you met us?"

"I did. I saw you before I saw Cleo. When I was around fourteen." He traced an umbrella tattooed on his arm. "I couldn't control when I'd get a vision. I couldn't conjure them, and I honestly still have trouble with it. But I'd go for long stretches without you. Then every few months, every few weeks, then every few days, there you were." The yearning in his voice was substantial and I felt my cheeks warm. "I had my first vision of you and me, of us together, when I was seventeen. I saw us in different futures—old, young, happy, angry." His mouth hung open and his eyes glassed over. "Alive. Dead."

After a breath, he said, "There are so many possible reactions and futures to every choice, that it's impossible to make the right choice every time. But I knew meeting you, befriending you, telling you what I am, what you are … It's all so fragile. And I'm sorry, Frank. I'm sorry I wasn't honest with you sooner. But the chances of things going well for us, for you, were so small, I couldn't risk it. Not yet, not until now, when the stakes are so high."

I chewed my cheek. "That's very manipulative."

"It is. But if you had the chance to stop a bad thing from happening to someone you cared about, wouldn't you take it?" He threw back the last of his champagne. "And I've seen a lot of bad things. Even when everything came out on Friday, the chances of you forgiving me were only around forty percent."

I listed to the side, my eyes like dinner plates. "That's why you were so … happy. When I came back. Chances were, I wouldn't." I suspected that's why Cleo came to greet me first, she made my return more likely, but I didn't want to lessen his confession by saying it.

He nodded.

I should be angry with him. His influence on my life was astronomical. But seeing him here, the way he looked at me now, with such adoration, I just couldn't manage it.

I poured the last drops of the wine into our cups, hoping pathetically that if he drank enough, he would want to kiss me again.

He tilted his head to drink and smacked his lips. I remembered the feel of that mouth. He would answer honestly, if I only asked him...

"I need to clean out my house. Maybe after the burial," I yammered in cowardice.

He stared at me earnestly, nearly glaring, until the silence was full to bursting. I felt transparent in his eyes. It was a relief when he finally said, "Sure, we'll help you. Are you ready to move back in there?"

He said *move back in* as if I were actually living with him. I didn't feel like my mother's house was really mine, and Ben's had started feeling more like a home this weekend.

"Are we both going to keep sleeping on your couches?" I asked, ignoring the fact that his couch was far more comfortable than my little bed.

His brows squirmed in postulation. He took several quick bites of his sandwich. I kept forgetting I was holding my own meal in my hands and followed his example. The food truly was wonderful.

Ben stared off into the darkening sky as if I had asked him a complex philosophical question. "You can stay as long as you're happy. But there's only one room." He leaned forward, elbows on his knees, with one pear slice wedged in his hand. He pointed it at me like a finger. "Your house has two rooms."

"Yes, it does." I replayed his words inwardly. "Thank you for noticing."

Ben snorted at my dumb expression. "You're welcome." He bit into the pear, sugary juice stuck to his lips, glossy in the setting sun. They were the sweetest pink. He had one freckle on the outer edge of his bottom lip, his tongue ran across it. I felt my lips pucker softly in response. *Oh, dear.*

He said, "Cleo wants to stick close to the two of us. It's hard for her to live so far away. And my house isn't a permanent solution. She needs to give my goddamn bed back. She has her own after all …"

Ben was the most important person in my life. It was easy to picture him within whatever space I inhabited. Cleo was more difficult to picture there, but even though we had only spent one day alone together, I cared for her. If I hadn't enjoyed my isolation so much, I'd probably jump at the opportunity to have a roommate.

"No pressure. The couch suits me fine," he assured, rolling his shoulders dramatically.

I frowned as I reexamined the effort Ben had put into this evening. There was nothing said here that couldn't have been brought up in front of Cleo, that couldn't have been brought up *by* Cleo. And she would have done one hell of a job convincing me, I'm sure. None of this was why he brought me up here, alone.

"Why did you kiss me, Benny?" I asked, shaken by my own courage. I swallowed hard, as if every pear I ingested was blocking my airway.

He scooted towards me, using his feet to drag himself. Every second he remained silent was like a splinter. I was riddled with holes by the time he cupped my heated face in his deft hands. He moved his thumb across my cheek.

"Because I've wanted to kiss you for the last thirteen years."

14

THE IMPACT of what Ben said hit me like a snowball to the face. The chill zipped through my skeleton, rattling my core. I had wanted him to tell me that, or something like that at least, in my most secret of fantasies since I was seventeen years old. Looking at him stung my eyes like smoke. This wasn't reality. Looking down, I dug small moons into my knee, asking my pain for assurance.

Ben's thumb touched the corner of my mouth, his other hand tilted my chin up. "You were driving me insane, just like you always do, but," he stroked my lip as he continued, "I don't know. You were just too close." My mouth hung open like a flytrap and he poked the corners of it whimsically, remembering our kisses. "And it's hard not to get swept up in the moment when a lady responds with such ... enthusiasm." He held his tongue between his teeth and leered at me.

My cheeks burned under his fingers and my defensive nature reared its ugly head. "Well, I guess being groped on a countertop made me think it was okay."

He snickered at my reaction. "Come on, Frank. I'm only teasing." He trailed a single finger up the side of my bare thigh. I shivered all the way down. "I *have* wanted to kiss you for the last thirteen years. Since I first saw you."

My emotions were dizzying and all over the place, littering the forest floor. Ben was warm and funny and playful and creative. He could have so much, but he chose to have so little.

"What is your deal?" I asked. Ben pulled back, affronted. He dropped his lingering hands. "You can't be this stupid. Why would you want anything to do with me? Friendship or other-wise? I'm not likable, or … or nice. I'm not trusting. I'm not—I can't cook! I don't know, I'm not good! I'm not good." I was shouting by the end. I hurt my own feelings, but I wasn't fishing for a contradiction, I just did not understand.

His affect was disappointed, almost pained at my admission. He held one of my hands to his mouth and kissed the skin of my palm. "Why would I want you to be any of those things?"

I'd been ready to argue, but instead was floored, totally. That was not the contradiction I'd expected, genuine or not. His words stopped my frenzy in its tracks, being so entirely unex-pected. He admitted I was not, what had I said? Good. Trusting. He knew that. And still, he kissed me. I had never accepted or even considered that if Ben wanted a person with redeemable qualities, he was smart enough to spend his time with a person who had them. The reality was, he had spent the last six years with me.

He braced his hands on the ground between us. He drifted forward into the empty space and held, giving me time to retract. I watched his eyes. There was such movement in them, they shifted like living things. Lustrous, brown eyes. They stared at my mouth, and I wished I knew what he thought of it. He tilted down and his face hovered so close to me I felt the swell of my lips quiver against his. He pressed them together with the lightest pressure. The tenderness was so much more terrifying than the hunger.

Ben pulled away after one kiss. "Now, whether you'd like to believe it or not, you *are* in a vulnerable place right now. So …" He forced his feet beneath him and stood up over me. He offered his hand. I didn't take it.

"Then why did you wait until this *vulnerable* time?" I spit the word out as if it were poisonous. I was annoyed and upset that he was so quick to step back. All I could see of him now was a dark shadow in the encroaching dusk. "It was even worse yesterday. Wasn't it? That didn't stop you."

His offered hand dropped a bit, but he didn't pull it back completely. It hung there in the air while his other hand rubbed his newly shaved head. "It's not that I didn't think about it before. But every time I came close it felt like … lying. You needed to know everything. About the magic. About the secrets, my age. The stalking, as you so generously put it." He finally pulled his hand away and closed his eyes against the setting sun. "I told myself, once you knew everything, then you could make an informed decision, or whatever people say. I probably could have waited longer, longer than yesterday, but, I … um … did not." He grinned, shameless. "However, I have a better perspective today. So." He held his hand out to me again.

Trying to remain objective, I supposed that was fair. If he had crossed the romance line before I knew about him, finding out later would have been crippling. A smarter person would be careful with Ben, not fling themselves into his arms so wholeheartedly. He *had* lied. I *was* vulnerable. Probably.

I finally took his hand, then picked up the empty food containers and cups, setting them into a not-much-better pile on the ground. I bent down, bunching up the blanket into a messy ball.

"Frank?" Ben whispered. My skin prickled unfamiliarly with the sound of my name in his mouth. I waited for another snowball-to-the-face confession.

"Yes, Benjamin?"

"Your ass is out." Ben reached forward and pulled the skirt of my dress to my thighs. He took the blanket ball from me nearly straight-faced, but his lips twitched at the corners.

"Fuck."

WE GOT BACK to Ben's house after dark. Cleo isolated herself in the bedroom and didn't welcome us home. I sat on the couch I normally slept on with Ben's blanket rumpled up beneath me. Even if it was my small, stained bed, it would be nice to sleep in a bed again. And it might be nice to have Cleo, an established witch, close. I was stunned to discover that living in my own place didn't appeal to me so much now.

Ben lowered himself onto the loveseat across from me and hung his head back. The couch was too short for him by about two feet, and wrapped in a sheet, he had to be much less than comfortable. Of course, he never complained, the idiot. It was hard to argue with Cleo moving in with me if it meant he could get off that itty bitty thing. As I saw his large frame overtake it, I thought this might erase some of my debt after his paying for the burial. Karma currency.

"I don't want to sleep in Pamela's room. It feels … spooky to me now. I'm assuming Cleo would be happy if I stay away from it?"

Ben's chin flopped forward, as he'd been dozing and I'd caught him off guard. He inclined towards me attentively.

"She would, yes. She's made that evident with her behavior in my room!" He shouted at her down the hallway. But his smile was there, and I knew that he didn't mind too much. "But we'll do whatever is needed. Cleo could have my room here, if she wanted. She could sleep here." He paused, letting that idea sink in before adding, "or she could have a room there."

He couldn't be asking to move in with me. I couldn't handle that today. And if he were, well, I doubted we would be getting some cool bunkbeds.

The two of us had slept in the same bed before, but it was always because someone had fallen asleep watching a movie or drifted off after a long day. It had never been intentional.

Ben wasn't my boyfriend. Thinking of him that way felt formal and strange and optimistic to the point of foolishness. Even without the expectations or the touchy romance, I was closer to him than I had ever been with another person. Sleeping with him—sleeping in the same bed as him—should not be a dramatic idea.

He was watching me, still and silent. I peered into those dancing eyes of his and Ben's face instantaneously fell lifeless. His mouth hung, jaw slack. He looked through me. I was afraid, but before I could say anything he shook his head to clear it. His following smile was utterly radiant.

He said nothing as he stretched out, completely relaxed, on his makeshift bed. He'd seen something. Something he liked. Me, letting Cleo move in, perhaps? Or Ben, even? I lifted my lip at my astounding ability to fold. That didn't mean I couldn't change my mind …

"You really are too monstrous for that couch. Let me switch you," I asserted as I gathered up his comforter.

"It's too small for anyone," he said, standing up and moving in close. He climbed over me acrobatically and molded his body to the back of the couch. He tucked his pillow I'd been using under both of our heads and spread his blanket across our knees.

Ben had touched my skin almost more than I could bear throughout our friendship, and I was now tucked into his arms. And I wasn't pulling away. With his elbow bent around me and the other arm burrowed under my head, we were close. This was what I would call close.

He kissed the space under my ear.

"I hope you're ready," he whispered as we drifted off to sleep.

I WOKE up feeling warm and squashed. I didn't understand immediately and felt the stir of claustrophobia, until I saw Ben's tattooed forearm hanging over me, off the edge of the sofa.

It wasn't the most restful night's sleep I'd ever had. I usually enjoyed being very cold with a lot of space to myself. But I preferred this to that all the same. I traced some of my favorite tattoos along his arm: a starburst, a window, an eye. There was an unusual artistry to them, their stark contrast against his skin, their simplicity. I wondered how the healing process would go if he gave one to me.

The tickle of my fingers woke him, and he arched his back, pushing his chest into me. He blew strands of my hair out of his mouth and flattened the mountain of it down close to my scalp until he could see me. "Morning, Frank."

He searched my hair with his hands until they rested against my neck. He draped them over my collar bones like silk, dipping and grooving along the ridges. He kissed my cheek quickly before swinging his leg high over my body and hopping to the ground.

"Best night's sleep I've had in a while." He beamed before he looked to the clock on the stove. "We have to be at the cemetery in two hours. I'll start the coffee."

I stretched my bones, twisting for weak cracks and pops once he was out of earshot, although if Ben was going to date me, he should probably get used to it.

I'd never changed out of Cleo's dress. It was wrinkled and baggy in all the wrong places. I gritted my teeth hoping that a wash would shrink it back to its normal sausage-casing elasticity. It looked like I'd be wearing my black jeans and a t-shirt to the burial.

I was almost obsessive with my personal hygiene routine in the bathroom that morning, in honor of my grandmother's memory, or something like that. I washed my hair with shampoo and conditioner and exfoliated my dry skin with a eucalyptus scrub I found in the shower. *Thank you, Cleo*. I blow-dried my hair until it bounced in winding spirals and even put on some make-up: mascara and a light lipstick. Once I had my old black jeans on and a wrinkled black shirt over my head, the visible contrast between my head and my clothes felt sort of like I was wearing a top hat and sweatpants.

I met Cleo in the hallway after finishing in the bathroom. She looked characteristically remarkable in a form-fitting black satin dress, her hair piled heavily on top of her head. She assessed me with a disgruntled expression. "What happened to the dress?"

"I was going to wash it first."

"Do you know how to wash that dress?" she followed up skeptically.

"Yeah, of course," I lied before turning away toward the kitchen. I would read the tag on the dress before I popped in into the washer tonight, easy peasy.

Ben was standing against the counter, sipping a mug of coffee and reading the newspaper. It was fitting for Ben in a way, but it was always odd to see a person reading the paper and not a webpage. I wondered if he drove to a gas station and bought it or if he stole it from his neighbors. So much effort for either case.

He lifted his eyes as I ambled through the kitchen archway. He slapped the paper onto his countertop for me to see. It was Pamela's obituary, small and unassuming next to the other grieving announcements.

"Pamela Marie Hughes …" I read aloud before scanning the rest silently. "She was sixty-four. I wasn't sure." The message was brief, listing the time and location of the burial. It mentioned her residence in Lehi, and my late mother and grandfather. The picture was several years old. They had downloaded it from her Facebook page. *Pamela is survived by her granddaughter, Francesca Lee Hughes.*

"Francescally," I read my name.

"It's got a nice ring to it," Ben complimented.

He was dressed modestly in a black crew neck and the exercise pants he'd worn when I first met him. We would make for a very somber bunch today, and although the occasion called for it, all of us matching felt unnatural to the point of theatrics.

I pulled my favorite mug out of Ben's dishwasher. It was white with a tiger painted underneath the word "Nashville." I'd found it at a yard sale five years ago. Ben refused to let me take it when I had moved to the city. He wanted me to "keep it at home."

I melted sugar at the bottom with a splash of hot coffee, added a bit of cream, and stirred. I then poured coffee to the brim. Perfection. I held my hand out silently until Ben gave his empty mug to me. Half an inch of cream at the bottom, no sugar, and I handed the steaming cup back to him. He stirred it in with a cinnamon stick.

Leaning over the counter, I worked on the crossword, and he worked on the Sudoku as we waited to leave. Cleo joined us in the kitchen after a while and poured herself a cup. She drank it black. Everything she did impressed me.

Once she had taken a delicate slurp, Ben addressed us both. "I see a few people at the burial today. I'm guessing they saw the announcement and decided to show. They're probably going to want to talk to you," he warned me gravely. "Can you be strong? Maybe be a little friendly to Granny's mourners?"

I curled my lip and glared at him. "I think I can manage."

Cleo snorted into her cup in disbelief. I glared at her, too. She didn't know me well enough to snort.

"We should probably get moving then, don't want to keep the party guests waiting." He grabbed his giant sunglasses off the table, handed me my own pair, and led us to the car.

THE TOWN CEMETERY was high on a lonely hill, squished into the south-east corner of Aspen Ridge. There had been rumors about the hilltop resting place when I was a kid, and every rumor was that the hill was haunted. This mostly was due to a peculiar plastic Jesus statue standing atop one of the plots. Fervid children had told me that the eyes glowed red on some nights.

Ben pulled into a corner of the scant parking lot. It was essentially a patch of asphalt, as there were no yellow lines or curbs. Gabriel Perez was standing outside one of the few cars in the lot, a shiny black hearse. I didn't like knowing Pamela's corpse was stored so close. It would be just like her to listen in on our conversations outside.

The pressure of the air was burdensome, almost soggy. It would rain soon. I raised my face skyward, attempting to smell water in the air, but all I could smell was that familiar perfume of death.

Ben and Cleo stayed close on either side of me as we approached the black cab. Gabriel appeared sorry and inviting as he reached his hand out to me for the second time. "Miss Hughes, so nice to see you again. I wish it were under different circumstances, of course. Mr. Bowen," he smiled and shook Ben's hand, seemingly more comfortable with him than when I'd left them in the office.

Gabriel was momentarily overcome by Cleo, his hand still reaching for Ben, his mouth flapping.

"Cleo Zaher," she said, taking the hand away from Ben and shaking it. Her smile was polite, but nevertheless, breathtaking.

Gabriel collected himself and regained some semblance of the composure he carried earlier. "Gabriel Perez, it's wonderful to meet another friend supporting Miss Hughes today." He held her hand a few moments too long before releasing her suddenly, as if shocked by a hand buzzer. He turned his entire body toward me, blocking Cleo from his view. "The plot is not far down the path. You may choose to ride with me in the car or walk if you prefer."

I was conflicted, torn between my aversion to small talk and my morbid curiosity. That my grandmother was dead in that car was incredibly unreal. I wanted assurance. I hadn't seen her since she had been rolled away in a blue plastic bag. Would she be wearing the dress I picked out for her? Was it necessary without an open casket or wake? Would she be wearing anything?

My thoughts were drifting toward the macabre. "We'll just walk behind you, thanks."

He nodded, understanding as always, and moved to get back in the driver's seat. I waited behind the hatch knowing I was so close to her casket, if I could only lift the lid a touch …

The car drove at a crawling pace onto a winding paved path at the edge of the parking lot. Ben put an arm around my shoulders while Cleo clasped my left hand. I felt undeserving of their gestures; I was still so unmoved by all of this. But as much as I avoided touching and being touched, the feel of the two of them was more than natural, it was right. Their power gushed into me, and I was unburdened, almost buoyant. I liked it too much to say no.

The hearse clambered up the steep hillside before crossing over a crumbling stone bridge. That such a fairytale element existed inside of this graveyard made me weary. We hiked the arch steadily and I saw no river or road beneath us. The bridge was simply there.

The headstones that surrounded me were as fascinating as they were depressing. Crosses and statues stood taller than me, or even Ben, in glossy marble and rough stone, wood and glass. They were all strewn about haphazardly. Each so different from the next, no HOA to stop the flamboyant or pursue the bland. I was tempted to wander the graves and read each name carved into this place, despite knowing that I wouldn't remember even one. There were a few people in the cemetery that appeared to be doing just that: shuffling, mildly interested, from one grave to the next like an outdoor market. We passed very close to a small and colorful stone painted with pastel zoo animals. The marker was circled in reflective balloons and tiny toy trucks. That one was the saddest, I think.

The hearse stopped next to a casket positioned above a person-sized hole in the ground. It was surrounded by green felt for some unknown reason. So, Pamela hadn't been in the hearse, I'd made the right choice to walk.

The coffin appeared to be wicker. Because I chose a biodegradable "green" model, they had skipped the embalming process. I couldn't assuage the inkling that she was not inside that basket at all. That it was empty. If it hadn't been for the stink, I would have ripped off the lid.

Gabriel exited the car with a passenger that looked very much like him, only younger, with a wider nose and no gut. His son. The two stood at the head of the plot, where there was a small crane set up, strapped to Pamela's box. People had evidently been following us up the graveyard without my notice, because they approached now, either alone or in couples. There weren't many; I counted five. A couple of the lone cemetery visitors I'd seen wandering around were paying attention, as if they wanted an invite.

"Would you like to say a few words?" Gabriel whispered at my side.

I thought that I absolutely should want to say a few words, and that these people who drove out here to pay their respects would want that, too. But as I stared down into the pit, any words of goodbye, or honor, or truth, simply escaped me. "No."

Ben squeezed my shoulder as the younger Perez operated the crane. The straps around Pamela grew taught before the box steadily began to rise. As it ascended, Cleo sang. It was gentle, all but secretive. I couldn't discern her words, at least not in any language I recognized, but the tone was painfully clear. It was such sorrowful, bereaved music, and the most transcendent gift she could have given anyone, alive or not. She crooned, more perfect, more alluring, than the song of any bird, of any instrument. And as tears spilled out over the lids of my eyes, I wished it were me in that box that now kissed the ground. That this song had been meant for me.

15

THE SONG STOPPED. I looked around disconcerted. We had all edged closer to the grave as Cleo sang, as if we longed to jump in after Pamela. I took an uneasy step away, as did most of the guests, when the spell of the music wore off. Cleo still held my hand, and I gave it a squeeze in thanks, though I was faintly horrified.

"We will handle everything here. Please feel free to reminisce with the other attendees," Gabriel coughed. He appeared shaken, even a little sick. I'm sure he had never experienced a burial quite like this one.

I was squeamish at the thought of talking with people who actually enjoyed Pamela. But Ben was right, I could be brave today. I didn't walk far from the grave when an elderly couple approached the three of us. Cleo and Ben didn't step away, which I was thankful for. I did not want to send the message that I was open real estate for hugging.

"Hello, Francesca," the woman said with a crazed smile. Her teeth were so large they looked like toes bleached white and aligned between her puffy lips. "I'm Tracy. I was a neighbor of your grandma's in Lehi. I think I even saw you waddle around her yard when you were just a baby." She smiled grotesquely again.

So, this was the gold-digging Tracy, after her husband's money. Tracy, that Pamela had journaled about. Then who—

"This is Roger Erikson," she said, gesturing to her blue-eyed escort. "He's a friend of mine. And Pamela's," she added.

It looked like Pamela had the divorce right. I hoped the ex-husband was a bastard, just to prove Pamela wrong about the rest.

Roger stepped up, "It's good to meet you, young lady." *Hate that.* "I'm so sorry for your loss."

I didn't extend my hand in greeting. But I was putting in a real effort to be kind today. "Thank you very much. For. Being Here." My sentence was filled with odd pauses, but the couple seemed consoled by my words.

"Will you be having a reception, Francesca? Please let me bring a dish! I can throw together a pomegranate salad like that," Tracy snapped her fingers.

Almost before she finished speaking, I started muttering, "No, no reception. That salad sounds ... good." Ben coughed at my side. "But no reception. Thanks. No." I worked on a smile, but she was visually offended at my dismissal.

The next in line to meet me started edging forward, giving enthusiastic Tracy the signal to move on. This man was alone. He looked to be in his fifties and very gray, with a gray polo, gray eyes, and graying stubble on his head.

"Hi there. I'm Jackson. Perry, Jackson Perry. I knew your grandma. Pretty well, actually. We'd get together from time to time. Talk. Quite a spitfire, Pams!" He grinned at some memory of her. That any man liked Pamela, or would label her evil nature as being a "spitfire," was news to me. "After she moved, to be there for you, I didn't see much of her. But I still think about her a lot, when I'm playing cards or having a smoke or something." I tried to get past the *be there for you* comment to picture my grandmother playing cards and smoking with this man. I couldn't do it. No way. The image was cartoonish. "I'll sure miss her," he finished sadly.

"Thank you. That sounds ... very nice," I said, and he nodded his head before stepping away. He seemed okay, Jackson. Other than his questionable taste in women.

The other two onlookers from the burial—I remembered them as two women—must have gone back to their car without meeting me, probably put off by the eerie effects of Cleo's song. Even the stragglers roaming the grounds were absent from the landscape. We were the only three, other than the Perez men, left on the sweltering hilltop, stinking sweetly of its residents. Ben, Cleo, and I began walking in the direction of the parking lot, finding the path quickly underfoot.

Halfway down, before we crossed the bridge, the cords thrummed. The cords in my chest were plucked. She was here, close. She was in the opposite direction of the parking lot, across the grounds. She was calling to me. My feet automatically turned in that direction, bumping against Ben. He stumbled and held onto me for balance, confused.

He asked, "You okay?"

I saw a small shed that housed the bathrooms at the source of the pull. "Yeah, I just need to pee. I'll be right back." Without thinking, I jogged toward the building, my breaths struggling in the oppressive heat. She wanted to see me. That's why she came. I thought of her reflective eyes in the darkness watching me, of her alluring and insidious nature. Still, I ran.

I swung open the metal door and stood in the center of the dank cement room, smelling old piss and completely terrified. I saw myself in the dirty mirror over the sink. A part of me was happy I wore makeup today. I was losing my mind.

I tried to feel her, to find her, as if I were a homing beacon. The vibration in my chest battered against me intensely, it was beginning to sting. She was right on top of me.

"Close your eyes."

I heard the raspy whisper just over my shoulder and I shut my eyes without hesitation, but not without fear.

"KEEP THEM CLOSED," she said from close behind me and pushed me back out the door. "Get ready to run." Her hair tickled the skin of my neck.

Then her powerful legs kicked behind mine like a ventriloquist holding a dummy, but with each stride, my boot hit solid earth and I managed to remain upright, though the hillside angled upward. She kept behind me until I managed an even and steady pace, then she raced out in front, keeping a strong hold of my hand.

"Keep them closed," she spoke louder now. "I won't let you fall."

We were flying. The wind whipped my hair in a frenzy, and I was scared. I heard the leaves rustle beneath and around us in a blur, smelled the soil and the sap. We ran like children, like we could leave reality behind us.

We stopped suddenly, I fell forward from the momentum, but Jessamae caught my shoulders and righted me. "Now open."

I opened my eyes to see the rising mountainside of Aspen Ridge. We didn't seem very high up, but we were far enough that I couldn't see a break in the trees behind or before me, where the cemetery should be. I searched until Jessamae stepped into my field of vision. She was wearing the same thing I had seen her in before. She put her hands on either side of my neck. I didn't flinch.

"There's my peach," she hummed. She was alarmingly close to me, her body nearly touching mine. I could hear her clothes rustle as she breathed me in. I inhaled her in return, and she smelled almost sour. It wasn't unpleasant; it was like the bitterness of resinous leaves. She smiled before she grabbed my arm and led me to some flat stones jabbed into the hillside, below a fallen aspen covered in shriveled gray mushrooms. Her thigh pressed to mine as we sat. It prickled nearly to twitching but I didn't pull it away. I wasn't behaving like myself at all.

"You buried your grandmother. How are you feeling?" She turned to me with concern evident on her face. That Pamela's murderer was worried over my well-being should have been surprising, but I wasn't surprised in the slightest.

"I'm okay," I mumbled, refusing the mirror of her eyes. I watched the movement of her scar instead. The line had lightened so much. A very old wound. "Not the hardest funeral I've been to."

She tilted her head, interested. The scar stretched with her sad expression. "Your parents?"

I was compelled by her, I wanted her to know me. I hated it, but I wanted her to know me. My attention fell to her lips to avoid those eyes. Wide. Dry. "My mom."

She tossed her head the opposite way, a cat considering me. She felt along the bones of my shoulder before she lightly touched my cheek. She pulled at my face, forcing my eyes to meet hers. I shivered; it was like looking into winter. "What was her name?" she asked me.

My lip trembled. My skin hurt where she wasn't touching me. "Allison." I felt like I was pleading with her for something. My eyes itched with unshed tears—I hadn't spoken my mother's name in months.

Her hands continued to feather softly across my exposed skin, my throat, my jaw. "What happened to her?"

I thought back to that terrible, terrible day in January. "Car accident. Our roads get … tricky, icy." I remembered the phone call, the way the snow fell across the headlights like stars. "People die on them every day." I traded my car in for cash within the week.

She made a clicking sound with her mouth in discouragement. "Don't get very lost in that memory. You are here with me now." She pushed my hair behind my ears. "Your father?"

I was sharing the deepest parts of me without any thumbscrews or pliers, I wanted so much to please her. "I never knew him. My mom, she said he wasn't father material. He wasn't interested in the title anyway." I thought of the journal entry that I had yet to tell anyone about, that I hadn't even discussed with

Ben. "But my grandmother knew otherwise." I didn't want to think about those things anymore. I'd put all my conscious effort into pretending they weren't camped in my brain like fat toads.

She appeared burdened by my confession. "I am sorry for what I did to you. I'm sorry I took her life before you could find out more about your past." She wasn't sorry for Pamela. It wasn't necessary for her to say it.

She stared into my face as if the sun rose and fell between my eyebrows, like she could never get her fill of it. It was unnerving. I had barely spoken to this woman. More importantly, she killed my grandmother. She stalked me in a much more imminent sense than Ben ever had. I didn't understand what was happening. My revulsion was there, somewhere, but it couldn't break through.

"Why did you ask me to close my eyes before?" I asked my hands, hoping if I avoided her face I might feel more like myself.

She laughed sardonically. "I heard your protector tell you about his intriguing magic."

I lifted my head, despite my efforts, in surprise. How had she heard? When was she listening? She noted my astonishment.

"I admit I've been rude. I've been listening, not all the time, but I have tuned into you from the mountain. Like a radio. The spell isn't overly complicated," she rushed. "Your friend said he can only see what you see, when he's inside your mind." She lifted her fingertips to my temple. "He wouldn't expect me to be in the bathroom with you. He wouldn't think to be looking. I thought if I could get you away before he could see me, then we would have more time."

"Were you listening to us on Sunday? At the glass house?" Blood rushed to my face, and I swayed, suddenly lightheaded.

Jessamae nearly blushed, I saw a small well of blood behind those tan cheeks. "I didn't want that to happen, I promise you. I was only keeping track of you. You were taken to an old witch. I didn't trust it." Her eyes were severe. "I heard you and your friend in the kitchen. Then you stopped talking." She shut those eyes, but not before I saw hurt flash in them. "I wanted it to stop. Then the window. It exploded. I ran once I understood what had happened. I went to the place you were staying, to explain, but I think I may have frightened you. I haven't listened to you since."

I easily traipsed past her violation of my privacy. Too easily. Much too easily. She could have killed us both, all three of us if Patrick had never gotten hurt. "But I didn't understand," she uttered. "Why have you kept me a secret from him?"

I shouldn't have had to say it. The answer was glaring. "You killed Pamela."

She pressed her lips into a firm line, resigned. "I did. But it had to happen. I believe he knows that. You were suffocating, Francesca. I could not sit by and watch it happen. I'm very surprised that he could." Jessamae looked faintly hostile when she mentioned Ben. "But I am sorry. I know I've hurt you, angered you. That's the last thing I want to do."

I wasn't angry. I didn't feel angry. But Ben certainly did, it was the reasonable response to what she did. "He must be so worried about me." I made no move to leave. "Why do I feel this way? Are you doing something to me? To my mind? What is this connection?" I gestured between us.

I sat down, woozy, and Jessamae moved in sync with me, reflecting me. We faced each other. Her eyes never left mine and she lightly grasped both of my hands in hers. I didn't trust her, had every reason to hate her, but I was putty between her rough fingers.

Her expression was brimming with excitement. "Your power reflects mine, I felt it before you did. I take, you give. You take, I give." She mimicked my back-and-forth action with her hands.

"I don't understand," I was so tired of feeling confused. She held the clarity I needed. I knew it throughout my insides.

She leaned in too close. I felt her exhale in warm puffs on my face, and when she spoke, I felt her words on my lips.

"We are life and death."

〰️

WE WERE LAYING in the dirt, side by side in the hot sun. I felt my skin sizzling beneath it, reddening. I doubted I would ever run out of questions for Jessamae, and as much as I wanted to leave, as much as I wanted to hate her, I couldn't ignore the overwhelming sense of wellness. "Can you hurt things? Like I heal them?" I asked.

"I can," she answered. "I can make people sick, make them weak. I hurt them inside. But I don't see much point in it. It's not as beneficial to slowly infect a threat."

"Not a warning kind of guy?"

"My presence is the warning."

I stiffened beside her. She made it so hard to not be afraid underneath it all.

She pushed herself up onto her elbows and peered down at my tomato sauce face with that chilling smile. "Do you blame the cobra for striking when it is attacked? Of course not. Nasty things should be left well enough alone."

"You sought me out," I reminded her.

Jessamae held my stare for several loud heartbeats. "I would not harm you, Francesca." Her words dripped sincerity.

"Call me Frankie," I asserted, wanting to stop that habit before it was too late. As if I would be seeing more of her.

She considered my preferred name and made a face. She didn't like that one as much. "Of course. Frankie."

She spoke with more formality than I was used to hearing. She seemed to exist outside of time, and it was difficult to guess an age for her based on her appearance. I had assumed somewhere between twenty-one and thirty-five. "How old are you?"

She didn't seem bothered, but closed her eyes against the sun's aggressive rays as she lay back down. "I was born in Virginia, in 1927."

"Holy shit." But my shock sounded insulting. "I mean,

Patrick was older than you, so …" I turned my lips down as if considering something menial. She laughed at me.

"We must sound very old to you. Witches tend to have their lifespans expanded further than an average human. But there are those like me, who can consume the vitality of others through some magical means or another, and the aging process may standstill, or even reverse." She was wistful. She enjoyed sharing with me.

"My father was a white man, my mother Japanese. My father had been shipped overseas after Pearl Harbor, he never returned to us. My mother was … persecuted. I lost her very young. But I had the most darling little sister, Eliza. Their loss was bearable, because I still had her.

"We were moved by train to an internment camp, not far from here actually. It wasn't until Eliza was taken from me, just after my eighteenth birthday, that my affinity presented itself." Her shimmering eyes held an old misery, a heart disease. I ached for her ache, despite whatever crime she may have committed at eighteen. "However, it was many years before I discovered the full extent of my magic. I believe my body to be somewhere in its mid to late twenties." She paused for a long time—I didn't think she was breathing. "I never discovered what became of my sister."

I scanned her up and down, baffled by the age of her mind compared to that of her body. She misread my expression and pulled at her clothes. "I'm not very presentable. I know that. I only carry a small stash of clothing with me. I don't normally wear clothes when I am outside. I take pleasure in solitude."

Me, too.

After I'd processed what she said, I choked on my spit. This deadly woman is running around the borders of our town, performing magic, *in the nude?* She was both a dream and a nightmare.

Jessamae was suddenly suspended over me, a hand on either side of my ribs. She blotted out the light of the sun, but she carried a more excruciating radiance. "I'm going to have to take you home soon. But I will see you again. Tomorrow night. Our potential … we have to see." She sounded greedy, fervent, at the notion. "Therefore, there are a few things I would ask of you."

I answered with a tentative, "Okay."

She beamed at me before listing, "First, you need to tell your friend I plan to see you. Whether he accepts it or not, I don't want him sneaking after you."

She was a demanding thing. I had a feeling that when I was alone again, I'd find her control issues irksome, if not scary. "Go on."

"Second," she trailed a rough finger down my throat. My breath left me. I couldn't get any air back into my lungs. Her finger stopped at my heart, hovering over my chest. "You need to work on your restoration. Do more than heal a life. Return a life." Her fingernail traced a circle through my t-shirt, I felt its imprint in my skin. "Use something small. Like an insect or a bird. Take all the help you can get, from your coven if they'll agree to it, from nature, from your blood. But it's important you try."

She couldn't have given a more daunting request. Resurrection wasn't in any of the memoirs. She was asking me to play God. I didn't know how to restart a life, especially if I was the one to take it away. Kill and resurrect, for practice! My teeth hurt, my skin hurt, but I didn't resist her. She gave me an electric jolt, its energy near pain as it held me in place.

"What else?" I stuttered.

She lowered herself until we were skin to skin. Her weight felt good on top of me. She tangled her hands in my hair and kissed my temple before whispering in my ear, "Close your eyes." I thought her tongue grazed me.

I shut my eyes with alacrity.

Her weight lifted. I lay there with my eyes closed, afraid to open them again. I then felt her hand in mine. Jessamae pulled me to my feet. I was standing, her strong arms wrapped around me tightly. She held me for some time.

"Open."

She stepped back, at arm's length, as I took in our new surroundings. She had moved both of our bodies in an instant. Even under magical means, the act seemed impossible. My head was spinning. "How ..." I uttered.

We hadn't traveled far. We stood at the base of the mountain, along a parking ditch for hikers. There was only one car, a black minivan, nearby. Jessamae loped swiftly toward it without answering my question. Her tangled white locks hardly appeared to shift in the breeze, as if she existed outside of gravity.

As I approached the van, I had an inkling it did not belong to Jessamae. Perhaps it was the sticker family—John, Jessica, Marissa, and Luke—on the back window. Or the cracker crumbs smashed into the seat cushions that I didn't brush away before swinging my body through the passenger door.

"Nice ride," I said as we pulled out onto the paved road.

She grinned wolfishly. "I couldn't take you too far myself. It's dangerous over long distances, particularly when carrying precious cargo," she explained as her smile grew. The fear and the appeal of her gave me whiplash.

She drove toward the center of town and eventually turned northwest, in the direction of my house. "Could you actually take me to Ben's?" I stammered. The question felt awkward, shriveling in the air. She didn't answer, but maneuvered a wide U-turn. She'd asked me to tell Ben about our plans, but she did not seem so happy about that now. "It's past—"

"I know where it is."

I nodded. I had no idea how I was going to tell Ben about this. I could sense his hurt and his worry already as I sat buckled into this sticky seat. If he could only get past the ... whole killing Pamela thing? As I thought the sentence, I felt awful, existing next to Jessamae. I knew the sentence was true, the awful feeling was real, so how could she undo all of that with a glance?

"Where do you want to meet tomorrow?" I asked. Regardless of my battling ethics, I knew that I would show.

Her expression sweetened at my question. "I'll pick you up. I know you don't have a vehicle," she looked at the sun overhead. "I'll be there at sundown."

I saw Ben's house in the distance—Jessamae turned the head-lights on, and they bounced off his windows. My nerves were completely fried. I sat with a murderer whom I did not want to leave, but whom I very much wanted to leave, to talk to Ben about why I abandoned him at my grandmother's burial, who had been murdered, the murderer of whom I did not want to leave.

She parked the van behind Ben's sedan. The chicken in me had been idiotically wishing he wouldn't be home. Jessamae turned to me, glum. She extended her hand and pressed it deli-cately to my chest. She held her warm palm to my skin as my heart puttered around under the pressure, waiting. The anxious organ eventually eased.

"Until tomorrow," she said, putting her hand back to the wheel.

"Okay." I popped the handle and stumbled away from the car. I brushed the crumbs off my butt, refusing to make any more eye contact with the woman as I approached Ben's front door.

The house was quiet and cold. I was too scared to call out to him. He wasn't in the living room. He wasn't in the kitchen. But I knew where he would be before I even crossed the threshold. I knew where he would wait for me. I finally slid back the patio door and stepped, again, into the heat.

He was on the ground with a burning cigarette held precari-ously between his fingers, leaning against the siding of his home as we did nearly seven years ago. How dramatic. There were butts and ashes all around him, as if they were sprouting from the cement. He had been waiting a long time.

He lifted his head and his expression stunned me. His eyes were hard as iron as he appraised me, revolted, under his dark brows. Nostrils flared, jaw strained, his entire face leaked whatever foulness with which I'd filled him up. His lip twitched as he pulled smoke into his lungs. He was so angry, so hurt. He glared at me, and my heart ached. He had never looked at me with such a face before.

He finally stood and pointed his cigarette at me in accusation. "What the fuck were you thinking?"

16

"LET ME EXPLAIN," I rasped. But I didn't want to explain. I wanted it to be like it was before he knew about any of this. I wished he couldn't see how Jessamae was with me, and how I never stopped her.

"What the fuck were you thinking?" he snarled. He stalked heavily closer, towering over me. I had never felt so small. "She killed your grandmother, Francesca! And now you're hanging out with her? Going on some freaky date with Pamela's murderer? How sick are you? How *sick* are you!"

His use of my full name made me feel like a stranger to him, almost more than his truthful accusations. "It's not ... I don't ... I'm sorry." I faltered, attempting to summon any words that would make him understand.

He was disgusted. "Why? Because I could see it happen?" He flicked his burning cigarette into the air.

I looked down at his bare feet. My voice was quiet. "For leaving." That wasn't entirely true. "For not saying anything to you. For making you worry." Better.

He leaned into my face, finding my eyes, his face twisted in fury. If it were anyone else, it would feel menacing. *But not Ben*, I said meekly to myself. Ben wasn't menacing.

"It's not about me, Francesca. Forget that I waited for you outside of that bathroom, without looking through your eyes so you could have some privacy. For half an hour! So you could FUCK AROUND WITH YOUR GRANDMOTHER'S KILLER ON A GODDAMN MOUNTAIN TOP!" Bits of spittle smacked my nose and cheeks. I didn't move to wipe them away. I thought I might be crying. "She is a *murderer*," he affirmed for me.

"I know what she did!" I finally yelled back in petrified desperation. "I'm not an idiot. I want to hate her!" Sobs punched my throat, and I swallowed them whole. It hurt. "But I can't! We have a connection because of this … stupid magic bullshit!" I was crying now, there was no denying the burn in my eyes. The tears trailed into my gaping mouth. "That's why she did it! Because our affinities reflect one another. I CAN'T HELP IT!" I wasn't sure how true that was either.

"She's forgiven then. She can kill whoever she wants to force your magic out of you? To be like her, or *with* her?" Ben tried to sound mocking, but to me, he just sounded miserable.

"It's not like that," I said, clinging to his lowered volume. "The link, I can feel it when she's close. When she's near me, it's instinct. That's it. Please?" I didn't know what I was asking for, but I couldn't endure his rage. Because all it did was illustrate exactly how much I'd hurt him.

He bared his teeth in distaste. "You failed to mention that, Francesca. Meanwhile, during your little tryst, we were all working to keep you safe from her." He turned away from me. How I must have repulsed him. After he gave me so much. The self-hatred pulled me under, I was drowning in it. But if begging saved anything, I would collapse gratefully to my knees.

"She was in the woods that night. When you cut your foot," he stated, putting the pieces together. I nodded fast. I would tell him anything he asked for, if it meant things could go back to good.

"And is all the holding and the touching, all the rolling around together, is that a part of your witchy phenomenon too?" he spat.

I didn't know what it was.

"It's just how Jessamae is," I scrambled, "She doesn't relate to people normally." I was reaching, but it was possible. "I'll talk to her. I'll tell her to give me … space."

Ben's face remained harsh. Things weren't getting better. "And you think Pamela's killer will grant you that wish, do you?"

I thought I may have found a way out of this, out from under his anger. "She'll have to. If she ever wants to see me again."

"And is that soon?"

His expression finally cracked. I saw his agony underneath. I had never wanted to lie more than I wanted to lie to him in that moment. But I was frantic to give him whatever he asked for. I nodded, ravaged, tears clinging to my lower lip. "Tomorrow."

He hung his head and was finished. He didn't look at me as he walked through the sliding door, back into the house. I didn't follow. I couldn't witness his suffering again.

It wasn't long before I heard his car start, saw the headlight's yellow glow from over the peaked roof, before he backed out of the driveway. Before he left.

I considered running after him. He would see me in the driveway, might even be moved by the pageantry. But I just didn't have the energy, or the courage.

I tripped down the hall to Ben's room. I was so ashamed of letting Cleo see my ragged defeat. But Ben, the only thing I had, had left me. I was crumbling. The night after Pamela died, when I thought I had never felt so lonely, was a frilly tea party next to this. It was all my fault. And this new loneliness made me dismissive of such an exhausting thing as self-consciousness.

I opened the door. She was sitting on the bed with one glossy leg crossed over the other, reading a book. She was the epitome of ease and relaxation while Ben and I had been shrieking like feral cats outside her window. While I crushed Ben, and he ruined me in return.

"Ben's gone." I worked to keep my voice from wobbling. A pointless act, seeing as my face and neck were shining with tears.

"I heard, as did the rest of Aspen Ridge." She flipped a page, indifferent to me. "You have to give him time, Frankie. Even a seer couldn't have prepared for the abhorrence and jealousy he experienced today." She glanced at me under her lashes, revealing her antipathy, before closing her book and setting it on the small, scratched table near the bed. Virginia Wolfe.

She didn't adjust her position, didn't move at all. She only stared at me with unimpressed anticipation, as if I owed her an explanation, and no matter what I said, it already wasn't enough. She obviously wasn't as affected by my fucked behavior as Ben, but it seemed she thought less of me now. I didn't like it.

"You heard everything we said?" I asked, dreading a repeat.

"Thin walls."

Forcing myself to meet her eyes, I whispered, "The connection is real." My hands opened at my stomach. I didn't want to fight anymore.

"I know," Cleo replied curtly. "I can understand magical compulsion." She twisted her hand around in the air as if she were on display. "But Frankie, you are to blame for your secrecy and lies. If you felt the need to see her, you should have told Ben. He's hurt. I'm beyond irritated." She released an exhale that seemed to weigh ten pounds.

I appreciated her honesty. And she'd stayed, after everything. I staggered over to the bed and draped myself upon it like a wet towel. It didn't smell like Ben at all anymore, it smelled minty and sweet. I buried my face in sheets like I was burrowing for lost comfort there. "You're right," I admitted, muffled through the fabric. "I just didn't want him to hate me."

The grief I should have felt this morning consumed me in large chunks. Because I had lied. Because I was weak.

A soft pressure tickled my head. Cleo was petting me. It was unfamiliar, but it wasn't terrible. I didn't think Cleo was accustomed to this stuff either.

"It isn't just you anymore. We're together, the three of us. You need to remember that." She continued to stroke my hair. She didn't say he would forgive me, or that everything would be okay. She wasn't a seer. But her touch felt nice. I never asked her to stop, and I never moved away.

Impossibly, despite the pain that I wallowed in, with Cleo's fingers woven into my hair, I sank like a brick into unconsciousness.

I AWOKE IN DARKNESS. My body was sprawled in the bedding like a beached, stinking squid. I took up most of the space on the mattress and Cleo was curled around me, filling the left-over bits of bed. By sleeping here, I was causing a lot of discomfort.

I pushed myself up onto my arms and, to free up some of the mattress for Cleo, curved myself away from her. My head swiveled around. We weren't alone.

I froze, terror-stricken by the imposing shadow. It was motionless in the corner of the room. My eyes still had not adjusted to the dark, I waited worthlessly for the shape to move in.

"I want to meet her."

Ben's voice was like cool water on a burn. He had come home. My chest hummed and my eyes swam. I wasn't fully awake. "What?"

He pushed himself off the wall. His feet didn't make a sound. "I'm going to meet her before you leave with her. I see it, and it's very unlikely that we kill each other," he grunted. "If she wants to be a regular part of your life—if you're going to let her, despite what she did—then she should know that I am too. She should know me."

Uncomfortable as the thought of the two of them together was, I couldn't deny him this. He was right. "Okay, Ben." I was immersed in gratitude because he came back at all. The rest was so small compared to that.

"And she should know to keep her claws to herself. She can't keep snuffing out lives she deems inconvenient." His candor was expected, but I winced. I hoped he didn't catch it in the shadowed room. He didn't need to see how repressive I could be.

"Okay."

He sighed, assuaged at my agreement. He ambled forward and gently crawled over the corner of the bed. Cleo's body was rounded from left to right across the pillows. I scooched with care closer to her slumbering form, to leave more room for Ben's tall frame. The three of us were now stretched horizontally across the queen bed. Ben mashed himself into the fetal position after his legs brushed the floor.

I was halfway to an agreeable placement when he pulled me closer to his balled-up body. He extended his legs to fit me against his chest before bending them back into place. We were doing something like spooning, if the spoons had melted and curled in on themselves. I felt like I was strapped into a baby's car seat, but I wouldn't move.

"I'm sorry," I uttered into the void, so softly I hardly made any sound to hear. I thought he might have fallen asleep. I rolled my head around, finding a flat stretch of his arm. When I was as comfortable as I was going to get, I closed my eyes.

"Okay," he said.

"HOW ARE we even supposed to catch a bird?" I asked the group as we crossed into the aspens that surrounded Ben's home. I awkwardly informed them of Jessamae's request once we had all woken up, piled on top of each other in a sweaty mound. After a lengthy silence, the two agreed to help me with the task. I wanted to start with a beetle, but Ben thought that the damage dealt to something so small might be harder to repair than it was worth.

Cleo ducked down under a low-hanging branch, maneuvering the wilderness well. "Getting the bird will be easy for me. *You'll* be doing the heavy lifting," she smiled. Seeing Ben wrapped around me like a belt this morning seemed to erase some of her disappointment in me. "There are witches that can communicate with and control animals—the leshy, the centaur, some shifters—but we obviously can't do that. I'm going to call them closer, singing."

"Why aren't we already doing that?" I complained, clambering higher into the trees.

"Because we don't want any neighboring ears listening in. We'll get far enough, then we'll block your hearing. You're very impressionable, Princess." Ben pinched my cheek from beside me. "And the song will get in your head."

I shrugged off his arm. "I've handled myself just fine, thank you. How come the song doesn't 'get in your head'," I hooked my fingers into quotes.

He smiled at my grumpiness. "Oh, it does." He reached into the pocket of the blue swim shorts he wore today, pulling out small orange nubs. "Earplugs. I have enough for both of us. Plus, I can leave my head and see through you or Cleo. It lessens the effects. All of Cleo's magic needs a mind to prey upon."

Cleo gave us a sly look over her shoulder, "That counts you out, doesn't it?"

Ben clutched his heart as if shot and tumbled into me. I pushed against his heavy weight, tripping over a root. I grunted, but loved the return of my playful friend. "Then what's our plan?"

He kept an arm around me as he strolled across the now level ground. "We'll make ourselves silent, a small piece of magic and very straightforward. Once a birdie flies close enough, Snow White here will make the call. Then she won't have to sing too long, and the risk of you flinging yourself off a cliff or becoming catatonic is low."

I watched Cleo move through the woods warily. I was beginning to trust her, but that her affinity could ruin my mind was disquieting, to say the least.

The clearing we stopped in was objectively pretty, though not as green as it should be. Locals had carved their names into the flesh of the aspens over and over. I thought the marred bark looked very much like Ben's skin.

Cleo, looking like the goddess Diana in a sundress, turned around to face us wandering behind. She reached into the chest of her dress, pulling out a lock of her hair tied in its center with twine. "I cut this earlier today." She set her hair on a bed of dead leaves. I searched her shiny lengths and couldn't find a single uneven strand.

Cleo then held out her hands and Ben took her right. They both watched me, waiting. Realizing I would complete the triangle, I rushed forward and grabbed each of their hands in mine, the lock of hair in the center at our feet. Lilting energy surged through my bones the moment our hands connected.

Ben gave my fingers a squeeze. "Using Cleo's hair for payment, we're going to channel each other and become soundless. We'll only ask for an hour. Remember, it's not that you hope it happens, it's that you know it will." He winked and shook his arm wildly, getting out the tension. "Let's do this."

I closed my eyes against the obvious scrutiny from the other two. I imagined my complete silence, and knew that in doing so, I was creating it. One hour of silence. I never feared for a moment that I would emit a sound, with Ben and Cleo branching into me, the possibility felt silly.

I opened my eyes to the excited gazes of my onlookers and let go of their hands. I tested my borrowed ability by jumping onto a dry, crackly stick. Nothing. It was spooky, like I had lost one of my senses again. I moved to kick a thick fallen branch, fascinated by the magic, and slipped, blundering down onto one knee.

"Shit!" I exclaimed, before slapping my hand over my mouth.

Ben chuckled and Cleo huffed out an exasperated breath. "We can still speak, only your movements are silent," she informed me with hoity-toity superiority.

"You could have said something. Literally."

Ben and Cleo separated and drifted noiselessly through the forest like disembodied souls. They were spaced out twenty or so feet apart as they moved forward; I hastily lined up with them, attempting to match the distance.

Though I could feel the hard-packed dirt below me, without the dragging sound of my shoes, I struggled for balance, at times panicked that I was floating. I couldn't keep my eyes from the ground long and checked in with my feet regularly. I made a poor hunter.

I would have to kill something today, I thought to myself for the hundredth time. Animals felt more innocent than human beings; they had never acted maliciously toward me. Picturing the frantic racing heart in my hands was nauseating. Especially considering my affinity had appeared so spotty since presenting.

If I *did* manage to succeed—which I couldn't quash my doubts about—I wouldn't use the same bird more than once. Surely being killed and brought back into your body repeatedly would leave some trauma behind, even for a bird. And I didn't want to take an entire flock for an experiment. I frowned down at my silent shoes.

A field mouse scurried out from under a rock nearby, lifting its tiny twitchy nose into the air. I looked to Ben and Cleo from the corner of my eye. Neither of them had heard the mouse and were continuing through the wood. I kept my mouth shut. Mice were so defenseless. A bird seemed … less so?

Shortly afterward, I heard fragile chirping in the trees above. Cleo was staring up through the leaves as Ben jogged noiselessly toward me. He stood behind me with his hands on my shoulders, subtly restricting.

"It's time to block your hearing, okay?" He whispered so quietly I had to strain my ears. He offered a construction-orange plug. They were squashed and oddly shaped.

"Used?" I asked with a lift to my lip. Ben shrugged in response. "I'll just plug my ears." I lodged my index fingers into my earholes, hoping it would be enough. Ben smashed the nasty plugs into his ears, then covered my hands with his, creating fleshy earmuffs.

Cleo watched our precautions until she decided we were as ready as we were going to get, then she opened her mouth and sang.

The trill was muffled, but the melody was there, enough that I started pushing against Ben's hands that sandwiched my head. He pushed inward as I fought. I wanted the song, I felt it whipping the air around me. I pumped my fists harder against him, batting my knuckles into his. His grip softened, but not enough.

Then, distracted, I watched our dainty target flutter downward toward the music. Cleo held her hands out as an invitation to the thing. My knees buckled in jealousy and hatred for that bird as her hands closed around it. The song stopped immediately, and I went limp. Ben held me up by my head, my legs wiggling like spaghetti and my neck dangerously taut. He lowered me down to my butt before patting my head in consolation. "Whew, that was a close one. I almost let go of you, Frank."

Cleo approached us, her hands caged the chirping. The agitation at Cleo's music swiftly morphed into horrified guilt.

Ben bobbed on his heels beside me, a thin switchblade balanced between his fingers. "I can do it if you want."

As tempting as it was to shuck the responsibility, I couldn't keep coasting on the backs of Ben and Cleo. The whole purpose of this was to push me into the same league as the two of them—three of them, if you included Jessamae. It was my fault the bird would die. I should be the one to hold the knife. I took it.

Cleo kneeled gracefully. She gripped the frightened animal held it out to me. Though it felt like my heart was trying to climb out my neck and escape me, I put the knife on my thigh and took the bird between my fists. It had a white chest and a deep black face surrounding its glossy dark eyes. Its loud chirping grew incessant and shrill. "It's okay, it's okay, you'll come back. You'll be right back." I hoped desperately that I wasn't lying.

I held the struggling bird in my left hand and picked up the knife with my right. I thought I was shaking, but I couldn't be certain. My vision was wobbly, I worried I might black out.

"I'll bring you back. I can do this."

I didn't look at Ben, I didn't want to see the understanding and encouragement I knew I'd find there. I held the knife, terrified, over the quivering breast of the bird. I steeled myself. For once, I would not be the passive bystander.

I plunged the knife, puncturing the feathered chest like a tough sofa cushion, and released a pent-up sob from my throat. It struggled in my fingers for the smallest of moments. The woods hushed as the chirping finished. The bird stilled, dead.

Where it lay felt like a hole in the air, and I was overcome with absence where the knife still jutted. I yanked the weapon roughly from the dead bird and immediately caught the stink of death oozing from it. "Why can I already smell it?"

I held the small bubble of blood under my thumbs and brought the bird to my forehead, hoping against hope I could put back what I'd taken. I mumbled pleas under my breath as I willed the wound to close in my hands and for the hole I had created to fill. The fume of death spread like goo in my fingers. I was tapping the bird body against my face. It wouldn't rise. *Please, please, please.* "Please, please, please."

I rubbed the sticky mess under my thumbs, making things worse. I was spiraling. I willed the chirps to fill the air and was met with only a taunting silence. I felt a hand on my shoulder and the exhale of Ben's useless affirmations in my ear. I squeezed the bird so hard, I feared I'd pop its organs. But this bird would never use its organs again. Its heart had been destroyed. I had killed it, and that was all.

17

I GRIPPED the animal between my hands savagely, close to crushing it. I begged in vain that whatever magic existed, wherever it was in me, to seep through my skin.

Ben touched my arm as if afraid. "Don't break it. Relax, Frankie." I felt my fingers ease around the bristled feathers. "That's it."

"It looks like you can't resurrect life. Straight-forward healing is a much more common affinity. Though I don't understand why Jessamae would be drawn to you, if that were the case," Cleo reasoned from somewhere nearby. My eyes were tethered to the hole I had made in the bird, the hole I had turned it into and still held in the air.

Ben braced his hand under my elbow and heaved. After noticeable effort, I surrendered and put my weight back onto my feet, the bird cradled loosely in my palms. He put his hands on my neck and forced my head up, searching my downcast eyes.

"Hey, hey, Frank, look at me." He rattled my head. "Frankie, look at me." My eyes flicked to his and back to the bird in rapid succession. "We'll still use it. Bird bones are a valuable payment for magic. It won't be for nothing." I was nodding but I mostly wanted him to stop talking—it *felt* a lot like nothing. "Let's take it back to the house. It will supply our very limited apothecary." He put an arm around my shoulders and led me toward the edge of the clearing.

"We need to conduct some sort of trial," Cleo insisted. "I watched as Frankie revived a dead daffodil. Although it might have not been entirely past saving." She ran through the forest quickly to catch up to Ben and me.

"Quite the pickle," Ben grumbled dismissively. He pulled me in closer to his body and kissed the side of my head.

"Why did you let me do that?" I whispered so Cleo couldn't hear. "You must have seen me fail."

Ben sighed, as if he was waiting for this question. "Telling you what I see could affect the likelihood of certain futures, Frankie," Ben explained in a strained voice. "The future is so intricate and frangible. If I get a vision, I could see a dozen possibilities. If I'm focused, I could see a hundred—and those one hundred visions could ultimately show only a few possible outcomes with insubstantial differences.

"If I told you the chances of success were twenty-five percent, you may change your behavior in some way and the reaction could decimate the chances of success in that particular time-line." He pulled his gaze back to the bird in my hands, as if he forgot what I'd done for a moment.

"Twenty-five percent?" I asked.

"It's just an example, Frank."

We hiked in silence for a while and Cleo had fallen several paces behind, undoubtedly distracted by the implications of my failure. Ben began making *pssst* sounds in my ear. I didn't react to the noise.

"I'm proud of you." I jerked my head away from the bird and up to his face. He smiled at my surprise. "That took guts."

I felt a new kind of shame at his words. "I'm not good at this. Look how messed up I am over a dumb little bird." The memory of Ben and the fire swirled before my eyes. "I'm not strong enough for this."

He waited a long time before responding. "It gets easier. Any people we take from, we try to make sure they deserve a little loss. Scumbags, to the layman, like the man Cleo chose for the third eye. Animals are always more difficult. Just remember that it's not for nothing, and we'll use everything we take. More so than the chicken or the beef we eat."

The argument made sense. It felt different to hold the desperate animal in my hands than to eat a cheeseburger, even if that was a cop-out.

I took a deep breath and nodded.

"Have you thought more about your … living situation?" he asked, undoubtedly to get my mind off things.

I said, "A little bit," when I hadn't at all. Between the burial, Jessamae's visit, Ben almost hating me, and now this, moving in with Cleo was the least of my worries. But Ben's general cheer told me the likelihood of my "living situation."

We broke through the edge of the trees. Now that Ben had brought it up to me, my back started aching dully from my cramped nights here. Having a bed to stretch out in would be a luxury.

As we padded across the grass, a breeze tickled my face. It took me a moment to understand why we were still in shadow though we had moved away from the forest's shelter. I looked up for the sun and saw a thick blanket of clouds stretched across the sky. It would rain very soon now. I heard the parched grass crunch underfoot and almost smiled.

A rumbling noise pulled my attention to Ben's house at the corner of the pasture. A big boxy truck was reversing into the driveway, an annoying beep ringing out from it. I turned to Ben, a confused scrunch to my face.

Cleo danced across the field in front of us, emanating pure joy. "Finally! It's here!"

"What is happening right now?" I asked.

"Cleo's bed has arrived," Ben answered before he pulled his arm away and turned around, walking backward in front of me. "So. All shit cut from the conversation, I did see the two of you living together, about nine out of ten times, for the last few days, but I need to make sure that you aren't actually hating it and just want to avoid conflict."

He held my wrists, guiding me, as he proceeded backwards around the side of his house. "So, I'll ask. And I expect nothing but brutal honesty from you: are you okay with Cleo living in your house?"

It was better to imagine two of us in that house than to imagine myself in the house alone, haunted by my mom and grandmother. I thought that once I was back to normal, or at least closer than I felt right now, I might want some quiet time to myself. Provided Ben kept this little gem across town.

"I am," I said with more conviction than expected. Whether it was fear, or loneliness, or my reaction to Ben's predictions—just as he'd warned—I wanted the two of them around. And Cleo was like a tether, keeping Ben close.

Ben beamed at me. He stopped several yards away from Cleo, who was talking to the movers from outside the driver side window.

I pictured Ben in my room with me, subbing out my twin bed for his queen, replacing the teen décor with some of his art, and maybe a fern or succulent on that hideous not-white-anymore cabinet. Ben would water it. I imagined the two of us in the same bed. The ability to feel him near me at the slightest movement was incredibly enticing. My mind ran away from me at the thought of his closeness. The spark he'd given me on Patrick's counter would be nothing compared to the fire he'd burn in my bed. My cheeks warmed as I daydreamed. The idea was so peaceful, my eyelids drooped. I could sleep right here.

The white and black bird between my hands caught me off guard. I'd felt a spasm, as if the little wings wanted to flutter. I lifted my thumbs from the breast, the blood had dried into the feathers, but I couldn't detect the gaping puncture I remembered. Its eyes opened. Its nervous head jolted left and right, clearly horrified. I flattened my hands out like a tabletop and the bird hopped up swiftly to its knobby feet. It promptly took off into the air, eager to get the hell away from me. Ben and I watched open-mouthed as it disappeared into the trees. The bird lived.

Ben wrapped his arms around me and lifted me off the ground. "I knew it! Just a case of the yips, typical Frank!" I clung to his shoulders, relieved.

"I did it! Oh, my god, holy shit!" It was imagining us together, I thought to myself. It finally diverted me from my self-loathing.

He put me back on my feet and kissed me fast. His lips were hard on mine for a heartbeat before he pulled away. Before I could react, he was grinning widely and ruffling my hair. "You are amazing," he said before turning to join Cleo by the truck.

One of the truths of my restoration dawned on me. My connection to Jessamae was otherworldly, but it was real. Balance. I may have had a choice in this, but I doubted I could stay away from her, particularly if she was near. And she would be, whether I invited her or not.

Cleo was now standing off to the side while Ben spoke with the movers. "How did these guys get your bed?" I asked.

"I left a key under the mat."

"Dangerous."

"So am I." She tossed her hair. "I only put it there the morning I met you. Ben told me about your grandma as soon as it happened. He said he saw the three of us together, so I made some preparations. Just in case." She was proud of herself, bordering on smug.

Confusion pinched my brows. A wrinkle would form there after this week. "How did you get to the bonfire? And back?"

She smirked, truly in great spirits today. "When you watched me dance naked and fainted?"

I remembered her shining dark skin. "It was blurry," I mumbled, embarrassed.

Cleo coughed into her hand to cover her giggle and I narrowed my eyes. I was a regular riot to these people. "We took my date's car. I drove him home after." A moment passed before

I understood her date was the one-eyed man. My mouth pulled down, nauseated. "Don't worry, we took care of him. He was healing fine when I left to meet Ben at the bookstore."

Their "date" must have left quite an impression on this man, other than the empty eye socket.

Ben trotted over. "These kind gentlemen are going to pack up whatever else you had here and meet us at Frank's."

I pursed my lips. Probably should have cleaned this week. Or ever.

THE MOVERS TOOK Pamela's bed and dated pine furniture out to their truck. They had the blue couch nestled between all that wood. I hadn't even noticed them lift it. I wasn't sad to see it go. Ben had asked they remove it all for an extra fee. I figured, since I'd be taking Cleo out of his bedroom, bathroom, and liquor cabinet, we were even on this one.

I told Cleo I would rather stay in my own room than move into Pamela's, which was bigger. Even though it was originally my mom's room, it felt nasty and unwelcoming behind that door, as if I still needed Pamela's permission to be in there. I was unsticking my youthful posters from the walls—they were so old they were falling apart in my hands—but my eyes kept wandering to my ugly, toilet-colored cabinet. It seemed more offensive than the posters. If I was going to keep it, I wouldn't keep it like this. I was halfway certain there were a few paint cans in the garage from when my mom first bought this house.

I passed Cleo's room in the hallway. Ben was helping her put her enormous walnut bed frame together. They sat cross-legged on the floor, bickering about what screws were the right screws to screw.

I moseyed easily through the now open space that was living room and kitchen. I grabbed a chilled beer from the fridge and took three quick gulps. I'd forced Ben to stop at Jim's on the way here. It almost felt like home seeing those cans on their own rack inside the fridge.

The garage was through the small kitchen, attached to the house. I opened the heavy door and flicked on the light. Something scurried under Pamela's Honda, knocking over various forgotten boxes in its path with a clatter. I clutched my chest in terror, choking on my own breath. Once I gathered myself, I crept down the few steps and timidly ducked under the edge of the car.

Shrewd yellow eyes stared back at me. It was a cat, one of the most solemn cats in existence, surely. It was gray with wildly long fur; it almost appeared to be wearing a cat-skin coat over its own. Between its hairy fringe was a wide, white-tipped nose. Its ears were oddly rounded, like a teddy's, as if someone had snipped off the tips. The animal somehow gave off the impression of both a lion and a wizard, both ugly and regal, like an old English king. Its bottle-brush tail swished lazily, as if it had never been frightened of me.

"Here kitty, kitty, kitty," I baited, tapping my fingers on the cement under the car. The cat was unimpressed, judging by its acidic yellow eyes. "Fine." I stood and charged back through the kitchen door. The fridge may have something more tempting to offer than my wiggling fingers, I thought, as I opened the white door that still held wedding invitations addressed to my mom.

The milk was spoiled; I wasn't sure if cats drank milk outside of cartoons anyway. The cheese had mold on it, and I didn't think it would be interested in an egg or my jar of raspberry preserves. There were a couple slimy slices of turkey stashed in a crisper drawer that seemed moderately appetizing. I closed the refrigerator and turned back to the garage only to, again, choke on surprise.

There it was. The cat sat just inside the closed door to the garage watching me, bored. This was a very quick and disconcerting animal. Displaying the meat for its consideration, I crouched onto my ankles. It took its sweet time deliberating. My thighs were convulsing in protest when it finally stepped a stately paw forward. Once within biting distance, it snatched the meat from my fingers viciously. After scarfing it back, it stared expectantly, waiting for more.

"What the hell is that?" Ben asked from the hallway.

"What does it look like?"

"I genuinely don't know."

"Who is this sweet baby?" Cleo pushed past Ben, and without question, adoringly lifted the cat into her arms. To my astonishment, it didn't object. It seemed to enjoy it, purring as loud as a garbage truck. She scratched its floofy head with blatant affection. "What's its name?"

"I doubt it has one. It was squatting in the garage. It just ate the last of the deli meat." The cat glared at me around Cleo's caressing fingers.

"Well, we can't keep calling it, 'it'," Cleo asserted. She adjusted the cat and lifted its tail to Ben's face, he jerked back as if slapped by the cat's anus. "What do you see?"

He squinted at the rear-end. "If the big fuzzy balls are any indication …"

I didn't like where this was going. "We aren't keeping it?" but it came out as a question. "I just wanted to give it a little food."

Cleo's affect grew frigid. "You want to send him out in the middle of summer to starve to death? Or did you want to keep him in the hot garage?"

Although this cat looked like the last thing that needed protecting, she had a point. I was still reeling from the brief death of the little bird and full of leftover guilt.

Cleo was crushing it with love, but its eyes stayed intent on me, full of human-like irritation. How could the thing dislike me? All I'd done was feed it. I suppressed the urge to extend my middle finger.

"We can keep it until it rains, at least. I'm not exactly a cat person."

"You aren't exactly a people person either," Ben added rudely.

"I'll go to the store for some supplies. I need to pick up a few things anyway," Cleo volunteered. I wasn't sure she'd even heard us over the purring. Even so, if it came down to it, I'd hurl the cat out the window in a few days' time. She rubbed her face in the forest of the cat's fur, by which he was either delighted or disgusted—it was impossible to tell.

I said, "You can take Pamela's car. I think it might be mine now. At least until the bank comes for it."

Her smile nearly brought tears to my eyes; she was having such a good day today. "Two cars. Perfect." She carried the cat to her room and retrieved her bag. "You two think of names while I'm gone." She held her hand out for the key.

"We aren't naming him! He's a guest in this house." I found the spare in a kitchen drawer, and without a word, she swished out the door.

There was an immediate formality to being alone with Ben now that hadn't existed before. I avoided any conversation by returning to the garage for the can of paint I'd originally sought before getting so upsettingly sidetracked.

I found a can on a metal shelf covered in spider webs. It wasn't white; the drippings along the edge of the can were a grayish-blue, and the label read "Smokey Sea." I hated the name but liked the color. My mom must have bought it for a project that she'd given up on. Either that, or the can's been here for decades.

I found a stiff brush and went back inside. I hurried past Ben's still form in the kitchen and down the hallway, noting the silver transient cat lounge across Cleo's bare mattress.

The cabinet was immense, taking up an entire wall of the bedroom with dozens of knobs and doors and drawers. I hoped there was enough paint in the can. The last thing I wanted was to walk into the hardware store looking for renovation supplies, when, by now, the entire town had heard from Scott that I was in mourning. And they were probably already gossiping about the moving truck that had just driven off.

I had called my boss before our hike earlier today and was scheduled to be back at work tomorrow, promising him grief every second before then. We would all be back in the swing of things come sunrise—Ben painting houses and Cleo doing whatever it was that she did. I still hadn't asked. The detail seemed so minor compared to everything else.

I began emptying out the cabinet cubbies of trash. Every corner greedily held scores of food crumbs, dust, and knots of my curly hair. The variety expanded, encompassing several dead bugs, some rock-hard gum, and something black and sticky that had dripped its way through two drawers.

I removed the drawers, planning to scrub them under running water, when I heard a clinking sound. Some metal glinted from the corner of the bottom drawer amongst the debris. It was an earring. I rolled it between my fingers. It was my mom's, a small gold hoop that finished in a delicate opal. I wasn't a sentimental person and had thrown out most of her things soon after the accident, but this sucker snuck under my radar. Well, it had made it this far, I decided, as I stuck it through one of the empty holes in my ear.

"Pretty."

I turned around, a little embarrassed, to see Ben watching me from the doorway.

"Didn't see you there," I mumbled. "What have you been doing?"

He sauntered into the room. "Cleaning out the fridge and unpacking a few things in Cleo's room." He studied the earring for a long time, as if I were on display, then he noticed the paint can. "Smokey Sea?"

I shrugged and motioned to the cabinet. He bent over and tapped my brush bristles against the can. They clanged. He sighed before he chucked the brush into one of the heaping black garbage bags on my carpet. Like a flashy magician, he pulled two large and satisfyingly soft brushes from the side pocket of his swim shorts. I took one, hiding my awe at his magic, and rolled my hair into a tumbleweed on my head.

I popped the paint's lid, and the smell of Ben filled the room. The stuff needed a lot of stirring but spread across the ugly exterior of my furniture nicely. Ben's strokes were much smoother than mine, so I would paint a coat, and he would paint over that coat. We worked for a long time without talking too much and finished before Cleo returned. Ben left the room to get a drink of water and I used the opportunity to wipe the swollen sweat bubbles from my forehead and neck. It had cooled today but the stuffy air persisted, turning the house into a sauna. Ben came back through the doorway and held out a dewy glass of water. I drank like an animal, letting small streams course down my neck and soak my shirt.

He was entertained by my thirst, watching me raptly. Then he touched his fingertips to my hair, and I froze, the glass still pressed to my mouth. When he pulled his hand away, it was smeared with Smokey Sea. I fluttered my hands along my face and hair.

He laughed at me, "You're only making it worse." He took my hand and held it to my eyes—it was coated in blue splotches.

He pulled off his shirt without warning, and my mouth filled with gooey saliva. He pressed the cloth to my forehead and tenderly wiped the paint away. He wrapped the shirt around my neck and kneaded it into my skin. I nearly whimpered at the glorious sensation.

Too soon he said, "There you go, though blue looks good on you." He threw his shirt on the floor where it fit in well with my stained and smelly clothes.

I didn't like that he stopped touching me. The something unfamiliar between the two of us persisted. "Are you still mad at me, Benny?"

Exhaling in a gust, he sat on the edge of my ratty bed. "I'm not sure, Frank. But if I am, it's not much. I just wish you didn't want to see her. And I can't be mad at you for what I wish."

Ben held my eyes assiduously. I wanted to tell him I didn't want to see her but saying that I *needed* to wouldn't help anything.

Suddenly, remembering the move today made me gasp. "I didn't tell Jessamae we moved back in. She won't know where to find me."

He sneered. It was unpleasant to see. "Don't fret about that, Princess. She's proven herself more than a capable tracker."

I lowered myself next to him on the bed. Wanting to alleviate his pain, mostly, I stretched a timid hand onto his and began tracing the prominent veins that decorated its back. He dropped his head backward as my fingers traced his blood past his elbow, around his shoulder, and close to his heart. I easily felt it thump through all the membrane. I thought I could follow every trail in his body. I could do this for days.

His hand snapped hastily around mine, stopping me as I reached his throat. His breaths sounded shaky in my ears. He used his grip on me to push me down to my back beside him. He moved onto his arms and held himself on top of me. His eyes were hypnotic in their motion. I lifted my hands to his shoulders and ran my fingers over his freckles, warming them. He leaned his head down and I felt his kiss on my neck, so soft, once, twice, three times. My pulse quickened and a deep blush built up steadily from my chest. He dragged his mouth along my collar bone and spoke into my skin, "Red."

His lips were on mine and we burned. My hand found the back of his neck and held tightly over the soft fuzz growing there. He kissed my cheeks down to my ear, his hot exhales tickling me. He wrapped his long arms around me and lifted us both off the bed. We floated for a delicious moment before we slammed back down to the mattress.

He made a sound deep in his throat, almost a purr, as his

tongue crept into my mouth. His hand burrowed under my shirt, and I arched my back, thrilled by his touch. His long fingers grazed my nipple, and an embarrassing moan escaped my lips. Hungered by my enthusiasm, he had my shirt off in one swift rip. It felt like I had Pop Rocks along my ribs; his bare skin was blistering on mine. My legs wrapped around his hips, which pressed against me in a tease. It wasn't enough. I needed the fire. His hand found the button of my jeans. I lifted my hips off the bed. The button snapped open, he dragged the denim down, and then his skin was on mine again, his tongue on mine again. *Yes!*

Ben held himself too far above me. *No!*

"See?" he growled, right before a slow knock sounded on the front door.

18

"I GUESS I BETTER ... GET THAT," I squeaked from beneath Ben's weight. He hopped off me like I had literally burned him and moved far back against the wall. I stood unsteadily, lightheaded from the heavy breathing, and buttoned my pants. I found my shirt tossed to the side of the bed and threw it over my head before toddling to the living room. The light had dimmed outside the house, turning everything to a soft gray. I hadn't noticed how late it was.

My hand trembled on the cold doorknob. It felt as though I was introducing a date to my parents for the first time. I couldn't shake the image as I opened the door for death.

Jessamae stood completely erect in the center of the porch with her arms straight at her sides. The overhead light reflected strangely off her otherworldly eyes. She scared me. It could have been that it was getting dark outside, because at night she was unnerving, terrifying even.

She had changed her outfit, though she remained nonde-script in jeans and a flannel. Her tangled hair had been braided and forced through an elastic at its end. It reminded me of when people braided the manes of horses. Her mouth stretched into a smile for me. My heart thrummed wildly.

"There you are," she sighed, reaching for my face. Resisting urge to lean in, I took another reluctant step back, sensing Ben in the room behind me.

I flapped my arm around like an injured bird, gesturing to the room. "Please, come in." She scanned the space over my head and her expression cooled dramatically. Ben was back there alright.

She stalked past me like a rogue toward a victim. She diffused her power throughout the room. It was like a living thing breathing against me, and I fought the instinct to shrink back from her. Ben leaned against the wall at the tip of the hallway, unimpressed. He never put his shirt back on and his tattoos were harsh in the dying light.

"Benjamin," Jessamae said as a way of introduction. His name on her lips sounded like an insult, and though he was much taller than her, she seemed to look down on him. "Lovely to finally meet Frankie's friend." She said my preferred nickname with much less resistance than she had on the mountainside, proving her familiarity with me and adding to her condescension.

Ben pursed his lips. "Look at the chutzpah on you."

Her expression was carnal. "It's well earned, believe you me."

"Sure. Nothing like killing skinny old ladies. Better than vitamins."

I hurried to get between the two of them, my lungs wilted against their weighted hostility. "Let's be cool, okay? A bit unnecessary but, Ben? This is Jessamae. Jessamae, Ben." I motioned to each in turn even though these pleasantries were useless.

Jessamae looked absolutely beastly. "As I said, lovely."

Ben gave her a disdainful smile but didn't gift her any verbal response.

Cleo, the angelic being that she was, chose this exceedingly uncomfortable moment to walk through the kitchen door. "Sorry I was gone for so long. I bought a few things for the house." Her arms were burdened with gigantic white paper bags. "There are a few more in the car if someone could—" she caught sight of Jessamae inching closer to Ben, "—help." Her pause was her only show of surprise. In an instant, her features switched from confused to composed.

Jessamae turned to the newcomer, and her expression lightened. "You must be Cleo. Pleasure." Cleo nodded in greeting, displaying nothing but polite interest. "Did you say you needed some help carrying things in from your car?" Jessamae continued.

Cleo didn't recover from that surprise quite as undetectably. Her eyes flicked to Ben and me behind Jessamae's back. "Sure. Thank you."

Two pale eyes shone into mine, before following Cleo back out the door, closing it softly behind her.

I was afraid to say anything out loud, knowing just how extensive Jessamae's hearing was, but I shot a warning scowl at Ben. If he couldn't be nice, then I'd end his little meet and greet right now. He only raised an eyebrow at me, unashamed. My head drooped. I couldn't blame him. This was his compromise and Jessamae wasn't making it easy for anyone.

Cleo struggled back into the room carrying just as many bags as the first trip. Jessamae held even more. My house was going to look like an entirely different building by morning. I felt a wave of gratitude for Cleo.

They piled the bags in the kitchen, and the silence in the room was awkward to the point of throbbing. Jessamae returned her attention to Ben. "The sun is going down. Perhaps you two should get going. I'll take Frankie off your hands."

A grin overtook Ben's face as if he'd been given a toy. "Oh, didn't you hear? Cleo moved in this morning! I was going to help her put a few things together. I'll be here when you get back." The intent was hardly veiled. Jessamae frowned but briskly regained her dignified contempt. Ben seemed to brighten at her shifting expressions. "Unless you would like to extend your invitation tonight to the two of us? I'm sure Cleo wouldn't mind putting this off until tomorrow."

Jessamae lifted her chin and stared him down. "Not tonight.

I'd like a little privacy. She is free to leave your supervision from time to time, isn't she?"

"And if she wanted me to come along, you wouldn't sacrifice her comfort just to be creepy, right?"

Her coy smile was mocking. "I wouldn't dream of it."

They both turned to me in anticipation, and I itched with stage fright. Cleo was following everything attentively but remained below their radar.

I was tired of this damsel in distress reputation I was being shrouded with when it came to Ben. Jessamae shouldn't view him as my savior, although that was absolutely what he was as of late. He made me look weak in front of her. I didn't want to say what I was about to. I didn't want him to feel inferior or snubbed, but, "I think the two of us would be okay." Ben's expression didn't change, and that was bad. "But I'll call if anything comes up, promise." He nodded once. I was more than eager to leave his icy presence.

∽∾∾

"HOW DID YOUR EXPERIMENT GO?" Jessamae asked as we pulled out of the driveway. She had returned in the same sticker-family van that she'd driven yesterday. I quelled my apprehension over ridding a family of their vehicle for one more night—Wednesday was practically the weekend anyway—and buckled my seatbelt.

"It was terrible, but it worked, if that's what you're asking."

She softened. "I'm sorry. I know it's hard to do. But it is what we are."

"Yeah, about that. I have some questions."

She returned her eyes to the road and dipped her chin in invitation.

"Can you, uh, this is going to sound stupid … smell life? Can you smell living things when they're around?"

A smile played at the corners of her mouth. "You sense death." She stated it with certainty. "Of course, you do. For me, it's not so much that I can smell life. All life smells differently, but I can sense it. I can read a being's vitality, whether they are close to death, or far from it. I think there's an evolutionary aspect to that. For example—" She turned off the main road and headed east. "I developed a very strong sense of sight in darkness, and for many years I was nocturnal because of it."

I coughed loudly to hide my gulp, spewing spit over the dash. Her grin doubled in size.

"I know it might be strange, but I prefer the night. We are naturally in tune with the moon, and as I strengthened, I developed other abilities. I could move silently, and at incredible speeds. The time it took to end a life halved, then halved again. There are even times when I can touch, without touch, if the urge is strong enough."

I tugged on my curls, remembering the strand suspended before my face as Jessamae remained on the other side of Ben's screen door.

"And abilities that will assist in your restoration will develop as you grow strong, too. It happens for all of us if we practice. Which is what we will be doing tonight."

"I have another question," I stammered. I hadn't allowed myself to dwell on it until now, but it was festering in my mind. If anyone could understand, it would be Jessamae. "Do you ever … eat any part of the things you hurt?" Jessamae bared her teeth, offended. "No, it's just, uh, when I was healing Cleo, the night with the window. I had her blood on my hands and I just …" I held my splayed fingers before me in horror.

"You ate it," Jessamae finished for me.

I nodded, desperate for answers. Specific answers, like: Don't worry, it will never happen again, you aren't crazy or cannibalistic.

Jessamae considered my wicked confession. "I have a theory," she finally voiced. "I take the vitality of others, their health, into my body when I touch them. If we balance one another as I believe we do, then you would be taking the inverse of that—injury, sickness—into your body. Finding strength in it. Was Cleo the first?"

The story of the pain junkie flashed through my head, brutal as a migraine. "No. Ben had a cut on his hand, and a black eye. But I can't remember feeling anything like that."

"Well, if his injuries weren't as severe, they wouldn't have had the same effect on you. Was hers a mortal wound? Was she close to death?"

I remembered her convulsing on the ground. It was a lot of blood, but it wasn't like I'd had any medical training. "I'm not sure."

"Yes, I suppose I could tell more than you if it was. At least right now. Just give it time," she consoled me, as if my upset was only due to my fledgling abilities. "An interesting theory at the very least." I thought she sounded like Cleo, and I didn't want to look at her. I finally returned my eyes to the road.

"What are we doing here?" I blurted instantly. Jessamae turned the inconspicuous minivan toward the hilltop graveyard, and the now-familiar rotten stench permeated the car.

Her eyes met mine, instilling both confidence and fear, "It's the perfect place for the two of us to test our potential." She drove the car steadily over the stone bridge, taking us into the forest of headstones. In the fading light of dusk, the different shapes threw shadows across the steep ground that almost seemed to break away and start lives of their own. I didn't see any grieving visitors tonight. We passed through alone.

Jessamae didn't give any further context for this evening's agenda, so when we pulled up to the freshly filled plot, panic skittered through my insides like a thousand spiders.

"What are we doing here?"

She gave me the courtesy of looking slightly uncomfortable. "You said you wanted answers about your father. I'm going to help you get them."

She left the headlights on and unfolded out of the driver's seat. I unbuckled my seatbelt. This was not going to be good; there was actually a decent chance it would be awful. But my curiosity had not been settled over the last few days—it had grown in me like a cancer. Who was this deadbeat that my mom didn't think was worth knowing?

Jessamae waited for me in front of the car, her eyes reflected in the headlights like fox's. "What does my grandmother have to do with us?" I asked.

"Come sit with me," she said, avoiding my question. She kneeled beside the dark rectangle of black soil that buried Pamela and pressed her hands to the surface of freshly churned earth.

An abyss was buried within the grave. I felt my grandmother's empty cavity in the earth, just as I'd felt the bird's void in my hands. I could sense a similar emptiness in the graves nearby, though not as strongly as this one, directly beneath us. Jessamae was right—I had a sixth sense. And as the smell continued to saturate the air, I bit back vomit.

Though I hated being here, I wouldn't say it. Jessamae had to have known anyway. A grandmother's grave didn't imbue any warm-and-fuzzies, and as disassociated as she seemed, that fact couldn't have escaped her. Part of me wanted to enjoy this night with Jessamae; it was insane and stubborn, but I kneeled next to her beside the plot.

Jessamae produced a knapsack I hadn't noticed her take from the car. She stretched it open like a lion's mouth and tipped it upside down over the grave.

Bones. Long pale bones toppled out of the bag like the worst game of Jacks I'd ever seen. "What the fuck?" I shook my head, straining for fresh air.

"Relax, my peach. They're the bones of a fawn. I took it down naturally this afternoon."

"What part of that is supposed to relax me?"

"It will help us. The bones will enable us to channel the

earth." She placed her hands into the soft soil, jockeying the bones, some still clinging with fur. "Put your hands here. Do you feel that? That power?"

With shaking hands, I reached for the dirt. Before I'd even made contact, I felt the vibration of energy coming from the soil.

"We're going to open the earth—"

"No." It was the first time I had blatantly denied Jessamae and the word tasted bitter on my tongue.

She didn't react. "Don't you want to find out about your father?"

"Not enough to dig up a corpse." The quaking in my hands had spread to my shoulders.

Jessamae slid her knees to the side until our bodies touched. The earth's energy combined with our connection, that simple touch, made me feel like a tuning fork in a paint-stained t-shirt. She was making me angry, using our link against me while we bent over my grandmother's body.

"I promise, everything will be back to normal by the hour's end. Your resurrection was successful before—"

"It was only a stupid bird, Jessamae. As in *small*."

She put her rough hand on top of mine. "I won't ask for such power from you tonight. We only need a piece of her, Pamela's consciousness, for the briefest of moments. You can channel me, and it should be more than enough, considering I was the one that … removed her from the body. We only need a few answers, then we will lay her to rest once more."

I couldn't say the plan wasn't alluring, but I couldn't say it wasn't atrocious either. "What exactly do you get from this?"

"You and I create a perfect balance. As my converse, you give me completion. And I have the same desire to discover your past that you do." Her eyes flashed and my elbows nearly buckled from the pounding force she was channeling through me.

The power made me feel … infinite. And the boundless potential made me afraid of myself, for the first time.

"We only need a second. One or two questions?" I begged

through my trembling. The energy wove through my blood, growing and stretching to the point of pain.

Jessamae grinned, "That's all." She rubbed her body against mine, took her hand away and pressed it to the plot. "Channel the earth, channel me. It will be easy. Channel the earth, channel me."

The dirt began to judder. "That's it," she urged. The ground shook apart as light and as amiable as soft Sahara sand. The clumps sifted, each clod of dirt separating itself.

"What's happening?" I was surprised at how steady my voice was—I felt like a snow globe trapped in a child's avid gyrating fists.

Jessamae was horribly excited. "We are opening a door."

The black square of ground almost appeared to melt under my fingers, and it became less than powder, sinking deeper and deeper. The fawn's dry bones were consumed by the earth. Soon, I was hanging over the edge of the grave, extending my arms underground, past their reach, as the hole grew.

"It's okay," Jessamae whispered over the hiss of dissolving dirt. "Move your hands up onto the grass, next to mine, just keep your focus on the same spot."

I tried to raise my torso using my weak core and nearly fell in. My hands flailed dangerously before Jessamae's strong fingers clutched my shoulders. The plot of land slowed, swirling lazily below me like dark waters. I smelled Pamela waiting beneath the surface, smelled her decay, and nearly puked over the edge.

Jessamae forced my hand to the dry grass that surrounded the grave. "Don't stop."

I planted my other hand and the swirling soil picked up the pace. It boiled and churned like a soup, the heat of it swelled skyward. The opening before me was a hungry gaping mouth, now deeper than I was tall. I could see the cream wicker of the casket peeking through the black like loose teeth. My heart hurt as I forced ragged breaths in and out of me. The casket appeared to rise, the illusion was nightmarish.

The last pieces of earth fell away from Pamela's box, and I leaned back, easing the intense pressure off my palms. "Not yet!" Jessamae yelled from beside me. I fearfully leaned forward once more, my muscles straining against the vibrations.

She was extending the grave a fraction at a time. I concentrated on giving whatever I could to her. The plot opened just enough to allow a few extra inches around the perimeter of the box below.

"That should do," she said, and I thankfully reeled in my numb arms. The shaking was gone. Jessamae lowered herself easily down the six-foot precipice and stood within the tiny edge of dirt along the side of Pamela. She lifted her arms wordlessly, like a parent would to a child. Holding her shoulders, she helped me down into the narrow gap. The moist dirt walls forced me onto the balls of my feet, my heels sliding along the bordering mud. My shins tapped Pamela's box as I worked to gain balance. It smelled like hell.

Jessamae circled around to the other side of the grave until she faced me. She slid her fingers under the flimsy woven lid. "Ready?"

I copied her actions, wedging my fingers under the lip of the lid. It should come off without a struggle, no metal hinges or clasps thanks to my cheapness. "Yeah."

It wasn't heavy, but there was a resistance, as if Pamela were pulling a blanket over her dozing eyes. It eventually released, and we lifted the head of the lid towards the shelf of grass above us, sliding it forward onto the ground until only a few inches hung out into the air. The stink overcame me, and I swallowed the ever-threatening sick.

There she was, or at least, there something was. This body was almost twice as big as Pamela was alive, and puffy. She was so swollen, she looked allergic to everything. Her skin was a mucky green and was streaked in a toxic-looking brown sludge that leaked from her nose, mouth, and eyes. I held my shirt to my nose but started heaving uncontrollably, my stomach tightening in convulsions. A strong wind whipped my hair before it settled into the steady stream, carrying some of the smell away in the breeze. My stomach relaxed.

"That's better," Jessamae said from across the body. The air tickled me as if to soothe my discomfort. Jessamae smiled at me in encouragement, then squatted onto the balls of her feet, somehow retaining her appearance of control and dexterity as she did so. "Come by the feet so we can touch, we'll need contact for the magic."

I dropped my shirt from my face and carefully skirted Pamela, stopping at her feet. Her shoes were open-toed, her flesh bulging out from them grotesquely, and her toes were painted an ugly shade of coral. Following Jessamae's lead, I bent down onto my ankles, leaning back against the soil enclosure to keep myself from falling forward again. I could only imagine what that swollen flesh would feel like if I lost my balance. "Oh, god." I belched acrid bile into my mouth.

Jessamae paid me no mind. She was intent, only allotting me a few cursory glances in her evident exhilaration. "Perfect, perfect. Remember what I said. We only need her consciousness for a moment, you won't need to resurrect her completely. You aren't ready for that."

I hadn't even told her of my appalling track record, particularly when I was under pressure or upset. I conjured the thoughts that filled my head before the bird arose this afternoon. Ben's face swam behind my eyes as I squatted before the bloated dead thing in the dirt.

Jessamae's calloused hands circled mine, and she set them onto Pamela's shin, which was miraculously covered in the black floral number I had given to the funeral home. The meat of her felt like a blooming mushroom, squishy. My head shook in instinctual protest and my hand flinched beneath hers, desperate to pull back.

Jessamae rested her other hand on Pamela's lumpy thigh, demonstrating what I should do next. I braced myself and arranged my left hand, mirroring Jessamae's position. Then she sat up straight, tilted her head back, and simply breathed.

All at once, I was engulfed in energy. My limbs filled with violent static that I couldn't contain or control. It was guzzling me, but for the first time, I felt strong. I pressed down harder into the goo of my grandmother, willing a piece of her back. My fingers dug into the dead skin like the spade of a shovel.

I thought the power would start trickling down my mouth and out my nose, as the brown sludge had in Pamela. Thoughts flicked past me like television channels, too quick to grasp. Ben, Cleo, Jessamae, cat, Ben, bird, Pamela, Mom, Pamela, Ben, Ben something. Something to do with Ben. I couldn't hold it! It was too much! I pushed it out of me, away from me, into the bag of bones under my hands. And it took from me, it drained almost everything from me. I choked back a scream but let out a cry.

A wet desperate inhale shuddered from the head of the grave. The air sounded as though it passed through a swamp to reach the surface in murky bubbles. The head twitched around violently, the bones inside snapping against the unnatural flop. Guttural sucking breaths kept pushing through the black mouth before her eyelids began to stretch against the spikes holding them shut. Thank god for the spikes holding them shut.

"What's happening to her?" I shrieked over the unearthly sounds.

Jessamae was stunned, her mouth split open in denial. This wasn't supposed to happen. "Pamela! Pamela, can you hear me?" she shouted at the monster.

But the body was not something to be reasoned with. The head rocketed around on the spine like a cursed bobble-head, the eyelids near tearing against the spikes. For once, I didn't need Jessamae to explain anything to me. I had done something terribly, abhorrently wrong. I hadn't brought enough of her back, or she was stuck somehow between dying and living. I had spoiled something beyond reason, beyond description. The head wailed shrilly against the wet muck in its airway. I thought it was pleading for death. I sure as shit would be.

The wind thrashed my hair around my face, stinging my skin. "Stop it! STOP IT, PLEASE!"

Jessamae held the tormented corpse down, but her touch did nothing to still the damned thing. There wasn't enough life in it. She could steal from the living, but this curse didn't live. She stood up, truly terrified now, and backed toward the wall of soil.

The arms of the scourge began to bounce. I searched the grave, frantic for a rock big enough to crush the skull, anything to end it, but there was nothing and there was no point.

I pushed my fingers to my eyes, pushing into the jelly of them, wanting to blot out this horror. I thought despondently of Ben, pathetically wishing he were here to shield me once more. I saw his dancing brown eyes in my mind, grateful for the illusion, when I heard the body give one last weighty flounder, and then silence.

19

MY FINGERS hesitantly left my eyes, but it took some time until they opened. The body was still confined to the weak box—ripped open like cardboard in some places—but it lay in a restless position. Where a joint could bend or break, it did, like a broken doll. Jessamae crawled down off the little ground she gained against the wall and leaned toward Pamela's head. I forced myself to look at it and recoiled. "Jesus Christ."

The eyelids had snapped their spikes and lay open. The eyes were discolored, the whites were the blue of a vein and the irises looked bleached. They stared vacantly, but somehow accusingly, back at me.

"No, no, no, no," I muttered as I turned to the loose siding of the grave and began to climb. It crumbled and slid under my hands, causing me to fall again and again. Thunder clapped overhead in the now dark sky. "Of course," I sobbed as I gripped the roots of the grass above me. I felt the milky eyes burning a hole in my back as I fell, my heels bending the woven casket beneath them.

"Calm down. It's dead," Jessamae chided, her arrogance returned.

"Shut up!" I yelled, heaving myself up on the grass. My repeated attempts left a decent-sized slot in the wall, and I got some leverage. My arms were weak, but my fear had reached Herculean levels. I heard several strands of grass rip from the ground but most held firm as I made my way out of my personal hell. My knee scrambled over the edge and gripped the earth.

Jessamae's hands brushed my back, she wasn't helping me,

just touching. Useless. "That was unexpected, but no harm done. We don't have to do that again if you don't want to."

I was nearly over to the surface. I hated that I, even now, was drawn to her, exacerbated by her touch, the urge warring with my new aversion to her. The hatred gave me the strength for one final, sweaty pull. I rolled to my back before staggering clumsily to my feet. I didn't want to catch my breath, I didn't want to breathe this air.

Careening down the hillside, swerving drunkenly around ugly headstones in the dark, I heard, "Francesca!" shouted behind me. It only spurred me on. Futilely I thought messages to Ben: *Help! Come to the graveyard! Please!* Knowing full well that wasn't how his affinity worked.

I crossed over the bridge in a craze, fearing ghosts and goblins hidden in the shadows beneath. Too afraid to look over my shoulder, I felt those blue and white eyes staring me down, as if I weren't only responsible for this torture, but for her death entirely. Maybe I was.

Air left me in dry hitches. My legs began to falter as I turned out of the cemetery. I'd reached the bottom of the hill, but the danger still loomed behind me. The hairs on the back of my neck itched terribly. I was sprinting without direction. The stink had only just started to recede. Thunder boomed again overhead before a lightning strike lit up the night.

The houses around me weren't the ones I wanted—siding, not brick. I had made a wrong turn. Even now, I wouldn't turn around. Circling the entire town was more attractive than facing whatever followed me out of the grave.

A beacon of light shook in my field of vision as I lurched forward in a jog. There weren't many streetlights in Aspen Ridge, but I had found one of the few. Heavy drops of water began splashing on my hot scalp as I shuffled toward the post. The rain was a relief from the constant heat but, regardless, added to my flooding despair and a hopeless bleating blared from me.

There was a rustling in the grass that surrounded me, all alone on the road. I allowed myself a nervous glance left and right. The weeds were moving. The stalks shook with a whisper —the whisper of air forcing its way up and through a dead throat. I pushed myself into a laborious sprint, knowing that snakes were far from the most sinister thing in town tonight.

An ugly red Volkswagen screeched around a turn up ahead, coming to a shrill and uneasy stop before Ben flung himself from the car. "Frankie! Frankie, are you alright? Is she here?"

He searched the nearby darkness for a sign of Jessamae, or maybe Pamela, as I ran to him. I jumped onto his chest, circling my arms around his neck and thanking him silently for finding me, wherever I'd ended up. I needed this touch like I never had before. His woodsy scent replaced that of death.

My lungs felt like cement sinking inside me. The rain was picking up fast.

"I can't breathe," I gasped, and I meant it. I hadn't run that fast since ninth grade P.E., and with my habit for slacking off, probably not even then.

He set me down and moved his hands to my shoulders. He bent down low enough for me to see him through my dripping hair. "Do you need to sit down?" he asked loudly as thunder echoed around us.

"No, I want to go home."

He turned me around and steered me toward the car. "There's a sweatshirt on the seat!" he yelled over the storm, running around to the driver's side. I gratefully forced my soaking hair into the hoodie, almost calmed by the warmth and Ben's heightened earthy smell.

He took off like a bat out of hell, and it wasn't long before I saw the familiar houses of my street. Once I could finally hold my teeth together with relative control, I sensed the weight of Ben's silence. His jaw clenched hard, his knuckles shone white under the glisten of rain. He was seething.

The house came into view through the downpour on the

windshield and I nearly fell out of the car as it rolled to a stop. My overwhelming desire to get indoors overtook my patience. I threw the front door inward with verve, the gale slamming it against the wall. I only gave Ben a few short seconds to follow me in before forcing it closed and twisting the deadbolt.

Cleo raced into the room cradling the cat in her elbow. It wasn't clear how much Ben had told her, or even how much he had seen. He walked wearily over the living room carpet and eased himself onto the floor. Cleo disappeared into the hall and returned with a quilt in her other arm. She threw it on Ben's lap, and he held his hand out for me. The gesture nearly brought me to sudden tears, so I hurried into his arms and under the blanket.

He tucked the blanket in around us both and stroked my hair until my breathing slowed. My lips plopped open, air wheezing in and out. I couldn't remember the last time someone had comforted me like this. If anyone had. I rejected even my mother's touch as a child.

"What happened tonight?" he finally asked once I'd been lulled out of a heart attack. Cleo, who had been absently stroking the cat, now settled him onto her lap after she fluidly gathered herself onto the floor beside us.

Budding tears seeped through my weak ducts. I gave up control, then simply cried, "I messed up!" My jaw trembled, I clenched it shut, grinding my teeth. "We were trying—we just wanted a few answers. Jessamae thought that together we could … I don't know, bring back Pamela! Just for a few minutes. Then we were going to put her back!"

Ben's brow came down hard over his eyes, but he just stroked the skin of my thumb and waited. The cat was batting Cleo's hair in an effort to regain her attention.

"But I messed up," I groaned again. "She didn't rise, like the bird, all I did was put just enough energy into the body to make it flop around, half alive, half dead. It was horrible! It was trying to breathe … I think it was trying to scream." I looked pleadingly at my friends. "Then it stopped. After a while, it went limp again."

Ben was more furious than ever. "Where is Jessamae?"

"I don't know. I left her in the grave with the body." I felt a small stab of shame at my cowardice and hurried to explain, "I just couldn't look at that thing anymore! You didn't see its eyes."

"I'm sure she can manage to put some dirt back on her own," Ben snapped.

I turned to Cleo for an explanation, but her face was just as murderous as his. What I had done was so heinous, they could barely look at me.

"I didn't know what would happen. I know it was sick ... twisted—"

"Jessamae knew exactly what she was doing," Ben interrupted and flexed the tension from his hands. "There are ways to talk to the dead without reanimating a corpse, Frank."

I froze. At the cemetery, next to Pamela's plot, I hadn't even considered that there might be alternatives. Was it because I was desperate for answers, or because Jessamae had asked it of me? I remembered the power coursing through me, to me, from her. I had never questioned if there was another way.

Ben's body went rigid beneath me, his gaze emptied briefly before he was right back to glaring. "She'll be here soon, a few minutes. You two will talk."

"I don't want to talk to her."

Ben had the decency to hide his pleasure about that. "Up to you, Princess. It's easy to change the future."

Knowing that she had used me to try out our ghastly team magic made me glad I had left her in the dirt with her victim. But she'd given me the choice, I couldn't deny that. Or how enticing the magic became to me. I shuddered to remember.

Cleo had yet to say anything, but her eyes were vigilant as she absent-mindedly stroked the purring animal in her lap. "What's his name?" I asked without a lot of interest.

"Amir." The cat appeared proud of the title, puffing out his chest. It was courtly, it suited him. I'd still toss him out the first chance I got. Amir could take care of himself.

A knock rattled the door. I curled my lip at my absolving attitude and left the comfort of Ben's lap to open it.

She appeared concerned and I didn't believe it. "May I talk to you?" Jessamae asked from the porch. Rain poured in buckets, her white hair stuck to her skin and her eyes looked bigger than ever.

I didn't answer her, I was still so angry and ashamed. But I left the door open, trudged through the living room—avoiding the furious glances—and entered my bedroom. Jessamae made no noise behind me, but I knew she would follow. I whipped around and confronted her immediately upon passing the doorway. I wasn't going to let her allure or our connection overcome my senses again.

"I take it tonight didn't go as you'd hoped," I said gruffly. She stepped into my room and closed the door behind her. I straightened my spine, pushing the unease I was feeling down into my heels.

"No, it didn't." She looked fatigued but unapologetic. "If I had known how it would go beforehand, then I would have taken more precautions. But it was still a success."

"Success! Are you fucking kidding me? We tortured a dead soul! I tortured my dead grandmother's soul! Who was dead because of YOU!" It was as if the heavy blanket of contentment that she had covered me with in her presence had been torn away. "We didn't have to bring her back to talk to her, did we?"

She was unbothered by my screams. Her tone was reproachful, her expression defiant. "No. I had faith in your abilities and your strength. It appears as though your friends don't have the same faith in your craft."

My snort came close to a growl. She was using this opportunity to insult Ben.

She twirled a strand of my hair around her finger, her regard for it twisted there was like spun gold. With strenuous effort, I clutched her wrist and pried it away from me. I held my breath and spit filled my mouth.

"I knew in my bones what you could do. I would never hide your magic from you." Her ghostly eyes shone with affection. "I know it's scary. I'm not going to push you, but I'm not going to shelter you either." It was as if she knew exactly how I'd felt about Ben as we were leaving the house earlier this evening. I didn't reply, I didn't trust myself.

Jessamae opened the door and stood quietly in its frame. She pulled a folded piece of paper from her pocket and left it on my shabby bookshelf. "Whenever you're ready." She slipped silently out the door and was gone.

I sank onto the bed and wanted nothing more than to burrow under the covers, but I'd thrown my rank comforter in the washer during the move. I took a big t-shirt out of my duffle bag and draped it over my body. It smelled familiar and I breathed deeply.

I didn't want to think about what I had seen and heard tonight. I didn't want the images to paint the walls of my head. I wanted to sleep more than I had ever wanted anything. So, somehow, I did.

WHEN I AWOKE underneath the shirt, I was chilly for the first time in months. Ben, unconscious, faced me on the bare mattress, his hands between his thighs; he was cold too. I got up as quietly as possible and crept down the hall. It was either very late or very early; therefore, very dark. The blanket we'd used earlier was gone from the living room floor. Cleo had taken it back. I retreated to the linen closet next to the bathroom. I felt my way through the shelves. There were no blankets, but I pulled out several thick, fluffy towels. I heaved the pile carefully back to my room and onto the mattress, stretching the quilt of towels across us both.

As my head touched down, Ben's eyes opened. I automatically slid the single pillow I had under his head, our faces almost touching.

"Did you see it?" I whispered.

He sighed. "Yeah … yeah, I saw it."

I took a deep breath, feeling a bit of reprieve. He had taken a fraction of the weight off my shoulders, just as he had with my pile of books in the bookstore. It was as if both our hearts were now pumping the poison that was the twitching, guttural thing I created. Knowing he had seen what I had seen, meant I was not as much alone. Keeping my hands close to my chest, I touched my forehead to his, and easily fell back into sleep.

IT WAS BARELY dawn when I began to stir again, a pale light filtered into the room through a small gap in the curtains. I passed out so early last night, I knew it was useless to try and sleep again. Ben's mouth pouted open, looking disgustingly sweet as he slept. To squash the temptation to touch those soft lips, I took a towel that was now tangled around me and got a boiling, skin-eroding shower running. Though I normally preferred my bathtub, I needed a different kind of clean today. I was due at Jim's Grocery at nine, which gave me just enough time to scrub at least one layer from my body.

Rain kindly tapped the window when I tiptoed back into my room, wrapped in my towel. I dug through the mountain of clothes in the corner, where we threw all the cabinet's innards before we painted it.

I found one of my polos in the pile and some jeans in the closet. I was almost looking forward to wearing them in the cool weather.

I turned away from the closet to find a pair of wide-awake eyes. I hacked out a cry of alarm, sounding very much like Amir.

His smirk became sheepish. "Sorry. I should have said something." Ben was leaning on his elbow and looked down. "Good morning, by the way," he addressed the pillow.

I clutched the towel around me tighter. Though boundaries and the lines of privacy had been so blurred between us, Ben still had never seen me naked and, after our bouts of kissing, I was feeling exceedingly shy. I had been kissed before—all awful experiences—and it wasn't like I hadn't had an orgasm—I also figured that out in my teens—but I always felt so unsure around Ben. I wanted him to find me … sexy. *Blech.*

"I need to get dressed," I said, sounding surlier than I intended, and shut myself inside of the closet. It was senseless, my dressing squished up against the cheap aluminum rod that filled the tiny space, bumping against the door as I jumped up and down pulling on my jeans.

I stumbled out, fully dressed. Ben hadn't moved from his position on the bed. He stared down at the pillow looking annoyingly delighted as I left him alone.

Hopefully Cleo brought home something for the fridge yesterday. It dawned on me that I should grab some groceries at work, aside from junk food and cheap beer. I made a mental note to ask Cleo for a list before I left. Aside from Ben, she was the most grown-up of our trio, and I didn't want to give Ben the satisfaction. I threw my hair into a ponytail as I walked down the hallway into the living room. My hands paused, clasping my hair, as I was buried in an avalanche of horror.

Where several perfectly packed boxes sat yesterday, there now was a faded blue couch. And poised stoically upon it, demonstrating impeccable posture, awaited the late Pamela Hughes.

20

HER SMILE WAS UTTERLY MANIC, the grin of a circus clown, as she watched me enter the room with blind, white eyes. The body was the dead thing I left in the ground. Green and blue, it covered twice as much cushion as Pamela did alive, like a swamp monster. A brown stain oozed from beneath her, soaking the blue fabric in rotten putrefaction. Pale worms squirmed in her crevices, I heard them in the leaking fluids of her. Still, she smiled, her fragile jaw quivering against the pressure.

"Francesca," she croaked, as if through puke in her throat. "Still the fat, little piggy I remember."

Had Jessamae left the grave open? Had Pamela's life returned to her somehow in that disgusting, festering skin-sock of spoiled meat? I sucked in weak bouts of air, intending to call for help. "No," I pleaded instead.

"Oh, yes." Her eyelids had been destroyed by the spikes; her eyes blared bright as hospital lights. Her hands made a sound like sloshing water balloons, and I fell back into the wall, knocking a picture frame to the floor.

Amir pounced from the dying house plant in the corner, claws out, onto Pamela's dirt-stained lap. As he landed, she was gone. The boxes were back in place, Amir's nails puncturing the soft cardboard surface. He frantically searched for the enemy, before darting inside a small opening in the box. I slid down the wall, crushing the broken frame beneath me as I hit the ground. She was gone. She was never here.

But she was. The cackle, the squelching of the maggots. The

eyes. Although … the smell I now always attached to death was curiously faint. Could it all have been in my head? Impossible.

Glass cracked beneath me. A small cut had opened along the lines of my palm. I pulled a crystal chunk out of me and inspected the frame for damage. The picture was one of the few I had of my mom and me. It wasn't taken on a heartwarming or even a memorable day. We were both standing in the then-green grass that surrounded this house. I was around twelve and Allison was dragging me into the trees for a hike. She smiled beautifully into the lens in the forefront of the photo. I slumped in the background like a hunchback with a Scott-straight smile. Whoever she was dating at the time took this picture. I couldn't even put a face to him. She and I weren't laughing together or hugging or anything like that, but we were both in it, and that was something.

I set it on the table. The frame was beyond repair. I flexed the fingers of my hand; the blood had dried. The cut would heal while I was at work. The thought was encouraging—I wasn't so defenseless. Then I thought of Pamela soaking in her own festering liquids, laughing at me, and the feeling vanished completely.

I stopped in Cleo's room, which was unrecognizable after her redecorating. Stylish and modern with accents of gold and emerald. She was in the corner digging at the edge of the old cerulean carpet as I knocked on her open door. I didn't ask what she would do with the bed if she pulled out the carpet, I asked about groceries. She already had a list written out for me. I suppressed a snort—this is what I wanted after all—and left to say goodbye to Ben.

"Do you want me to drive you?" he asked, his eyes still on the page of the little lined sketch in his hand, a chunk of charcoal suspended above the surface. The notebook was one of mine, but he always had some chalk on him. He'd need to go home and change before work. He was most likely on thin ice after taking so much time off for the burial.

I toyed with the doorknob, aiming for nonchalance. "No, I have Pamela's car now. I'll drive myself."

From the corner of my eye, I saw Ben pause in surprise. A familiar blank look appeared on his face, but again was fleeting. "Sounds good, call if you need anything." And he went back to his sketch.

I crossed the room, wanting to kiss him goodbye, but I still felt embarrassed and a little afraid of something. I chickened out and touched my lips to his cheek before I disappeared.

My hands trembled on the steering wheel, which was stupid. I wasn't the best driver, but I had never been in an accident, had never even struck a curb or a lamp post. It smelled like factory fresh plastic in here. Why Pamela had bothered to buy a car, when she left the television about as often as a solar eclipse, was beyond me. I pressed the big white button to start the engine— my own car had been a key starter. Her gear shift was in the center console—my own had stuck out to the right of the steering wheel. Still, this was just like riding a bike. A big metal death trap of a bike. I swallowed hard as I put the car in reverse.

"Chicken shit," I growled to myself, tired of my constant tremors. I slammed my foot to the pedal and zoomed backwards out of the garage, crushing a box of clothing donations that had been left near the tailgate. They were ugly anyway.

I drove too fast, overcompensating for my anxiety. When images of snow and headlights began to permeate my blustery surroundings, I started naming the things that passed me by, "Power line, fence post, fence post, fence post, fire hydrant, truck, house, car." It helped. But as rain continually slithered across my vision, my list grew louder, filling the car with thunderous noise.

After what felt like a very long time, I turned into Jim's parking lot, relaxing into the smelly upholstery. I didn't realize how tightly I held my muscles until I let go of the wheel.

Scott was clicking a mouse infrequently. He squinted at the screen as if he either couldn't see what he was doing, or he didn't know what he was doing. His tie was black today, his shirt sleeves rolled up. He looked like a waiter at a chain restaurant.

"Miss Hughes!" he exclaimed once he caught wind of me shadowing him. He spun his little chair to the center of his desk. "Welcome back! Whelp, I'm sorry to hear about the, um, you know, misfortune you've had to deal with these last few days." His mouth pressed into a hallmark straight line, like a worm. He was already stumped, out of consolation. "Are you feeling better?" he asked, as if I'd had a cold.

"I am, thank you."

He nodded his head happily.

"I'm going to start on register," I stated without asking for permission or waiting for direction. He sputtered a bunch of nonsense, ruffled by my assertion. I shut the door to his office and jogged to the front of the store. I couldn't risk the autopilot tasks, like stocking or mopping. My mind was not allowed to wander today.

I was as friendly as I ever was to the customers, which is to say I wasn't, but I was never blatantly rude. My bravery in the car this morning, if you could call it that, made me feel strangely unaffected by the people around me. What used to needle me— essentially everything—couldn't break the immense shield I'd put in place.

I worked through my break, afraid of stopping for too long. When my mind was in danger of drifting, I became more absorbed in the details, reading aloud the ingredients of every soup can, one at a time, as I was finally forced to stock. Then listing the colors of the specks in the linoleum I swept underfoot.

At four o'clock, my useless cataloging had done its job and I clocked out. I pushed a cart efficiently through each aisle, plucking the items Cleo requested from the shelves, as well as some garbage for me and some red peppers for Ben. He ate them like a normal person would an apple.

I rang myself up, which was against the rules, but I'd run out of patience. Besides, I would be paying for everything today. I reached in my cart for the last thing, a jar of dill pickles, to find them already held out for me. The hand was withered and grotesque, spotted in deep welled spots of liquefaction and decay. It held the jar steady.

"Couldn't live without your slop, could you, little piggy?"

I wouldn't look up. I was hallucinating again; this Pamela was not real. My upper lip began to sweat. Keeping my stinging eyes fixed downward, I shoved the crumpled bills into the till.

"What? Afraid to look your sweet old granny in the face?" My hands were shaking now. The quarters kept tumbling out of my fingers, clinking against the plastic as I dropped them. Coins spilled to the floor, and I finally punched the drawer closed.

"Look at me." I looped the plastic bag handles around my arms, leaving the cart and the pickles at the checkout counter.

"LOOK AT ME!" the sulfuric voice bellowed into my ear. I didn't want to, oh, how I didn't want to. But I was so thrown by the howl that my visceral reaction was to do exactly what it demanded.

It was worse. Somehow the aberration was even worse.

Red bloomed on the sloughing flesh of the face. Not the expected red that skin turns with heat or excessive drinking. Red red, brick red. Like paint. It gave the nightmarish woman an artificial cast, a plasticity. Her eyeballs were dissolving in their sockets, buried too deep in her skull, almost retracting inwards like a frog's. I was falling, running, taking short, panicked breaths, afraid to turn my back. Why wasn't anyone helping? Screaming? Anything?

The insane smile was there. Pamela had become something beyond horrifying. "Pretty thing, aren't I?" She belched through the spider webs filling her throat. "Although, I don't know why you chose this ugly rag to bury me in." Her green hands tugged at the stained floral fabric of the dress. "I love to show a little … skin!" With that, she yanked the neckline down past her breasts exposing the open lesions in the skin of her chest. They were like tar pits dotted across her, filled with living, moving things, either relishing the muck or trapped within it.

A whimper bubbled through my lips. I dragged my eyes away from the terror that was my topless, rotting grandmother. I searched for someone, a witness. The store was empty and silent. The lights had shut off. Everything outside of Pamela's reach vanished in darkness. This wasn't possible. My head whipped around, panic-stricken, as my feet finally began to slide backward. Helpless, I looked back to Pamela. She was shaking her sagging, eaten flesh at me like a graveyard strip show, giggling at my fear.

"Want a taste?" she teased. "Your girlfriend did!" She laughed and laughed and laughed.

I was running, running backwards, but running. My ankle knocked painfully into another checkout counter, and I flipped forward. The bags hanging off my arms that I'd forgotten until now were heavy and cutting into my skin.

"I'll see you at home, sweetheart!" the hag shrieked after me as I fled out the door, blinded by the sun after the inexplicable darkness inside.

I was sweating profusely, which the rain washed away, cooling me as I sprinted. I gave a silent word of thanks for automatic key fobs as I still struggled to open the tailgate. I hurled the grocery bags inside in a giant heap of mashed bread and dented jugs.

As I pressed the button to start the engine, I looked back to the store, expecting the corpse to hobble after me. Pamela was nowhere in sight. A few customers were walking in and out, wheeling towering carts through the parking lot. Nothing was amiss at all. It was the same absence of the abnormal I had felt seeing Pamela so still on that blue couch, an absence that made my heart collapse. She was probably watching me now.

I raced through town. "Tree, tree, cat, car, house, garage, grass—" Knowing that if I stopped to think, the fear would overtake me and I'd drive into a telephone pole. I sped the car into the garage while the door was still opening, driving over the same crushed box of clothes that littered the driveway. "Driveway, box, sweater, something purple."

I slammed the door behind me and turned the deadbolt, panting in the kitchen.

"Hey. Where are the groceries?" Cleo was putting some pretty glass plates into our kitchen cabinets. She looked over her shoulder, suspicious at my empty arms, and took in my shaken appearance. "How was work?"

"Uh, work, yeah. Work was okay. The groceries are in the car." I gestured to the closed door.

She studied me with patience. "You locked them out?"

I was feeling very stupid, I must have imagined everything. A guilty conscience could be a nasty bitch. "I just … forgot they were out there." I turned back the lock and opened the door, searching the garage with wide eyes. Nothing.

When I offered no explanation, Cleo strutted past me through the door. She lifted the Honda tailgate and found the food strewn across the trunk and backseat; they must have really been flying around. She gave me an irked frown. I stared at her, trying to look innocent but waiting for her to ask. Instead, she stacked the mess neatly back into the plastic.

"I'll get you some reusable bags," she said, and left me alone in the garage.

༺

WHEN BEN WALKED through the front door, I jumped from my feral position at the kitchen table, ready to bolt. Cleo had sat across from me for the last hour, calmly folding some of her clothes as I freaked.

Ben held his arms up, conveying he wasn't a threat, before he opened them to me. I rushed into them, unrecognizable to myself but starved for healthy human touch. His hand found the back of my head and held me to him. "Looks like Gran is back in town?"

I nodded against his chest.

"I've been texting you all day, are you alright?"

"Is that what's going on?" Cleo asked from the table. "Frankie's been making Amir jumpy all evening." I glared at her, certain Amir would get through this hard time. She placed a pair of silk pajama shorts atop the perfect stack. "Reanimation?" she asked Ben.

"Based on what Frankie saw at Jim's, I'd say no." He let go of me and paced around the kitchen rubbing his head. "There's something very wrong here. I'm not getting any visions of this thing. I've only seen through Frankie in real-time when she's threatened by it—the end of the resurrection, today at the store."

"I saw her this morning too," I admitted. "I thought I was imagining it. I'm still not sure what was real." I allowed myself to remember fully how she looked on a couch that, as of yesterday, was buried in a landfill somewhere, and then in a dark empty grocery store which I knew to be filled with people at the time. "Is Pamela's ghost haunting me?"

"I don't think so. But this is not something I'm an expert in." He gnashed his teeth before he addressed Cleo. "The body is rotting, but it's changing. And she was very …" he searched for the right word, "cruel. Thriving on insecurity and fear. Really cut into our Frank." He gave my shoulder a squeeze.

Cleo traced her mouth with a perfect fingernail. "I've never dabbled in the dead. Have never even tried to speak to them. What do you know?"

"I've tried to communicate with someone, once. But I dealt with the spirit, not the body."

Despair gripped me, we were dealing with something unknown to us, something malicious that could alter our surroundings, or at least our perceptions. Something that Ben couldn't warn us about.

"We should at least try to get some wards up while we figure out exactly what we're dealing with," and Cleo took off for her room.

She returned to the kitchen table, arms overflowing with what appeared to be craft supplies. Ben was now circling the perimeter of the house doing some version of his psychic fields that he conjured at Patrick's. When I asked to help, he told me in my current state, I would be of no help to anyone.

Determined to be of more use than Amir, who was now batting the strings and ropes that hung over the edge of the table with fervor, I plopped myself down in a chair and scooted uncomfortably close to Cleo.

"Are we making wreaths?" My voice was too high. I squeezed the seat of my chair until I had control over my hands again.

"Sort of. We're weaving enchanted materials together, and then we will hang them over the doors and windows. They'll keep unwanted forces out. Or they'll at least create a challenge for them."

I fingered the textures she had laid out, taking particular interest in a pile of long black, silky strings. Touching the familiar strands, recognition slapped me. "You made my bracelet with these."

Her head remained down but I saw her mouth quirk. "You needed the enchantment that night. Or you would have gone into shock."

I lifted the pile of black thread, strangely tempted to run it across my cheeks, my lips. Too soft. "Is this your hair?" I yelled, astounded. Her smile stretched further, she only flipped her flowing smoky locks over her shoulder and kept braiding.

She taught me the pattern to weave, and I completed a few smaller plaits. They were nowhere near as intricate or as eye-catching as Cleo's results. If I crafted bracelets, no self-respecting person would wear one, even if I begged. I knew this because Cleo told me so. But with a sigh, she dejectedly declared they would do. When she started spitting all over my work, I reared in offense. "You could just throw them away!"

She rolled her eyes and smirked. "It makes the magic stronger. Using my hair and saliva is like putting an extension of myself in the ropes. Then the object can do the work for me. From far distances and over long periods of time." She was still grinning as she hung her ropes over the doors and windows of the house.

"I'm still learning, alright? It's been less than a week."

"You have made that abundantly clear."

Ben who had been laying on the floor for an hour in seer concentration, sat up in agitation. "Sorry, we'll be quiet," I said.

"The volume is fine. I know what we have to do." He put two fingers to his head and fired. "You'll call Jessamae. You have her number."

I remembered the slip of paper she left on my bookshelf. I had been afraid to look at it, thinking it would somehow hurt Ben's feelings. That was, of course, under the cocky assumption she had left some deep profession of love on the paper. It was only her phone number, and I was a narcissistic idiot.

"Can she get past your ward?" Cleo asked from the kitchen. She stood on the counter hanging her hair ropes like curtains around the window over the sink.

"I think she'll be fine," he said. "The ward is against the non-living. Jessamae is a cold-blooded, psychotic crone, but I assume her heart beats."

21

THE RINGING SOUNDED bizarre in my ear. It seemed out of sorts to get ahold of someone as otherworldly as Jessamae via my cellphone provider rather than through some cosmic alignment or phoenix call. After the third ring, she picked up with a, "Frankie," though I had never given her my number in return.

"Yeah, it's me," I redundantly confirmed. "Listen, we have a problem. It's Pamela. She's alive and dead at the same time. And she's here. She's, sort of, following me. Haunting me. We don't know what to do." My voice rose in pitch throughout my spiel, ending as a shriek.

The line was quiet for a while. I held the screen out, fearing we'd been disconnected, but the call timer clicked on. "Jessamae?"

"May I talk to Benjamin? I assume he's with you."

I hesitantly handed the phone to Ben, who put the phone to his ear with an unfriendly expression, as if she could see his distaste for her. "Yes?" He listened with little patience. "No." Pause. "No." Then he looked at me and obvious worry creased his eyes. "Yes." He hung up the phone and handed it back to me.

"Well?" I asked, slightly stung at being left out.

Ben's irritation sizzled. "She's on her way, going to apport into your bedroom apparently." He smiled with zero humor. "She must have been lingering close by."

"Apport?"

"Like teleporting without the tech," Cleo answered, again amused by my flowing cape of ignorance. "Not many witches can do it. Prices are high, and even with payment it's enormously difficult. She's very practiced in the craft." She stared, placating, at Ben. "But I think we already knew that."

Apporting sounded like what she had done with me after the funeral, to return to the car. I kept the fact that she could move multiple bodies at once to myself.

Ben forced out a breath in resignation and then busied himself hanging the last braided rope over the garage doorway. I was no interior designer, but I thought the hanging additions looked rather chic, at the least the ones that Cleo made, and I saw no reason to ever take them down.

A door opened down the hall, and Jessamae was there. It made me uncomfortable, to know she could do that into my room. She measured me, head to toe, her eyes fierce. "Are you alright?"

"Fine," I answered, hovering nearer to Cleo and Ben in the kitchen. "You haven't seen my grandmother today?" After all, Jessamae was in that grave, too. She was the one that killed Pamela in the first place.

She shook her head.

"Did you bury the body after I ra— after I left?" My tone was accusatory, I felt the blame for this piling on top of me and I was fighting against the burden of it.

"Of course I did. If the body was truly alive, it could never have dug itself back out. She was too frail, even on her best day."

I was having a hard time breathing. Each inhale was not enough. "If she isn't alive, then what the fuck is she?"

"Has it touched you?" Jessamae asked, stepping closer to me.

I thought back on the hellish apparitions. "I don't think so. But she's messing with my head. This morning, I saw her sitting on our old couch—I threw that piece of shit out yesterday! And at the store, all the people inside but us disappeared, and it was dark. Oh! She held a jar of pickles! A real jar," I added, hoping the information was useful.

"Is the body decomposing?" She was closer again. I hadn't noticed her move.

I thought of the black fissures, of the dribbling fluids. I closed my eyes against the memories. "Very much." Undeterred, the images clouded my mind. Those gooey white eyes. The skin. "And her skin, it's red in some places. On her nose and around it." I circled my hand before my face with my eyes clamped shut.

When they opened again, Jessamae was wired, her eyes bouncing around as if speed-reading. "It's a demon. And an angry one. At least that's what I believe. I had a friend, quite some time ago, who had an affinity for necromancy. His constant trials summoned something that had similar traits to what Frankie's describing. But it's hard to say. Not all demons are malicious and not all use human hosts."

My face remained neutral in light of her ridiculous theory. But this whole thing, my life, had become quite ridiculous.

"I'll have to return to the plot, then I can make sure the entity is using the physical body and isn't just an apparition or some sort of phantom." She rushed to the door as if to leave immediately.

"I'm going, too," I insisted. This was the only way I could be certain. Regardless of what Jessamae reported back, I had to see for myself.

"Okay," was all Jessamae said, but her face lit up.

"We'll take my car," Ben announced. As fed up as I had been over their pissing contest, I was grateful. Going to the graveyard alone with Jessamae again was more than dangerous, it was stupid. She had proven she was more interested in testing our limits than anything else. And I couldn't trust myself when I was alone with her.

It was getting dark now, and though it was irrational, I was becoming very afraid of the dark. "I have a flashlight in my closet." I turned to retrieve it, and I screamed.

A crazed red face with no eyes smiled at us all through the window. Though the sockets were only filled with a sickly jelly, I knew she could see perfectly, had probably been watching us this whole time. She gave that clogged-sounding cackle of hers and waved. As her hand tipped back and forth, her grin stretched, ripping the delicate green flesh around her mouth.

Ben said, "It can't come in." But she didn't have to. Watching us all exist in this house, a house she's more than familiar with— we couldn't hide from her, and we weren't safe. Who knew how long the wards would hold, and what she could do when they failed.

"What do we do?" I asked the room, spellbound by my grandmother. The light from the living room illuminated her, holy and malevolent. With the glow, I could see them. I could see the flies surrounding her. I tried counting them in their buzzing, but there were too many.

Pamela noticed my fixation on the things. With a theatrical air, she lowered her jaw like a drawbridge. Wider and wider, her jaw unhinged. The skin surrounding her mouth split entirely, snapping up to her cheek like a broken rubber band. And though I couldn't hear her, she visually inhaled a gust of squally air. Her ruined chest expanded, and the flies were sucked in.

She shut her mouth and rubbed her empty belly at the taste. She stood dead still in anticipation, giddy. I felt bile repeatedly tickle my throat. Before long, a fly crawled out of the mess that once was her eye. Another crept out of her swollen sticky nostril, but it perched on the tip of her brick-red nose in no hurry to leave. Pamela took a bow once, twice, still, the fly stuck to her like an obedient pet.

Amir leaped up to the window frame, spitting like a fiend and swatting the glass. The dead woman was delighted by the kitty, pawing at him and bouncing around. Without warning, her reaction flipped. She stood tall, her red face imperiling and enraged, and hissed. Her hiss shook the windows, rattling them in their frames. Amir zoomed into the depths of the house, I watched him disappear in an instant. When my head rocketed back to the window, Pamela was gone.

I looked to the other three for something, reassurance or vali- dation. They all were frozen, all with matching expressions of shock and horror. The uniformity was cartoonish, and I started giggling uncontrollably. The laughter became hysterical, braying, hyperventilating. When my noises heightened the confusion and fear on their faces, I laughed harder! I collapsed in a bubbling heap on the carpet.

Cleo whirled around, chasing after Amir, while Ben and Jessamae swarmed me, my body convulsing with hee-haws and snorts. Their hands reached for me at the same time in the same places, as if they were a single person with eight limbs. They fought like lions over a zebra carcass.

Cleo broke between them with a pitcher of water and poured the whole thing on my face. I sputtered through the cold flush, gulping for air, throwing out a solitary chuckle or tear like the final kernels of popping corn. I took a clean breath, then another. "Thank you."

"We need to get to the graveyard. Now," Cleo said. She turned to Ben. "Get your keys."

I stood and weaved to the kitchen, flapping my polo in the air to dry it. So much déjà vu. I got a glass and held it under the tap. My hand shook violently as it filled. I pressed my body into the counter, hiding my spasms from the omnipresent eyes behind me. If they knew how I was spiraling—more than they already suspected—they would only focus on me, would suggest we all stay here, or worse, they go without me. I gulped the water quickly to hide the visible sloshing, dropped the cup in the sink, and marched purposefully to the door.

I strategically placed myself in the middle of our ragtag group as we filed to the car, very much terrified of standing out front or trailing behind. The paranoia reminded me of how I felt about Jessamae, how I still sometimes felt about her—the sense of being watched—but multiplied by a hundred or more. The smell of the rain as it soaked the dry earth did nothing to soothe me, but it wasn't for lack of trying. I was breathing like an asthmatic pug.

Ben rigidly sat behind the wheel. I tucked into the passenger seat as Cleo and Jessamae slid into the back. It was uncomfortable, to have Jessamae there. We all felt it, and we all kept quiet about it.

Not a single word entered the car that night. Rather than growing accustomed to the silence, it only bit at me harder, and after we drove over the cemetery bridge, I practically barrel-rolled out of the frigid car. Ben parked farther away from the plot than Jessamae did. He couldn't see like she could in the dark, and we had to hike up a steep incline in the misty rain to reach the grave. My flashlight wasn't enough for the ominous night, only providing a small circle of illumination—a head-stone, a single flower in a dying bouquet.

I smelled the dead bodies beneath me as if I stood on a squishy stack of them, but I was not repulsed. I was comforted. The weakened stink on Pamela was unnatural and wrong. Dead things should smell as such.

Dark soil filled Pamela's grave, but it was loose and uneven. "Is this how you left it?"

Jessamae was quiet for so long, I looked up. She was kneeling with her hands pressed to the dirt and she paid me little attention. "No," she finally said when she registered I'd been speaking to her.

Was this some sort of trick of Pamela's? Filling the hole so haphazardly forced us to check. We had to check. It seemed like a setup, like a trap. I cracked my knuckles over the edge. My knees and shoulders hadn't popped hard enough since I'd practiced my affinity. It was making me all the more antsy.

Ben stood very close behind me and I heard him clap his hands together. "Well, let's take a look, shall we?"

He grazed the back of my neck before he kneeled at the foot of the soil patch. Jessamae already stood at the head, and Cleo skipped to Jessamae's right side. So, late to the party, I took the remaining side—the body's left, our right—and set the flashlight on its butt in the corner.

"We don't have much time, so," Ben pulled his switchblade from his canvas pants, "everyone, take a turn."

He expertly flipped the blade around to face himself and ran the silver slash along his inner arm. Blood welled briskly. He passed me the knife with a sad smile of encouragement. I made a matching slice in my own arm, accustomed to the sting after last weekend, but unhappy with the practice. And I passed the knife along.

Eventually, Cleo returned the knife to Ben, and we all put our hands to the soil. Blood had gathered at each of our wrists, and it mixed with the dark tossed earth.

The dirt began to whip wildly, and for a moment I envisioned the ground splitting open and swallowing us all, closing in over our heads. But in a flash, the loose burial opened like curtains, and it stayed that way. Compared to the work of Jessamae and me, it was virtually instantaneous.

As we scraped our way down the muddy edges, the death stink deepened just as it had before, and my trembling eased. Then I relaxed my mind and searched outward. There it was— the abyss was here, in this casket. Maybe the vile thing that haunted me really was just a projection or a ghost.

Jessamae and Cleo grabbed the casket lid on their respective sides.

"Ready, you two?" Cleo asked with impatience.

Together, the four of us easily raised the lid and pushed it over the shelf of grass above. I didn't want to look. I dreaded an empty casket even more than I dreaded a decomposing corpse. When I heard Ben curse angrily beside me, I looked, and had never felt such regret.

A sob gurgled up through my chest. I bit my lips closed and smashed my hand hard to my mouth. Controlling my cries did nothing for the spasms that racked my body.

The casket wasn't empty. It was occupied by a very dead Gabriel Perez.

❧

THE HYSTERICS WERE THREATENING to break me. Ben leaned over the body, needlessly checking for a pulse— something we all knew he wouldn't find—but I appreciated his doing the chore. Even in death, Gabriel's eyes were full of fear. I couldn't help comparing it to Pamela's dead face: blank, void of any emotion at all. More than anything, the undeniable truth that this death was on my hands buzzed around me like a swarm of flies. I had killed this man, as sure as if it were me to wield the knife or the rope or the hands that finished him off.

"Who?" Jessamae asked. I'd almost forgotten the other two were there somehow, in the tiny, dank grave that was now Gabriel's. Cleo was somber and Jessamae confused to the point of rage. She began searching the spaces around the body in a determined frenzy.

"It's the director of the funeral home, Perez," Ben said. He sounded exhausted, looked it too.

Cleo moved closer to Gabriel's head, everyone was examining him, touching him. Everyone except me. "Why him?"

Ben turned to glare at Jessamae. "Demon?" he asked.

"Yes," she answered without giving him any attention. "It dug its way out, killed, and refilled Pamela's casket." Her hands delved deftly into the pockets of Gabriel's slacks.

"What are you looking for?" Cleo asked.

Jessamae fished out a small keyring, a cell phone, and a wallet. "Insurance," she said. She stopped ferreting around the body and stared at me. "Are you ready to try again?" I didn't need to ask what she meant.

"Are you serious? What the fuck is the matter with you?" Ben shouted, straightening his hunched shoulders. His hatred radiated from him and filled the grave. I wanted to move away, toward Jessamae, but that certainly wouldn't help anything.

She ignored his hollering completely, had eyes only for me.

As horrendous as her experimentation was, I couldn't deny that her faith in me was … nice. I also couldn't deny that I wanted to try again, so much. Gabriel didn't deserve to die. I wanted to put him back on his feet. But I remembered the wet, animal sounds Pamela emitted when I'd tried before, and I became light-headed.

"No," I told her.

She nodded, unsurprised. "His absence won't go unnoticed." She turned around and dropped her hands to the dirt walls. Small, evenly spaced footholds appeared along her side, and she climbed out easily. I readily followed her up and out, Ben and Cleo behind me.

"He's going to be heavy. I'll need some help," Jessamae stated as she sized up Gabriel from above.

Cleo took a dazed step toward her. "Help with what exactly?"

"We can't leave him here. We don't know what the demon's done and if he can somehow be traced back here. And if they find him in this grave, Frankie will be in hot water, indeed," she answered.

"If they find him with us, won't that be slightly more incriminating?" Cleo rebutted.

"That won't happen."

I was dissolving, afraid to speak. I only wanted to get out of here, away from the dead man who had shown me such kindness. But, "Jessamae's right. We can't leave him here."

Ben had been reticent for too long. I found him behind me, his arms crossed tightly over his chest. Gabriel had gotten under his skin too.

He walked to the edge of the hole in submission. "Once more, with feeling," he said, and he, once again, gripped the handle of his blade. Once we had all cut into our arms, I promised to heal each of them afterward. My first cut was beginning to scab.

"Lift on three?" Ben asked, eyes on the body.

"I don't want to drop him," I whispered, my mind on the lime I couldn't lift a foot off the ground.

Ben watched me twitch in the dark. "Yours is already healing. How about you pull the car up here? Please, Frank?" He might have noticed what I was fighting, the urge to flee or faint or cry, all of it. I nodded, grabbed the flashlight and Ben's keys, and took off into the mist.

Once I left the unseen protective boundary the others provided, I was sprinting. The circle of sight from my flashlight jerked around in a fitful web. I couldn't see anything.

Everything was a threat. I hurtled downhill. My heart kicked out at me as I tried to stick to the path. The panic was smothering. I lost control of my feet on the slick grass and my chin hit ground, my teeth clapping together loud enough to echo. I flexed and slid my sore jaw, and felt sticky blood when I touched it. A fanatic laugh clicked out above me, clear and close. Very close.

I stood and lurched forward. I was steps away from the car when I realized my hands were empty. "Shit, shit, shit!" I dropped the keys when I fell. I shone the unsteady flashlight behind me. I saw the muddy skid where I slipped, but the grass was too tall to see through clearly. I muttered pathetic pleas under my breath, afraid to leave the illusion of safety that I got from the car. Finally, the beam of light bounced off something reflective, metal, in the grass about twenty yards from me.

"Are you scared, little piggy? Do you want your mommy?" A croak drifted through the night.

I steeled myself, gritting my teeth. *Don't fall.*

I was off, scurrying low to the ground like an animal, darting for the keys. "Call her, call for your mommy!" the voice wailed. The flashlight bounced against my thighs as I moved, shining into the sky, over the grave markers.

I reached the spot and clawed for the keyring, taking a grip of mud along with it.

"Where's your mommy!" it screamed as I leaped into the

driver's seat and threw the flashlight behind me. I wrenched the car in drive and floored it, staying in first gear, terrified to shift and stall. I was halfway back before I flipped the headlights on. I'd been too afraid of what I would see on the hill, of what they would reveal. I thought I'd been afraid of the dark, but it was the light that terrified me now.

Ben, Jessamae, and Cleo stood around the body at the top of the hill. The hole had been filled with packed soil, the surrounding grass shockingly clean of the stuff. I popped the trunk latch and sped to the back of the car.

Ben put a concerned hand around the base of my skull.

"I'm fine," I lied. "Just hurry."

All eyes were on Gabriel as he floated gently up into the air and to the trunk. He hovered over the space, too tall to slide in easily. I wiped more blood from my chin and grabbed his shins. His legs were stiff with rigor mortis—I couldn't bend his knees! Tears sprang into my eyes.

"Here," Jessamae said, approaching the trunk.

"No!" I shouted. "I can do it, just ... keep him there for a second." I held his calves with renewed determination.

I needed to push oxygen into his muscles. I could do that. I didn't want to break his legs, and I worried that's what Jessamae would do as a last resort, or first resort even. Thinking of Gabriel's compassion, knowing he was one of the few individuals I didn't openly detest, the knee began bending beneath my fingers. I was restoring the muscle of his leg. That's it. And afraid of taking it too far, traumatized by what I knew I could do, as soon as his legs bent just enough to force him through the edges of the trunk, I released him.

I slammed the latch shut over his petrified face.

22

BEN and I stood over Gabriel's lifeless form, cold on the kitchen floor. Jessamae declared immediately upon arrival that she was off to fetch his car—which we'd assumed had been one of the three in the cemetery lot—as well as whatever else needed hiding. Cleo demanded she escort her on her quest, distrust evident on her beautiful face. They grabbed the Honda key fob and were gone within three minutes, only staying long enough to assist in carrying the corpse into the house from the garage.

"Do you think, if I could get rid of the rigor mortis, it would help him? Or make it worse?" I asked.

Gabriel's legs were stiff once again, now bent at the knee, and his neck was twisted. It looked uncomfortable, for him and for me. The stench clung to him powerfully, filling my house with death fumes, but it didn't affect my gag reflex anymore. The comfort that came with it remained.

"Princess," Ben said delicately. "He's dead. I don't think there is a better or worse anymore."

I lifted my lip. "Yes, I noticed. But I mean, maybe I could do this a little bit at a time or— should we freeze him? Maybe I could fix him at some point, you know?"

Ben's expression was too gentle, and I hated to see it. "Maybe. But we don't have a freezer big enough. Unless you wanted to cut him up."

My eyebrows shot up. No, I did not want that.

"But there's something else we can do. I helped Patrick with a bit of magic a while back, a sort of timeless spell. It should stop the decomposition until we have a better idea."

"And why exactly did you need a spell like that?"

"Oh, we don't have time for that story, Frank."

My eyes flicked to the window and back, nervously anticipating hollowed eyes. It was still blustery and wet outside, but that wouldn't last forever. It was the middle of summer in Utah … flies a body would attract. "What do we have to do?"

"Do you think you could help me get him into the bathtub?"

I was inundated with uncertainty as I stared again at the body. Even with the strong arms of Cleo and Jessamae, we struggled to get him into the house. It hadn't yet started to bloat, but I guessed him at about 240 pounds, give or take a few dumbbells. *That's a lot of limes*, I thought.

"Not by hand," I whispered. Picturing my soft arms beneath Gabriel stiffened my resolve. "Okay, we'll levitate him. One more time." I pulled open the silverware drawer for a small paring knife. "Would my hair work?" I asked, tired of the grisly practice.

"Not as well. The hair of a siren is valuable."

"Fine," I spat as I cut into my hand, opening the scab the picture frame had made earlier. I passed Ben the knife.

"Do you want to hold my hand?" he asked.

Channeling him would certainly help, but if I couldn't build my magic muscles then I would have to start hitting the gym. "No. Ready?" He nodded.

I opened my body to the air, feeling its gentle flickering around me. Gabriel began to gradually ascend. My focus was the lower half of him, and I was proud that he was relatively level as he floated. But once we reached the hallway, the tendrils of air began to weaken. I sensed a claustrophobia, the walls closing in. His feet began to droop and drag. Determined to do this one thing right, I grabbed the broken picture frame that still lay scattered on the kitchen table and dug the edge into the closing wound of my hand. As the blood welled and ran in deep red pathways down my elbow, Gabriel stabilized three feet off the ground.

Once we had him lying in moderate comfort within the porcelain walls of the tub, blood was dripping off the tips of my fingers. I'd cut deeper than I thought. Ben's eyes widened, he appeared both inquisitive and impressed. I held the wound under the bathroom sink and let the water run. "Now what?"

He stepped closer to me. In the small space of the bathroom, heat pulsed from him. It felt strange in combination with the icy waves that emitted from Gabriel, like I was trapped in a car engine. "We need some herbs and a few other plants. I have most of them at my house. We submerge the body in water, toss in those extra ingredients, and it will work as well as a freezer. We won't even have to thaw him out afterward."

I glared at him but thought the whole thing sounded something close to good, considering the circumstances. "Let's wait for the others to get back before we leave. Jessamae ..." I shuddered to think what she would do to him if I weren't here to stop her.

Ben folded his arms over his chest. "I could go alone. If you want it to be quick."

I hadn't even considered it. When Cleo left with Jessamae, I was relieved knowing neither would be alone. Pamela took advantage of me whenever I strayed from the group, and even if she didn't follow Ben and corner him, she would absolutely have her fun with me. "Let's give them another hour."

He seemed more at ease after that. "I can do an hour," he said and squeezed past me.

I spared another glance for Gabriel spilling out of my bathtub before I turned to follow him. "An hour for what?"

He was in the kitchen, digging pans out of low cupboards. "To cook a decent meal. Have you even eaten today?"

"Yes," I answered defiantly. He raised an eyebrow at me, but I wouldn't elaborate. I'd had a bag of chips from the vending machine at Jim's about twelve hours ago. I could take care of myself, or I could at least try.

"What are we making?" I asked, butting in front of him as I

opened the fridge. My arm had stopped dripping, but my hand was caked with the red stuff.

"Something easy, won't have much time for a banquet. Soup and grilled cheese."

I nearly smiled at the thought of comfort food. I pulled out enough bread for four sandwiches and the block of white cheddar I bought today. If Cleo wanted it for something else, she was going to be disappointed. "We're making one for the vampire? Does she even eat people food?" Ben asked as he ignited one of the burners.

I stifled the biting tone that now stood at attention behind my tongue. "I guess we'll find out."

I was halfway through my meal and Ben was dunking his sandwich in my creamy tomato soup knowing I saved it for the end, when Cleo and Jessamae came through the garage door. They were debating something.

Cleo's eyes rolled to her hairline. "He's overrated, that's all I want to establish. You have to be more than a sensationalist, you need substance—"

"All he is, is substance. Substance without the distraction. If you could have seen the immediate reactions from literary critics when Beckett appeared on the scene of those, comparatively, stuffy modernists …"

Ben's cheeks puffed out, full of soggy masticated bread. He'd stopped chewing to watch them and looked a bit green around the gills.

"Swallow," I reminded him under my breath. He tried, but the lump of food clogged his airway.

"Did you find the car?" I asked much louder than I needed to, interrupting what I'm sure was a fascinating conversation.

Cleo's perfect dark skin almost reddened under Ben's astonished stare. "We found the car at the cemetery. We parked it in the garage. We checked the funeral home for anything incriminating or demonic. Nothing appeared amiss."

"Where's the Honda?"

"In Ben's driveway. We felt it prudent to check there, too." If I had thought to call, they could have grabbed the herbs we needed. But something told me Ben wouldn't take kindly to Jessamae stepping foot in his garden. Now that he'd swallowed the mammoth bite that threatened to choke him, he did not appear pleased with Cleo's behavior.

"Sounds like you two had quite the field trip." He made zero effort to hide his displeasure. Cleo stared him down, her chin jerking up. Their battle of wills ended in seconds.

Ben sighed in defeat. "There's soup and sandwiches on the stove. Please, help yourself, Cleo," and after a fat pause, "Jessamae." He stood up from the table, clearing our plates.

Jessamae assessed him coolly. "I will, thank you."

He gripped the edge of the sink in a brief respite from his unstable mood, then turned around with a pleasant smile for me, gesturing to the front door with a wave of his arm.

"Right," I said as I stood. "Gabriel is in the bathtub. Please leave him be. Both of you." Cleo would do whatever was logical to her and I couldn't trust either one with a dead body. "We're going to Ben's for some herbs to keep him … fresh?" My face twisted at the word, making Cleo smile.

"What herbs? You have an entire apothecary in your home, Benjamin?" Jessamae asked.

He spoke to the door when he answered, "Everything but a prescription pad. And a few things I can pluck from the mountainside."

"Things?" she asked, interest increasing in her pitch. "I know these grounds. I can retrieve these 'things'."

Ben still hadn't turned around, instead, he leaned forward and began smacking his forehead into the door. He must have picked up that habit from me. We watched him go about it for ten or fifteen thumps until he rested his head there. Suddenly, he whipped around, fast enough to make me jump, and grabbed a pen and a slip of paper—it looked like an old receipt—from a kitchen drawer. He jotted down a quick list on the back and held it out aggressively to Jessamae without a word. She took it from him politely before he clutched my elbow and pulled me to the door.

"By the way," Jessamae called out to us as Ben opened the door, "there was a message from the dead man's son on the funeral home answering machine. He was supposed to be home hours ago."

༄

BEN PICKED the correct leaves and blossoms from his garden while I sat in the dirt and strung rubber bands around the bundles. The moist air combined with herbs smelled heavenly, and the few crickets that had ventured out after the rain, into the night, called to one another. If outside were always like this, and the bugs would agree not to be too loud, I thought I might enjoy it.

Whenever I had a few seconds between handfuls, I sent nervous texts to Cleo, asking if she and Jessamae were alive and well. I had never had so many people to keep track of before and fretting over them was positively taxing.

As we returned to the car and drove across town, Ben chatted to me about the necessity of a garden at both homes to fill out the gaps in his current herb collection, virtually having an entire apothecary at our fingertips. We'd need feathers and bones. He prattled on, listing millions of obscure plants that I'd never heard of before when I couldn't contain my anxiety any longer.

"How do we kill this thing, Ben?" I stared out to the road, tormented by what I had done. Because I brought it, this demon, into being, I had ended the life of one innocent man. Who would be next?

I heard Ben's rub his bristly head. "I'm not sure. All demons are different, what works for one won't work for another. Sort of like us." The band Cake played on the fuzzy radio. I liked this song, or I would have ripped it from the dash. "All I know is, we need Jessamae. I see her with us, she's necessary, but I can't see any more than that."

"You didn't see Gabriel?" I kept my voice as neutral as possible. I knew he was blameless in this, but I had wondered.

He sounded angry when he answered. "No, I didn't. I didn't see the murder, and I didn't see him in the casket either." He knocked his knuckles against his skull. "The demon—I've only seen it through your eyes, in real-time. Whenever I've tried to see it coming, it's like trying to hold water, worse even. Like trying to catch shadows. I come up empty every time."

He pulled up to the house, put the car in park, and rested his head on the steering wheel. This had been eating at him for a while; he just hadn't said anything until now.

I lifted a timorous hand to his head and stroked the short down of hair, so soft, like velvet. It had been growing so rapidly since our touching took off, he had already shaved it again. He let me pet his head with his eyes closed for a while. We had entered the early hours of the morning and I was bone-tired. Though I was afraid of seeing Pamela and of her seeing me, I thought if I could just keep my eyes closed, I would never know. And maybe I could live with that. With my hand brushing against Ben's head, I began to drift.

"Come on, Frank. We need to take care of Gabriel before morning."

I pushed against my heavy, heavy eyelids. My arm had fallen back around Ben's shoulders. He looked over at me with wide eyes, energized and awake. His hair had grown another inch. I bit the inside of my lip, wishing momentarily that we could trade affinities, and opened the door.

I didn't know how long we'd slept, but Jessamae was back. There was a neat pile of leaves and pretty-petaled flowers on the table.

"About time," Cleo snapped. She lounged on the floor, reading. Jessamae seemed to be napping against the wall before we came in, because she sat up and pushed the tousled white hair from her eyes. The more time I spent with her, the more human she became to me. I didn't know if that scared me or thrilled me.

Ben strummed his fingers through the plants on the table, checking for accuracy, no doubt. Everything he needed would be there in spades, no doubt. He took an armful with him down the hall, a second tote full of herbs in his hand. I staggered after him, still floating between conscious and not as much.

He already had the faucet running when I came in. Reaching around him, I held my hand under the water. It was freezing. Gabriel was clearly dead, obnoxiously so, but it was details like this that solidified the truth.

I crouched down beside Ben and reached into the tote of greens. "One of each?"

Ben was sprinkling pastel purple blooms into the water. "Might as well do two or three. Better safe than sorry."

I flung in sprouts and leaves and sprigs and stems. Once the tub was full of water, Ben turned off the faucet and stood. The water was beautiful, like something out of a self-care article in a teen magazine. And if Gabriel's brown eyes weren't so alarmingly open beneath the surface of the water, it would have been inviting. It was like we were the first responders to an accidental drowning, and that meant that Gabriel still looked like Gabriel. It was almost like we still had time.

"I'm going to sleep. We can do more tomorrow. Later today, I guess."

Cleo and Jessamae watched from the doorway. I pushed between them to get out of that room.

Cleo must have done laundry today, I thought, seeing my folded old comforter on the mattress. I sighed in relief as I took off my clothes and crawled beneath the blanket in my underwear.

The door opened, and Ben snuck in, shutting the door against the light of the hallway. Slowly, as if I were already asleep and he was afraid of waking me, he took off his shirt and tossed it into the closet. His torso was so long. Miles and miles. He slid down his pants. It was rude to watch, but I watched. The veins along the lean muscles of his arms were evident, even under the sheet of tattoos and the weighted dark of the bedroom. His back was to me, and I realized the freckles that spotted his face and shoulders continued down his broad back. When he turned toward me, blue in the small strip of moonlight I'd allowed through the curtains, I was struck dumb at all his skin. His eyes met mine. He knew I'd been watching, but I held his stare.

He climbed into bed in his boxer-briefs. Years before, when I could have sworn I was only a friend to him, he told me he rarely wore underwear, and I wondered if he wore them now for my benefit. He shouldn't make himself uncomfortable for my sake …

Crossing over me, he pushed his back against the wall and very gently placed his arm on top of mine, almost nervously. He was so rarely timid with me. I turned around to read his expression. He looked imaginary. I thought there was a chance I might already be asleep and dreaming. Because the way he looked at me made me feel beautiful.

His fingers trailed along my neck, tickling my collarbone, and sleep was the farthest thing from my mind. His thigh slid between both of mine. "I felt so far away from you today," he whispered.

I inhaled, the dirt and smoke and paint of him almost erased the ever-present death. I inhaled again. His hand pressed against my chest, over my thumping heart. "There." I felt him smile beside me.

There was an unexpected knock on the bedroom door before Jessamae glided inside. I bolted up from my indulgent position between Ben's arms and swallowed hard. My mouth was suddenly dry.

I was under the blanket, but I pulled it up to my chin, feeling exposed. Ben sat up behind me and I could sense his aggravation like needles in my back. He kept his arm curved around my hip in my lap. It wasn't a showy touch for her benefit, but he didn't pull it away either.

Jessamae sat at the foot of the bed obtrusively. "I'm going to stay in the living room tonight, in case the demon shows up again. Also, I'd like to be close. The morning's preparations should start early."

"I don't remember Frankie issuing an invitation." Ben's voice was dead cold.

Jessamae ignored him and continued to stare openly at me, as if we were the only two in the room. I still hadn't forgiven her, but that wasn't why having her so close made me feel conflicted.

"That's fine, Jessamae," I said. She reached out and caressed my ankle. It was somehow just as intimate as Ben's naked chest currently pressed to my back. He knew it too, his fist clenched in my lap. "You said a necromancer had problems with demons before. Will any of that help with Pamela?" I asked, partially for the critical information and mostly to take the attention off me.

Her fingers walked along the curve of my calf, and Ben's teeth were grinding in my ear. "Maybe. It's worth a try."

"Can we get ahold of them somehow? The necromancer."

Her shoulders twitched subtly. It was a weary act coming from her. "No, that won't be possible." She stood up, and absolutely disinterested in Ben—who was practically biting my neck in irritation—kissed me lightly on the forehead. "He lost the battle with his demon. He's dead."

23

WHEN MY ALARM blared through the room, I cursed it to hell. I cursed Jim's Grocery, Scott, and every decision I had ever made that brought me to this morning that began far too early. After Jessamae left our room last night, Ben kissed my cheek and turned to face the wall, away from me. An understandable reaction that kept me up for another hour before sleep finally took me. He still faced the wall now.

I slid out of bed carefully. The alarm did nothing to rouse Ben, whose long arm was thrown over his eyes like a blindfold. He'd set his own alarm for an hour from now, and he would have to turn that one off himself. I took clothes suitable for work from my closet and crossed the hall in my underwear.

I refused to entertain the tub, but it was hard to ignore the rotten floral funeral home stink, the hand resting against its edge, the black spikes of hair jutting from the water. His loafers were surprisingly clean, the cuffs of his pale-yellow shirt buttoned. His hands were sandy brown in color, human. That was good. But when I caught the glint of a gold wedding band on his finger, I looked away.

I gave myself a slapdash sponge bath with a wet dish towel and some hand soap. The nerves at leaving my little pack of misfits were increasing every second as I got dressed and put my tangled, lumpy hair into a bun. The memory of sludge pouring from Pamela's green flesh was like the clamor of my alarm, and my heart seized every time it hit me.

Jessamae was still asleep beneath a woven blanket in the

corner of the living room. Cleo must have loaned it to her, because it wasn't one I recognized.

Amir slinked between my ankles as I grabbed a granola bar from the cupboard. I broke off a corner for him and he gobbled it up. The cat stared up at me sadly. "That's all," I chastised in a whisper as I ate half the bar in one bite.

As I chewed, chocolate chips fell out my mouth and I brushed them off my shirt. Lifting the other half of breakfast to my lips, I met Jessamae's pale and watchful eyes across the room. I sucked the dry bits out of my teeth before I opened my mouth. Swallowed a burp. "You're up."

"I don't sleep much," she said solemnly. "But you're awake quite early."

"I have to be to work by seven. Stocking." I glimpsed longingly at the coffee machine. No time.

Jessamae stretched, even this early she appeared distinctly feline. Amir watched her but never approached.

"I'll go with you," she asserted and neatly folded the blanket. "Why?"

She swept her white hair over her shoulder. It was criminal for someone to look so striking at this time of day. "Because you're in danger. And because I know I'm not wanted here." But she wasn't at all put off by the latter. She said it matter-of-factly.

"Sure ... just give me five seconds." I rushed back into the bathroom and gargled some mouthwash, checked my shirt for offensive stains, and layered on a bit of deodorant. I never had to look presentable for Scott and the grocery gang, but if Jessamae were joining me ... Sighing at my slip down the insanity slope, I flashed Gabriel a sad thumbs-up and joined the witch out in front of the house.

Ben's car nosed up to the curb out front, and the Honda was nowhere in sight. "Shit!" I'd forgotten they left the Honda at Ben's last night after the car switcheroo. I must have been more tired than I thought; I didn't have time to walk now. I couldn't drive a missing funeral director's vehicle.

Jessamae gave a throaty chuckle. "I can take you." She saw my apprehension. "I'm sorry if it's unusual. We thought it might be better to leave the car. If both are seen here outside the garage, it might make people wonder. Neighbors talk in small towns."

I bit my lip. I was certainly taking up more than my fair share of the town's attention as of late.

"Okay, thanks. I might even be early," I said without enthusiasm. "But will you take me to Ben's after my shift? I left some clothes, and I can grab the car. I'll park behind the house, so you won't have to take me everywhere."

After a long pause, she nodded. "I haven't made payment for my magic since yesterday." She eyed the house.

I looked over my shoulder and saw Amir watching us from the window. I turned back to Jessamae. "No."

She sighed with impatience. "Give me a moment." She closed her eyes, her hands extended at her sides. I stood awkwardly beside her, wondering if I should sit on the lawn to wait.

Her eyes flashed open and her head cocked to the right, to the tall yellow grass. She pulled a pocketknife from her loose canvas pants with relish.

"Don't move." I didn't know if she spoke to me or the grass.

A crispy sound swished within the field. A snake. I took a step back, despite what Jessamae may have just asked of me.

Her steps were soundless, her legs bent deeply. She became predacious, so quick and low to the ground. Her head cocked again, though I hadn't heard anything.

She sprung without warning, her feet flying out behind her as she landed on her hands. Tall grass shook around the struggle. She didn't squeal or grunt or cry—anything I might have done. There were a few violent thumps, a puff of dirt rose to the air, and nothing more.

"Jessamae?" I called hesitantly after the grass had stilled.

She popped from the grass like a daisy, a smile on her face and a fat garter snake in her fist. "A plant wouldn't do."

"Why didn't you use your affinity?" I asked as I hiked through the straw.

"Even though it's a sacrifice to another, it's of benefit to me. It wouldn't work."

She showed me her kill, her pose reminded me of pictures some people took after they'd caught a fish. Proudly displaying their skill. There was a bloody hole in its head.

She rolled up the snake like it was loose yarn and tucked it away in her pocket, sliding her knife in along with it. I didn't ask why she wanted the dead thing. I didn't care much to know.

She molded herself painfully close behind me. She was only a few inches taller than me, and we fit together like forks. I felt her chest inflate against my back.

"Ready?" She breathed into my ear. I shook off any feelings of skittishness and admittedly hoped Ben was still sound asleep.

"Ready." *Please, be sleeping.* And we were gone.

We reappeared behind Jim's loading dock. I'd felt nothing as we traveled, not the wind against my face or the changing terrain.

Jessamae lowered her arms to my stomach. The scent of her skin, like bitter greens fresh in the rain, dominated the air. I'd finally escaped the stink of decay. Her arms squeezed my middle, tight against my ribs. I relaxed inside them for just a second before I pinched myself inside my elbow. "Thanks for the ride."

Her body lingered. I leaned my head forward and she allowed me a small distance. "What will you do in the meantime? Do you live around here?" I'd never asked her before, but surely, she had to shower and sleep somewhere.

She stalked along the side of the building. "More or less. But I'll be inside with you."

I was shamefully eased by the idea. Jessamae was such a formidable opponent. "Won't you get bored?"

"I assure you I won't." She smiled frighteningly and led the way inside.

The overhead lighting was much too bright this morning, my eyes felt swollen and tingly beneath them. I grabbed two sickly-sweet bottled coffees from the beverage aisle and held one out for Jessamae. She looked bemused at the offering, and read all the ingredients carefully with raised brows. "Have you never had one of these?" I asked.

She popped the top. "Not like this. I make coffee when I can." She took a sip and her eyes gaped open. "I've always liked the taste."

I took a couple more with me to the back and stowed them in my apron for later. We didn't open until nine, and Scott wouldn't be in until at least then, so I didn't feel too bad about flipping a milk crate over for Jessamae, giving her a seat while I worked. She never looked away distracted, never fidgeted with her nails or her hair, and she never offered to help, which would have really moved things along. She just watched me stock with rapt attention.

"So where do you live then?" I prodded, because I was so ill at ease under her ogling. I felt like a milk-lifting sideshow attraction.

"Nowhere, all over. After I discovered what I could do, when Eliza was taken, I lost control of my affinity." She swirled one calloused finger along the lip of her coffee. "And I had to leave for a while. I became quite the outdoorsman." She smiled but her eyes were sad. "Then I met members of our kind, even made a few friends. I stay with them from time to time. I actually intended to see an old acquaintance in Nevada when I felt your pull."

"You live outside?" I asked, dumbfounded. She had given a lot of information to me, but my mind clung to that detail.

She laughed at my outrage. "I enjoy it, Frankie. If I didn't, don't you think I would have acquired my own house by now?"

I bit my tongue. I didn't want to invite her to stay for any sort of long-term vacation. Though I could feel myself once again thawing towards her, she would always be unsettling and intense. I was already unsettled enough by Ben's long, freckled body.

Ben would hate it if I invited her to stay, not that it was up to him. Regardless, even with Ben in my bed, I couldn't always keep myself under control when it came to Jessamae, and I didn't want to find out what exactly that meant. When I remembered her hushed breaths, the feel of her tongue on my ear, I blushed like a fool. I held my red face to a milk jug to cool it down. It smelled bad.

"What are you doing?" she asked reasonably.

I hoped my coloring had normalized when I turned toward her. "Just smelling. I thought that one smelled spoiled."

She scrunched her nose, and I knew what she was thinking: they all smelled like that.

Once I finished stocking, it must have looked suspicious for Jessamae to follow me around the store like a trainee or a tethered balloon. However, no other employee asked if she needed any help, or scolded me for bringing in a person who was clearly a friend. They seemed to avoid the two of us entirely, even the customers.

The thrumming in my chest that I'd experienced earlier at Jessamae's closeness hardly distracted me today. Instead, I would just lose track of myself and wind up inches from her side. I never felt myself moving, but would gravitate toward her constantly, like a moon in orbit. The farthest Jessamae ever strayed was an aisle or two, but she would always return to me within minutes.

In those few small moments, I heard and saw things—things of which I couldn't be certain. Crazed laughter over my shoulder that sounded like an echoing crow caw. Wet breath on my neck that I'd manically swipe. I'd spin around, and I'd find nothing. I couldn't be sure if they were demonic, or if my fear was getting the better of me when Jessamae was out of sight. Pamela had proven she didn't mind an audience when she stood outside our window last night, so why was she being so evasive now? At this rate, I'd lose my mind before we could stop her.

I clocked out at one. I went into Scott's office to grab my phone and keys off the long side table where employees regularly dumped their belongings. Scott was chugging along like a steam engine, typing on his computer one key at a time. I stood with my back to him and my hand on the door, waiting for him to say something about Jessamae, or worse, the state of my apron. He didn't say a thing. When I peeked over my shoulder, he continued typing as if I wasn't in the room. Perhaps my luck was turning.

Walking to meet Jessamae at the check-out counter, I saw two texts from Ben light up my phone screen:

I hope you made it to work ok. I would have taken you.

The second was a picture of a jelly donut with a single bite taken out of it.

"Bastard," I whispered.

"What's so funny?" Jessamae asked. I was smiling, my eyes cast down on my phone.

"It's nothing," I said, putting it in my pocket as we exited. "Jessamae," I started, already feeling so weird and conceited, "What am I to you?"

She stopped in her tracks, then pushed her hair back from her face to see me clearly.

"I mean, with Ben, he and I are sort of … romantic." My tonsils itched at the word. I sounded like such an idiot. I stared down to her boots. "And I think, the way you touch me, it makes him wonder about us. And I think it makes him upset." That was the most chicken-shit, half-assed way I could have put it. I covered my eyes, mortified.

Her hands pulled against mine until I could see. "I know it upsets him." She was smiling, and my anger simmered beneath my blush. "But he needs to understand, and it sounds like you do too, that what you and Ben have, it's sweet, but it's young and it's fleeting."

She wove her fingers through the loose hanging coils of my hair and lowered her voice. "What you and I have is much more than that. It's balance." She kissed my left temple. "It's timeless," she kissed my right. Pressing in even closer than she was already. "We are inevitable."

She leaned her face in, and I almost let her do it. I wanted her to—desperately I wanted it. But I forced my feet back. Ben was probably watching now, whether he wanted to see or not. I couldn't drag him through this with me.

Jessamae was only a little disgruntled. "You told me how you think Ben feels about this. Is that all that's stopping you now?" She stepped away from me, and I wouldn't admit to her how wrong that felt. "How do you feel?" She walked toward the spot where we had arrived this morning.

How did I feel? Excited, terrified, powerful, helpless. Like a stranger, and like I had been waiting to be this person my entire life. An erupting Pandora's box of emotions that I wasn't ready to confess to anyone yet. Above all else, she made me feel confused.

"I don't know," I muttered. Jessamae grinned at me, satisfied. "But I do know about Ben!"

Her smile grew patronizing as she held her hand out to me. "I won't do anything you don't want me to do." I saw the loophole in her words, and I didn't clasp her hand in return.

Without pause, she wrapped me in her arms. She rubbed her hands against my shoulders, bumping her forearms against my side-boob, getting very comfortable, enjoying herself. "Benjamin won't see a thing. If that's what you want."

"That's not—" We took off.

And appeared in the familiar yellow skirting of Ben's home.

"What about payment?" I asked, distracted from our discussion.

"I took care of that while you were getting your things."

I didn't want to see the extra bulge in her pockets.

When, again, Jessamae didn't release me from her powerful embrace, I pushed her sinewy arms from me. Being here alone with her, at his place, the place I'd been very alone with Ben for years, scraped against me like gravel. I could smell his coddled herbs from here. The scent spread throughout my insides and smelled a lot like guilt. She pulled the keys to the Honda from the flatter of her two side pockets. The other had definitely grown.

"Could you wait outside?" I didn't want to explain myself, and she didn't ask me to, though she did look slightly put out. Maybe she had hoped I'd ignore Ben's feelings and invite her giddily inside.

"Okay. I'll be waiting in the car." She cupped my chin, pressing her thumb into the dimpled cleft, and left.

Ben never locked his doors. I used to think it was crazy, but I now understood he had other ways of stopping intruders, or he'd see them coming. If only that were the case for Pamela. I let myself in the front door.

Though Ben had been back here to change and shower since Cleo moved in, everything was exactly as we left it. Ben's blankets were roughly littered across his living room, his green sheet at the foot of the loveseat. I rubbed the silky fabric between my fingers and lifted it pathetically to my face. The smell was faint, but it was Ben. No matter how many times he told me, and no matter how often he was there to prove it, I wanted some sort of evidence of his affection to hold on to. A smell. The sheet was probably too big, and Ben would notice if I took it. I folded the sheet and set it back on the arm of the couch.

I perked my head up in alarm. There was another smell now, a much stronger one. Something was burning. Had Ben left the stove on? All day?

Around the corner of the archway, smoke curled lazily from a stack of paper on the counter. It was the *Tribune*, the same newspaper that held Pamela's obituary. A bright spark flashed below the smoke.

I rushed forward to put it out, ready to grab the paper and throw it in the sink. But as my fingers touched the thin pages, the spark grew like a white spider. I clutched the paper and the edges ripped off in my hands.

The newspaper was being held down; I couldn't lift it. The spark continued to flesh out, extending in several directions with one thick base in the center. A hand.

"You know what I do with little piggies?"

I released the crumbling paper and fell back to the linoleum floor, closing my eyes and sliding myself backward with my feet.

Heat flashed against me and burned my face. My eyes peeled open. I didn't want them to. I prayed for fire and nothing else.

Pamela was imminent over my cowering form, her face entirely red now, her eye sockets hollow and dark. Flies entered and exited her open mouth, clinging to her chalky old teeth. Her dress had begun to disintegrate from the rotting flesh of her torso, hanging open in large cutouts that displayed her corpse like a paned window.

Her hands and her feet were burning, devoured in flames. The orange tongues of fire danced along the dead woman's skin as if she were made of paper. She held the newspaper between her flaming palms, and read her own obituary. Her ugly smiling face lifted back to mine, her eyes elated though empty. She threw the burning print behind her where it continued to blaze on the counter.

She trampled toward me on burning legs like a toddler, her bare feet leaving sputtering fires in their wake, melting the linoleum flooring. She considered me madly as I backed into the living room, nearly paralyzed with fear.

Then her legs seemed to give out, she tipped forward like a timbering tree. Her knees hit the kitchen floor and her torso fell forward with a smack, shaking the furniture. She was only inches from my feet. She didn't stir. She lay there like the dead woman she was, half-consumed in her own flames. Her scalp was corroded through with blistering black holes.

I straightened my torso, lengthening my neck as I examined the terrible sight of her, hoping against hope that she would never move again. I gulped down my spit, and bent forward at the waist, toward the body. I had to know.

Slowly, inescapably, her forehead began to rise. It lifted leisurely, as if inflating. My breathing hitched, and I began to cry. I couldn't move. Still, the head rose, little by little, until all I saw was red. Browless eye sockets took up half the terrible face and the nose was hanging slightly away from the cheeks, like a damaged prosthetic. That wide mouth stretched, a skinless hole. I was frozen, I couldn't even blink.

Pamela held her lunatic countenance, her chin resting on the ground as if decapitated. Her empty eyes held mine and a single fly crossed what was once her lip.

"I COOK 'EM!" she shrieked. And I screamed.

Her laughter resounded as her body erupted completely in flame, her eyes and mouth disappearing into the forest of fire. She clawed at my shins with her burning fingers, scratching the denim of my jeans and singeing the meat of my calves. I pulled myself on fumbling hands, cracking my elbows on the hard floor, desperate to keep my bare skin from her touch.

My screaming hurt my own ears. I was wailing, kicking at the fire uselessly. The rubber of my soles dripping to the floor.

Pamela loved my fear, cackling as her flaming form climbed up my knees. My jeans were on fire and melting to my skin.

"Mmmm, something smells good." The frog's voice bubbled from within the growing inferno. "Tasty little piggy!"

"No, NO!" I tried to stand, to run, but the fire was heavy, sitting on my legs and feet. I planted my hands and pulled. Pulled for my life. *Snap!* Somewhere in my right foot, I had broken a bone.

The front door slammed violently into the wall and fresh air pervaded the house.

"Here she comes! Here she comes!" Pamela mocked in a sing-song voice. "Always coming for her peach, isn't she?" She seemed to roll her fiery shoulders salaciously and laughter reverberated off the walls of the kitchen.

Jessamae's hands were under my arms, and she yanked at me fiercely. My body straightened in the air, taut against Pamela's weight. The flames were eating me, digesting me like a snake from bottom to top.

Pamela continued to cling, the bones of my legs straining. I started to cough. My middle cramped, hacking out the black poisonous smoke.

The hand of fire seemed to lift from me. It danced at the two of us in a wave. And in an instant, the fire was gone.

Without the resistance, Jessamae careened backward with me in her arms. We pummeled into the living room wall as if thrown. But Jessamae would not rest. She stood immediately, her legs trembling as she readjusted her strong hands under my pits. She dragged my limp and charred body through the front door and far from the house, gravel rolling underneath me as I scratched along the ground.

Once she released my arms, I twisted to the side. I yacked out the rest of the smoke and some bile. My guts clenched and heaved until I puked that sickly sweet coffee all over Ben's driveway. I dragged myself farther, skinning my stomach on the pavement. I sucked in clean air like gaseous ambrosia. It was exquisite. It was everything.

I couldn't feel the ground beneath me. I couldn't feel much of anything below my waist, for which I was thankful and terrified. I looked back to my legs, knowing the sight would be nightmarish. It was worse.

My legs were a molten swirl of red skin and black denim. Any cloth that remained had fused with my skin. The bottoms of my boots had melted away completely. I couldn't see the bottoms of my feet, but the skin must be completely cooked.

Jessamae flopped down on her back beside me. Her words

had a touch of volume now, a mumbling hive full of anger. Her hands fluttered close to my back and away again repeatedly.

I laid in a miserable tangle of burnt flesh. The sun was out again, and the sheer amount of warmth and light threatened to smother me. It baked my skinless muscles. A siren wailed in the distance, getting closer every second, but I couldn't move. Everything felt fuzzy and numb— even my painful cough had dulled to a rumbling between my ribs. I faced the forest I'd been led to the night Pamela died. Through the slit of my heavy lids, I saw movement there, between the limbs and trunks. A patch of color swaying unnaturally. It was her.

Pamela was dancing behind the home she burned. She jumped and twirled like a child that didn't have full control of their legs. As if she felt my stare, she turned to me. Her smile was so wide I could see it from here, a patch of yellow surrounded by that unreal red face. She waved happily at me, and everything went black.

24

I WAS BEING TOUCHED. The fingers were foreign, not deft like Ben's or rough like Jessamae's. They prodded the dainty lines of my throat. Remembering Pamela dancing in the woods, my eyes flashed open, and I was crawling, the raw skin of me shredding on the tough grass, so I flipped my body over and felt woozy. I couldn't stand.

"Whoa! Slow down! It's okay. I'm an EMT." E-M-T. I took in the white shirt, a small blue logo. "You were in a house fire." The speaker came into focus under the bright sun. Sort of young, in his late twenties or early thirties, with a friendly face and a full circle of dark hair that covered him from crown to shoulder. He looked like Jesus. "Do you remember a fire?"

I stared back to the house. The door was hanging open, which I didn't like. It was like looking at a family member naked. The windows were all open—white smoke drifted into the breeze from most, but the smoke from the kitchen was heavy and dark. People shrouded in black and yellow moseyed in and out the door. Jessamae was gone.

"Miss? Can you hear me?" the man asked nervously. There was a grouchy-looking older woman standing behind Jesus, scrutinizing beneath caterpillar eyebrows.

"Yea—" I croaked before the coughing fits began again. It was like a brick was lodged into the jelly lining of my neck. Jesus helped me to sit up and heartily patted my back until my body was finished. I cringed away from his touch. My skin burned anew with every movement.

"Yes," I said in the same bullfrog croak without the cough. "How long?" Each word was agony.

"Not too long," he glanced behind him at the grouch before he elaborated. "Fire was called in twenty minutes ago. A bystander saw the smoke. Medical wasn't dispatched at that time. Then the owner of the home called emergency services. Told us he'd been informed of the fire, and a friend of his had stopped by to pick up a few things. You," he pointed helpfully at me, "and that you were not responding to phone calls."

I nodded. Ben knew about the fire, knew about Pamela.

"Miss, you have suffered severe burns," he said formally, motioning to my ruined lower half. "And we will transport you to the nearest medical facility."

Before he finished speaking, I shook my head. I didn't have insurance, and even if I did, a ride in an ambulance was more than I could afford. "I'll drive."

My head was spinning like I'd coughed up all the air in my brain along with everything else. I examined my body. I was pleasantly surprised to find a shirt—only the hem had been destroyed. But my arms were a very angry red and my fingertips had started to bubble. I didn't want Jesus to examine my legs, but they were hard to miss. Where my jeans hadn't burned away, they had adhered to my skin like a black plaster. But I knew they were healing. No hospital should see that.

The young EMT looked again at the woman who shook her head silently. "You are in no state to drive—you're seriously injured. Do you have a friend you can call?"

Jessamae didn't have a car. Cleo didn't have a car. Ben was working, but after seeing our latest disaster, he should be on his way.

"Sure," I mumbled over the sandpaper scraping my tonsils. I pulled my phone out of my front pocket. The screen was oddly warped, colors shimmered through the black. It was done for. But hoping to assuage the paramedics, I tapped my phone fruitlessly and held it to my ear.

Ben's Volkswagen turned into view down the lane, and I exhaled in relief. "That's Ben," I told Jesus.

Ben twisted between the firetruck and ambulance at a jog, his stiff white overalls crunching roughly with every step. He didn't look at his home, but I'd never seen him scared like this. I did my best to scooch away and sit up on my own.

He didn't say anything. He kneeled over me and virtually shoved the EMT to the side for all the care he showed him. Jesus looked to the woman for instruction but moved out of Ben's way.

Ben held up strands of my hair for inspection. Some of them were broken and smelled horrible. Then he ran his hands over my forehead and neck, down to my heart. His touch was so soft and careful, it reminded me of running the smooth bristles of his paintbrushes over my cheeks when they were fresh from the package. His fingers landed down just below my navel and pain choked me. He stopped the exam without touching my legs.

The caterpillar woman cleared her throat, but Ben paid her no mind. He crawled smoothly behind me to inspect my back. He made a noise between a growl and a cough. That burn on my stomach was growing in volume, so loud, overwhelming in its heat after he'd touched it. I felt his chin rest on my shoulder, light as a feather.

"Frank," he whispered only for me, "I don't think you can walk."

I swallowed the black phlegm building in my throat. "I can."

I heard a sigh as Ben stood up and turned to the paramedics. "I've got her," and he held his arms out to me. I took them and pulled, a small noise seeping through my clenched lips. The burning hadn't stopped. I was still in the fire.

Ben held me as I was, waiting for the pain to recede, but we had to get away from these prying eyes. He met my stare, and I could practically hear his thoughts: *Brace yourself.*

He scooped me into his arms, his hand below my butt. I'd yet to feel pain there, but I wasn't concerned about that. The hand that held my back was like a rake in my muscles and I choked on a cry. He marched me away from the disgruntled and worried EMTs as fast as he could without jostling me, but the friction against my back brought tears to my eyes.

The Volkswagen was just outside the circle of firefighters and their truck. The Honda was farther away than I remembered it being. Jessamae had thought to move it.

Ben set me gingerly in the passenger seat, and I leaned forward away from its touch.

I was quiet for most of the car ride. My back was howling, and the smell of my hair was potent in the tiny space of the car.

Ben let me suffer in silence for a those few minutes, but couldn't keep his emotions pent up any longer than that. "It nearly killed you this time."

I wanted to tuck my face into my arms, but I knew it would sting. "I know."

His teeth ground together like stones in water.

"Your kitchen—"

"It's only some shitty linoleum, Frank." He rubbed his head in agitation. "I watched you burn. The fire was melting you, and I watched! You! Burn!" He slapped his hand back to the wheel with each word. I felt the force of the beats in my chest. "I didn't understand. I called Cleo, told her to report it. Then I called the police to get an ambulance there. I couldn't see the extent of the damage because you fainted." He clawed again at his scalp, his fingers leaving long paths in his skin, and I saw the affliction in his eyes. "I had to lock myself in the bathroom of the house we were at today."

His miserable stare drifted and I knew he was playing the scene back for himself like the meanest home video. "I had to watch. I had to see the end, if you made it out. But the whole time, I thought I was watching you die."

I worried about the skin on his head, that he would wear it away. His eyes became shiny, shimmering in the sun. I wanted to jump from the car, from his life. I couldn't stand the sight of the welling tears.

"I was watching you die, and I couldn't stop it. It was killing you and I had to keep watching." His mouth hung open and his glossy eyes stared away. "I don't know which was worse."

I remembered my wish to trade affinities the night before, and I took all that wanting back. I'd never seen Ben in such pain. I couldn't imagine the devastation if our roles had been reversed. His experience sounded so much more than terrible, so much worse than my own, and I was almost sorry he'd come into my life at all.

I buckled the seatbelt over my wounds and ignored all the anguish.

BEN CARRIED me over the threshold of my house, and it was even worse than the first time. Pain had exploded beneath my knees, and I was crying again. Jessamae sat at the kitchen table with Cleo, who had a restless Amir in her lap. As he bit savagely at her hands, Cleo surveyed my ravaged skin-suit, her lovely face creased with worry. Despite my reluctance for a roommate at first, my heart grew squishy at the concern in her eyes.

"I'd normally draw you a bath filled with herbs and tinctures, but because our bathtub is still occupied," Cleo said irritably, "I made a salve."

Jessamae was intent on a pile of what looked like salt. Her eyes were red from the smoke. She had on a new set of clothes—the blush-colored silk top almost certainly belonged to Cleo.

She seemed reluctant to look at me, and when she did, her eyes were haunted. Jessamae was filled to the brim with ghosts.

"I am sorry, Frankie. The house—everything looked normal

from the car. There was no smoke, no heat. I had no idea." She looked slightly out of her mind, her head too loose on her neck.

"I had no idea," she said again. Her upper lip kept pulling away from her teeth in a neurotic snarl. Her shame and her rage were wringing her like a wet rag. I shied away in the limited space of Ben's arms.

Pamela was hunting me. She'd been watching, had followed me to work, had followed me to Ben's. And the second I was alone, she'd trapped me like a fly under a glass. I survived, but living was excruciating.

Ben set me down gently on the tile, the carpet too abrasive for my skin. I screamed at the contact. He brought the salve to my side.

I scooped up a handful of the green goo Cleo had made. The instant relief on my palm was better than any medicine I could imagine. My arm stopped in the air, hand full of gunk. I was too afraid to touch anything.

Ben stuck his own fingers in the goop of my charred hand and lifted the back of my shirt. No matter how careful he was with whatever was festering back there, once his fingers made contact, the pain was baffling.

"Jesus Christ!" I was bombarded by the image of the EMT trainee.

"Do you want to go to the hospital?" Cleo threatened, and I turned her down with a cough. I'd already rejected Ben's offer to take me. It may not be instant, but there was a big risk they would notice my accelerated regeneration. Plus, no insurance.

"I'm sorry," Ben whispered, and again brushed the cream against my skin. Knowing what to expect, I clapped my mouth shut and clenched my teeth. Once Ben had a thick layer of green goo on my back, I sighed at the startling relief. It was wonderful.

I looked down at the black husks over my calves. I still couldn't feel any pain below my knees.

"We'll have to cut your pants off you. Your legs have already started to heal to the denim. We need to do it now—it won't be pleasant," he warned.

"It's okay. I, uh, can't really feel parts of them right now."

Ben inhaled sharply and closed his eyes tight. After several tense seconds, he eyed me steadily. His composure renewed. I heard a gust of air and looked to Jessamae. I saw death reflected in her pale eyes; she was crazed in her fury. Ben was trying to stay calm for me, Jessamae clearly was not.

"Just do it," I gritted to Ben.

He took a knife out of a large pocket that lined the side of his overalls. Cleo tossed an aggrieved Amir aside and held my feet to the ground.

"I can't feel them," I reminded her.

She said, "Just in case, then."

"You'll need a tight hold," Ben forewarned. "But don't worry, Frank. You won't be conscious for the whole thing. And you don't want to be awake for what I need to do."

Ben leaned over me, wielding the knife, and unfastened the button of my jeans expertly, one-handed. I snuck a bashful look at Cleo, but her eyes were glued to my lower extremities. He slid the knife between the denim and my skin. I worried for only a moment about its sharp steel, when he sliced past my zipper. My thighs burst free from the fabric like burnt cinnamon rolls, red and puffy with yellow bubbling blisters. My jeans had removed some of the skin, but at least they hadn't fused. I wished I had a belt to bite down on, whimpers had clawed their way between my teeth.

Ben positioned himself lower for leverage and dragged the knife past my thighs. He cut through cautiously, but only an inch or so below the knee, my skin began to stick. Ben peeled the denim away and my slimy lining went with it, sticky and elastic and transparent.

"What—what is …" He was pulling my skin off, piece by piece like a rubber sheet, but what he left behind was worse. My legs were radiating like an overcooked pizza, speckled in blacks and yellows, oranges and pinks. Where the jeans didn't cling, my skin was crusty and hard. Underneath the sticky outer layer looked like a discharging watermelon, pink throbbing muscle oozing yellow pus. Random sections would rock me with paralyzing pain, bucking my legs hard beneath Cleo's restrictive hands. I hadn't blinked since the de-gloving began.

Ben was speechless as he shucked away the last of my jeans and the skin of my ankles. His focus was all-consuming. Tears clung to my lashes, blurring my vision.

Ben cut into the black rubber of my moto boot and the sock beneath. Bits of cotton had melted into my feet so deeply that it tore from the sock rather than from my body. He snipped around the islands of fabric, his intent to get the boot off before anything else. At long last, he threw the mutated leather to the ground. I could see my toes past the dots of sock in my body. They were black nuggets. They looked frostbitten. But my toenails shone white and strong in the charred mess of my feet. I wiggled my toes, and they responded. Though I couldn't feel pain, I could move them. I watched them wave at me across the vast distance of damaged meat, and lost consciousness.

WHEN I CAME TO, I was gum. A chewed blob. I opened my eyes to the kitchen ceiling. I hesitantly lifted my head and surveyed my legs. The chunks of sock were gone, and from the knee down, light bounced off my skin's shiny sheen. They were covered in Cleo's salve. I wondered if I should bandage them. I didn't think they looked any better than before.

The others were seated at the kitchen table above me. Ben's eyes were already on me. He didn't look surprised to find me awake. Jessamae and Cleo were bent over the table. I couldn't see what held their notice so tightly. Bottles and jars stood at attention beside them. Every now and then, Jessamae would sprinkle their innards onto the tabletop.

"What's she doing?" I asked Ben. My voice at least sounded better.

His focus darted to my stomach before he answered. "She's trying to discover the name of the demon," he stated quietly. There was no humor in him, and it broke my heart. "Clearly, this demon deals in fear and fire. That cancels out a lot of possibilities: al ana, gorgon, kroni, things like that."

Nervous at Ben's furtive glances, I assessed my stomach. My shirt had been lifted to my ribs, and there was a scabbed line along my left side that I didn't recognize. I poked at it stupidly. It was harder than a scab—it had been superglued shut.

Ben cleared his throat. "It had already closed by the time I got to it, but it closed around a rock, from my driveway." I'd never seen him so pale. "I had to reopen it and pull it out."

I ran my fingers over the incision again. "How did you know how to do all of this, Benny?"

"I've taken my magic too far once or twice. I don't have super healing powers like you, so ..." I thought of a few of his tattoos, the ones that burst from his skin like mountain ranges, layers and layers of scar tissue. My aching skin pimpled in gooseflesh. Ben didn't appear embarrassed, and he never stopped appraising me.

My anxious eyes flitted to Jessamae. "How many types of demons are there?"

"Hundreds and hundreds," she stated, focused on the table.

"Pamela," I started, already winded. "She was dancing in the woods before I passed out." With strenuous effort, I forced my torso up onto my elbows. It didn't pain me as much as it had after the fire. But the burn in my back was alive and well.

"It was an *it*. Remember, it's not your granny anymore," Ben interjected above me.

"Does it even matter at this point? It has her face. It's red, but it's hers." I swept my blistered hand through my matted hair. It stank. Sections of it were singed and destroyed, hardening into brown balls.

"It matters," Jessamae asserted. "It matters very much." She dropped a clear liquid from an eyedropper onto the table where it sizzled like bacon. She sat back in her chair and a shiver jiggled my spine.

"It's a royal," Cleo gasped. Even Ben, who hadn't been paying attention to the other two, clasped both his hands behind his head in distress.

"What exactly does that mean?" I snapped, working my way slowly into a seated position. My ass seemed better now, there was less pain. I dreaded the next step, but I needed to see the tabletop, and I refused to ask for help after all they'd done for me today. I tilt my weight forward and touched my cooked toes to the tile.

Cleo held Amir close to her face, squeezing him. His eyes bulged. "Royals can practice magic."

I placed the bottoms of my feet down to the floor, one inch of skin at a time. "A demon that uses magic? Like witches?"

"In a way," she said through the mess of cat hair. "Their magic works against nature, ours is dependent upon it. Where we require balance, sacrifice, they require nothing."

I hoisted myself onto my feet and yelped. I'd forgotten about the break I heard at Ben's. A bone in my foot. I felt a wetness beneath my soles, pus beneath ruined skin. But I stood—for around five seconds. Then the throbbing took over and I listed backward. I caught myself on my hands, which were healing well, and lowered myself back down to my butt. Though I was obviously struggling, Ben never moved to catch me. God help him if he did.

"Will you bring me the scissors?" I asked him with whatever dignity I had left.

Ben, though standing by as I crashed, jumped up with enthusiasm and combed through the junk drawer. He held the blade, putting the handle in my palm.

I pulled the fried bunches of curls forward and started to cut. Hacking away, I felt a vicious pleasure watching my burnt ringlets fall to the tile.

"So they can do anything?" I asked the room from behind the scissors. "All-powerful? Really?" Ben watched me slash at my hair with a grave set to his mouth. I looked through its curtain, and everyone stopped to watch me.

Jessamae returned her eyes to her work. "No, not anything. Their powers are specific to them. Each royal holds individual abilities."

"Also like witches. They're sort of the witch antithesis," Cleo added.

I snuck a glance to the window from under my uneven levels of hair. There was nothing I could do about it, but I needed to know if Pamela was out there, observing, waiting until I was alone.

"How do we know everything it's capable of? Just wait and see? Keep a list?" I was yelling. I was scared. I took out a large curl with a satisfying snip. I wasn't sure if that one had even been damaged. Suddenly Ben was there, his hand over mine.

"I think you got it," he whispered, pulling my hair behind my shoulder. I elbowed him in the rib, my teeth bared in aggression. I resisted the urge to scream and rip my hair out by hand.

"Fine."

Cleo put her fingers to her temples. Amir took advantage of his moment of freedom and zipped out of the room. "We only need an advantage. That's what Jessamae is doing, Frankie. Asking for a name."

I'd heard there was power in a name. On television.

Running on stubbornness alone, I heaved myself—my hands on the seat, the scissors mashed beneath my palm—into one of the remaining two chairs around the kitchen table. I felt like bubble wrap, blisters bursting and wincing with every point of contact, but I succeeded. I adjusted my weight, held my feet in the air, and sat at the table. Complacent.

Jessamae was bent over her pile of colorful granules of various sizes. The pile smelled of resin—it smelled like Jessamae. She sprinkled minerals over the anthill as if spicing a stew.

It only took a pinch, something soft and brown, like cinnamon. Flames erupted in the middle of the table, and I cringed back like a kicked dog, holding my hands in front of my face. The salt pile was burning, and my skin keened terribly at the sight. The fire danced in strange shapes, leaving splotches of salt unscathed until they formed a single word.

"Paimon," I read aloud.

A loud shudder sounded from down the hall, like a giant zipper. Or a giant tambourine. It rattled so raucously, the wooden door bounced in its frame with the pressure. A chill worked its way over my new skin and around my neck. Because a folk band was not hiding out in our small bathroom. Something else was.

"You've got to be fucking kidding me," I whispered.

25

GABRIEL BROKE through the plywood door like a battering ram, splintering it to pieces and smashing a head-sized hole into the opposite wall.

"He's alive!?" Ben shouted over the destruction, backing away to the front door as the leaden body lurched towards us all.

Death clung to him. It was wispy and faint, but there. "No, he isn't." My feet couldn't hold my weight, not yet. I pushed myself away from the table, sliding my chair across the tile.

Gabriel, gaining some strength and balance, straightened. He did appear alive, almost as I'd seen him at the funeral home. The illusion was broken by the soaking wet clothing that clung to his thighs and gut. A flower petal stuck above his eyelid like a stye. And his expression was vacant as the moon. Dead. Utterly and unquestionably dead. But still he pitched forward on uncertain legs, a low groan spilling from his lips before some long-swallowed water dribbled down his chin.

"Mr. Perez? Gabriel?" Ben yelled over the sounds of the dead man. "Remember me, Ben Bowen?" At the name, Gabriel did seem to pause, a chord plucked somewhere in his sloshing mind.

I leapt at the possibility that his memory functioned, even existed. "I'm Francesca Hughes. You helped me, remember?" His head rotated from Ben to me gradually. He appeared to understand, though no emotion touched his face. He lost interest in Ben and took a step in my direction. He extended his soaked fingers out to me, as if to shake my hand.

"He remembers!" I thought of his hand clasping mine at each greeting, always the professional. I held it out to him from my chair, momentarily forgetting my burns, and he grabbed it instinctually. It was slippery and very cold.

He lifted our joined hands up and down in an unwieldy imitation of a handshake. I smiled at him, unsure of what he could see through those deserted eyes. Then his shaking gained velocity, jerking my arm around painfully. He pulled me closer to him.

I yanked and yanked. "Gabriel, you're hurting me!" The chair caught between two tiles and tilted forward, dumping me on my busted feet. Gabriel held most of my weight and I stayed vertical.

His stomach was touching mine now. The reek of decay spewed out of his open mouth. He made gurgling, grunting sounds, louder than before. My attention latched on my hand. He would crush it in his, when an unexpected force on my throat crashed into me like a wrecking ball. He was choking me! The lining of my throat, still so raw and charred from the fire, felt like it was exploding, flaking apart in his hands like ash. I couldn't breathe, I couldn't cough.

My hand constricted into a desperate fist as I pounded at the arm that held me. Something hard dug into the skin of my palm, and it took me two punches to see it. The scissors! I never dropped them after my haircut. I squeezed the handle frantically and I stabbed. The open blades punctured the side of Gabriel's neck, all the way to the handle. And it didn't affect him in the slightest. The handles simply protruded from his neck like a plastic tumor.

Ben clawed at Gabriel's fingers, trying to force his release, enough that Ben's bones stood out under his skin. I watched the knuckles in surreal detail, they were like great plates threatening to break through. The dead man didn't budge.

My vision began to fade. I was suffocating. Ben changed tactics, moving his hands to Gabriel's chest. He stood at my side, his arm against mine, then he took a deep breath.

Everything seemed to slow down and melt. Under Ben's

touch, Gabriel was hurled backwards, skidding across the burning salt pile, and slamming into the kitchen counter. I fell to my knees and gulped the barbed wire-like air. I couldn't get enough as it scraped along my insides. My knees radiated pain to such an extent, they felt nuclear.

Gabriel was blundering, but was upright fast. He wasn't angry or hurt, he didn't brush the clumps of salt from his clammy skin. He was fixated on me, a red flag before a bull. His arms spread, and he charged.

Cleo brought down a heavy wooden cutting board onto his head and he went down. A gash opened on the back of his skull, and his skin flapped languidly against the bone. The wound did not bleed. It was dark as mud, open and dry.

Cleo held the cutting board over her shoulder, prepared to swing again. Her arms didn't shake, and her eyes didn't waver. And when Gabriel lifted his substantial weight onto his loafers, she brought the board down hard. The crack of his skull could be heard around the block. His knees bent with the impact, but he did not fall. Instead, he ripped the cutting board from Cleo's hands, and slapped the board into the side of her face. The force of his strike carried her across the room and to the floor.

Keeping a hold on his new weapon, Gabriel turned once again to face me as I cowered on my knees. I backed into the living room, shredding my skin along the rough carpet. There was nothing I could do. I couldn't summon any energy and I couldn't slow him down. I watched his approach helplessly and waited for the blow that would push me out of consciousness. I prayed for it before he killed me.

Gabriel thrashed to my side. He raised the cutting board, and his arm fell like a dead fish to the carpet at my feet.

Ben filled the empty space where the arm once was, his enormous knife in his hand. Ballistic, Gabriel garbled out a roar, fluid shooting from his nostrils. He lunged ferociously at Ben and kicked him square in the chest. I heard an eerie snap as he went down. Broken ribs.

As he bent over Ben's wobbly form, Jessamae appeared. She hovered several inches off the ground, reaching Gabriel's height. Her hands made a type of crown around the back of his head, thumbs folding over one another at the ridge of his skull. Her expression contorted with outrage and his scalp began to sizzle, melting away like a spark through gunpowder. Relentless, Gabriel stayed solidly on his feet. Jessamae let out a seismic screech, furious at her failure. Fire spread around Gabriel's scalp, igniting his hair.

The burning was so recent and familiar, I covered my face. But Gabriel hadn't tired one bit. He beat at Jessamae's hands with his remaining fist, crushing her fingers.

"Nothing is working!" Jessamae shouted as she descended the ground. She cradled her fingers to her chest. The fire that had engulfed Gabriel's head smoked and shrank. He turned to face us in the living room. Before he could pursue me for a final time, Ben swept his long legs into Gabriel's knees, sending the dead man's nose smashing into the tile beneath him.

The smell of death overpowered the smoke. He was dead— the stench proved it. Jessamae's affinity had failed her because, "He's dead! You can't kill him if he's already dead!" But he had to be something. Somehow both and neither, floating in between.

I crawled over Cleo's unconscious form and pulled Jessamae down to me. I felt the electricity shoot between the two of us. My heart hammered against my ribs—it was hard to breathe around. I lifted myself to my knees, the lightning between us smothering the pain. Our affinities linked like a scorching chain—it was both unbearably hot and wonderfully thrilling. I held her hand in mine.

I pressed my free palm to Gabriel's temple on the floor, which was only bone and thick congealed jelly. Nothing happened. Jessamae's broken fingers still hung loosely at her side.

"Do it!" I commanded, and she clapped her injured hand to his temple.

The lightning under my skin tunneled into the brain between

our hands, and the power of it was staggering. A brief memory surfaced of touching a low voltage cattle gate when I was five, my body seizing, my jaw clamping.

Now, as Gabriel convulsed between us, emitting a haunting groan that seemed endless, it was as if that memory of the cattle gate, that shock, had transformed into a drug. A drug that I liked. Loved even.

His face rebounded with fleshy slaps repeatedly into the tile, dark fluid spattering with the contact. He shook and shook while he choked on the static. Fear returned to his eyes. Gabriel gave a final pitiful wail, and was still.

~

"HOLD STILL."

"I am!" I couldn't stop shivering. If the expression "shaking like a leaf," held true, I was shaking like a grove, an orchard, a forest. "Forgive me if I'm a little unnerved, Jessamae."

I was bent over Cleo. Her lips were parted, and her eyes were barely discernible through the slits of their lids. Ben held her head in his lap while Jessamae hovered in petulant agitation. Gabriel lay wet and smoking, his brain exposed, in the middle of the room like a rug in need of cleaning. My fault. All my fault.

I, again, lowered my shaking-leaf hands to Cleo's head. There was redness and swelling that would certainly bruise, but I could fix that. What I was afraid to touch was her mind, to mess with it. A concussion was a much more complicated injury than Ben's broken ribs—I'd felt two fractures inside his chest, and I'd mended those first—and was, therefore, a much more dangerous one. But the others demanded I try.

It was so easy with Ben, my hands beneath his shirt as he smiled for me. I didn't feel so incapable, even with Jessamae's shrewd eyes on my back. But the second I pulled away, the reality of our situation crashed down as heavy as the dead man in my kitchen. I didn't have time to process it, seeing as how Jessamae immediately ordered me to Cleo's side.

Ben stilled my fingers on her scalp. "Think happy thoughts, Frank."

I squinted at him, almost offended. What would we do about Gabriel, his family? He was past fixing now.

"For Cleo?" Ben asked, sensing my grief and my self-hatred.

At his reminder, I stared sadly at Cleo's face. Happy thoughts. A memory pushed tentatively at me, like a dog nose to the palm. It was a feeling. The feeling of Cleo's fingers pulling softly through my hair. Though Ben had left and I was falling apart, her touch helped me and I slept beneath it. That was a nice feeling.

Cleo's head quavered side to side, but I held on firmly. I could almost feel her nimble fingers in my hair.

Her skin warmed beneath mine, as if she had a fever. Her eyes opened. Her head shook vehemently now, but I wouldn't let go. It wasn't finished. While I rode the wave of a memory, the bump on her head improved—the swelling shrank. Watching the transformation miraculously eased some of my ache.

Cleo looked lost, then frightened, then angry. She tried to sit up and Ben held her down. "Easy slugger. He got you in the second round."

"What happened? Where is he?" she asked. Her eyes zagged below her low lids until they caught sight of him. The body sizzled, though it lay in its own puddle of tub water. The blood-less arm lay like an art exhibit in the middle of the living room. Her shoulders eased, one answer down. "What happened?"

"It was the name," Jessamae explained as I moved to hold her broken fingers—the pinky and ring—between my palms. There were multiple cracks in these bones. She flinched at the contact, then closed her eyes while I worked. "It was booby-trapped."

I focused on the breaks. The electricity between us had become a force we could conjure, like the air or the earth, and it didn't overcome me now as I held her hand. I wasn't afraid. Mending bones was as natural as breathing. I thought of Ben, of Cleo. I looked up to Jessamae's peaceful expression, and I felt the bones shift beneath her hot skin.

"How did you find the name?" I asked, curious about her salt ritual.

"I used a sample of the funeral director's skin," she informed me without emotion. I balked, sickened. Though that seemed senseless, considering the state of Gabriel now. "The demon either knew we would take the body, or it was meant to dig its way out. He was obviously after Frankie. It would have hunted her, searched the town until it found her."

"Pai—" Ben's freckled hand clamped down over my mouth.

"It was probably just the first time, but let's not take our chances, yeah?"

I nodded beneath his fingers. "But now that we have a name, we can learn how to stop it?" I asked Ben, then looked at Jessamae.

She evaluated the body, her mind churning. "At least, it will tell us what it's capable of. At most, it will give us a weapon to use against it."

Cleo climbed to her feet cautiously, her hand on her head though the wound was gone. "I'll start researching the name, see what sort of information I can find. But first ..." She walked down the hall, through the gaping hole that was the destroyed bathroom door. We heard the shower running straight away.

I needed a plan for Gabriel. The body was completely obliterated—not exactly the image of a heart attack or a suicide. Nevertheless, I didn't think I could stomach leaving his family to wonder for the rest of their lives with no closure.

I stood and opened the fridge. I took out a beer. On second thought, I pulled out another.

I hadn't given myself the opportunity to delve into the minutia, but after healing all of them—Ben, Cleo, and Jessamae—of their extensive wounds, my own healing process had accelerated exponentially. It hurt to stand, but I could do it. As Jessamae drank vitality and life, I drank pain and death. My lip curled in loathing as I plopped down heavily onto the water-logged carpet. I smacked the crown of my head against the wall behind me, and having assumed the position, began to chug. The corpse smoked on, but the Gold Star made me feel closer to myself than I had in days. A shower wouldn't do that for me.

Ben slid down the wall beside me and swiped my other beer. I snorted at him but figured he probably deserved it after saving my life. "Near-death experiences don't make this shit any better," he said after a swallow. I held my finger up, warning him against anything further.

"The demon can reanimate again or—" Jessamae started before I held up the same finger to her.

She watched the two of us gulp, short-tempered. "Is that the only thing you have?"

I raised an eyebrow and pursed my lips. "What else could you ever need?"

She grimaced and pivoted to the cupboards, foraging through the storage until she uncovered a bottle of hard alcohol. Cleo wasn't a beer person either. Jessamae poured herself a few fingers of bourbon, shot it back, and immediately poured herself another.

She sat stiffly against the other wall, sipping the heavy brown liquid and watching steam creep from the bathroom like a euca-lyptus-scented ghost. Having no door and no shower curtain—if that was the foreboding sound we'd heard before Gabriel's rise —Cleo was virtually showering across the room.

I finished my beer, burped with my mouth closed, and flat-tened the can. I delicately laid back onto my hands and stared at the fissures in the popcorn ceiling. With a sigh for the man I'd destroyed, I surmised, "Fire the only option for him now?"

Ben slapped the top of my thigh, and I barely winced. "Or an explosion."

My closet supply of C-4 was running a bit low for that. It

appeared that Gabriel was doomed to fall to the element that just would not quit. "We'll have to get rid of the car, too," I rationalized. There was no point in crying over spilled milk, even if the spilled milk was a husband and father who treated you like you were worth a certain kindness. "Maybe we could manage a small explosion."

Jessamae continued to drink without speaking, watching the tendrils of steam unfold. She was lost in that vast, old mind of hers, searching for answers. She needed that drink. And I needed another. I made a second roundtrip to the fridge for two beers, dropping one in Ben's lap.

Cleo hustled from the bathroom to her room cleanly, and very nakedly. I choked and averted my eyes, working to hide my coughing fit.

Ben chortled beside me. "Easy." He looked like he wanted to pat me on the back then thought better of it. "You'll get used to the sight. Believe me." I doubted that. He appeared to understand my thoughts and smiled at me. "Ready for a shower?"

I assessed myself—I was a pile of pink and red, sensitive shit. Practically inside out, even with the regeneration I'd accomplished. My toes were still black, but the dark stiff shell was cracking, the red gleaming underneath like magma. I sat in my underwear and burned grocery store polo, lacking the energy to feel weird. My hair was a sea-witch disaster and my throat felt bruised. I couldn't see my backside, but I thought that was best. "Am I that bad?"

"Yes," he said, unabashed. He lifted one of the ugly cut clumps of my hair. "A bath then?"

"A cold one?"

"You got it, Princess," he agreed, standing his can on the wet carpet. "I'm mixing Cleo's salve into your water," he said before grabbing the bowl of medicine—it had been knocked to the ground, but the thick goo was unshakable. Ben took in the lingering steam from the hallway. "Good thing you won't need hot water." I nodded and followed him down the hallway.

I found a fluffy towel in the linen closet, a little embarrassed at Cleo's doing all the grungy laundry, and I redundantly swung open the shattered remains of the bathroom door. Ben and I navigated the small space carefully—water covered the floor, along with the shower curtain, the shower rod, wooden shards, and herbs. My chest rubbed against his ribs as he passed. His warmth made my mouth pop open. But he let himself out, shutting the strip of wood behind him.

I crossed my arms carefully over my middle, my hands on the burnt edges of my polo. I tugged it up and over my chest.

"Let me know if you need some help in there!"

I brought the fabric back down and glowered through the door's opening. Ben flashed me a wink and lifted his beer to his lips. I raised my middle finger and turned back to the tub.

I was afraid of the water. I was afraid of anything touching me. I dipped my hand in and felt renewed relief. The water held a slight green tint from the salve.

I lowered myself in on trembling arms clamped on the walls of the tub. The shock of the temperature and of the contact was brief, then I exhaled for what felt like the first time. Nirvana. I balanced on my butt, floating the rest of me in the wonderful water, working to forget the tub's last inhabitant.

I sat for so long, from time to time needing to rest my tender back against the wall, that the water warmed to match my temperature. Confident in the skin on my hands and face, I spread my body wash across my cheeks gently. The homey smell of lemon stung my eyes. Denying tears, I scrubbed it viciously across my cheeks, shedding flakes of the smoked skin from my fingers.

I drained the water and spun myself around in the tub like a break-dancer. I dipped my head under the tap, my ab muscles screaming, and shampooed my hair under the faucet's cool stream. I stepped out shivering, but refreshed.

Wearing a pair of cotton pajama shorts and Ben's shirt he left on the floor yesterday—the shirt promoted Doug's Famous Hot

Hot Hot Sauce—I threw every shred of clothing I could find into the washer.

Everyone was in Cleo's room, I heard them talking while I poured twice the recommended soap level into the machine. I grabbed another beer before I joined them.

"There are different variations on the name, but I've found two that look good for us."

"Most of it, but not all of it."

"Of course, they couldn't get everything right, but you have to admit, this one in particular looks promising."

When I stepped through the door, Ben skipped past me to the shower. I'd been in there so long, there had to be hot water by now. Jessamae stood behind Cleo who was typing speedily into a sleek and fancy computer. Her carpet was gone, though the bed hadn't moved. The hardwood needed work, but it was a great improvement, nonetheless. "What looks promising?"

Cleo glanced at me before she nodded to a verbose PDF. "First," she pointed a finger at me, "we desperately need an internet upgrade. Your connection is pathetic."

I lowered my brows. I could barely afford the bill as it was. "What looks promising, Cleo?"

She turned back to her screen. "This was published by a professor of theology and the occult. The name is a little different, as you can see." She was obviously unwilling to speak the name, but this article depicted a demon called "Paimona."

"Powers include apparition, secret knowledge, creation of visionary hallucinations, and reanimation. It can reanimate dead bodies for long periods of time. It doesn't mention arson or fly consumption, but it's not bad."

I knew the flies were specific to Pamela, not Paimon, but that hardly seemed relevant. "We need to take care of Gabriel," I dictated. The information they were digging up was essential, and that was all well and good, but I couldn't pull my attention from the man. "Need to make it look like an accident. Today."

Jessamae blinked at my demand. "Because he and his car

have been missing for over twenty-four hours, I think the mountain is best."

"Then he'll still just be missing."

"We'll call in the smoke." Her colorless eyes were sympathetic. For me, not for Gabriel. "His family will know by today's end." It was the best I could hope for.

"The Honda is still at Ben's place," Cleo reminded.

"Don't drive that car!" Ben called from the bathroom. I didn't even hear the water shut off. He leaned into the room, the same fluffy towel I'd used wrapped around his waist. "You don't know what the … *thing* could have done to it. Especially since it used to be Pamela's."

"Can we take your—"

"Transmission is a bit testy. Give me five minutes."

26

THAT'S how our little troop ended up together, on the side of a mountain, with the cadaver of a funeral director locked in his own trunk. Ben and I had taken Ben's car, while Jessamae and Cleo drove Gabriel in his hatchback—the body bothered the two of them very little. We took different paths at different times to get here so the cars wouldn't be seen together. Nearly three hours had passed since we were discussing this at home.

Jessamae and Cleo arrived first. They were sitting against the trunks of a couple aspens that shone yellow in the headlights when we pulled up.

"Let's move him to the driver's seat," Ben insisted before our car doors even thudded shut.

It would look like a murder, which was the simplest setup on account of the fact that it *was* a murder. Gabriel was already dead when we found him—there was nothing we could do to change that. They might find water in his lungs, but either way, his family would be completely blindsided, and we would not be tied to it. That was the plan.

Jessamae's strong legs lifted her swiftly from the ground with no help from her arms. "We already moved him."

Cleo stood up and dusted herself off. I stared at the two long enough to insult them. Strong, yes. But strong enough to move the immense limp weight of Gabriel? "How?" I asked.

Jessamae looked from Cleo to me pragmatically. "It's a simple magic. Accepting strength from the earth." I'd have to write that one down. My soft arms couldn't lift a fingerprint.

Ben retrieved the gas can that we'd taken from my garage. It was meant for our lawnmower, but I hadn't mowed the lawn all year—the grass was also dead—and the can was full. He was somber. All evening his arms swung instinctively upwards before he let them fall to his lap. His head needed a break—he'd nearly worn it down to the bone this week.

Repressing the few memories I had of Gabriel was difficult, but repression was my go-to, and I was good at it. It would get easier.

"Okay. Shall we?" He turned to Gabriel's car.

"Wait! Just a second!" I shouted. He still deserved an explanation. I jogged like a goon in Ben's flip-flops over the dirt and rocks to the passenger side of the hatchback and shut myself in with the body. My breathing was so loud inside, when present company didn't breathe at all. The ugly perfume of him was loud too, but it didn't turn my stomach. All life had left him, and that was natural.

Gabriel did not get a peaceful exit from his life. His eyes were open and restless in death—he had been so scared. Of course, his body had been totally decimated, but it was the fear he harbored that twisted my insides.

"Hey, Mr. Perez." I frowned at my idiocy. Though, admittedly, I thought there was a chance he would answer. He'd surprised me before.

I searched his face for something I'd never find, something like forgiveness. His mouth was open in a childlike pout. I bet he had grandchildren.

"I never wanted this for you. I never wanted this for anyone, I guess, but you more than most." Gabriel had no words of comfort for me, and as unfair as it was, I wanted that from him. Salt clung to his forearm that rested so near mine, as if he were crystallizing. His left arm lay across his lap, like it was a jacket, or a handbag.

"I wish I could take it back. Or that I could help your family, maybe." One of my eyes prickled painfully. "I don't know if you were a good man. But you were nice. And patient." I gave his face one more guilt-ridden glance, wishing frivolously that I were a braver person. A person who would have saved him when she had the chance. "Thank you." My right eye overflowed and striped my face. "I'm sorry. Gabriel."

As I touched the door handle, static blasted angrily from the car radio. The sound transitioned into a ghostly song that struck a memory: "Dream a Little Dream of Me." It wasn't the original, it was the Doris Day adaptation. My mother had loved this song. I moved my hand back to the handle, giving it a frenzied yank, but the door wouldn't budge. The music faded in and out, as if finding its station.

"Such pretty words for a stranger. I'm not surprised, two fat peas in a big fat pod."

I jerked the car handle with all the strength I had, nearly cracking the plastic.

"Too bad your grandma didn't get such a pretty goodbye. What did she get? Survived by her granddaughter, Francescally."

"Get me out! Please! Get me out!" I wailed, crashing my shoulder painfully into the door. I seized the handle and this time snapped it clean from the door with a clack.

"You're alllllll alone, blue as can be," she croaked. "Is the baby scared of her sweet granny?"

A single red finger poked out of the tape deck, squirming for purchase. The fingernail was thick and black. "Baby's got no one left. Daddy never wanted her."

Ben appeared at the window, panic-stricken. He was shouting something, but my ears were numb to him. Tears for Gabriel still hung in my eyes, blinding me. I rammed my body uselessly into the door.

"She's wet for the witch who killed grandma."

Ben threw his weight into and away from my door, his grip on the handle. Then he began to slam against the window. His collision didn't make a sound. The car rocked with him. I lifted my feet and began kicking at the windshield. The force was torment on my soles and healing bones. The glass held.

An entire red hand now protruded from the tape deck, scraping and pulling at the edges. "And what happened to baby's mommy?"

I leaned back, and with all my power, stomped on the searching fingers. They crunched like beetles under my flip-flops.

As I pulled my pink legs in for another hit, the windows exploded inward, showering me in glass powder and rocking the car like a hurricane.

"SHE DROVE INTO A SNOWBANK RATHER THAN SEE BABY ANYMORE! KILLED HERSELF! KILLED HERSELF! KILLED HERSELF!"

The broken beetle-shell fingers slithered back into the machine, receding like snakes into grass. "KILLED HERSELF! KILLED HERSELF!" On and on, the screaming.

Ben grabbed me under my arm and pulled. I grasped the jagged edge of the shattered window and heaved with him. My skin tugged against the sharp remains, tearing my clothes and my burns until my feet dragged across the dirt.

"BURN IT!" I cried over the endless wailing of the radio, backing over the rough terrain until I crashed to my back, then crawling still backwards away from the sound. "BURN IT NOW!"

Ben gripped one of my arms, though I was leading him now, and followed me, rambling unheard words.

The heat pushed against my back, making me tingle with residual fear. I watched it over my shoulder, unsure of which threat I ran from anymore. The broken door handle was still gripped in my fist.

Jessamae and Cleo circled the hatchback, Cleo wielding the gas can and Jessamae igniting the fuel in her wake using Ben's copper lighter. Cleo splashed the potent liquid through the crushed window, covering Gabriel in the fuel. Jessamae promptly reached the lighter into the opening.

The upholstery blazed to the car's roof in seconds. The flames climbed up Gabriel's stomach and chest. It wasn't long before the fire found the paperwork Gabriel had kept in the backseat. He was a man who took work home with him.

"KILLED HERSELF! KILLED HERSELF!"

Jessamae stood before the hood, her eyes reflecting the orange glow of the flames like taillights. Her vengeful expression belonged on the face of the demon I feared. Ben pulled me in tight to his chest, protecting my head from what he saw coming.

Cleo lifted the hood of the car and scattered the last of the gasoline below it. She bolted for the tree line as Jessamae approached the inferno. She lifted her hands above her head before she brought them down in a firestorm. Fire burst from her like an imploding star, eating her with heat and blinding colors. She channeled it without burning—she was both magnificent and terrifying. I couldn't look away even as my eyes burned.

Almost instantaneously, the engine blew in a bright ball of fire, lifting the car like a bucking stallion. The screaming cut off abruptly, and not an echo remained.

Warm bits fell from the sky like the heavy rain of a dream. I heard them everywhere, showering the four of us as thick black smoke billowed into the sky. I watched the fire swallow the machine from under Ben's arm, a Rottweiler full of kisses and teeth. It devoured the car and the man inside, touching the sky in tall, graceful swirls. But dogs could turn, and I still didn't trust the element.

Through the flames, I caught glimpses of Gabriel Perez driving his hatchback over the mountainside. His head tilted too far back on his spine, and his single hand limp on the seat, leaving the wheel untouched and lonely. His face began to crack in the heat. Layers of him furling back like the thin skin of an onion, like a blood-red flower in bloom. Until I saw teeth.

Jessamae stayed near the flames. She watched them with

affectionate glass eyes until the smoke clouds were too thick above the tree line. "We need to move," she said without much urgency. Her eyes were bright and her cheeks flushed. She was still riding the wave of ecstasy with which the fire surrounded her. I envied the rush that visually flowed through her. I felt sick and hurt and sad. And ashamed. Shame buried me.

Of course, Ben was there, lifting me, guiding me. I hated that he needed to. My lip quivered and I hated that, too. I hated so much about me.

He towed me to the passenger seat like the fragile thing I was. Cleo was already in the back, piling her heavy hair onto her crown. Jessamae entered the car stoically and focused on her phone.

In half an hour, she would call the police. Optimally, someone else would report the smoke by then. She was not publicly connected to me or Ben or Gabriel. If they asked her for her iden-tifying information, she'd give the address of her ally in Nevada, claiming she had been hitchhiking across the country, camping on public lands. Her look fit the bill—her camping equipment was still stashed somewhere in these very woods. She would claim to have been on a hike when she saw the smoke.

But just minutes after our departure, Ben uttered the words, "Don't call." And that was the end of any conversation.

The quiet hurt. Because I knew the demon's words ricocheted inside our skulls like a song. But unlike the other three, the song became a soundtrack to my own macabre movies. Movies that starred my mother. In my mind, I made her drive onto the ice wearing different expressions over and over: grief-stricken, resolved, laughing like a demon. How exactly did she hold her mouth? Were her eyes open, were they full?

When she killed herself.

No one spoke. The screams carried on. And, again, I sobbed.

I SHUFFLED through the living room with my eyes on the floor. I felt my baby cheeks heat under their stares, knowing they were remembering the melting man. Remembering those things about my mom. I left the bedroom door open because I didn't want them to think I needed to be alone, though I did. I plummeted through the sheets on my stomach. I grunted in pain when my legs touched the fabric, and stuck them out of the blankets like bait. I wished I still had some Cheezy Poofs. I didn't feel hungry, but I didn't care.

No one came in after me, thank god. I prayed for sleep, which refused to come. That seemed fair. I just lay there unmoving, my favorite pastime only a week or so ago. The earthy scent of Ben on my sheets ruined things for me. Made it comfortable.

It was very late, at least I assumed it was late by the numbness in my arms, when Ben shut the bedroom door behind him. I didn't look at him, but his gait was louder than Jessamae's. I considered feigning sleep, but that had never worked with him in the past. Might as well get this over with. I pulled myself up onto my elbows and creaked around to face him.

I couldn't do it. His face was so full of tenderness and compassion, my words gripped the lining of my throat. I couldn't do it, not if he was going to make it so easy on me.

"Will you give me a tattoo?"

Ben was nonplussed, but only for a moment. He didn't smile like I wanted him to. "Butterfly on the small of your back?"

"Anything," I answered too quickly. "I don't care."

He nodded. "I just need to run to my car." He left in a hurry.

He nudged the door open again holding a needle, a razor, and a little plastic puck full of black ink. He loped into the bathroom and returned with a brown bottle of hydrogen peroxide. Sitting on the corner of the bed, he set the razor and the ink on the nightstand before pouring a healthy splash of the bottle onto the needle. "It's going to sting." Good.

The needle was thick. He surprised me when he dragged the point across the skin—above my right thumb, below my wrist—

rather than poking me. My hands, particularly the backs of them, were in good shape. The skin firm and real. Beneath the v of my thumb and index finger, he drew a simple leaf, rounded at the base and pointed at the tip, strewn with dainty veins. He traced the lines two or three times until they turned red. It didn't sting as much as I wanted.

He switched from needle to blade. Wet with hydrogen peroxide, the edge was dull enough to stick in like a rake through rough soil. I was bleeding a lot, enough to obscure the image in a red puddle. Ben pulled off his shirt to soak up the torrents.

"Hold," he instructed, and I held the soft cotton to my hand —it smelled like fire—while he opened the small well of ink. "Okay," I held the shirt away at his word. The blood had already stopped. He dipped the point of the needle into the ink and returned to his work. It hurt graciously now.

Ben never checked my expression, and I appreciated that. He focused only on my hand. From time to time he had to reopen the wound. He swiveled the blackened point through the cavern below my thumb relentlessly. It was really burning now. Every few runs around the leaf, he would dip the needle into the ink and start again, periodically dabbing at my hand with his stained shirt as blood continued to ebb and flow.

The pain had faded by the time Ben was satisfied. He tilted my wrist this way and that, observing the symmetry, which to me, was obvious. The lines were clean and thick. He leaned in and touched his lips lightly to his work, leaving a delicate stamp of black and red across his mouth.

I forced a smile and held my hand up in admiration.

"She loved you, Frank. You know that."

Not enough. "Yeah. Yeah, I know that." I watched the leaf on my hand, waiting for leaching blood that never came.

He didn't demand my attention. I was worried if I looked at his face I'd start crying again. I could feel it building inside my head like a storm. I counted the sunspots across my knuckles in the lamplight.

"Did you know about her?"

I sucked in a lot of air, preparing for a long-winded defense, but "I suspected," was all I could say.

"Why didn't you say anything?"

"I didn't have to tell you that," I growled in response.

I felt Ben shake his head. The mattress shivered. "That's true."

I wrapped my arms around my knees, ignoring the pain of my shins. I hoped that Ben wouldn't touch me. "The cops said it was an accident, ice on the road. So, there was no point in talking about anything else."

Ben didn't respond to that. His stare was a heavy thing on the side of my face. I rubbed my chin over my knee.

"She was—would be sort of—up and down. She would be happy and dancing and carrying me along outside and taking my picture," I whispered. The words were too light, they floated in the air between us. "And then, when I didn't like any of that, when I complained, I think it made her sad a lot of the time. When I moved, I told her it was because I hated it here. That all of her effort made it worse." A tear dripped down to my nose, but I wouldn't give in to them. Not again. "She was just … in her room a lot. Stopped cooking. Stopped doing a lot of things. She was acting like me."

I pushed the bone of my chin harder into the bone of my knee, and my jaw was beginning to ache. I could see too easily in the darkness now. "Honestly, it didn't bother me. I was happy with it, I think. She was finally leaving me alone." Ben remained motionless on the bed, I wanted him to look at something else. Wouldn't that be the polite thing to do?

"She called me. Before the crash. I was working. It was inventory, so we had to stay late—it only happened once every few months. I didn't answer and she left a voicemail. It wasn't like a final goodbye, nothing like that. She said she … just wanted to hear from me. Said maybe we could go to a movie or something that weekend." I had never said any of this with my mouth, it was hard to describe exactly what was scary about it. "I don't like movie theaters. We hadn't gone to one together since I was a little kid."

"Do you still have it? The voicemail?"

I shook my head, grating my face along my knee. "I listened to it twice. I deleted it." My eyes stung because I wasn't blinking. I didn't want to shut my eyes. "She never mentioned driving anywhere, never said she was leaving. She called at 10:52." Confusion shaped my features as I relived the details of it. *Wrong*. "She didn't say, 'It's your mom.'"

Ben swallowed and the sound of it boomed throughout the room. "What?"

"Every time she's called me, ever, she always started with, 'Hey, Frankie. It's your mom'," the inflections and tone matched hers perfectly. "She didn't say it."

"Maybe she just wanted to talk to you."

"I think you're right." Which is exactly why I was right, too.

"Did something happen? Something that would lead her to …"

He didn't finish his sentence and I shrugged halfheartedly. I wouldn't have noticed if something did. I spent so much of my life purposefully ignoring my mom, almost angry at her for her differences. Her volume, her lack of shame. It was a habit I clearly didn't break in my twenties. Something could have happened, and I would have never asked.

I waited for the debate, for Ben to say we couldn't be certain she'd done it. That it probably was an accident. That she wouldn't want to leave me. I didn't hear any of that. He stretched his long body out beside me and then propped himself on an elbow. "Pajamas?"

I paused, then shook my head again. My clothes were uncomfortable and I chased that discomfort. I knew I was punishing myself for something, but that didn't stop me.

Ben's fingers reached for my side. I could feel energy coming off them. It tickled my stomach. He put his head into the crook of his elbow and looked at me with shiny eyes. "I'm not sure what the demon wants. It hasn't killed you. But it's hurting you. It won't stop." His fingers twitched. "We can't keep waiting."

"What do you mean?"

"Set a trap, disable it, banish it. Whatever. But we summon it. We can't let it have the upper hand again."

"Okay." But we both heard the indifference in my voice. I knew we would never get the upper hand. It would use every person I connected with, had ever cared about, against me until I was totally alone. Just as I had always wanted.

27

UNLIKE WHEN I'D lain alone, with Ben in my bed, I practically leapt into sleep. The shift in consciousness was jarring and I didn't recognize my dream for what it was.

I dreamt of myself. I didn't look as ruined. I was mostly whole, but I was afraid, terrified even. The body that held my eyes, that I now watched myself through, danced. I jerked my arms and legs up as if on strings, twirling fast. The other Frankie fell to the ground and scurried away from me. I reached for her trembling hands, which were pulled up to protect her face. *Don't be afraid*, I thought. When I heard the insane cackle swell from my lips, I woke.

Once my blood slowed, I was disgruntled to discover how comfortable I was. Ben was absent from the sheets.

I lifted the blankets to inspect my damage. I nearly gagged at the sight. Under the covers, my bed was coated in flakes of skin that looked like rock salt and gravel. Pieces of black chips were scattered around my now pink toes. Like my shins, they were an ugly spackling of yellow and vibrant pink, like untidy Easter eggs. They were much better than yesterday. I smashed my boobs down so I could see my belly. The incision had faded to a shiny line, only a few chunks of glue remaining.

The sight of my hand distracted me. The black lines of the leaf were so stark against my freckled skin. The tattoo had nearly healed, the top layer peeling lightly away, thin as black feathered silk.

Whether due to my injuries or maybe my laziness, I was the last one up. It was finally Saturday. I figured someone would have overslept, other than me. After I moved my laundry from the washer to the dryer, I found everyone in the kitchen. Ben and Cleo were seated at the table with steaming mugs of coffee, and Jessamae stood at the counter fixing her own. They had clearly made multiple pots by now; this one was nearly full. When I walked up behind Jessamae, she smelled like Cleo's bath scrub and my own rosemary shampoo. She'd showered here and she smelled fantastic.

Her coffee was repulsively light, so much cream and sugar. She must have loved the bottled stuff we'd had yesterday.

I took a mug from the cupboard and felt a bud of sadness over my favorite tiger mug that I'd never use again. Everything in Ben's kitchen had been thrown out. This mug was offensively blue and bland.

As I went through my coffee ritual, I sensed Jessamae's eyes on me like laser beams. You'd think I was painting a masterpiece or performing open-heart surgery for the intensity she showed in her observation. Once I'd achieved the perfect coloring, brown sugar, drank deeply. A small smile lit Jessamae's face as I finished.

"Today's the day," Ben interrupted my small moment of peace. "We're going to need some supplies. Summoning a royal takes a list." He was in one of the t-shirts I'd stolen from him after high school, a crew neck that read "Hold Your Horses!" over a colorful depiction of a girl petting a pretty pony.

"Supplies?" I groaned.

Jessamae said, "A being of sky, earth, and sea."

"Thank you, Raiden." Ben translated, "A bird, a mammal or reptile, and a fish."

Cleo shook her head over her mug, tired of their bickering. This was certainly not the first sign of tension between them.

"I've been off and on with the police and insurance all morning. They're going to want to talk to you today, Frank." Ben's stare was like a reprimand.

Lying shouldn't be too difficult on that front—the fire had

started in the kitchen. In a panic, I tried to put it out myself and had gotten hurt. The only thing I'd really have to lie about was the extent of the burns. Minor redness, healing well. I could even send them pictures at this point. I took another gulp of coffee.

"The remodel is going to take time. A lot, to be honest." Ben spoke impassively. "Do you mind if I crash here for a while?"

My cheeks bulged with the burning liquid as my throat suddenly closed. My mouth puckered tighter than a librarian's asshole. I felt the stares of the others hone in on me. I swallowed hard, it was like forcing down a hot rock, and nodded violently. "Of course, Benny." I aimed for the same casual tone he used. "As long as you need." I quelled the giddy fluttering that threatened to rise from my stomach like puke.

He smiled, happy. "There's bagels in the fridge if you want to toast one."

Cleo returned her attention to nothing in particular—gratefully off me—as I pulled a cinnamon raisin from the refrigerator and popped it into the crumb-crusted toaster. "I can get the animals today. It will only take an hour or two," she offered over her mug.

Jessamae watched me conspicuously. The weight of her dissatisfaction hung on my shoulders like buckets of water. Ben's question did this and I did not have the energy to stretch stupidly between the two of them today. "I'll go with you."

Cleo's head swiveled to me in surprise. "Will you?"

"Yeah, I mean, three live animals. Kind of a handful." Her arched eyebrows stayed near her hairline as she clearly summed me up. "I'll go with you," I stated again.

"Okay. Finish your breakfast and take a shower, please." I glared at the toaster. I was living with a bunch of clucking mother-hens.

THE SUPPLY SHOPPING was much easier than expected: no hiking, no fishing, but literal shopping. Cleo had to stop at a Payless along the nearest strip mall first, my boots now scraps in their dumpster—they'd smelled too bad to keep in my own trash can. I gave her my credit card and asked for the cheapest pair of sneakers they had, to which her mouth turned down in indignation.

Once my tender feet were socked and shoed, we walked into the wonderfully air-conditioned warehouse of a PetSmart thirty minutes out of town. I picked out an especially hefty Comet Goldfish. It only cost a quarter, which was a tad nauseating as I held the sad little life in a Ziploc. The bird was more expensive but still the cheapest in the store, an Andrew Jackson for a zebra finch. I was more comfortable giving the bill for the pretty bird with the vibrant orange blush. No life should cost a quarter.

I strolled the quiet aisles full of lizards and guinea pigs, checking price tags. I stopped beside the enormous snake terrariums in disgusted fascination. Cleo continued to survey displayed prices for the most inexpensive land species. She turned the corner toward the turtles.

I stared transfixed at one of the coils, alone in the glass box. It appeared to be young, maybe a baby, and was coated in the strangest assortment of colored scales I'd ever seen. It was a striking bright white, which covered most its length, but was patched in unanticipated oranges, blacks, and browns. Its face was … almost cute. Its nose was wide, its head more of an hourglass than a triangle, and its eyes were big black orbs with white spots of light, animated eyes. It had an intelligent air and its stare held mine in a way that made me want to pet the icky skin.

The sign told me it was a female junior piebald ball python. It was over a hundred dollars. A lot over. A batshit amount over. For a snake—a snake whose life would only last the day. I squeezed my hand into the pocket of my shorts for the cash Ben gave me. Two sweaty twenties.

"Mice are a good price," Cleo said, walking toward me.

Without realizing it, I had my hands pressed to the glass of this terrarium, my cash crushed under my palm like I was desperate for a reptilian striptease. The snake slithered closer to the barrier, gazing curiously at my fingerprint smudges.

"This is the one," I blurted. "I can feel it, we need this one." I pointed to the python waiting patiently in its cage.

Cleo tapped her foot to the laminate. "I didn't realize you were a snake lover."

"I hate snakes."

Her eyes narrowed and flicked to the price tag. "We only have forty dollars, Frankie. We don't need to spend the money just to kill it. Move on." She strutted past me toward a very bored teen employee that appeared to be counting hamsters. She abruptly turned around, "When you have these gut feelings, are they generally valid?"

"It's a coin flip, I think."

She pursed her lips. "A mouse it is then," and continued toward the blue smock.

CLEO WAS bemused when I gave the cashier the two twenties while repeatedly whipping my head back toward the snakes. I couldn't explain the compulsion, so I didn't try.

We walked prudently to Ben's car, encumbered with animals. Cleo held the bagged fish and the boxed bird, as well as smelly fish flakes and some birdseed. I held a small box full of holes for the two mice I bought—they seemed so breakable, I thought there was a chance one might keel over at a strong breeze—as well as pellets for them. The cashier looked perturbed by our purchasing food and no cages or bowls, but I decided that if they were going to die, they deserved a decent final meal.

I slid with care into the passenger seat—I suck at driving stick—adjusting the mice in my lap. Cleo set the bird at my feet and plopped the fish into the center console. I felt the weight of the mice shift steadily throughout the confines of their cardboard, and my shoulders tensed with apprehension.

The bird chirped erratically, flapping against its prison. "Quiet, please!" she ordered, and so it was. The silence of the box was chilling. Cleo nodded at the mute fish and zoomed onto the main road.

"There's a great coffee place around here. My treat," she trilled as she swerved dangerously into a hidden drive-thru between two ugly apartment buildings. I gripped the mice box roughly in my hands, willing it to steady during the crazed turn. The rodents hurried from corner to corner. I scowled at Cleo. "Sorry," she shrugged and turned to the dingy black speaker. "Could I please get a large iced mocha with whipped cream and a triple iced Americano? Thank you." She pulled forward without a response.

"I don't like mochas."

"You'll like this one."

A pale girl with vivid red hair and nails like a cat stood inside the window. She ogled blatantly at Cleo as she popped open the glove compartment, pulling out two metal tumblers. "Would you use these, please? Thank you." She held the two cups out the window for many moments too long while the girl took her fill.

"Thank you!" I yelled, shocking the girl out of her stupor. She visually shook herself and took the cups from Cleo, brushing her fingers as she did so. Cleo smiled radiantly until the girl disappeared into the darkness of the building, then she let out an irritated *pfft*.

She pulled into a faded parking spot behind a towering brick wall after taking our drinks and doting out an overly generous tip to the girl. The mocha was wonderful and cooled my insides all the way down. I poked at the whipped cream with several fingers and licked them clean.

"Cleo, what do you do? For work, I mean." I'd yet to see her leave for any sort of shift, yet she clearly had no problem with money. She'd virtually furnished our house on her own.

"I teach adult language courses. Mostly online." She sipped her dark beverage from behind expensive yet simple sunglasses.

My eyes widened. "What language?"

She licked the coffee from her full lips. "French, Spanish, Italian ..."

Of course. I repressed an eye roll, and took a long pull through the cold metal straw.

"So, Ben's moving in. For a while. That's convenient," she mentioned off-handedly. "I assume he'll be staying in your room?"

I sucked the liquid from my teeth. "I'm not sure. I guess so."

"And Jessamae. What are the two of you, anyway?"

I slammed my head back into the headrest. When I felt the mice scramble on my knees inside their box, I placed my fingers on the edge apologetically. We were gossiping like a couple of preteens in an online chat room.

"Ahh ... I don't know. I don't know what to ... do anymore." My focus lingered on the box, the subtle movement calmed me. "It's hard for me to stay away from her. She makes me feel ... things. Strong. Capable." I remembered the power electrifying me when we touched, and I inflated with guilt. "Brave."

"Ben treats you like you're a very fragile thing. True." I didn't like that she compared the two of them that way, when I hadn't even said his name. "But we both know it's because he's afraid to lose you." I couldn't look at her or respond. "Do you like her as a person? Outside of the power?"

I shook the ice around my cup. "I don't really have a lot of time to think about it. I spend my free time being just terribly, terribly ... scared." I hadn't said it in so many words before, and the honesty of it made my jaw hurt. Cleo heard the sincerity in my tone and watched me quizzically. "I don't want anyone to get hurt. Again. And I don't want to die." The words were true. As little as I appreciated it, sitting in my room, drinking myself numb within the confines of my bed, I did not want to die. I was petrified of losing the small comforts I had. Petrified of being nothing.

Cleo turned to face me, folding one leg up in her seat. "This is going to work, Frankie."

"What's going to work?" I bellowed unreasonably. "We have nothing! We can't win! All we can do is bring it in close, make it real convenient to kill us all! Fuck!" I flung my stupid delicious drink to the floor, covering my legs, the door, the bird, and the mice in coffee. They scurried and squeaked wildly in their few inches of space. I was instantly contrite about upsetting the animals. I petted the side of their boxes.

I popped my knuckles and tried to breathe. "I'm sorry," I murmured out of obligation, though in truth I wasn't at all.

Cleo held her pose during my outburst, her eyes glued to my performance. "If you're finished," she raised an eyebrow, "I was going to tell you that Jessamae and Ben have a plan." She held her coffee close to her chest as though she feared I'd rip it from her clutches and toss it out the window.

～～～

OUR ARMS WERE STACKED with furry, winged beasts as we approached the front door. I'd cleaned the coffee from the floor mats with napkins from a McDonald's, and only once I finished did Cleo offer to clean the mess by magic. I was tired and nearly regretted throwing the caffeine.

Ben opened the door before I could try. The boxes dug into the skin of my elbows, and he kissed my head as I slid past him. I set the bird and mice on the table and slumped into a chair.

"Why haven't you given me a tattoo, Ben?" Cleo accused from outside.

"As if you'd ever let me mar that pretty skin of yours."

"I'd still like the offer," she snapped. She dropped the fish unceremoniously beside the other doomed creatures and strolled to her room. The little fish seemed shaken, but he had seemed that way when we bought him. I could hear the hearts of the poor white mice thumping within their cage. The bird had returned to its panicked flapping, rattling its box across the table. I didn't want to kill them.

"Your legs look great, Princess," Ben complimented.

I peeked at them under the table. They were a vibrant rose, like a sunburn fading in the shade. I'd forgotten about them as the pain left. I spun the meat of my calf for inspection. The scar I'd gotten running through sagebrush when I was six had been erased. New skin. "Thanks."

Ben seemed in too good a mood.

"Where's Jessamae?" I asked, wondering how long she remained in the house, alone with Ben, until coming up with some reason for leaving. Two minutes max, I thought.

He took a deep breath of Jessamae-free air. "She's finding a spot. We're stronger in an environment of balance."

I raised an eyebrow. "Cut the fortune cookie bullshit, please?"

"A circle, Frank," he replied in exasperation. "If we can find a circle in nature, we'll be more effective within it."

Fair enough. Nevertheless, our possible "advantage" made me reevaluate the competition between us and the demon Paimon—the devil required no balance at all. The harder we tried, the worse I felt.

"She found something." Ben's eyes zoned off into the distance. "She had to. She'll be back soon. Four thirty-seven." He blinked away the premonition and refocused his attention on the dusty old clock leaning against the wall on the kitchen counter. "Only twenty-seven more minutes of peace," he said with a disheartened frown. Then his brown eyes seemed to darken. "We need to talk. Review the plan together."

"Right, Cleo said something about that." *After I threw an iced coffee under your dash.* "What exactly does this plan entail, Ben?"

Uncertainty morphed his face before he seemed to fortify himself and meet my eyes. "I'll let her give you the details."

And at exactly 4:37 p.m., Jessamae entered quietly through the heavy garage door. Her arms were empty, it was as if she just walked in off the street. Which she did. She had either apported or she ran the entire distance. The Honda was still at Ben's.

She was excited. "It exists. The best I could possibly hope for. Is Cleo ready?" She looked expectantly between Ben and me. "We need to move. It's a long drive. Night approaches."

28

IT WAS OF ABSOLUTE MAGIC. As we hiked away from the car into the oncoming darkness of the hillside, I had imagined a flat circle of grass or even a bald patch of parched dirt. It was the inverse of my puny imagination: a small, surreal circle of bleached aspen trees huddled together in an isolated mob, as if the encroaching pasture were poisonous. The edges of the copse rounded perfectly, uncannily. They stood familial and lonely and other in the center of a hidden valley between towering ridges of rock and fallen pines. The crowd of trees was like a harsh and towering audience, and my incompetence gushed through me as if my heart pumped it rather than blood.

The mice peered up at me from the cardboard box in which I purchased them. "Only a little while longer." *One of you might go free.* "We will," *might*, "get through this." The clerk at the pet store said they'd only need a few pellets, but I dumped the whole bag in the box. I hoped they gorged themselves to death before we got to them.

"Beautiful," Cleo called. Ben carried the cardboard birdcage and Jessamae had the goldfish swinging lightly from the bag in her fist. Cleo, unburdened, raced ahead.

"We'll just catch up then!" Ben yelled after her. She didn't look back.

Crossing into the circle felt like climbing into a brambly bush. The trunks were packed so tightly together, they were like thick layers of veins in tissue. We wove our bodies through the white stripes, raking our hair and clothes across sharp, invasive sticks, until we deemed ourselves centered. Jessamae thrust the fish bag into the crook of Ben's arm and started scouring the ground for dead twigs.

"Fuck you," Ben breathed just loud enough and piled the trapped animals onto a mess of crispy leaves.

"A fire?" Cleo turned curiously to Jessamae.

"A small one," she replied, clearing a tiny patch of earth between the trees. "We could easily lose control. Care is necessary."

I kneeled to the ground and began sweeping the leaves aside. They were too flimsy under me. My hands and knees sliced readily through them, creating a leafy dust. I cradled one of the broken brown things in my hand until I felt the capillaries plump and green. I twirled the healthy stem between my thumb and pointer finger and scowled. "I still don't know this brilliant plan I'm supposedly about to perform." I ripped fleshy green strips off the leaf and watched them flutter to the ground like plucked wings.

Jessamae teetered sticks expertly above the bare dirt. "It isn't complicated. You've done it before."

Ben, who was circling our group with his palms facing outward, creating a psychic field, snorted at her lack of explanation. I appreciated the commentary.

"Well, I've done a few things before. Could you give me a clue as to which thing it will be this time?"

"Perez." Pause. "Remember?" She sighed. "He was neither alive nor dead. He was something in between. Or something outside. But, together, we ended him. We can do that again."

I remembered the crumpling funeral director sprinkled in with bursts of fire and graveyard dirt. "We got lucky with him." I flicked the broken stem in my fingers to the ground. "He wasn't even the final boss. He was an old funeral director, and he about killed us."

Cleo's eye roll was so powerful, they pulled her head back on her neck. "Your grandmother's body gives the demon means to move, but it also limits it. It's vulnerable." She pulled out several loose strands from her heavy hair and draped them throughout the surrounding branches of our aspen cage.

"You broke its hand," Ben added. I felt attacked when they all worked together like this. "Right? You broke its fingers inside the car." He finished his circle and stood behind me. "If we can kill the body, the demon leaves. Nowhere to call home."

I shuddered, imagining the bug-infested red skin that covered Pamela's bones. I'd have to touch it. "We should have brought beer."

Cleo said, "You just need to survive long enough to get your hands on it. Ben and I are here as distractions." She glanced balefully my way, as if I had planned any of this and were using her on purpose.

Jessamae stood. The kindling was propped in a perfect teepee. "Ready?" she asked.

I stood up and brushed the dirt from my backside. Ben gave my shoulder a slap and stepped forward, rigid on my right.

"Nope," I grunted. "Let's get this shit show on the road."

Jessamae, Ben's lighter in hand, flicked the wheel against the teepee. A spark ignited within the dry sticks. "Stand at four points around the fire. Cleo east, Ben west, Frankie north."

I didn't know where north was, so Ben steered me to my place. The fire was already growing at an alarming rate.

"Channel the element. Channel each other." Jessamae stood and held out her palms. In the setting sun, her rippled tan limbs were like the branches of another ghostly tree, leading us deeper into the wood. Cleo grabbed her hand readily. Ben followed her example with hesitation and distaste evident on his face. The two then reached for my hands—Ben gave an encouraging squeeze—and our circle was complete.

The flame spread fast. "Channel the element, channel each other," Jessamae repeated.

The scent of the plumes epitomized the burnt and blistered summer that had ravaged us all this year. My thin skin cringed under the heat. I doubted I would ever feel comfortable channeling this element.

Despite its small beginnings, the flames danced nearly to our shoulders within mere moments. I was certain I did nothing to assist in fostering the damn thing. I hadn't felt the consumption, the flame, as I had in the past. I only felt sweat drip under my arms, and the two hands in mine—Cleo's silky palms and Ben's supple scarred skin.

Once the fire was deemed stable, Jessamae curved her spine around to reach the critters behind her. "Cleo," she stated simply, handing her the white cardboard box bouncing with the cries of the terrified bird inside. Cleo's gaze hardened in the light of the fire, she pulled her shoulders down and straightened her head on her swan neck.

"Ben?" Jessamae continued, more a question than direction. Ben pulled an amorphous plastic bag from the giant pocket of his shorts, a golden flash bobbed in the reflective water like a toy, blissfully unaware. I prayed the fish wasn't already dead. Or that it was.

"Frankie." My own name was like a foreign tongue in my ear, and I flinched. Jessamae was at my side, though I hadn't seen her move. She bent behind me, into the box of mice, and straightened with one trapped in her fists. I was glad I wasn't the one to choose between the two animals.

The rodent hand-off was smooth. Tiny paws scratched the ditches of my hand. Jessamae twirled the soft baby hairs on my neck before she left me clutching the luckless little ball.

Jessamae returned to her position, her eyes on the flames. The fire seemed to grow taller under her attention. Her voice, which naturally commanded the space it filled, took on a new kind of authority that rang steadily between whistles of the wind.

"In the name of the air, the land, and sea, we evoke you, hiding in plain sight."

My hair stung my face as it whipped in the sudden gale.

"With wings that sculpt the air, we evoke you."

From the back pocket of her pants, Jessamae pulled out her pocketknife. The wood grain of the handle shone in the fire before she tossed it to Cleo.

Cleo's full lip quivered. She clutched the knife tightly as she caught Jessamae's eye. She seemed to find encouragement there. She opened the lid of the box just enough to allow her shimmering hand inside. She didn't grope long before she lifted the bird free. The anguished twittering stopped, and my brow furrowed in revulsion—magic. Cleo squeezed the compliant prisoner in one hand and opened the small blade in the other. She pointed it over the heart, and I felt a familiar ache in my own chest.

"The wings," Jessamae spoke like a Sunday-school teacher, ruler in hand.

The muscles of Cleo's neck stood out, her throat pulsing harshly in the light. She turned the poor thing over to its feathered belly and gripped the pretty wings in her fist before she sliced them from its back.

It was so little, it didn't make a sound when it fell to the ground, and it was mean enough to survive the cuts. The former bird bounced around the dirt in a horrifying dance that made my eyes sting and my jaw clench in anger. I watched it impatiently, hating it.

Cleo tossed the dead wings into the flames, which swallowed them up like a monster. She efficiently plunged the knife through the suffering remains of the bird, and it graciously stilled. She set it back inside its white box, which would make a decent coffin. She threw the knife, blade out, to Ben and stood straight as a soldier. Her face was stone.

Ben, who had been waiting with his hand out for the knife, caught it. He cut through the knot of the plastic bag.

"With the tail that cuts the sea, we evoke you."

He needed no further clarification. Ben dunked his hand into the sagging bag to capture the fish. It slid between his fingers expertly before he got a solid hold. The bag became a dark puddle at his feet before he sawed through the gold scales of the tail. I thought he could have made a cleaner job of it, but eventually the little fish also fell to the dirt, and an orange shimmer was thrown to the fire.

This one had a harder time righting itself on the ground. The puddle of mud swaddled the fish, and without the tail, it could hardly budge. Though it was obviously trying, trying hard, to get away. Ben did as Cleo had, and stabbed through the goldfish, and its fruitless attempts to flee ceased.

He let the dead fish lie and stood. Unlike Jessamae and Cleo, he walked the knife the few feet over to me and offered it. The handle was warm. I looked to the once shining orange fish, now a muddy, cakey thing, and resented Ben. It could have been that fish couldn't show pain, couldn't make sound, wasn't covered in a soft white down and squeaking hopelessly in my hands, but I resented Ben for how easy he had it.

"And with the paw that packs the land, we evoke you."

I couldn't imagine something smaller than the baby pink paws desperately clawing at me. It had four paws.

"One will work, Frank." Ben spoke softly.

"Both wings were used," I reminded him, sparing a glower for Cleo. "I'll take all four." As much as I detested myself, and my friends, I knew four would strengthen the spell and I was sick of the coddling. I pinched the four paws together and readied the knife.

Doing it, the amputations, was easy enough to scare me. The knife went through each struggling limb like a fresh vegetable. Celery. I cried the whole time. The final cut bit shallowly into my lurking thumb. The shriek of the animal and the shock of the cut made me drop my victim like the handle of a hot pan.

I cast the pink things into the flames and dropped down simultaneously, knife poised. I stabbed the white ball before it could touch the ground, my blade sinking into the dirt. It was tiny enough that only once was enough. It stopped struggling. I stayed there, on my ankles, hands on the knife, for a very long time. Then I yanked the blade out of the earth, the mouse still dangling from it, and walked to Cleo's side. I slid the animal from the blade and set it in the box with the dead bird. I slipped Jessamae's knife back into her pocket without a word.

When I returned to my place in the circle, I tipped the surviving mouse into the surrounding trees. I wished it sped far from this place, before it ended up dead like everything else. I loathed us all.

"In the name of the air, the land, and sea we evoke you, hiding in plain sight." Jessamae didn't spare me a glance, her sea glass eyes reflecting the flames as if fire lived inside her. She looked wild and strong. "We evoke you, Paimon."

And with that, the bonfire died. There was no sputtering or flickering. The flames went out, instantly. In the tight copse of the trees, I couldn't find the moon. I could have been alone, in the pitch velvety blackness. I may as well have been.

Laughter echoed everywhere.

All that kept me grounded was the slow shifting of dead leaves, someone transferring their weight in the circle. I resisted the urge to crouch down low and crawl away from here, to follow the mouse I freed. I couldn't see the monster hiding in the dark. I couldn't see anything.

Laughter rang out again, beating around us like sleet. The gruesome scene we'd played out had succeeded. Paimon was here.

"You called?" Pamela's throat had cleared of the graveyard muck. The voice was deep, more masculine than feminine, but it was clear. It cawed above and around us as if it were its own army.

"Hello, Paimon." Jessamae lost some of her intimidation in the darkness. Paimon clearly agreed; it laughed in a ridiculing echo.

"Well, if it isn't the thing that's titillated my grandchild so," it hissed. "You're a brave one, I understand what she sees in you." The branches above us creaked in the black sky as if a panther darted across them. "And, of course, that full pink mouth of yours."

"You aren't the body you wear, Paimon," Jessamae shouted, unsure of Paimon's location. "Come out of hiding!"

Though my eyes were beginning to adjust to the darkness, it wasn't near enough. Now I only saw a tangled web of dense black that bobbed and swayed all at once. The treetops moved as if filled with hidden heavy birds.

A spark mercifully illuminated the night. Cleo had bent down and nurtured the kindling stealthily. Jessamae had crossed the clearing with her jaw angled up toward the knot of trees. The flame reflected off her scar, amplifying its distorting effects. Ben hadn't moved, but he felt farther than before.

"Gladly."

Ben rocked his head to the right and searched above me. I followed his furious stare. The trees gave no hint of movement and the stillness was sinister, until suddenly Pamela was there, so very high in the trees. Not as if she had moved, but as if she simply became.

I chided myself for using my grandmother's name. Because the thing that watched me now was not Pamela, was not human. Not even close.

Orbs that shone pale in the firelight like silver dollars zeroed in on me. The head flicked with unsettling speed, like that of a bird or something with too many bones, from me to Ben. The red of its concave cheeks creased in a haunting and ravenous smile that was entirely for him.

"The piggy brought her chaperone." The tongue slipped around the mouth. The spit stuck to the skin there. "Does she make you watch from the closet, Benny Boy?"

Cleo, moved by Paimon's fixation, shifted toward Ben with a protective arm extended. Paimon's eyes in Pamela's unnaturally stretched sockets jumped to the movement. "But why did you come? Forcing a square out of a triangle?" Its head jerked on its neck. "Who wants you here?"

Cleo stiffened, but she was otherwise unmoved.

Paimon giggled and scuttled through the trees, red arms hyperextended, too quick to track. The boughs shook, and shriveled leaves rained down like dead skin from a scalp. They littered my hair and arms. I swiped them from me in a panic. They looked like bugs, they felt like bugs. I remembered how Paimon hurt me in Ben's kitchen, how it had become fire. Fear suffocated me. Sweat wet my forehead and palms, sticking to the dead debris.

Tree limbs shivered lower and lower, spindly branches snapping on all sides of the circle. It was cycling around us as if down a drain. I bent down in a silly sort of defense.

I stared straight ahead, through the feeble light of the flame, to Cleo behind it.

Paimon. I saw the red skin peeping through the trees. Without stepping, without lifting a foot, it moved closer to Cleo. Over her shoulder, just out of sight. Its metallic eyes held mine as it licked its yellow teeth. Its mouth was just behind her, curving around her neck, its tongue so near the skin. She had to know its breath on her throat. Its mouth unhinged—

"Cleo, behind you!"

She whirled around to nothing. Paimon was gone as if it had never been. I jerked to my left, to Ben.

"BOO!"

Paimon was there, only the width of a whisker from me. Its mouth trickling sticky drool onto my head.

I expected a nightmare and met nothing less. With each appearance, Paimon had snapped Pamela's corpse into new horrifying shapes. It was tall, my head barely clearing its engorged stomach. It bent forward like a crone, as if its spine were too long for its body. The arms broke from the torso at the wrong place, nearly in the neck, and were long, too long, the elbows peaking above my head. The knees on which it stood were inverted, protruding backwards like a bird's. Every square inch of the barely swathed cadaver—the floral funeral dress stretched around it as taut threadbare strings—was grotesquely bulging and sinking, a big bad wolf filled to bursting with stones. Things moved under the sores of the skin … living things. I heard them wriggling not a foot from my face.

"What's my scared little piggy want from her granny?" It tromped forward on distended crocodile feet. Its arms lifted for an imminent embrace.

Before it could wrap itself around me, its serpentine neck seemed to clench, held back from the rest of its body. It was fighting to breathe, vying against something unseen. I backed away while I could, until I sensed Jessamae at my back. Her hand extended past me, over my shoulder. Her fingers were tight and bent viciously. As if around a throat. She was choking it.

Over heaving breaths, Paimon's silver eyes found Jessamae, and anger seemed to emanate from the blinding lights of them. It vanished from my side and reappeared at Jessamae's back. Before I could warn her and before she could react, those long hideous hands pressed, unexpectedly gentle, against Jessamae's temples.

She swayed between those hands, her eyes rolled in their lids. She pulled at Paimon's massive wrists, but her efforts were weak and it scared me. I rushed to her and helped her pull. "Let her go!"

"You want her? Of course, you do. Take her!" Paimon laughed maniacally and threw Jessamae forward into my flailing arms before, once again, disappearing.

"Jessamae? Jessamae, can you hear me?" I slapped her. She was limp on my chest. I rolled the two of us over, flopping her on her back. I leaned in above her face. "Jessamae!" Her pale eyes opened in an instant, her abrupt return to consciousness making me gasp. Her hands grabbed my wrists hard enough to hurt. I leaned away from her.

"Where you going, Peachy?" The words came from Jessamae's mouth, but the voice was not hers. "You know you want between these legs." She rubbed her strong limbs together crudely. The smile pulled her lips to their breaking point. She had more teeth than I remembered.

"Jessamae?" Cleo called from behind me, her voice uncharacteristically unsure.

Jessamae didn't even gift her a cursory glance. Her glass eyes reflected my fear back at me. "Come on," she whispered. Her hips surged beneath me, a moan escaping her lips. One hand reached for my mouth, tracing my lower lip. The other inched to her side. I settled into her touch, and she purred in response.

My eyes were on that hand; it crept along her thigh, over her round hips. Her fingers trailed along the skin peeking between her jeans and her shirt. To her pocket.

To her knife.

29

WITHOUT THINKING, I attacked Jessamae's writhing body, my knees climbing to her stomach. Her wrist flashed silver, and the knife came at my throat. My hands clamped around her muscular arms, pushing against her power, shaking with the strain. "Jessamae, this isn't you! Don't let that thing do this! Jessamae!"

Cleo and Ben were on either side of us, on their knees, pulling the knife away from my neck and attempting to restrain Jessamae. But she reacted quickly and, catching Cleo by surprise, swung the knife to the right, slicing her in the cheek. The cut welled red.

"Jealous, pretty?" Jessamae waggled her tongue. Then, taking advantage of our diversion, brought her weapon down to her left. The knife sunk into my hand.

I cried out in fear at the sight; the blade impaled it entirely, its tip poking out my palm.

Ben's grip was already on the handle. "Ready?" he asked me.

"I know you are," Jessamae said before throwing herself at Ben.

He couldn't foresee her actions—the movements were Paimon's—and Ben was blind to her. Regardless of who called the shots, Jessamae was unhinged. She scratched and clawed at Ben's neck and chest.

"Is this what you wanted, Benny?" She ground her hips on his stomach. "You wanted us both?"

I wrapped myself around her torso, trying to ram her off him.

She went for his eyes. Her fingers clutched his cheeks, her thumbs pressing hard to his lids.

The knife still stabbed through my palm. I wrenched my arm around and slapped her again, the knife dragging through her skin. She was pulled forward, toward Ben's head.

He bucked her with his hips, then used his knee to get her off him entirely.

I crawled to her head, my hands on her jaw, the knife still in place. "Jessamae, listen to me, you are stronger than this." I tried to conjure happy thoughts. Ben, Cleo, Jessamae, us.

Paimon smiled at me with Jessamae's mouth. "I will take them all from you."

"Leave us the fuck alone!" I screamed, shaking Jessamae, shaking Paimon. I squeezed her cheeks until I felt her teeth behind them. The skin began to warm, to burn. Jessamae's eyes rolled in their sockets, the whites hardly discernible from her irises.

"Francesca?"

It was her. Jessamae. She was afraid, her moment of control tenuous. When she pulled against me, I let her. She squirmed from my grasp, flopping through the leaves. Her head flipped from side to side, trying to spin off her spine. Her body would jerk and drop; she was having convulsions. She reached the barrier that Ben and Cleo had made from air and hair. She threw herself past the invisible wall with a grunt. She cried out, her hand at her temple. Then she fell to the ground and stayed there.

Maybe I wasn't in the clearing at all. Jessamae broken on the ground seemed far away and unreal. I felt like a dreamer, going through the motions as I did the night Ben took the third eye, but I hadn't been dreaming that night either.

"Jessamae?" Cleo called, her hand at her wound.

"Jessamae?" Paimon mocked.

We turned to the noise. Paimon had taken Jessamae's place in the circle. "Granny's killer left the circle. One down."

ITS MOUTH NEVER CLOSED; the lips had been ripped away. Its eyes never shut; Pamela's eyelids were torn through. I couldn't predict the thing because it was as emotionless and deranged as a black hole.

"We killed Gabriel," I stammered, wanting to be brave.

"I killed Gabriel," Paimon corrected with glee. "He visited my grave with headstone markers. *You* only took care of the body." It inched its face closer on its unnaturally long neck. "And you did take care of it, didn't you?" It gaped at me with its insane wide eyes.

"BLEW HIM UP! BLEW HIM UP! BLEW HIM UP!"

Cleo interrupted its screaming and began to sing. I plugged my ears immediately, recognizing the moment for what it was— a distraction. But without Jessamae, the plan was destroyed. I was powerless.

Paimon's did nothing but laugh. "That trick won't work on Granny, little mermaid."

Cleo shut her mouth, but her eyes were glued to the demon, holding its attention. I clenched my hands and felt a searing pain. The knife was still wedged into my palm. I reached for it slowly.

"Does your face make you sad, little mermaid? Is it hard to be so pretty, pretty?" Paimon stomped closer to her on its strange feet. "They tried to fuck the mermaid, didn't they? All of them! Kiss you, squeeze you, sell you, take you! All of them! Until you drove them craaaazzzyyyyy," it sang its horrible secret.

Cleo said, "They tried." Her lack of feeling jabbed at my spine and pimpled my skin.

"Did you like it, when your last husband-daddy jumped off the bridge? Did you like it, little mermaid?" Paimon was close enough to touch Cleo now. My hand paused on the knife's handle. *Please, no.*

Cleo's face remained controlled. "I loved it."

I didn't know if her disgust was for Paimon or for the guardians of her past, but her eyes flared with such disdain, she seemed capable of anything. Towards anyone. And I took a step back from her, not the demon.

"Oh!" it cooed, clicking its blackened nails together. "I like you. The pretty makes you brave, little mermaid." Its wide-open smile was too close to Cleo, its coin eyes vacant. Its tongue, purple and pointed, slithered from its open mouth. It stretched across the space between them as if to kiss her. Cleo didn't budge. Stone.

The demon tongue retracted. Though its expression hadn't changed, Paimon seemed to sober. It held her eyes, for once, serious. "But what if you weren't?"

It ran a broken finger—one of the fingers I'd stepped on—down its chest obscenely. It dug a fingernail through its own skin, puncturing the rubbery layer, and ripped downward like a zipper.

Insects poured from Paimon's stomach, the perverted, bubbling, red surface slicing open like a preternatural C-section. Black beetles, buzzing swarms of pests, hundreds of scurrying spiders. Endless shiny flies. All bursting from its middle in a gushing torrent. They flew and crawled from Paimon's insides and over Cleo's skin as if she were dead and rotting.

Cleo couldn't contain her own scream as the bugs coated her like a pulsing straight-jacket. She promptly shut her mouth to the onslaught. Ben conjured a psychic field around Cleo's face, his hands held out from his chest. The bugs covered the field in its entirety in moments.

I could see flashes of Cleo's eyes through the piling insects, they shot about in panicked circles, looking for a way out, a rescue. Her honey iris found mine and her fear was crushing. Then she toppled backward into the trees, her struggles ringing in our ears. Her shaking was hardly perceptible through the blanket of pests.

Paimon turned its red head in Ben's direction, so unhurried and deliberate, its movements demented. Just as slowly, it held up its hand. The demon extended two fingers.

∼∞∽

"BENNY BOY!" Paimon turned to its new focal point. "What about baby Benny? Let's see …"

I turned to Ben, heartbroken and disgustingly curious. I shook my head against what was inevitably coming. Ben never talked about his family or his parents. That he got himself emancipated was explanation enough.

Paimon cocked its head hard enough to crack bone, the lining of its throat bulging out, visible through its red skin like a snake digesting a rat. "Benny scared Mommy and Daddy! And they didn't want him anymore, did they? Boohoo!" The crying noises resounding from that elated smile were beyond disturbing.

I didn't want this. My curiosity evaporated instantaneously under Ben's stressed glower and hard eyes. I tugged at the handle in my palm, quelling a shriek. The knife didn't move. My hand was healing around it.

"He scared the nanny, scared the little boys and girls at school, didn't he, Benny? Daddy took him away, no more school, no more nanny. Daddy stuffed the creepy baby in the attic. Locked you in the attic, didn't he Benny? FOR YEARS! It was so scary, wasn't it Benny? All alone!"

I didn't want to react to the sad story, and I didn't want to feel sorry for Ben. If I softened in the slightest, something terrible would happen to him. Paimon wanted me to react. I was the only one left after all.

"Benny Boy dreamed of my grand-piggie and he'd cry, cry, cry." Ben's eyes flicked to me for an instant. "That's what she was to the creepy boy, a chance to be loved for the very first time," Paimon said as if choked with tears in a baby's high voice.

"How bad does it hurt, Benny Boy," the demon leered sickeningly, "that she prefers my killer instead?"

I stared resolutely at Paimon. I wouldn't face Ben and see his reaction. It would make things worse for everyone if I saw even an ounce of hurt or shame in his eyes. I yanked at the knife, a small cry escaping. Then my pain was beyond notice, even my own.

Paimon was going to touch Ben. Its long, crackly fingers curled close to Ben's raised hand. Before it could make contact, the red digits met another psychic field. The arm was blown back on its high shoulder with a pop—one of its many bones. Ben was shaking with exertion, his blank façade beginning to fracture. He couldn't protect Cleo and fight Paimon off at the same time.

"That hurt, Benny Boy. But you seem tired. Creepy baby can't do this, can he? What's it gonna be, Ben? You or Cleo, Cleo, you, you, Cleo." Its devil fingers pointed from one to the other in a chaotic gesture using both hands. "Oh, it's just so hard!" It held its hands to its cheeks and the shriek reverberated throughout the circle.

But we all knew who Ben would choose. I moved, tripping around the pathetic flame, reaching desperately for Ben.

"Daddy didn't save you then, and he won't save you now." Slobber dripped from Paimon's mouth. It didn't have to wait any longer.

Cleo's shield held, it stretched below her neck, down her chest.

And Paimon thrust its clawed hand into Ben's stomach, driving its way up to his ribs.

"NO!" I leaped on Paimon's curved back, ripping the pocketknife from my hand with a spurting squelch. I plunged silver into red, up to the hilt. I stabbed again and again into the dead skin, sensing the pain beneath my fingers.

Paimon tore its sharp fist from Ben's torso, dropping him in a pile of his own blood at its feet. It shook me like an animal, stomping across our small fire, snapping the kindling, dimming the flame. My legs swung wildly, like pendulums above its backward knees. I clung my feet around them, pulling myself in tighter to the beast. I stabbed its back like a pin cushion, eating its pain, gaining strength. I cut into it voraciously, hungry and only growing hungrier.

The first wounds I'd inflicted were already closing, I stabbed with renewed conviction, the handle of the blade pushing through the skin. I couldn't stop my magic, I couldn't stop the wounds from closing. But I would continue, no matter how futile. Paimon roared in outrage as I embraced its humped back. Its lengthy arms couldn't reach me here.

Ben barely stirred, and the field protecting Cleo began to recede, inch by inch. The buzzing was deafening.

White light flared over Paimon's shoulder. Using the knife as leverage, I peered over its massive frame.

It was Jessamae. Her legs weren't steady, but she had returned, and she was herself. She lurched between Paimon and Ben's prone figure, unwieldy but incredibly fast. Her shoulders barely passed Paimon's boney hips. Using that to her advantage, she reached her calloused fingers into Paimon's flapping, open guts, as it had to Ben.

"You!" Paimon screamed down to Jessamae. It circled its hands around her throat. "Why do you help them? You and I are the same!" Its voice shattered, as if it were the sum of a thousand voices. They shouted around us in a horde.

I was aware of Jessamae's hands digging around in Paimon's chest cavity. I could feel them through the layer of meat. I stabbed with purpose now, carving the flesh like a Halloween pumpkin. Thick blood driveled, closer to purple than red, along my knuckles.

"Humans took your sister from you! Cut your face when you fought!" It shook her with each word. Though she was dipping in and out of consciousness, Jessamae's hands remained inside it. "How many did you kill then? How many have you killed SINCE?"

I saw its depraved features mirrored in her eyes. Gone was the wide smile—its games were over. Paimon seethed with untethered rage. Jessamae reached further into its mutated organs, causing a lot of damage as she burrowed.

"You killed me! You took the life from this body and drank it for yourself!" Spittle flew from its cavernous jaws. "And you expect my granddaughter to care! You are worse than this, Jessamae Mori. Worse than a demon wearing a corpse. Because you are a monster who wants to be accepted by those lesser than you! You are completely, pathetically, alone!"

The word rang out from the beast, the gust so powerful it blew through Jessamae's hair. Cleo's muffled cries were the only sounds left. The psychic field around her face must be nearly gone, along with Ben's consciousness.

The hole I'd sliced into the back beneath me was too small, it continually shrank as it healed. I tried to force my fingers through, gathering them together like a crow's beak. It was like forcing my way through the earth. I beat at it senselessly. We were out of time.

Paimon circled its immense hand around Jessamae's head, palming her like a basketball. The demon tightened its grip, its nails prodding the skin of Jessamae's face, and with only one hand—the fingers of its left still crunched and broken—hoisted her from the ground.

Jessamae didn't kick, didn't struggle. Her eyes were now level with mine, her tan face, surrounded in fingers, darkened in the dying light of the fire. Tears filled those eyes. I couldn't see past the reflective water to her icy irises. The darkness grew thick around me. I pounded the knife in desperation, it hit at an angle and slipped from my bloody fists. I punched at the demon who took everything from me, who held the last thing I had in its hand.

"I ... killed ... Pamela." Jessamae squeaked out of her

crushed windpipe before Paimon heaved her weight upwards and threw her skull to the ground.

"No," I whimpered through my sticky throat. "No. Goddammit!"

Her head bounced off the hard dirt with an ominous clap.

I didn't know if Jessamae needed to get the confession off her chest or if it was the last clear thought in her unbalanced mind after Paimon's intrusion. But I despised her for those words—they meant she had given up. Paimon won.

"Oh no, Francesca!" it called to me without turning back. "It wasn't enough. They weren't enough to save you, were they?" The monster stood tall on its wrong legs, its voice inundated with the behemoth confidence it had nearly lost. "Everyone you care for is dead, you can't hide behind their legs anymore. Climb down and avenge them. Face. Your. Fears!"

My head lifted at one contemptuous word. *Dead*—were they dead? I found no holes, no voids, in the copse around me. My friends lived, barely, perilously, but they lived. The only darkness I felt was stunted and blurred. It was entombed in the abomination beneath me, in the mess of purple entrails. Pamela's heart.

I slid down from Paimon's back, putting pieces together, considering Jessamae's final words. *I killed Pamela.* Pamela was dead, though Paimon was not. The demon resided in her dead body. It existed around her frozen heart.

I stepped over Jessamae's twitching form, focused on Paimon looming over me, nearly twice my size.

"Look how brave she's being." I rounded its left side, its broken hand, to the mad mutation of my grandmother's face. "If only your mother were as brave as you. She would have been proud." Its silver eyes shone brightly, the only light now, as the fire finally puttered to ash.

Paimon reached to caress my cheeks, its torso open, its hand and shoulder broken, its back full of holes. Because it wasn't a ghost, it was a body.

"I have a request. A last request," I said. The pain of my friends surrounded me like the fire I'd lost. It warmed me, comforted me, just as the smell of death comforted me in the graveyard. Their pain meant they lived, and I rejoiced in its presence.

"How precious little piggy is." Its hands met my burning face, its pain drowning in my bloodstream. Whatever Paimon had imbued in Jessamae's mind, it was powerless here, against me. "But nothing can be done for you now."

I drove my own hands into its center, drawn to the emptiness. I found it hanging like a cocoon, and cradled it in my palms as I'd cradled the bird.

"You're wrong." As my skin made contact with the slimy organ, Paimon's face flattened, shock erasing the psychotic joy. I felt the tissue spasm and stretch at my touch. Paimon's pain grew and I drank it in, channeling it back into Pamela's dead heart.

The demon scratched my face in a vain attempt to remove my arms from its chest, but the heart pumped between my fingers. Paimon screeched in agony. It could not survive a living host.

"Cry for me, Paimon," I whispered. "Cry because it hurts." The words were lost to the screams. The heart beat hard, pumping the purple sludge. Life entered the body.

Paimon's head tipped back on its spine, and those uncanny silver eyes shone up into the night, erasing the stars. Paimon was breaking, its enormous bones snapping inside the skin and muscle. Its feet curled backward, as if losing their innards. Paimon fell to its side, seizing violently against the beating heart in my hands. I wouldn't let go. I fell forward with it, sliding on my knees, covered in sticky, freakish blood, its smell pungently caustic and curdled.

Its arms were shrinking and floppy, the mammoth bones now shards within them. Paimon howled, its face almost human.

"Francesca!" The wail wasn't Paimon's, the voice wasn't

Paimon's. "Francesca! Please! End it!"

It was Pamela. My grandmother begged to die. She controlled her voice for one final plea. All I could hope is that she hadn't been trapped all this time, that I only just now resurrected her consciousness.

A feather-light touch brushed my ankle. With my hands still wrapped around the heart, I looked down.

Jessamae had dragged herself to my side. Blood matted her hair, turning the strands a shocking crimson. She offered her hand, mere inches from the ground. Her red fingers trembled with the effort.

Paimon was stuck between living and dying. Pamela was stuck between living and dying. Just as Gabriel had been suffering there. I reached for Jessamae's hand, Paimon's blood mixing with hers in the wells between my fingers. Lightning coursed through us both, the pain of the seizing body humming in my blood. I towed her forward—stronger than I'd ever been—closer to the horror. Close enough for her to reach a finger out, and simply touch.

The body shook and cried, Pamela and Paimon contorting against the electric jolt. It was frothing at the mouth, its stomach acid and saliva fizzing up from its throat. The heart pumped faster and faster, thumping against my palm like a cornered hummingbird. I thought I heard a final sigh from the dark ruined mouth before the beating finally ceased and the body dropped in a motionless, transfigured heap.

~∞∞~

A VAST VOID GREW, larger than any I'd ever encountered. I wondered if we'd managed to put a real end to Paimon, and two deaths coincided within the carcass. I had my doubts.

My interest left the broken menagerie on the ground. It had nothing else to offer me. Jessamae, on the other hand, did. The damage to her skull was substantial—her brain was hemorrhaging. I clasped her shuddering hand, and all the harm she had suffered flooded into me. Her injuries were so extensive, she offered a feast. Her skin was warm. My fingers climbed to her scalp, the source, and the heat burned hotter.

"Ben is dying," I heard from outside my banquet. Hands raked against me with irritating persistence. Gone were my concerns of complicated concussions and brain trauma. I drank it in gluttonously. "Ben is dying, Frankie."

I was insatiable, there was hardly anything left. Still, I ran my fingers along the fissures of her scalp. I felt a strange sickness there. I poked my soaked fingertips between my lips, sucking the blood clean. It made me almost sleepy, heavy.

A strong hand slammed into the side of my head and my vision exploded in stars.

"Jesus!" I held the sore, it was already beginning to swell. Jessamae's face came into focus through the glimmering blur. "What the hell, Jessamae?"

She yanked my arm roughly. I bowled forward into the pit of dead fire. Ash blew up into my face, coating my nostrils in gray dust.

"Help Ben. Now, Frankie!" Jessamae as she stood, her energy renewed. "He's nearly dead."

Comprehension rocked me and I whirled around to face Ben's inert form. His chest wasn't rising, and his middle was missing from him. His blood had soaked through the hard-packed dirt.

I scurried to him on hands and knees. "No. No, Ben. I'm sorry! No, no, no." I latched onto his ankles and pulled myself closer. My hands trembled over the open hole in Ben's stomach. I covered it. The blood, he had lost so much. Paimon tore through his stomach entirely, as well as punctured one of his lungs and re-broke the ribs I'd repaired two days ago. I sensed it all beneath my palms, but the rush, like the one I'd felt from Jessamae's wounds, didn't come.

"I'm sorry, Benny, I'm so sorry! Don't do this, don't die. I can't do that again! I can't try again, please, Ben! Not you!" The injuries didn't sustain me. I felt nothing. I couldn't pull pain from a dead man. "I'm not ready, Benny! I CAN'T DO THIS!" My face was numb. I couldn't stop shaking. Tears filled my mouth as I begged him. "PLEASE, BEN!"

He'd become so pale, his freckles stood out like flecks of ink. His lips were gray and still. There was no vibrancy, no color. This wasn't Ben—this was a horrible ghost, a doppelgänger. I ran my shivering fingertips along his eyelids, his cheeks.

I remembered our kisses, what they did to him. His health, his blush, his bright shining eyes. I'd never seen him so alive. I threw myself onto his chest and pressed my mouth to his.

"Please! I'm so sorry, I'm sorry!"

Jessamae, who'd been hovering over me uselessly, moved away from us. She bent to the ground across the clearing. Cleo. I couldn't think about her now. If she were at death's door, Jessamae would have told me.

I forced my lips to Ben's in desperation. Holding those smoldering memories between us in kisses. Remembering the years before, his smile, both teasing and genuine. The hundreds of small and beautiful moments we've shared. They were everything. And I sobbed at the possibility of losing any of them, filling Ben's lifeless mouth with my sticky cries. "Please, Ben. Don't die."

I'd stained his lips and cheeks and chin with Jessamae's blood. "I'm sorry." I held his face. My forehead met his, our noses rubbing together, side by side. Any piece of me, I gave to him, skin on skin wherever I could reach. I kissed his mouth once more. He was cold. "I'm sorry." My tears tangled within his eyelashes. I closed my eyes.

I felt an unforeseen and unwelcome relief from my own pain. The chest beneath me stuttered. Warm.

"It's … okay."

30

"FUNERAL DIRECTOR MURDERED, remains and car burned."

The Salt Lake Tribune was draped over my thighs, my legs crossed on my bed. I didn't have a laptop and I couldn't afford one. I'd walked to the town gas station at dawn to buy the newspaper, as well as a sickeningly sweet bottled coffee and some powdered donuts. I'd filled out the little pink slip inside the paper and put it in the mailbox upon return. I could afford a Sunday subscription … if I still had a job.

The sun was rising gracelessly as I returned, but Cleo was still asleep. I lugged a bottle of her bourbon into my bedroom with me, took two shots, and dipped back into sleep for another three hours.

I couldn't put it off any longer. I lifted the coffee to my lips and winced at the taste. I didn't prefer hard liquor, but had splashed the bourbon into my cold morning Joe as soon as I'd made enough room for the stuff. I was going to need it to get through this. I shoved a donut in my mouth as a chaser.

6, Aug. Friday evening, the day he was reported missing to the authorities, the remains of Gabriel H. Perez, proprietor of Perez Family Funeral Home, were recovered near the Rock Chuck Hiking Trail outside of Aspen Ridge, UT. The scene was discovered after several smoke sightings were reported to the volunteer fire department. The source of the fire was a car explosion. Perez was found inside the blazing car, which was registered in his name, gasoline residue both on his person and his vehicle. The autopsy found no smoke in Perez's lungs, indicating the fire was started postmortem. The case is currently being investigated as a homicide. "What happened to Mr. Perez isn't fair. I hope that whoever is responsible gets what they deserve for what they did to him and his family," says a recent customer of Perez Family Funeral Home.

I meant what I said. The reporter called the day we fought Paimon, leaving a voicemail. I returned their call the next day, hoping for some information about the investigation. I asked if the fire had spread. She replied grudgingly that it had, but had since been contained, plainly thinking I was terrible to be asking about anything other than Gabriel. I'd been too afraid to ask if the police had any leads, worried that I would appear suspicious, and instead spoke the words that now appeared on the page.

"Need another?" Cleo asked from my doorway, a bottle of Irish whiskey sloshing in her fist. I nodded without looking up, rolling the now empty bottle I'd taken from her in the general direction of my trash can. I held my mug in the air.

Cleo wasn't the same anymore. Not only had she swallowed dozens of insects—inhaled them—the bugs had worked to eat her alive. Though the swarm dissipated into the surrounding woods once Paimon fell, by the time I put my hands on her, Cleo was missing enough skin to make parts of her nearly translucent. Healing her took almost as long as Ben. Under Jessamae's scrutiny, I didn't lap anything up and I remained in control.

Nearly losing Ben was a sobering experience.

Now, Cleo's glowing skin was a patchwork quilt of lights and darks, the scars encompassing her entirely, though the worst of it was on her arms and legs, having been the most exposed. Her face healed cleanly—almost—having been protected throughout much of the attack, thanks to Ben's efforts. She had two light scars where bites had been deepest, one on her proud nose, the other on her upper lip. I wondered if I would continually touch her, the effects might improve in time. I wondered if she hated me.

She gave me another shot and held the bottle to her chest. "How long are you going to hide from us?"

I took a calculated swallow with my eyes on the paper. "I'm not hiding."

I was hiding. We trekked back to Ben's car as the sun was rising yesterday. Jessamae and I had buried the nausea-inducing monstrosity that was somehow both Pamela and Paimon outside of the copse of trees while Ben and Cleo caught their breath. I wouldn't burn the body, having seen Paimon on fire before. Submerging it was out of the question. The nearest body of water was twenty miles away and I didn't trust the corpse to stay beneath the surface. No one could ever see what had become of Pamela Hughes.

I silently hoped that Pamela's re-death would qualify as payment to move the earth for her grave. Jessamae, having guessed my thoughts, said that each sacrifice had to be made with the intent purely for payment. So I had to cut my fucking arm again. I'd wiped dried purple blood from the blade before I did it.

We rolled the body into the hole in an everything-comes-full-circle sort of black irony. Staring down at the empty sockets and lipless mouth, the head looked closer to human than it had in the night. But not human enough. Thinking of the week leading up to that burial, thinking of Gabriel, I jumped into the grave, teetering on the big, deformed carcass. I scrambled for balance, reached up over the edge for the same pocketknife I'd use to carve a hole in its back, and hacked the thing's head off, one nick at a time. The reek was unbearable. I was sweating by the time it detached.

Jessamae hadn't said a word as I pulled myself free, covered to the elbows in what looked like crushed blackberries. When she'd reached out to me, I shrank away. I didn't want to be comforted. I needed a break from touch, and I needed a break from magic. I laid the box containing the wingless bird, the paw-less mouse, and the muddy remains of the fish onto the monster's body to be buried. All my victims.

Ben and Cleo didn't ask questions when we returned. We were all bloodstained, torn, traumatized, and smelled like hell; I didn't draw attention.

I drove us home, stalling the clutch sporadically as we went. I was the only one who hadn't suffered a life-threatening injury— my only scar being an ellipse on the front and back of my hand, just above my tattoo—and it had seemed polite to offer. Other than the whining of the transmission, it was eighty-seven minutes of uninterrupted silence. I used each of those painfully long minutes to relive the horrors I'd endured and the horrors I'd committed. The latter was what kept me locked away in my room for the last twenty-four hours.

Ben went home yesterday as soon we exited the car. He didn't come back.

Cleo was in the bathroom for over two hours after I'd unlocked the front door. I didn't want to disturb her and held my pee into the evening. I was dehydrated anyway.

I had no idea what happened to Jessamae. I hadn't seen her since.

"Of course, you aren't," Cleo patronized, bringing me back from my reverie. "But I happen to know you haven't had food since Saturday." She clearly didn't see the donut wrapper in my trash. "Breakfast is on the table." She turned for the door with a flap of her silk robe.

I drank my whiskey, grounds being the only remnants of the coffee, and fell back on my bed. It was going to be horrible, the way they would look at me—abandoned, betrayed, disgusted, terrified—but I couldn't stay away forever. I was very hungry.

I rolled from the center of my bed, no longer fearing the orange stain there; I was a stain. I studied the cabinet that lined my bedroom wall. It was still empty, all the doors and drawers hanging open immodestly as I took in the darkened color. "Smokey Sea," I mused. Better.

The mouthwatering smell and sizzling sound of bacon on the stove greeted me unexpectedly in the hallway. I thought Cleo might be a vegetarian. I'd never seen her eat meat.

All three of them were in my kitchen: Ben stood at the stove, spatula in hand, whistling an unfamiliar tune. Cleo sat at the table with a glass of whiskey to her left and two slices of wheat toast to her right. Jessamae perched beside her, a glass of booze and ice held in both hands, her eyes far away.

"Um, hey," I said to the crowd, perturbed at their unknown gathering.

"Morning, Frank," Ben called over his shoulder. He slid some fried eggs onto a plate of bacon and toast. I opened my mouth to thank him, but he set the dish in front of Jessamae. My eyes just about popped out of my skull and rolled around on the tile.

Jessamae forked an egg onto her toast, digging in. "Thank you, Benjamin."

Ben pointed his spatula at me. "Over-easy?"

I blinked away my stupor. "Yeah. Yes. Please."

He turned back to his frying pan—it was definitely his, mine were all blackened and scratched—and cracked an egg using only one hand. "Did some of your kitchen stuff survive the fire?" I asked.

"No, this is new. Your pans offend me." He flicked the pan, the egg turned prettily in the air and landed again with a slap. "There's coffee in the pot."

I shuffled forward, pulling a new mug from the cupboard. I

turned and found a tower of boxes blocking the living room window.

"Wow."

"Yeah, I packed up most of my things yesterday. I will, however, have to go back at least every other day to check on the garden. But this beauty right here—" he shook the empty egg carton "—will fit twenty-four seedlings. The humble beginnings of our *second* garden."

I opened the flaps of a few of Ben's boxes, my mug held carefully in one hand. Art supplies, movies, two very colorful boxes of clothes. I stopped when I saw a bag of second-hand books. I bent down, running my hands along the worn covers. "My books."

"Remember those?" Ben asked as he slid my eggs onto a full plate. "They were supposed to distract you from the death of your granny. I figure the sentiment still applies."

I smiled for the first time in what felt like a decade and sat down. "Thanks, Ben." I dipped my toast into the yellow pool of delicious yoke. "I should probably invest in real furniture. Like a couch. Maybe a queen bed."

"I'd pitch," Ben offered from the stove. "Considering it would be my bed, too. For a little while."

I paused with my fork halfway to my mouth, a gooey bit of egg white dripping. When I remained mute, Ben looked at me, a lift to his eyebrow. I nodded crazily in response, hoping my face wasn't red. I brought the fork to my mouth, but it was empty. The egg had flopped passively into my lap.

Amir leapt to my legs as if from nowhere and gobbled up the eggs from my sweats. I knocked him back to the tile with great enjoyment.

Jessamae, finished with her food, pushed her plate forward and dabbed at her mouth with a paper towel—I didn't have any napkins. "Frankie. I'm glad you're up." She stood to pour herself some coffee over the dregs of whiskey in her glass. "I need to be leaving after breakfast." She leaned against the counter with her mug to her lips.

I burped into my hand and pounded a fist against my chest, bacon having lodged itself in my throat. I coughed. "Why? To where?"

Ben took a seat beside me with his own plate and mug. Cleo stopped eating to listen.

"I have some affairs to attend to. I've been very ... preoccupied, in Utah with you. There are other people, other witches, who have been expecting me."

I gaped at her, feeling spurned. She had never mentioned leaving before now, and it may have been vain, but her absorption had led me to believe she was here to stay.

During my day of quiet masochistic thought, I had often considered her reaction to Ben and me, when I'd clung to his limp, sallow body with such desperation. Maybe how I felt about him wasn't so young and fleeting after all.

Cleo dropped her eyes and held a small piece of toast under the table for Amir. Ben's eyes stayed on his eggs.

"Oh. Yeah, okay. That's ... fair." This had to be the most chaotic aftermath to a killing she had ever undergone. And I'd only given her reasons to leave. I couldn't imagine what she suffered, having Paimon in her head. Then to drag herself back to the fight, only to have me lick at the blood of her skull like a dog.

No, I couldn't blame her. But I did.

"I'm sure I won't be able to stay away long," she consoled over the rim of her glass. "And you have my number."

I was nodding with my Scott-straight mouth. "True." Despair leaked throughout my organs at the thought of her being away from me. I didn't know where she was going. But if she wanted me to know, she would have told me. This was some sort of punishment. I returned my focus to my food but tasted nothing.

Jessamae finished her coffee and set the dish in the sink. "I wish I could say it's been a pleasure. Benjamin," she nodded genially, in good spirits with him.

He dipped his chin to her in return. Their friendliness made me queasy.

Jessamae's face fell. "Cleo." Her disappointment was tangible. Those two had similar interests and got along as normal people might. I wondered how long it would be until she could have an easy conversation with another human being.

Cleo became stone once again. I hoped one day to be able to decipher when it was a defense mechanism and when she was just plain apathetic. "It was good to meet you, Jessamae." She held her eyes until Jessamae looked away.

"Would you walk me out, Frankie?"

I pushed my plate away and stood from my chair. "Of course." My guise at nonchalance slipped entirely and the words came out somewhere between sarcastic and total asshole. I marched through the front door without waiting for her.

Heat immediately crushed me and pushed my dark mood further into the shadows.

"I'm sorry, Frankie," Jessamae said from behind me. "There is someone that I have to see. And there's another I need to track down. I need time but I will be back."

I flipped around with my arms folded. "I understand. We need to get back to our ordinary lives, or whatever." Her sea-glass eyes were astute, but I held her gaze. "I just don't see why you asked me to 'walk you out.'" I quoted with my fingers, a bitter twist to my mouth.

"Don't do this, Frankie." She lifted a curl of frizzy, slept-on hair and twirled it around her finger. "I will be back. I promise. Call if you need anything. Okay?" She kissed each of my temples as I held perfectly still. It kindled the memory of us behind the grocery store, when she spoke of balance and inevitability. Liar.

She leaned her forehead into mine and I relaxed unintentionally, falling into her touch. Our link thrummed as if saying goodbye as well. "Okay."

Her hand tangled itself within the roots of my hair, she held me to her with fervor and I nearly felt her pain, emotional pain, as if it had shape. Even if it were possible, I wouldn't have taken it from her. I felt savage pleasure because she was hurting.

"You were so strong. I'm proud of you, Frankie." She breathed me in one last time. "Goodbye, my peach." She released me and walked backwards, eyes on me throughout her retreat. At the edge of my property, without a bag, without anything at all, she spun on her heel and was gone.

I watched her run for longer than I'm happy admitting, until I was watching the empty air around the aspens, searching for flashes of her pale hair between the trees.

I trotted back into the house, feeling as though I weighed less now. Knowing I would never take the first step and call Jessamae.

I paused with my hand on the knob, a familiar pull in my middle. I looked down and lifted my foot in alarm.

A snake edged up over the front step of the entryway, its needle tongue exploring my scent. I timidly eased my foot back to the stair. A junior piebald ball python, a female, and a baby. It was the snake from the store, I was certain. No snakes like this could be found around here. She inched her way closer to me, and I felt an immediate nurturing instinct for the animal. She'd come all this way. She'd come here for me. She was mine. I bent down and extended my hand, unsurprised when she slunk up my fingers and around my wrist.

Cleo and Ben were finished in the kitchen when I walked in with her. Knowing she was safely around one of my forearms, I grabbed my bag of books, and toted them to my room.

Cleo's door was closed when I passed it in the hall. I pathetically worried that they were either watching us through the blinds or breaking in Cleo's new bedroom rigorously. The latter was a small worry, one that got smaller each day I spent with them. But scarred or not, Cleo inspired great insecurity in me.

My bookshelf was just a plank of wood screwed directly into

the wall, but I liked to see books on it, and the six that I owned appeared pitiful, shoved to one side.

I dropped the bag on the floor and gently set my pet amongst the blankets of my bed. I scratched her head naturally and she leaned into my hand. Her tongue tickled my thumb and I felt only adoration for her. She'd traveled so far.

I clutched several paper spines and lined my new books along the shelf. Once all but my VHS tapes were aligned, the shelf nearly full, I took a moment to appreciate the colors of them. Then I began to pull and replace them, organizing them by size, from biggest to smallest.

"Looks good, Frank." Ben was leaning against my door jam.

"Do you have any to add?

"I don't think they'll fit. You might need an actual bookcase if you keep this up." He strolled across the room, turning to flop on the bed.

"No!" I gasped, gripping his forearm. The snake stretched herself up tall on her heavy tail in curiosity.

Ben froze, stunned. "That's a snake." I didn't see surprise on his face often. He must have given my head some privacy while I was outside.

"It is." I sat down beside her, petting her scaled length. "I saw her at the pet store the other day. I wanted her, but she's pricey."

"So … you stole her?"

"No, she was on the front porch."

He eased himself onto the edge of the bed. "You hate snakes."

I tickled her chin. "Yes."

Ben held her intelligent stare and extended his hand to her. Her tongue flicked against his palm. "Mmmm," he breathed, "she'll stay with you." His eyes shut in concentration before he took his hand back. "A familiar. What's her name?"

I sensed she wanted up and I took her in my hands as if she'd asked. Her elegant head rose to me in inquiry.

"A familiar?" Her tail dangled over my legs. The white of her looked too clean and too bright for my sweats.

"An animal that chooses you, a witch, to care for. To protect. She'll understand you. In time." Her ribbon tongue flicked again. "No ordinary pet."

I was grateful for the explanation. I already felt a kinship for the reptile that I'd rarely ever felt for human beings. She was mine. She coiled inside my hands like a croissant.

"A baby?" Ben asked, rubbing her flat head.

I nodded. "She'll grow."

He watched her settle into the nest of my palms with affection. "She'll want for nothing."

I smiled at the idea. "I need to buy her a terrarium, and some food. Frozen mice, no live ones." I shuddered at the memory. "Maybe I'll make a whole day of it and look at new beds."

"I'll go too. You'll need someone with taste if you're buying actual furniture."

"Plus," I uttered shyly, "it'll be sort of your bed. Right?"

Ben watched me from the corner of his eye. He then unwrapped the reluctant snake and set her gingerly on the bed. He reached out to me, and I stared at his hand like a bear trap. At my awkward dithering, he grabbed my fingers and pulled me closer beside him.

"How are you, Frank?"

"Fine," I barked. "I'm fine. Did you, um, sleep at your place last night?" I spoke to his hands. I hated how vulnerable I felt.

"I did. I needed to take some time. I thought we all did." He swept the wild bangs of my hair away from my face.

"Yeah, especially Jessamae." Embarrassed by my admission, I grabbed the newspaper from my end table and plopped it into his lap. He held it warily and read to himself. Nothing took him off guard—he already knew. When he didn't comment on what I said, I prodded, "You two seemed very cordial this morning. I'm sure you knew, bet you loved to see her go."

He didn't take the bait I laid out for a fight. "I saw that she would leave, yes," he admitted calmly, flopping the paper back to the nightstand. "But I feel a little differently toward her now. I don't like her, but I don't want to hit her with a shovel."

"Why?"

"That night ... she didn't have to stop you." His hand lifted back to my hair. He shouldn't be touching me. "I tried to see my own future, and in so many of them, my sight went dark in minutes. But she stopped you."

"I would have tried," I begged for solace from him. "If you didn't make it. I was scared, but I know I would have tried."

"You should probably work with a few more birds, maybe a dog. For practice. Before you do another human resurrection. Don't you think?" His hand moved to my thigh. "So, in a way, I'm in Jessamae's debt."

Ben's scar was as unlike Cleo's as it could be. Rather than a dusting over his entire body, the hole in his stomach took layer upon layer of tissue. A giant pale crater wrapped his torso in hard new skin, erasing the tattoos that used to exist there. It took nearly an hour to close his organs and mend his bones. The skin took just as long. It didn't match the rest of him, it was lighter, a little pink. The baby skin growing was like a rising tide—slow, patient, and a freakish thing to watch for us both. Then there was the bruising. But he lived. Because of Jessamae.

I cleared the moisture from my throat. "I'm sorry."

"You were amazing, Frank. You broke it." I pulled away. I wanted no more praise for what I was and what I'd done. "But why didn't you tell me?"

"That I get off on injuries and death?" I erupted crudely. "Why didn't you tell me about magic all these years? You hated Jessamae so much for what she was. I didn't want you to hate me."

"I didn't hate her for what she was. I hated her for what she did." He spun my tightly balled body around to face him and put his hands on my knees. "To Pamela, to you." He put his chin between them, resting it on his thumbs. "Control comes with practice, Princess."

"Did you not see it, when you had your visions of my affinity?"

"I only see, Frank. I can't feel. I didn't know how it would affect you."

I set my hand on his skull. He'd shaven again and it was velvety soft. "Why didn't you tell me?" I whispered. "About your family."

He closed his eyes and left them that way. "Why would I tell you about that? It's like you said, I don't have to tell you anything." I winced at the memory of confronting my mother's true cause of death.

"Fine," I said, stung. "It's just … I hope you do."

His eyes opened, the lovely swirls of browns, blacks, and yellows dancing in the light streaming in between the curtains.

Feeling brave, like maybe he needed me to be, I leaned forward and put my lips to his. I could practically taste his hurt, but it was replaced promptly with hunger. His hand entered my hair, his thumb stroking the tips of my cheeks to the corner of my eyes. He took my bottom lip into his mouth so softly. Then he pulled away.

"Control," he said. "We both need to practice control." He stood up.

"When do you want to go?" I asked dolefully, wiping the traces of him from my mouth.

"I can't until after work. I'm going in for a half-day. I don't see them firing me yet, but I am definitely trying their patience." He bent to kiss my temple, and I was slightly mollified at the flush of his neck.

"I wonder if I work today."

"You did." Ben stared absently at the wall. "But if you call within … the next two hours, and tell Scott you were hurt in the fire—he already knows a fire happened—he'll let you come back on Wednesday." He blinked the future away.

I would put it off as long as I could. An hour and fifty minutes. "I can unpack some of your stuff while you're gone?"

"How chivalrous of you, Frank." He smiled at me, more teasing than genuine. "You've grown so much."

"Keep it up and I burn it all." I shoved past him to the living room.

Ben called a goodbye to Cleo, who was emptying Amir's litter box. He explained our evening plans to her.

"We need a couch. Maybe some artwork would brighten these walls?" She held her chin in her hand and surveyed the lifeless living room. "I guess we could use something of Ben's, but diversity is a must. Should we say five o'clock?" And she returned to her room without a response. I smiled to myself. She sounded like Cleo, and almost looked like her, too.

"Later, Princess," Ben winked and dropped a light kiss on my mouth. He pulled my heavy knotted hair forward and covered my face. "Maybe give this thing a wash. It looks like Cthulhu." I shoved him in the chest. He laughed at my irritation and jogged out the door.

I rolled my eyes and pulled open several boxes. I found a box full of books—no way these would fit on my shelf. The three stacked on the top of the pile were the tomes we'd borrowed from Patrick. He had to be human again, and he probably wanted his things back.

I opened the first book. I had never gotten around to studying this one, the book on eradication, and now that Jessamae wasn't an imminent danger to us, I didn't see much point in doing so now. But curiosity got the better of me and I turned a few blank pages. There was a very short family tree. It was written in multiple inks in different handwritings, added to as the years had gone by. It was more of a line than a tree, there were so few branches.

The first entry, the root of the not-really-a-tree, belonged to a Charlotte Dorothea Flock, and there was no birth or death date. Beneath her name, it merely said "16th century." I couldn't resist searching for Jessamae's name, but the youngest entries of the tree looked to be a pair of siblings, twins: Anthony and Madeline Wood, each with the birth year of 1843.

There was no way to know from this if the authors only recorded magical family members, or if the lack of conception had led to such a bare family tree. Either way, there was no telling which names had magical affinities and which didn't, because, after the diagram, there was only one entry in the book. It was printed in curling black script on the right-hand page, in what I guessed to be German. And printed on the left-hand page, in a blue and hurried scrawl, was what I took to be an English translation:

She took everything. The mistress who came in the night. Her hair is light as the moon and her eyes, the green of first spring. She, who played with the children, who braided the hair of our brides. The first message from God was a single sick sheep. Its milk spoiled, its wool full of pests. Once it fell dead, the entire flock perished. Not a single animal bled. Our horses, our oxen. Dead. She came each night, she comforted the bitter men in their homes. She held the weeping children to her breast. She took, she took, she took! Once she drained our women of their fertility, she took their children's love. They no longer wanted their mothers. They wanted her. She took our very souls from us. When I witnessed my young son lose his anger, his fear, his will to live   to her! I ran! I ran from my family! All I am is a warning, to those who encounter the life thief! The witch! Beware Charlotte Flock and all whom she births! A curse to us all!

EPILOGUE

I MISSED HER ALREADY. But I wouldn't return to Francesca until I found what I needed. The sun felt hotter here in Nevada than it had in Aspen Ridge. I traveled almost entirely at night. But I was close now, to the contact I initially sought when I traveled west. Until Francesca so tragically ensnared me.

Benjamin would take care of her. He couldn't resist his protective impulses, no matter its annoyance to her. Cleo, so strong and so intelligent, an unexpected treat that one, would live in Francesca's house with them both, another form of defense against those who might wish her harm. I had repeated similar mantras for days, and repeated them now as I hurried up the long desert drive.

This town was even smaller than my Francesca's, an unassuming collection of hermits and castaways. Jack was just another recluse in this place. His home was small and dusty, his warnings hung unseen in the air, as his ancestors hung their enemies to keep visitors away. Much more effective than any sign, that was for certain. I wouldn't succeed without his help.

Allison Hughes purchased that Aspen Ridge home two years after Francesca's birth. Records indicated she'd been born in a suburb outside of Las Vegas. The Vegas covens were expansive and talented. I wouldn't approach them all. I needed Jack in the elimination process. If the man I hunted was no longer in Vegas, I would find someone there who knew of him, who knew of his power. Only once I had a name would I return to Francesca. Once I knew the name of her father.

· · ·

IF YOU ENJOYED THIS STORY, please consider leaving a review on Amazon and Goodreads.

ACKNOWLEDGMENTS

I am incredibly grateful for Lake Country Press for believing in this story and giving my characters life, as well as the LCP author family—especially Kirsten and Beka—for their friendship and tear-jerking enthusiasm.

I am grateful for my friends—Chris, Austen, Powell, Brittany, and Jessie—for giving PEACHY a chance, and actually finishing it. Especially Chris, if he gets a tweed jacket.

I am grateful for my siblings—Shay, Tan, Madi, and Max—for believing in me and knowing PEACHY would be a book one day. Especially Shay, for loving the characters as much as she did and for designing the original image I used as a working cover graphic. I'm grateful for my brother-in-law Mitch as well as my nieces and nephews—Camryn, Emmy, and Finn—for their constant support.

I am grateful for my dad, who never let me forget I am a writer, a real writer, the best one he knows. And for my mom, whose faith in my potential is unwavering and has championed all my achievements.

And I am grateful for Dylon, who makes me better, and without whom, I would have never written this book.

But most of all, I am grateful for the readers. I hope you picked up this story, and it made you feel something.

Thank you.

ABOUT THE AUTHOR

Raised by a welder and a Jack Mormon in the small town of Wallsburg, Camri Kohler worked her way to the grid city, Salt Lake. Camri earned her BA in English from the University of Utah before completing her MLIS at the University of Illinois. Camri is an archivist at PBS and spends her free time with her partner, her dogs, or her tomatoes. She is a mess of unresolved issues which are the primary inspiration for her writing.

ALSO BY CAMRI KOHLER

Coming Soon…

Pared

Buried

Ingram Content Group UK Ltd.
Milton Keynes UK
UKHW040750240423
420680UK00004B/289